MW01182041

Back From Iraq

The story of a traumatized soldier's quest

For love and peace

In a frightened world.

HANNA SAADAH

The entire proceeds from the sale of this book

Go to charities

Via the Oklahoma City Community Foundation.

2

Hanna A. Saadah
Copyright © 2009
Tele: (405) 749-4266
ALMUALIF Publishing, LLC
4205 McAuley Boulevard # 400
Oklahoma City, Oklahoma 73120-8347
Web Site Address: www.almualif.com
or www.hannasaadah.com

Library of Congress Control Number: 2009933856
Copyright Certificate Registration Number: 1-220824481
Effective Copyright Certificate Registration Date: 07.22.09

ISBN 10: 0-9765448-3-0
ISBN 13: 978-0-9765448-3-8
ISBN-Library of Congress-0-9765448-3-0
SAN 256-467X

Saadah, Hanna Abdallah 1946—

Books by Author:
Loves and Lamentations of a Life Watcher (Poetry)
Vast Awakenings (Poetry)
Familiar Faces (Poetry)
Four and a Half Billion Years (Poetry)
The Mighty Weight Of Love (Novel)
Epistole (A Novel in Letters)
Back From Iraq (Novel)

To Order On Line:
www.almualif.com
or www.hannasaadah.com

Disclaimer
This novel is 100% fiction.

Cover design

By

Oklahoma Artist

Angel Peck

To Judy

Summary

Back From Iraq is the story of a soldier, Scott Thornton, who after spending two years in war-torn Baghdad, returns to Oklahoma City a shaken man only to learn that he has to go back to Iraq again. Changed by his traumatic experiences, he becomes repulsive even to his own family. "What have they done to my son?" says his father, Howard. "Scott never came back from Iraq. He never came back..." says Nancy, his wife. The entire novel, which transpires over a period of four months in 2006, reaches into the deep, dark past of the 20th Century when Baghdad was a beautiful city and then races across the war-torn Iraq to the present day. The church and the cemetery frame the novel while Baghdad, Al-Qaeda, the US Armed Forces, the Oklahoma City Police Department, and the Department of Human Services are interlaced into a web of love, intrigue, terrorism, despair, and fear.

Transference—the mighty albatross of the unconscious mind—spreads its wings, soars high in the mental sky, and then alights upon the characters' minds with mystifying consequences. A kidnapped, five-year-old girl is the linchpin that holds the plot together and the axis around which a heroic father, a libertine mother, a maverick military mentor, and a green-eyed, sainted maiden revolve. The bloody threads of Al-Qaeda are woven into the novel's tapestry on fear's foreboding loom creating a memorable quilt bursting with forbidden pulses.

"Once fear conquers your heart, the only means to overthrow it is to hurl yourself back into it, over and over, until it runs away from you instead of you from it. Waste no time reasoning with fear, Scotty; its only antidotes are reckless courage and blind faith." These proverbial words of Peckford, Scott's military mentor, provide the ideological scaffold from which the novel hangs as a tour de force of Fear and Peace instead of War and Peace.

*"**Back From Iraq** is an extremely accurate accounting of a returning combat veteran. Any one who reads this book will have some insight into why we are not the same persons we were before we went to war. A great thanks to the author for telling our story..."*

J.G. Baughn
Owasso, Oklahoma
U.S. Navy
Vietnam Combat Veteran

Prologue
(*We Are Our Thoughts*)

We are what we think and only our minds represent our true identities. When our thoughts change we also change, for our thoughts are the rightful monarchs of our souls. Hence, whatever changes the way we think also changes what we are, making us but the look-alikes of what we used to be. Of the many forces that change the way we think, the mightiest force of all is experience because it combines all of the forces of life that continuously remodel our brains.

Of all the emotional forces that color our experience, fear—with its many misshapen faces—is the darkest and the most ferocious. Once it infests the mind, it can become permanent and uninfluenced by reason or reality. Severe trauma, physical or emotional, is fear's mother from whose womb fear flies out crying into the night. This fear, which hides in the dark dungeons of memory, is the demon of the Post-Traumatic-Stress-Disorder-Syndrome and the driving force behind this action-filled novel.

The omniscient narrator, by peering into the minds of his characters, spies on their thoughts and reveals their naked truths to us. We are rendered privy to their mental and emotional developments as the novel unfurls its intrigues before our eyes. Baghdad, Al-Qaeda, the US Armed Forces, the Oklahoma City Police Department, and the Department of Human Services all play their parts while love, desire, betrayal, despair, and fear play havoc with the characters' hearts and minds.

The entire novel, which transpires over a period of four months in 2006, reaches into the deep, dark past of the 20th Century when Baghdad was a beautiful city and then it races across the war-torn Iraq to the present time. A kidnapped five-year-old girl is the pin that nails the plot together and the pivot around which a heroic father, a libertine mother, a maverick military mentor, and a green-eyed, sainted maiden revolve.

"Once fear conquers your heart, the only means to overthrow it is to hurl yourself back into it, over and over, until it runs away from you instead of you from it. Waste no time reasoning with fear, Scotty; its only antidotes are reckless courage and blind faith." These powerful words of Scott's military mentor provide the ideological framework from which the novel fights its war against fear in order to win its peace.

HAS
7.17.09

Chapter One
(Issues)

"Why are you telling me all this? I'm closing my ears. I don't want to hear any more."

"But he's your brother and you're my friend. Whom am I going to tell if I can't tell you?"

"Nancy, it can't be true. You're dreaming. Scott is a good man. I don't want to hear any more. Here's $20 and you can pay the rest. Good-bye."

Jane left Nancy staring at the paintings on the walls of La Baguette. One showed a sailboat in a storm, and the other a harbor with two sailing ships, one hoisting the French and one the Italian flag. There were other paintings, but she liked the sail ships best because she could gaze at them and sail away from her boring life. She never really wanted to become a wife or a mother but both wifehood and motherhood surprised her at the same time, at the prime age of twenty-four. Four years later, burdened by a life she did not choose, she still yearned for her old freedom, for her single days, and for her big city, Dallas. Her eyes drifted with the windy imagination of the sails. *"One day, I shall set myself free and sail away,"* she thought, *"sail away to where I can be myself again. I'm a caged wild bird awaiting freedom."*

The waiter came with the bill, looked at the two uneaten plates, and politely inquired if the food was okay. Nancy smiled back at him with blue, sheepish eyes and muttered, *"We just wanted to talk. The food was a good excuse, but we were not hungry."*

Hurrying home in the heat of August along the congested May Avenue left little room for patience. The motorists fought for every inch of road, the traffic lights barely let a few cars through before they turned red again, faces sweltered into red moons behind dirty windshields, and air conditioners groaned under the unforgiving sun while the car engines guzzled gasoline as fast as it was ladled down their throats.

"*Scott was too good of a man,*" thought Nancy as she waited in traffic on the hot avenue. "*He was born good, grew up good, and remained good until the day he came back from Iraq. He was the perfect gentleman while we dated, never pressed me for sex, never cussed, never drank, never misbehaved, never lied, and was never unkind. All my friends envied me because he was such a perfect husband and father. We had two normal years before his reserve unit was called up for service.*" Her thoughts swallowed her as she approached home, dreading yet another encounter. "*What will he be like this afternoon? Poor Sara. She will only remember her dad as a psycho and her mom as a libertine.*"

Quietly, Nancy entered the house from the garage. Scott, absorbed in his computer, hardly noticed her. "*Pornophile,*" she muttered as she passed his office and glanced at the obscene screen. "*Shameless and tireless, still at it since morning, and thinks it's okay. Scott never came back from Iraq. He never came back.*"

She returned from the bedroom, went into his office, stood behind him and began rubbing his massive, muscular shoulders. On the screen were men and women in unspeakablc positions performing sexual acts of infinite variety. With eyes still glued to the screen, Scott reached for Nancy's hands and stroked them gently without saying a word.

"Baby, why don't you turn this thing off and come sit with me."

"Humm, what's on your mind?"

"Nothing, I just miss my husband."

"When do we pick up Sara?"

"At four o'clock."

"What time is it now?"

"Two."

"Okay then."

Scott got up, and with an effortless, sweeping motion, whisked Nancy into the bedroom, threw her on the bed, closed the door, unbuckled his belt, and unzipped his fly.

"No Darling, not now."

"You said you missed your husband."

"I did, but ..."

"Well, your husband misses you too."

"No, not now, please."

"Why not? Do you have anything better to do?"

"Yes."

"What?"

"I want us to cuddle and talk first."

"Talk about what?"

"About Iraq."

Scott stopped, gazed with surprise at Nancy's quivering face, zipped back his fly, buckled back his belt, and sat beside her on the bed.

"I'm sorry if I hurt your feelings, Babe."

"Women need attention a lot more than they need sex. You haven't learned that yet, have you?"

"What would you like to know about Iraq?"

"What was it like? What happened to you? Why did you come back so changed?"

"Nothing happened. I was in Communications. It was relatively safe."

"Did anything shocking happen? Were you ever afraid? Did you see any action? Did you meet any native women?"

"No, Babe. I was in Communications and we were in a safe, isolated place."

"How about your buddies?"

Scott paused, smirked, frowned, seemed perturbed, and then laughed it off with a wave of his hand, "My buddies were fine too, all except Jimmy Kaminski who was sent out on a patrol and was blown up. Everyone in his Hummm...veee... died."

All of a sudden, when Scott stuttered the word Humvee, his mouth became contorted into a frightful spout, his eyeballs froze in their sockets, his whole head began to shake uncontrollably, and his neck swelled up at the throat like a bullfrog's. Nancy held her breath and was afraid to stir. She watched him slowly thaw and return to the conversation just like an epileptic who regains consciousness after a spell without recalling that it ever happened.

"He's from Minnesota. He carried a picture of his fiancé in his wallet. Her name was Frannie."

Nancy knew that she had to change the topic from Humvees and buddies but her mind was still too startled to come up with anything neutral and distracting. Pornography seemed safe enough because talking about it had not provoked an explosion before. Hesitantly, she inquired, "What turned you on to internet pornography?"

"We were lonely men and had time to kill. It was an outlet. Doesn't hurt anyone."

"It hurts me to see you do it."

"Why? I've never been unfaithful to you. Some men watch television, some drink and gamble, some take drugs, some womanize, and I distract myself with pornography. There's no harm in it and I don't even like it. It's like taking a bad-tasting medicine because it makes you feel better. It's just a real good distraction."

"Distraction? Distraction from your wife and your daughter?"

"Distraction from what's in my mind."

"And what's on your mind, Darling?"

"It's not on my mind. It's in my mind, Babe, and I can't get rid of it. But if I keep myself distracted, it doesn't seem to haunt me as much."

"Why don't you tell me about it then?"

"I'm afraid to talk about it because I'd have to relive it."

"Do you also watch pornography when you're at the bank?"

"Oh, no! You can't use the bank computers or phones for personal matters. Besides, my work distracts me enough that I hardly need another distraction."

"You know that you can lose your job if they catch you doing it?"

"How can they catch me if I don't do it there?"

"Somebody is liable tell them."

"They don't care what I do when I'm at home. They

only care if I don't close on enough loans."

"Do you still love me?"

"What a question? I adore you and Sara."

"If you adore us, stop this disgusting habit."

"I can't. It's my calming outlet. It keeps me from going insane."

"There are better ways to stay calm than this. Why don't you see if the doctors at the VA Hospital can help you?"

"Help me with what? I'm not sick. Besides, going to the hos-hos-pi–pi-hospi-hospi frightens me."

Scott had trouble articulating the word hospital and by the time he finished the sentence beads of sweat had formed on his frowning forehead.

"Let me get you an appointment with a private therapist then; my mother knows a good one; her name is Dr. Small."

"You've been discussing me with your mother?"

"Oh, no. We were just talking and ..."

"Nancy! I've only been back a month and you're already plotting against me?"

"Oh, no Honey. I love you and I need you, but what you're doing is not healthy and you obviously need help to stop it."

"In that case, since you think I'm such a weirdo, perhaps I should volunteer and go back to Iraq."

Scott got up and walked back to his screen, leaving Nancy alone on the bed. She lay there motionless, stunned, gazing at the ceiling fan with disbelief. *"What have they done to him?"* Ruminating over her life before and after Dallas, before and after Sara, before and after Scott, and before and after Iraq threw her into a vertiginous daze. Her eyes turned round and round with the ceiling fan. She began to feel dizzy and nauseated. While considering whether she should run to the toilet or resist her vomiting urge, she was startled out of her reverie by Scott's clear, nonchalant voice, "I'm going to pick up Sara."

In a panic, Nancy rushed out of the bedroom screaming, "Wait. Wait. Let's pick her up together."

On the way to Scott's parents, Nancy stroked Scott's hairy arm while he drove. She was afraid to say anymore because she didn't want to make him mad. He didn't have a temper before Iraq but he did return with an explosive one indeed, one that had been grafted onto his kind, native stem. At first, Nancy thought that it was a temporary graft but now, after one month without any sign of change, she realized that the graft had taken and that realization caused her great alarm. Even his parents noticed how changed he was. Of course, they were afraid to say anything to him but they did to her. They practically thanked her for putting up with him: "Nancy dear, we're so glad you understand. You have such a calming influence on him."

Jill and Howard were in their swimming pool playing with Sara. "Hope you brought your bathing suits with you," were Jill's greeting words. "Sara isn't ready to leave Grandma yet."

"She isn't ready to leave Grandpa either," said Howard as he put his arm around Sara and Jill.

"Okay then, watch what Daddy can do."

Before Nancy realized what was happening, Scott jumped into the pool, making a huge splash.

"Daddy, Daddy, you forgot to take off your clothes."

Scott, like a heedless child, charged Sara and began to splash her with cupfuls of water.

"Stop it Daddy. You're splashing water into my eyes. Please Daddy, please stop, you're choking me…"

Sara, blue with cough and wheezing, buried her face in Grandma's chest while Howard got in between Scott and the girls and held his son's arms, hoping to stop his reckless splashing. It didn't work because after some intense wrestling, Scott pushed his dad under water and chased after Sara and Jill who were trying to climb out of the pool. Sara let out a frightened scream as Nancy rescued her out of Jill's arms and ran with her into the house, leaving Scott and his parents in a heated discussion.

"Scott, I'm your dad, not your child. You don't push your dad under water. What ever happened to your mind? You used to be so calm and reasonable."

Jill held Howard by the arm and led him out of the pool whispering, "Honey, let him be; he'll calm down if we leave him alone. Go into the house, check on Sara and Nancy, and get him some dry clothes so he can go home. I'll stay outside with him."

Scott continued to splash and play, hardly aware that he was alone in the water. Jill sat on a chair and watched her child-like son with salt in her throat. *"He can't be trusted. He's dangerous. Poor Nancy. Poor Sara. Dear Lord, what have they done to my son?"* With these thoughts on her mind, Jill wiped her tears and, feeling overwhelmed, ran into the house.

Sara sat shivering in Nancy's lap, holding on to her mother's neck as if she were drowning. Howard stood at the window and dolefully watched his son play alone in the pool as if naught had happened. Jill brought a towel, wrapped it around Sara, and asked her if she would like a sandwich.

"I don't want to go home; I want to stay here with you," was Sara's answer. Nancy handed Sara to Jill and went back to the pool, where Scott was still jumping and splashing, unaware.

"Baby, it's time to go home. I need you to get out of the pool. I brought you a towel."

"I'm not finished playing. Have Sara and Mom come out and play with me."

"Scott, Honey, everyone's tired. Let's go home, please."

"All right, I guess. I'm tired too."

"Here, wrap this towel around you before you go into the house. Your dad has some dry clothes waiting for you."

As Scott, dripping copious amounts of water, went into the house, Jill, Nancy, and Sara walked out from the other door and sat under the large green umbrella. Jill held

Nancy's hand and the two looked at each other with sad, knowing eyes. There was a lot to be said but not with four year-old Sarah in her mother's lap. Soon, Scott walked out with a cheerful demeanor, carrying his wet clothes in a black trash bag. Howard walked close behind him with a hyper-vigilant expression as if ready to intervene at the slightest hint of trouble. Nancy handed Sara, still pale with wheezing, to Jill and whispered in her ear, "Call Jane. She and I had lunch today." Then, holding Scott by the arm, she led him to the car.

"I'll drive and you can sit next to me. Wouldn't you like a woman to chauffeur you back home?"

"But what about Sara?"

"She wants to spend the night with your mom and dad."

"When will she come home?"

"Tomorrow, silly. When you return from work, you'll find her waiting for you."

"What's in the bag?"

"Your wet clothes."

"Oh, is today Sunday?"

"Ycs, Darling."

"And Sara will come home tomorrow?"

"Yes, Darling.

"I have a headache. When we get home, will you lie with me and hold me?"

"Yes, Darling."

Scott stroked Nancy's bare arm while she drove, laid back his head, and closed his eyes to avoid the sun's glare.

When they arrived home, Scott went back to his computer without saying another word to Nancy and, for the first time since his return, Nancy began preparing dinner for two instead of three. Slicing tomatoes with the long kitchen knife, she became aware of an inner restlessness as she squeezed the handle with inordinate force. *Why do I feel so angry? He still loves me. He may be strange but he's also harmless. He's back to work. He's a good provider. Why do I feel so intimidated by him? Is it because we're going to be alone all night? I don't remember ever feeling that way before, even the first time I spent the night in his apartment. That's when I should have felt intimidated, not now! What am I afraid of then? Maybe I'm afraid of myself, afraid of doing something to him while he sleeps. Oh, that knife is getting too heavy for my hand."*

When dinner was ready, Nancy started toward Scott's office then changed her mind, returned to the dining room, sat down in her usual chair, and spooned her glass as she called, "Honey, Darling, dinner is served."

Chapter Two
(Whispers)

When August softened into September, Oklahoma sighed and began splashing its eye-pleasing fall colors onto streets and yards. Pansies, mums, and sweet potato vines vied for attention as they flaunted their bright carnival attires at cars and passersby. Nevertheless, the gentle softness in the mist belied the tumult in the Thornton homes.

On Tuesday, September 5, 2006 Scott, after the long Labor Day weekend, went to his work at the Hartland Bank in downtown Oklahoma City while Nancy dropped Sara off at school and then hurried to her salon at the northeast corner of May and Britton. Her first appointment of the day was Jane and she had not talked to her since their quarrelsome lunch at La Baguette a month earlier. *"Surely, she knows by now. Surely Jill would have told her something. She can't still be angry with me."* These were Nancy's thoughts as she tidied up her station, prepared her trade tools, and got ready for her first client.

Jane had been her friend long before she and Scott started dating. In fact, that was how it all began. As classmates in high school, Nancy and Jane spent much of their free time together. During those high school days, they became each other's confidants and spent long nights talking about personal issues. Once during their junior year, when Nancy was spending the night at Jane's, Jane got in bed with her, told her that she was madly in love with her, and kissed her passionately on the lips. Nancy was so alarmed that she ran out of Jane's bedroom and, by mistake, took refuge in Scott's room. Scott, a senior at the time, woke up startled when he saw Nancy standing by his bed, screaming at the top of her voice. Quickly, he got up, gathered her into his champion-swimmer arms, calmed her down by telling her that she was having a bad dream, and reassured her that everything was going to be all right. He then carried her back into Jane's room and told Jane, who appeared equally startled, that Nancy was just having a nightmare. That night, after Nancy calmed down, Jane apologized to her and the two settled down into what became a more profound and accepting friendship.

After graduation in 1996, Jane got her real estate license and began working with Jill and Howard at the family-owned Thornton Real Estate Agency. Nancy went to a beauty school in Dallas and found work at a salon in the Doubletree Plaza. They remained best friends throughout, visited each other during vacations or holidays, and shared their most embarrassing secrets.

Scott must have had his eye on Nancy ever since that night when she came into his room screaming, but nothing happened between them until Nancy became pregnant while working in Dallas. The father of the child, she said, was a certain Rick whom she happened to run into at a bar when she was lonely and drunk. She had a one-night stand with him, did not even know his surname, and never saw him again. When she found out that she was pregnant, she came back home to see Jane. By that time, Scott had gone to college on a swimming scholarship, graduated with a business degree, had his own apartment, and was working at the Hartland Bank as a loan officer. When Nancy told Jane that she wanted an abortion, Jane had no idea what to do except to call Scott and ask for his help. Scott came over to Jane's apartment and took Nancy out to dinner. They talked until midnight and began seeing each other frequently from that point on. Within three months they were married and when Sara was born he adopted her and thus became her legal father. The only two who knew Nancy's secret were Jane and Scott. As for Nancy and Scott's parents, they simply assumed that Sara was Scott's child because, at that time, Scott was making frequent business trips to Dallas.

Jane walked in smiling and, as if nothing had happened, gave Nancy a long, warm embrace. Of course, Nancy was not about to broach the awkward topic again and began trimming Jane's hair as usual. They talked about the wedding of Angela and Gregory, about the Funeral of Ed, and about the latest hairstyles. Nancy inquired about Flora, Jane's live-in lover for the past four years, and wondered if she had recovered from her gallbladder surgery, and Jane asked if Sara liked her preschool teacher, Mrs. Mann. Then, when Nancy began coloring Jane's hair, Jane asked, "And how is my dear brother doing these days?"

"Scott is happy to be back and at work."

"Has he changed any of his habits yet?"

"Well, he still likes his computer and his new books, if that's what you mean."

"Have you seen Mom and Dad since the swimming pool incident?"

"No, but mainly because we've been busy with our lives and Sara's."

"And how are you two getting along?"

"Oh, just fine."

"Nancy, you don't have to spare my feelings. Mother and I talked at length. You can tell me the truth."

"Maybe we can have lunch together sometime this week? It's hard to talk here."

There was anger in Nancy's eyes, which did not go unnoticed by Jane. "How about today? La Baguette at 12:30?"

"Okay, I guess, if you promise not to get upset and leave me staring at the sails."

"What sails?"

"I meant to say the walls. There was a painting of two sail ships when we were last there."

"I remember that painting now."

"Well, you promise that you won't get upset?"

"I'm sorry. I just wasn't ready to believe that my brother had come back so screwed up and weird."

"I didn't want to believe it either. Let's not say any more here... Voila. How do you like your hair?"

Jane and Nancy spent a good chunk of the afternoon whispering their thoughts to one another. It was hard to begin, but once the conversation took off, it was hard to stop. *"Old friendships get better with time and with hardships,"* thought Nancy as she kissed Jane on the cheek and hurried back to work. *"I need to get him help before he gets any worse. I'm going to make an appointment with Dr. Sylvester and tell her everything. She'll know what to do."* While in her car, Nancy dialed Dr. Sylvester's office.

"Sheri, this is Nancy Thornton. Do you have any openings today?"

"No, Mrs. Thornton, I'm sorry. Can it wait till tomorrow?"

"Tomorrow will be fine. What time?"

"I have a four o'clock open."

"I'll take it."

That night, Scott tucked Sara in, told her a beautiful bedtime story, and stroked her back until she fell asleep with a smile on her face. Then, as usual, he went back to his computer and books. Nancy took advantage of that time and wrote down her thoughts for Dr. Sylvester, making sure to mention all pertinent details. When she had it all down, she hid the paper in her purse, turned off the bedroom light, and tried to sleep.

Her thoughts were confused because the very man who had married her to save Sara from an abortion was also the man who was torturing her mind and causing all sorts of questions to haunt her. Although she was never in love with him, she did recognize that, with time, she had grown fond of him because he was a most honorable husband and father. Nevertheless, at twenty-eight, she was still very attractive and capable of luring other men if living with her damaged husband were to continue to be so difficult.

Of course, if he were to change back to what he was before Iraq, she would never leave him especially since Sara and he adored each other and Sara had no idea that he wasn't her biological father. Moreover, he was a very good, considerate lover, the best she'd ever had, notwithstanding all her free years as a single Dallas woman and her clandestine escapades during the past two years while he was in Iraq. Sleep came painfully to Nancy's exhausted eyes but, mercifully, it rescued her before Scott came to bed. Indeed, because of his late-night computer-and-book routine, the only time they had made love since his return two months ago was on his first night home.

After that unusual night, Nancy realized that something had happened that had radically changed him. She cringed when she recalled that when they went to bed, instead of holding her in his mighty arms, kissing her gently, and telling her how much he missed her, he did something totally unexpected. He slowly undressed her and then asked her to stand naked in the middle of the bedroom. Standing there, he looked at her for the longest time then asked her to turn her back to him, bend over, and look at him from between her legs. While in that awkward position, he lifted her upon him and made violent love to her while she was bent over and he was standing. Caught by surprise, she was unable to reach an orgasm, which he did not seem to mind at all. Then, when it was all over for him, he dropped her on the bed, turned his back to her, and fell asleep without saying a word. He did not want to snuggle, stroke her back, play with her hair, and kiss her finger tips as was his habit after lovemaking.

She lay next to him for the longest time, sleepless, confused, feeling like a used rag tossed into the laundry bin with one haunting thought that tirelessly nagged on her mind, *"Whatever happened to him?"* Throughout all her single days, she had never been subjected to such humiliation. She had always reserved the prerogative to say stop whenever her lovers became too aggressive or mischievous. But on her husband's first night home, she couldn't be assertive nor could she ask him to leave, which in her single years she had done many a time without a second thought.

Dr. Sylvester, her parents' physician of thirty years, also became their family physician since they married. Nancy was more comfortable with Dr. Sylvester than with her own parents and Dr. Sylvester treated Nancy like her own daughter, the daughter she never had. Since it was the last appointment of the day, Dr. Sylvester did not feel rushed and gave Nancy all the time she needed. Nancy told her the entire story, stopping occasionally to wipe her eyes or blow her nose, while Dr. Sylvester listened attentively without saying a word. When Nancy was through, Dr. Sylvester looked intently at her and poignantly asked, "Did you ever love him?"

"No, I'm afraid not."

"Does he love you?"

"Yes, I'm afraid so."

"And how about Sara?"

"He adores her."

"Except for his paraphilia, would you say that he's still a decent husband and father?"

"Para what? What is that?"

"Paraphilias are a diverse group of mental disorders featuring obsessive preoccupations with myriad sexual perversions."

"Is that what he has?"

"Most likely."

"And it can come on just like that?"

"No. It usually comes on slowly starting at puberty."

"He never did anything like that before he went to Iraq. I've known him for years. He's always been a straight arrow. We never even had kinky sex."

"Is he changed in any other way?"

"Well, he used to read about sports and watch a lot of TV. Now he's reading books about the old classics."

"What old classics?"

"I don't know; that's what he calls them and he talks about them all the time. He talks to me about Mesopotamia, Sumer, the Greeks, the Romans, mythology, and so many other things I've never heard of."

"What was the last thing he talked to you about? Do you remember?"

"Last night at dinner, he told Sara and me the story of Antigone."

"Really, how unusual! We're going to need a good psychiatrist for that one."

"You mean that's more important than the para

25

whatever?"

"The paraphilia. Well, it suggests a change in intellect, which may have preceded the sexuality issue.

"Could mental trauma bring such changes on?"

"I'm not sure; I suppose it could. I need to call Dr. Mellon on that one."

"Who's Dr. Mellon?"

"A psychiatrist friend of mine."

"But Scott doesn't think that there's anything wrong and refuses help."

"You've already tried?"

"Yes, of course."

"Then we're in deep trouble."

"Why is that?"

"Because seeking treatment has to be voluntary."

"So what do I do with him then?"

"There isn't much you can do."

"Could he revert to normal on his own?"

"You mean without treatment?"

"Yes."

"I don't think that's very likely. These disorders are usually hard to reverse even with proper medical and psychological treatments."

"You mean I have to live like this for the rest of my life?"

"The way it looks at present, you can either tolerate him or leave him. There might not be a middle of the way solution."

"Oh my God. What have I done to deserve this?"

"Let me talk it over with Dr. Mellon and I'll get back with you. In the meantime, don't do anything foolish."

"Do you think it would help if I took him to church?"

"Would he go? Did he like going to church before he went to Iraq?

"We used to go every Sunday. The last time we went as a family was the Sunday before he left. Since he's been back, Sara and I have been going alone because he refuses to leave his computer and books. If he's not on the computer, he's reading. That's how he spends all of his free time."

"He certainly has undergone a radical change in character, not only sexually, but also intellectually and spiritually."

"He sure has and we're his victims. Should I make an appointment for next week?"

"Next week? For you or for him?"

"For me, of course."

"Oh, yes. That's a good idea."

Nancy drove home with a mind full of conflicts: *"I'm trapped with a son of a bitch who loves me and adores my daughter. Most of the time, his head is in the clouds and his dick is in the computer. I live with a ghost who doesn't even see that there's anything wrong.*

My life was screwed the moment I screwed up in Dallas. If I hadn't gotten pregnant, I wouldn't have married Scott and wouldn't have had to put up with him now. One day without my pills and my life was reset on a crashing course.

Oh well, Scott will be home before me today but he won't miss me. He'll miss Sara though and will call me to find out if I have forgotten to pick her up from preschool. I'll tell him that I had a doctor's appointment and asked my mom to pick her up instead. I'll have to stop by my parents anyway and then I'll head on home. I wonder what classical stories he's going to tell us at dinner? Damn the red lights; I've hit every one of them so far."

Chapter Three
(Church)

Sunday the 24th of September, the last Sunday of the month, was greeted with a titillating sunrise. Bird gossip could be heard tattling in the trees surrounding the Thornton home in The Greens. The freshly arriving sunrays inebriated one silly woodpecker that pecked irreverently at Sara's window until it woke her up. Blanket in arms, she half-somnambulated to her parent's bedroom and stuffed herself between Nancy and Scott. Nancy, who was already awake, tucked Sara underneath the covers and continued her contemplations behind the heavy bedroom curtains that held the morning out.

"I'm taking him to church today, no matter how hard he tries to resist. Instead of his computer and books, he's going with us to be healed by God. As sinful as I have been, he needs the church much more than I do. I hate to breakup this marriage and lose my security. I need to bring him back from Iraq and if Dr. Sylvester can't help me do it then God will have to. God will have to for Sara's sake because Scott is a much better father than I am a mother. Oh, God, just this one favor please. I'll make him a wonderful breakfast and You make sure that he won't say no to church."

Scott ate heartily while Sara sat in his lap. Nancy said very little and bode her time until breakfast was over and Scott's tummy was happy and full. While Sara pretended to help her dad clear the table, Nancy rinsed the plates and placed them in the dishwasher. When all was done, her heart began to pound as she prepared her face to frame the question. She was taken aback, however, when instead of retiring to his office, Scott startled her with, "Are you taking Sara to church?"

"I was planning to. What are your plans?"

"I was going to read a bit and then play with my computer."

"Why don't you come along with us? We haven't gone as a family since you came back."

"I know."

"Well then, why don't you come along?"

"I'm sorry but I can't do it."

"And what's preventing you?"

"I can't stand to hear them distort the message of Jesus."

"What? The church distorts the message of Jesus?"

"All the time. Churches have become a competitive, tax-exempt industry; they merely use Jesus in order to increase their congregations. On top of that, instead of settling their differences in a Christian way, churches multiply like rabbits, which means that they are all corrupt. The message of Jesus is very simple and speaks of The Church as one unified body."

"And since when have you become an authority on religion?"

"I'm not an authority but I'm able to think for myself."

"Why don't you come along then and listen only to the words of Jesus."

"What Jesus? Jesus has not been to church for two thousand years."

"Won't you at least come for Sara's sake? All the other children come with their parents. Do you want Sara to be the only exception?"

Scott was stung by Nancy's sharp point. He paused, looked at Sara standing between the two of them, and mumbled, "I guess not."

"Well then? Let's all get dressed and go. I have a feeling that something great is going to happen today."

Scott gazed at his pajama bottoms and bare feet, flexed his toes in a spasm, and ran his fingers through his thick, brown hair. Then, smiling at Sara, he sighed, "Sara baby, would you like me to go to church with you?"

"Yes Daddy."

"And why's that?"

"Because after church, they'll let me have donuts if you'll stay for coffee."

"And are the donuts that good?"

"Uh-huh."

"In that case, let's all get dressed and go to church."

"Oh, thank you Lord; I owe you one," thought Nancy with votive gratitude as she hurried with Sara to get ready.

St. Michael's Church was well-situated on the Hefner Lake Drive overlooking the water. The pastor, Father Elias, was a most holy man, loved and revered by his congregation, and the one responsible for moving the church from downtown Oklahoma City, where it was languishing, to its present, propitious location. In the ten years since the move, the congregation had grown from a mere two hundred to four thousand strong. In fact, he was the one who performed the wedding ceremony for Nancy and Scott five years earlier.

The Thorntons walked into the church just as the service was starting and barely found room in the back pews. To save on space, Scott lifted Sara onto his lap and wrapped his lithe arms around her. The mass began in the usual manner with organ music announcing the entrance procession. Father Elias, preceded by the alter boys carrying the cross, made his way to the altar while the congregation stood up with heads turned toward the center aisle. After the introductory rites, the greeting, the act of penance, the absolution, the two readings, and the reading from the Gospel, Father Elias surprised his congregation by asking Father James, his young assistant, to give the homily.

Although Father James had been with the church for less than a year, he had succeeded in these few months to make a strong impression on both its youth and its adults. He was articulate, kind, tall, handsome, and very playful. Many believed that when Father Elias retired, he would be the one to replace him as the church pastor. Besides his high seminary education he was also a true scholar and had wonderful ideas on how to improve the Christian spirit among the congregation. In fact, he had just submitted a treatise to Father Elias about Original Sin in which he argued that belief in Original Sin is necessary because it equalizes Christians and leads them to humility, two necessary conditions for salvation. Given his scholarly reputation, when Father James took the stand, a deep expectant silence supervened as eyes and ears focused their attention on this most impressive man of the cloth.

"Dear God, please let him speak directly to Scott's heart. Let this be the most holy homily Scott has ever heard. One more time, Lord, just this one last time..." Nancy was still praying when Father James, with a most distinguished voice, began his homily.

"We are all sinners, born sinners, and will die sinners unless redeemed by our Lord Jesus who died on the cross to save us from sin. We are all sinners because none of us is perfect. We are sinners because only God is perfect. And we are all sinners because our fore parents, Adam and Eve, disobeyed God's command and committed the Original Sin by partaking from the Tree of Knowledge. Their sin is our sin, their guilt is our guilt, their downfall from heaven is our downfall, and only through Jesus Christ can we be redeemed and elevated back into God's grace. If there is anyone among us who is not a sinner, let him stand up and declare himself. Otherwise, let us all bow our heads in silent prayer and ask our Lord, Jesus Christ, for forgiveness."

All the heads bowed in silence, all the heads that is, except Scott's. From the corner of her eye with mounting trepidation Nancy spied Scott as he surveyed the scene, put Sara into her lap, stood up, raised his arm like the Statue of Liberty, and with a soft but determined voice addressed the prayer master: "Father James. Father James. I am not a sinner."

All the bowed heads suddenly looked up with startled disbelief while Father James stood motionless, staring at Scott's tall, erect, military form with raised arm standing in the back pews.

"I'm not a sinner, Father, nor is my innocent daughter Sara, or my wife Nancy. I am an honorable citizen who has recently finished two years of service in Iraq. We are a good family with a clear conscience and we live a peaceful, loving life."

"My friend, if you've come to pray, please respect this place of worship, sit down, and pray with the rest of us," pleaded Father James with a weak, quivering voice, obviously forgetting that he was the one who said: "If there is anyone among us who is not a sinner, let him stand up and declare himself." The congregation, like pointing hounds, froze with heads turned back and eyes fixed on Scott.

"We are not sinners, Father. We are all good people here, normal people, and living normal lives. Why are you trying to burden our peaceful souls with guilt instead of enriching them with joy? The story of Adam and Eve is one of the many creation fables. Jesus who knew of it never taught us that it was true nor did he teach that we are all sinners. On the contrary, Jesus said let the children come unto me for theirs is the kingdom of heaven. Jesus is a kind and loving father; He is not a severe, guilt-riddling God. It is most cruel of you to saddle us all with unjustified guilt about myths and forces totally beyond our control. Christ never used guilt or fear as tools. He used love and kindness instead. How can you call yourself Christian when you don't preach in the spirit of Christ? How can Christ, who taught us all forgiveness, not forgive us a sin that we didn't even commit?" Having said that, Scott bowed his head, sat down, lifted Sara back into his lap, wrapped his stalwart arms around her, and kissed her on the head.

"*Oh, dear God!*" thought Nancy, with eyes closed and hands clenched, "*I'm married to an idiot. Please have pity on us and forgive us, oh Lord. And please forgive this blasphemous husband of mine and lead him back to Iraq so we can regain our peaceful lives.*"

At the other end of the church, with a blank unseeing stare, Father James clasped the Bible to his chest and tried to redress the congregation but his cottonmouth prevented him from voicing a response.

Father Elias seized the moment, hurried back to the pulpit, put his arm around Father James's waist, and motioned to the congregation to stand. He then looked at the choir director and nervously said, "Hymn thirty-seven, please."

Suddenly, the choir with the entire congregation exploded in unison as the organ spewed: *Joyful, Joyful, We Adore Thee.* The unusually loud hymning was rendered even louder by Father Elias's exuberant conducting. Scott stood up and joined the merry din, with Sara on his arm and Nancy by his side. *"The weirdo is singing!"* thought Nancy while she kept her eyes on the hymnbook. Everyone else—including Scott— looked straight at Father Elias. When the hymn ended, Father Elias motioned to the congregation to remain standing and, looking at the choir director, said, "Hymn forty-four, please."

When *Holy, Holy, Holy* ended, having been sung with equally boisterous gusto, he asked for hymn sixty-five, *Holy God, We Praise Thy Name.* When that hymn was finished, he rushed through the Holy Communion—a calculated violation of the most sacred of rites—and dismissed the congregation with: "The mass is ended; go in peace."

Quickly, Nancy nudged Scott to get up and pointed him in the direction of the door. The Thorntons walked out in solemn silence, escorted by two thousand gazing eyes that followed them through the swinging double doors into the churchyard, into their car, and all the way up the Lakeshore Drive to the top of the hill. No other car left the parking lot. Little groups coalesced and grew into one large circle at the church entrance. Through her tears from up the hill, Nancy could see Father Elias in the center of the circle, like a white pupil in the middle of a black eye, conducting with both arms what appeared to be a most heated discussion. Scott, on the other hand, was driving unaware, listening to a Lennon and McCartney song on the radio: *"All the lonely people, where do they come from, where do they belong."*

"Lonely people indeed, that's what we've become now that we've lost our church," thought Nancy as she eyed Scott, driving obliviously, entirely immersed in his wondering mind. *"He doesn't seem to recall that he has just caused an embarrassing scene. What am I going to do with*

him? He no longer fits in society. Aberrancy, that's what his middle name is. I'm married to Scott Aberrancy Thornton. Where on earth is he taking us now?"

"Baby, Baby, where are you going? You've missed your turn."

"It's a surprise."

"Please don't. I can't stand any more surprises."

"Sara honey. Do you like surprises?"

"Yes Daddy, yes, yes. I love surprises."

"Well then, just wait and you'll see what Daddy has in store for you."

Scott continued east on Memorial Road, passed underneath the Broadway Extension, and turned south on Kelly, entering the Memorial Park Cemetery from its West Gate. Nancy was alarmed because a suicide murder had recently been aired of a father who, before shooting himself in the head, shot both his wife and daughter in a cemetery in Tulsa. Although she attempted to hide her fear, it stuttered through her hoarse, quivering voice, making it barely audible.

"Scott! Scott! Why are you taking us into the cemetery?"

"I need to look for something."

"Scott, please, we're tired. Please turn around and let's go home."

Scott parked facing the graveyard, got out of the car, helped Sara out of her car seat, and together they walked around to Nancy's door.

"If you want to know how come I returned from Iraq a changed man, you'll have to come along with us."

Curiosity supplanted fear as Nancy, without saying another word, jumped out of her seat and walked with Scott and Sara toward the graves. The sun shone from above, giving them all rather short shadows, which seemed to amuse Sara as she skipped and pranced holding Scott and Nancy's hands. Methodically, Scott went from grave to grave, up and down the long rows, carefully examining each name and date. Time passed slowly for Nancy and Sara who became quickly bored with Scott's fastidious scrutiny.

Nevertheless, they stayed with him until he reached the end of the third row where they found a bench to sit on, leaving Scott to prowl alone up and down the remaining rows. When Scott reached the end of the fifth row, Nancy called him and said, "If you would tell me what you're looking for, I could help you."

"Peckford."

"Man or woman?"

"Captain Theodore Peckford."

"Old or new grave?"

"This year."

"I'll start at the other end."

When Nancy stood up to go, Sara pointed to her back and said, "Mommy, Mommy, you have writing on your jacket."

"Oh, no," said Nancy, taking off and inspecting her new, pink jacket, and then examining the bench where her back had leaned. "Scott, hurry up. I found it. Come and see. It's on the bench."

With light, eager strides Scott ran to where she stood, approached the bench, and began to read: *In memory of Captain Theodore Peckford who gave his life for his ideals. Born, Oklahoma City, 1955 / Died, Iraq, 2006.*

Nancy could not control her curiosity. "What does all this mean? Why a bench instead of a grave? It seems a bit ambiguous, doesn't it? Gave his life for his ideals instead of his country?"

Scott did not answer. His face swelled up, became contorted, turned pale, and his red eyes quivered with moisture. In a Thomas-like gesture, he ran his fingers over the writing with disbelief. Then, sitting down, he ran his fingers through his hair, lowered his head, and faded away into the deep, dark dungeons of his memory. Awed   by Scott's sudden metamorphosis, Nancy and Sara stood by the bench a while and then wandered away among the near-by graves. What they saw every time they glanced towards Scott was a motionless, melancholy man with bowed head and eyes peering deep into the earth.

After half an hour of graveyard wandering in the

afternoon sun, Sara began to show signs of fatigue. Afraid to disturb Scott's mournful trance, Nancy took Sara back to the car and waited there for Scott to join them. Another half hour passed but the statue on the bench showed no signs of life. She could see him in the distance, catatonic, unaware, as if frozen in a time that had long passed away never to return.

"Who is this Peckford," wondered Nancy, *"and how come Scott has never said a word about him? I need to find out more; I need to get him to talk; I need to know what happened to Scott while he was there to cause him to become so changed that I no longer recognize him."*

The afternoon sun swooned into shade underneath the giant trees that still clung to their leaves in spite of the impending fall. Birdsong bubbled down from among the branches, burst in mid-air, and vanished into the footless halls of silence. After a short nap, Sara woke up in the back seat, rubbed her eyes, and murmured, "Where's Daddy?"

"He's still at the bench where we left him."

"When's he going to take us home?"

"Why don't we ask him?" Saying that, Nancy dialed Scott's cell phone. The ring must have startled Scott because he abruptly stood up, looked around as if bedazzled by the silence of the graves, saluted the bench with taut, fervent sinews, and, without bothering to answer his phone, marched with tall, military strides towards the car.

Chapter Four
(Confessions)

That last Sunday of September was like an action-filled play; it lasted a while and when it was over, the theater emptied and everyone went home. The congregation went home, Father Elias and Father James went home, and the Thorntons left the graveyard and drove back home. For the rest of Oklahoma City, the remains of that day sailed across a sunny afternoon and harbored into a calm, eventless evening.

But Nancy, being an only child, was in the habit of visiting her parents in Edmond on Sunday afternoons. Peter and Frances Bradford, who taught school at Casady, met Nancy and Sara at the door with constrained smiles and weathered faces. *"Dear Lord, someone has already told them,"* thought Nancy as she watched them embrace Sara while avoiding eye contact with her. After milk and cookies, Sara settled down in her own little corner of the living room with Beaver, the family mutt, in her lap. Sitting with her parents at a safe distance, Nancy cleared her throat and started the conversation with a muffled voice that Sara couldn't hear.

"Okay, what's wrong?"

Quietly sipping their coffee, the Bradfords looked at each other, gazed through their living room window at the browning backyard trees, and said nothing.

"Please stop pretending. I know that someone has already told you," whispered Nancy, trying very hard not to attract Sara's attention.

"Father Elias called and talked to your dad," confessed Francis Bradford with avoidant eyes staring at the carpet.

"What did he say, Dad?"

"He told us what happened at church, asked us to pray for Scott's sanity, and wondered if you would be kind enough to give him a call during your lunch break tomorrow."

"Good, I was planning to do so anyway. Oh, what a

37

frigging mess," snapped Nancy as she stood up and began to pace.

"Did you know that his boss was there?" asked Mrs. Bradford after Nancy finished pacing and sat back down.

"Mr. McMaster? Oh, no! I hope that doesn't mean he's going to fire Scott."

"Maybe he won't if Scott would make amends with Father Elias," groaned Peter Bradford in a low, un-assuring voice.

"You don't understand, Dad. Scott doesn't think there's anything wrong with what he did."

"God only knows what will happen then," interjected Mrs. Bradford as she crossed herself. "Even God runs out of patience after a while. Tomorrow, the whole school will find out and your dad and I will get all sorts of looks. At our age, notoriety is not a desirable thing."

"This is going to hurt my business," hissed Nancy as she gazed at a flock of black birds swirling away beyond the backyard fence. "Surely, some of my devout clients will start going to other salons and that will definitely thrill my competition."

"What does hair styling have to do with church?" grumbled Mr. Bradford. "We may be making too much out of this. He's only been back three months. Give the kid some time, for God's sake."

"I'm giving him time, Dad. I'll give him all the time he needs, if he'll change back to what he was. I just don't think he wants to and Dr. Sylvester seems to agree with me."

"How in God's name did you manage to get hold of Dr. Sylvester on a Sunday afternoon? Did you page her for such a silly thing?"

"I went to see her last week about some other stuff that Scott had pulled," explained Nancy as she turned away from the window. Then, giving her mom and dad a curt look, she added, "I'm sorry for the short visit, but we really need to go. I still have a lot to do. I'll talk to you guys later." Nancy then walked up to Sara with a furrowed forehead and commanded in a strangely abrupt voice,

"Come on Sara, say goodbye to Beaver and give Granny and Pop hugs; it's time to go."

After dinner, Nancy got Sara ready for bed and called on Scott to tell her a bedtime story. When, after a while, Scott turned off the lights in Sara's room and retired to his office, he was surprised to find Nancy sitting on the love seat waiting for him.

"Hi, Babe. Nothing worth watching on TV tonight?"

"Who's Captain Peckford?" retorted Nancy with a high-pitched voice. "You said that if I went with you into the cemetery you would tell me why you returned a changed man. Well, I did, and you'd better deliver."

Surprised by Nancy's demanding tone, Scott stood at attention and saluted her while staring at his patriotic picture-in-uniform hanging on the wall above his desk. The computer screensaver flashed the figures of naked women, swirling like dervishes, dancing to no music. In response to Nancy's firm insistence, Scott's mind had apparently taken leave of the moment and traveled back to Peckford. The salute endured as Scott postured like a mime and reveled in his reverie until Nancy's hissing voice whisked him back to reality.

"Scott, look at me; I am your wife and I have a right to know."

"It's a long story, Babe. Tomorrow is Monday and I have to be at work at eight."

"I'm not going to sleep until you tell me. Wasn't it enough what you put us through today," snapped Nancy, unable to conceal her anger.

"What was it that I put you through? I thought we had a lovely day."

"Have you already forgotten what you did in church?"

"Father James was the one who invited me to declare myself and so I did; what's wrong with being honest?"

"You disrupted the holy Sunday service and you can't see anything wrong with that?"

"You blame me for speaking my mind? Would you

rather have a yes-man for a husband?"

"Your behavior was inappropriate."

"How's that?

"Well, never mind, you won't understand. Now, tell me who was Captain Peckford," cajoled Nancy with a faint smile that belied her consternation.

"Make room for me. I want to sit by you," said Scott as he took one last glance at the swirling women on the computer screen before he approached Nancy.

Nancy moved over to the right side of the leather loveseat, making ample room for Scott who gingerly sat and wrapped his mighty arm around her bare, bony shoulder. "It's a very long story, Babe. I'll tell it to you one day. We both have work tomorrow. Let's get to bed early."

"The only time you've gone to bed early was on your first night home. You've not gone to bed with me since that night. I feel like a widow because my husband is too busy with his books and computer to notice me."

Tears dripped down Nancy's quivering cheeks, her face took on a forlorn look, her chest heaved with suppressed ire, and her breasts bellowed up and down as if she were starving for air. Then, like a wounded animal, she shrieked, "You've not made love to me for twenty-seven months, damn it. I want to know what happened to my man. You can't keep me in the dark forever. I have a right to know what..."

Gently, Scott shushed Nancy's mouth with his fingers and began wiping her tears, one eye at a time, just like he did five years earlier when on their first date she asked him to help her get an abortion and he offered to marry her instead. The déjà vu must have struck them both at the same moment because a sudden silence gasped as they looked into each other's knowing eyes. After a polite intermission, Scott got up, opened his desk drawer, and retrieved a photograph of Captain Theodore Peckford in uniform standing underneath a palm tree in what appeared to be an oasis. Then, with a doleful tone and downcast eyes, he muttered as if talking to himself, "That was the last time I saw him."

"Why? What happened to him?" sniffled Nancy as she pulled the picture out of Scott's hands and peered into it as if trying to decipher all the meanings concealed within its frame.

"He had me drive him to the oasis and asked me to leave him there. He said that a secret unit was coming to pick him up at sunset. Before I left him, he asked to me take his picture and then gave me the camera as a souvenir."

"So, why's that a big deal?"

"I obeyed him and drove back to camp without questioning anything he told me."

"And what happened next."

"When at roll call he turned up missing, they asked if anyone knew his whereabouts."

"And did you tell them?"

"No."

"You didn't tell them?" glared Nancy as she laid the picture down. "Why didn't you?"

"Because I believed that he had a secret mission and that no one was supposed to know his whereabouts."

"And then what happened?"

"Administration launched an investigation and questioned me because I was the one last seen with him. Of course, I told them what I knew but that was a week too late. They never found him." Scott picked up the picture, went to his desk, and reverently placed it back in the drawer. With back turned to Nancy, he couldn't help stealing another glance at the naked dancers on his screen before he returned to the couch.

"Did you show them the camera he gave you?"

"No. It was a personal souvenir."

"Well, is he dead or isn't he?" inquired Nancy with obvious agitation.

"His body was never found but his dog tag turned up a month later in a Basra flea market and was brought to our unit by a local spy."

"So what are you saying then? I'm confused."

"The administration thinks that he was a deserter."

Scott swallowed the last word with a tedious gulp.

"Deserter?"

"They interrogated me for several hours because they knew that we were close. I told them everything I knew but that was not enough. They wanted to know all the details of all the conversations we had ever had and I had to write a complete report about the ideas that he had shared with me."

"Ideas? Oh, I see."

Nancy grappled with the concept of ideas as she studied Scott's face.

"Well, tell me then, what kind of a fellow was he and what kind of ideas did he share with my husband?"

Nancy's tone was deliberately cynical but Scott did not seem to notice. He continued to answer Nancy's questions as if she were the committee in Iraq.

"He was a scholar of history, philosophy, and ethics, and he had many beliefs that were considered dangerous."

"Dangerous? How can beliefs be that dangerous? What on earth do you mean by that," interrupted Nancy, unable to hide her frustration at the way the conversation was going.

"Well, for example, he believed that our invasion of Iraq was based on false information that was deliberately fed to us by Al-Qaeda."

"Al-Qaeda? He's crazy and so are you if you believe such nonsense. Why would Al-Qaeda want us to invade Iraq?"

"Because they wanted Saddam out and they wanted up to do it for them."

"And why did they want Saddam out? I thought that he was helping them."'

"He controlled them and they didn't like that. They wanted to kill Americans and Saddam wouldn't let them."

"So Saddam was protecting us from Al-Qaeda? I think that both you and Peckford are mad."

"Saddam was not interested in killing Americans because he didn't want the US breathing down his neck."

"So, according to your and Peckford's theory, Al-

Qaeda fed us the wrong information and got us to invade Iraq so that it could kill our young, brave soldiers on its own turf. Right?"

"Well, Peckford explained that Al-Qaeda's strategy has always been to kill us with our own powers. On 9/11 they used our jets as bombs and now they are using our military might to squander our resources and to expose our soldiers to their deadly fire power."

"So, you must believe that Al-Qaeda is smarter than the US."

"Peckford believed that our most deadly military error has been the underestimation of our enemies, especially Al-Qaeda."

"And is that why Peckford deserted?"

"No, he's too patriotic and too intelligent to do something that stupid."

"So why did he arrange to disappear that way and why did he choose to use you as his accomplice?"

"I'm not smart enough to know. But I am sure that Peckford was not a deserter. He was a very deep thinker and when he couldn't get them to think out of the box he became frustrated with them."

"Assumptions?" jeered Nancy, shaking her head with disbelief. "How can anyone believe such nonsense?"

"The suicide rate among our soldiers in Iraq is higher than what it was during the Second World War, Korean War, or Vietnam War."

"What does that mean?"

"It means that Al-Qaeda is successfully killing us with our own powers."

"Who's perpetrating all these rumors? I don't believe a word you said," shouted Nancy, no longer able to restrain herself.

Her emotional reply again went unnoticed by Scott who continued with his explanation in the same automatic tone as before.

"So far, more than fifty of our soldiers have committed suicide." When Scott said that, he put an imaginary gun to his temple and pretended to pull the trigger.

"Don't, Scott," screamed Nancy as she pulled his hand back. "You're lying. Why hasn't this made the news?"

While every now and then stealing a look at his computer screen, Scott continued unperturbed, "Seven of the fifty killed themselves after returning to the US and two of these also killed their wives before they put the guns to their own heads." This time, Scott put his imaginary gun to Nancy's temple and pretended to pull the trigger.

"You're sick," screamed Nancy as she moved her head away, stood up, and plugged her ears. "I don't want to hear anymore. I was proud of you before, but now, you've made me ashamed because you're talking like a traitor."

"I was commended for my good work and received an honorable discharge," retorted Scott, with a resigned, sheepish voice.

"So what changed your brain then?"

"Peckford. He taught me a lot about many things and he confided in me."

"So, whatever happened to Peckford since he was so smart and knew it all?" taunted Nancy with a smirk then, noticing that Scott was glancing at the screen again, followed it with, "Turn off your damn computer. Is it possible for you to have a conversation with your wife without these naked dancers between us?"

"He didn't want them to find his body," replied Scott, as he got up and stood between Nancy and his computer.

"What? Who? No one can disappear without help. Did you help him? Oh, Scott! Are you mad? You can go to jail for that."

"I didn't help him, Babe. He was my superior officer, and he ordered me. I told the committee everything I knew."

"Everything?" queried Nancy with raised eyebrows.

"Well, everything except for the camera because it was a personal gift."

"What did he have you do?" Nancy paced as she

prepared her face for the threat. "You'd better tell me if you want me to stay with you."

"He asked me to take his handgun, his uniform, and his shoes back to camp and to leave them on his bed. He said that his secret mission required that he not be uniformed or armed. When I left him in the little oasis, he was barefoot, in his underwear."

"Did you ever find out what happened to him?"

"Nobody knows. The committee found a note in his uniform, which they showed me when they were questioning me."

"Go on, damn it. What did the note say?" glared Nancy as she stood face to face staring Scott in the eyes.

Calmly and out of memory, Scott proudly replied, "It said that when a soldier is forced to choose between his country and his orders, the hero sides with his country and the coward, with his orders."

"And what are you, a hero or a coward?" spewed Nancy with hands on waist.

Scott flexed his massive biceps as he reparteed, "I was a coward while in Iraq, but now, I'm feeling more like a hero. In Iraq I obeyed my orders but here I'm going to obey my country."

"Really! And how's that?" smirked Nancy, as she stood looking at Scott's mighty arm still defiantly flexed upward.

"By educating myself, by refusing to remain ignorant about current events, and by speaking my mind without fear of repercussion." Scott rattled his answer briskly as if he were stating his name, rank, and serial number.

With a cynical move, Nancy reached up and gently un-flexed Scott's defiant arm. Then, pointing it behind him at the obscene screen, she remarked, "And you do all that with Internet pornography, I suppose?"

Unperturbed by her scornful cynicism, Scott brought his arm back, placed it lovingly on Nancy's bare shoulder, and said, "Don't be silly, Babe. That's just my distraction; my bad tasting-medicine that I take because it makes me feel better. I really spend most of my computer time tracking Al-Qaeda chatter."

With an abrupt motion, Nancy pulled his arm off her shoulder and, staring at him with irate eyes, came back with, "And the violent, inconsiderate, upside-down sex we had on your first night home, and the jumping in the pool with your clothes on, and the incident at church this morning were all designed to attract Al-Qaeda chatter, I suppose?"

With no awareness of propriety, Scott calmly explained, "The sex position was something I saw in a porno movie at camp, and I couldn't wait to try it out when I got home. But I must admit, trying it wasn't nearly as good as watching it, and when it was over, I didn't think it was worth repeating."

Nancy's eyes moistened as she remembered that horrible night when she was tossed like a used rag and spent the night gazing at Scott's back as he slept unaware. Scott, on the other hand, did not notice her consternation as he eagerly continued defending his actions. "The splashing in the pool with all my clothes on brought back memories; it was something we did in the Euphrates when we wanted to cool off, and that is definitely worth repeating."

"*The son of bitch forgot that he almost choked Sara,*" thought Nancy as she gazed in amazement at her transmuted man.

Unmoved, Scott continued his defense, "As for the scene in the church, Father James deserved everything he got, preaching guilt as he was to a God-loving congregation."

"And the fact that you haven't touched me since your first day home," queried Nancy with irrepressible tears flooding her eyes. "Does that mean you now prefer pornography to me?"

"I haven't touched you because I feel guilty and ashamed," replied Scott as he lowered his head and stared at his feet.

"Ashamed and guilty of what?" quizzed Nancy with utter exasperation. "I'm your friggin' wife."

"I feel guilty making love to my beautiful wife in my comfortable home when, everyday, my buddies in Iraq are dying at the hands of Al-Qaeda."

"And if you feel guilty, you stop loving your wife?"

"It's hard to be amorous while grieving. Give me time, Babe. I've just returned from hell and it's hard to snap back after losing so many friends."

"Is all this grief because Peckford died?"

"Not only Peckford. So much has happened that you don't know about."

"Like what?"

"Like the fact that I wouldn't be here if Peckford hadn't saved my life."

"But you said you were in communications and that your life was not at risk?"

"Something horrible happened and he risked his life to save mine."

"Why don't you tell me about it then?"

"I don't want to remember it. I don't dare to remember it. I'm afraid that if I tell it, I'd have to relive it."

Saying that, Scott put his shaky arms around Nancy and fell into a pensive silence, which Nancy ignored as she went on with her interrogation.

"Well, are you or are you not going to talk to me about Peckford?"

"He was a remarkable man."

"In what way?"

"He was a true leader and led us with his mind and with his heart. He was a scholar who taught us how to think for ourselves and when to doubt and when to question."

"And what was your relationship with him, Scotty."

"He was my idol, the man I wanted to become, the intellectual father I never had, and I loved him."

"More than you love me?"

"Not more, just different. He opened my eyes and ears and taught me how to understand history, philosophy, poetry, politics, cultures, and art. We had long, wonderful discussions that forever changed the way I see things."

47

"What was the most important thing he taught you?"

"He enlightened my mind and taught me to question dogma."

"Dogma? What the hell is dogma?"

"Everything that we have been brought up with and taught."

"Is that why you questioned Father James?"

"Perhaps?"

"That's not you Scotty. If I had known that you were going to become a philosopher, I wouldn't have married you. I cut hair for a living, remember? I used to be able to reach your head but I can't anymore because your haughty head is up in the clouds now. I wish you had never met this Peckford. He changed you so much I no longer recognize you. All of sudden you are a mighty philosopher that no one understands," retorted Nancy as she pried herself out of Scott's overwhelming arms. "You weren't like that before you left! Boy, you must have really fallen under the spell of this Peckford devil. Well, guess what Mr. Plato, he's no longer here and you're no longer in Iraq. You'd better snap out of it if you want me to stick around."

Nancy's crimsoned face meant every word she said and Scott knew and feared that determined look.

"Don't talk like that, Babe, and please don't ask me to be less than what I am. You and Sara are my whole life and I could never make it without you." Saying that, Scott tried to hold Nancy in his arms again but she pulled away and wiped her tears with her bare palms.

"I just want my Scott back," gasped Nancy as her tears mellowed down her anger.

Restraining his impulse to wipe off her tears for fear that he might be rejected, he cautiously handed her a tissue paper, which she accepted. Then, affirming with unwavering resolve, he continued, untouched by her sorrow, "The old Scott is gone, Babe, and he will never return. You need to get used to the new Scott, the better Scott."

Hearing that, Nancy's eye sockets went suddenly dry with anger as she reparteed, "Do you mean the porno Scott or the heathen Scott? Which one is the better man? I say to hell with you and all porno heathens like you."

"But I'm ..."

Nancy stormed out of Scott's office, went into the bedroom, slammed the door, and locked it with a snap. Scott heard the lock click into position; it sounded like a guillotine and he felt his head begin to roll. Instinctively, he put his hand over his neck, ran his fingers through his hair, gazed at his bare feet, and squeezed his toes. Then, he got up, unlocked his desk drawer, took out one sleeping pill, and went to the kitchen for water. When he returned to his office, he pulled Peckford's picture out of his drawer and gazed at it as if searching for answers. It was long after midnight before he finally turned off his office lights, curled his tall, lean body into a fetal position onto the small loveseat, and fell asleep.

Nancy listened as she lay quietly in bed, her eyes open wide with anguish. *"He'll come after me,"* she thought. *"Surely he will. He won't be able to sleep without me. Although he has too much energy, he'll still have to get tired of reading at some point. I can wait him out. Sooner or later, he'll need to have sex. Porno can't possibly satisfy a man like him. He must need it temporarily only because, for some contorted reason, he's not ready to face me. I bet that when he gets hungry enough, he'll forget all this porno and philosophy shit and come groveling for sex. When he gives in and comes back, I'll make sure that he'll never leave again."*

The night stood watch as Scott slept and Nancy tossed. The only one at peace at the Thornton home was Sara who was having entertaining dreams relating to her adventurous day with her daddy. She would wake up tomorrow in a good mood and go to her preschool as if nothing had happened. Mrs. Mann, her teacher, would also treat Sara as if nothing had happened although, just like at Casady School, the word would also be out at the St. Helena School that Sara's father, Scott Thornton, had disturbed the Sunday service at St. Michael's Church on the water.

Nancy's thoughts ramified like ivy and kept her awake as the darkness slowly stole towards the light. *"Damn, it's getting late,"* she thought as she tossed between her side of the bed and Scott's. *"I'd better unlock the door. He'll be coming in any minute now. What a screwed up mess I'm in. I broke up with all my lovers when he returned, thinking that he'd be hungry for me. I wish I hadn't because I'll have to find me a new lover now. Richard Straight has been after me for years. Dick Straight? What were his parents thinking? Oh, how funny is that?"*

Chapter Five
(Repercussions)

Monday, the 25th of September, was busy with awakenings. The first to awaken were the truckers and pickup drivers, followed by the bus and SUV drivers, and the last were the sedan drivers. The roads were tandemed with cars vying for the better positions in the long, serpentine lines. Dreamy drivers were multitasking— scanning their radio channels for music and news, talking on their cell phones, sipping their coffee, and smoking their cigarettes all at the same time. *"The busy hum of men"* rubbed Oklahoma City's yawning eyes and pried open her crimson eyelashes that gleamed all along the slumbering horizon.

Scott negotiated the winding traffic with remarkable ease, slipped onto Tenth Street from the Broadway Extension, turned left on Hudson, parked, and leapt the stairs to the Hartland Bank on the ninth floor. Little did he know that Breena, the bank's gossip diva, had already shared with the entire ninth floor what she had heard about the St. Michael's Church Sunday service. As he made his way to his office, pairs of eyes escorted him all the way to his seat. Unaware, he settled down and began working on the pending loans stacked on his desk. He worked diligently and tirelessly until Breena marched into his office with a cup of coffee and a folder. Taking a sip from her coffee, she laid down the folder on Scott's desk and said in her sensual, nasal tone, "The boss wants you to take a look at this and be ready to discuss it with him at lunch. You need to be in his office at twelve." Having delivered her message, Breena sat down on one of the two chairs facing Scott's desk and eyed him while he browsed through the folder. Then she took one more sip of her coffee, crossed her legs, pulled her skirt up a bit, and sighed, "All of a sudden, you've become famous."

Scott continued to browse through the folder, utterly deaf to Breena's solicitous remark.

"Yes sirree, you're our overnight famous man."

"Huh," nodded Scott, still focused on the folder.

"Huh! Is that all you have to say?"

"Say what?" mumbled Scott with head still buried in the folder.

"Say something, General. I'm the official staff delegate, and we're all dying to know what really happened." Breena's nasal tone must have barely scratched Scott's attention shield because he repeated her words without reflection, like a preoccupied popinjay.

"General, delegate, happened?"

"You're hopeless. You need to hear what people are saying. The last I heard was that the Pope was preparing an excommunication."

"I was in communications in Iraq."

Noting Breena's exasperation at the lack of attention she was getting, Brenda snuck in and sat on the other chair facing Scott. Like a pair of curious kittens, Brenda and Breena eyed every move that Scott made as he continued to study the folder, unperturbed by their feline antennas. When he finally finished, he raised his head and, realizing that Breena and Brenda had been staring at him awhile, cleared his throat and asked, "What's going on, ladies?"

"You tell us," meowed Brenda and Breena in unison.

"Tell you what?" barked Scott with an abrupt wag of his hand.

"Tell us what happened at church," beckoned Brenda with a reassuring gleam in her eyes. "We've heard so many versions and don't know which one to believe."

"That was a private matter and this is a bank. You're paid to work, not to gossip."

Having said that, Scott buried his head back in his loan folders ignoring Breena and Brenda's intrusive giggles, which sputtered for a while before fading away into the bank lobby. Indeed, Scott continued to work, absorbed, unaware, with one eye on the clock so that he would not miss the noon appointment with his boss.

"Scotty, come in son," came his boss's words upon hearing Scott's knock at twelve o'clock sharp.

"Sir, you wanted to see me?" said Scott as he walked in, stood erect in front of James McMaster's desk, and handed him the folder.

"At ease, son, you're no longer in the army," commanded Mr. McMaster as he took the folder. Then, with a softer tone, he inquired, "Hungry for some Mexican food?"

Before Scott could answer, James got up, came over to Scott, put his arm around his shoulder, and escorted him out of the office to the elevator across the hall. While waiting for the elevator, Scott remarked, "Sir, you forgot to bring the folder."

"Ah, we don't need folders for lunch, son," replied Mr. McMaster as he rubbed his abdomen with his palm. "Just around the corner there's a new Mexican restaurant that I haven't tried yet. What do you think?"

"I'm sure it's fine, Sir," answered Scott as he followed his boss into the elevator.

Going down, the elevator picked up lunch goers from several floors, boisterous young men and women eager for a break, older men and women with long resigned faces, and visitor clients, some of whom seemed ill at ease in a packed compartment. Many of the passengers took a second look at Scott on their way out, and several even whispered to one another while exiting the building. Although unnoticed by Scott, this hushed notoriety did not escape his boss who tried to hide his feelings by engaging Scott in idle chat all the way to the restaurant. After a brief wait, they were seated in a remote corner, chosen by James for its quiet location. When the waiter came, Mr. McMaster ordered a taco salad and Scott, an enchilada special. Then, out of respect for seniority, Scott sat quietly and waited for his boss to begin the conversation.

Mr. McMaster, a distinguished looking man in his early sixties, had been the CEO of the Hartland Bank for over fifteen years and was the one who hired Scott right out of college. After a short learning period, Scott proved to be a star employee with an enormous capacity for hard, productive work. At one year, Mr. McMaster promptly promoted Scott to his present position as chief loan officer.

Unsurprisingly, Scott proved exemplary in his work ethic and inimitable in his prolific output of high-quality loans. Over time, Mr. McMaster came to value Scott's opinions in commercial loan matters and depended on his detailed financial analyses in making his final decisions. Given their excellent professional relationship, it was indeed obvious why Mr. McMaster felt a bit awkward at broaching a non-work related topic with Scott and why he chose an off site location for his discussion. It did not help matters that James McMaster was also a good friend of Scott's father with whom he had done a lot of steering work for St. Michael's Church.

The taco salad and enchilada special were consumed in polite quietude among perfunctory comments about work and weather. Finally, Mr. McMaster cleared his throat and with an awkward cough began the conversation.

"Scott, you know how much I respect you and value your exemplary professionalism as a member of my staff."

"Yes Sir," nodded Scott.

"And you know that your father and I have been friends for a long time."

"Yes Sir," nodded Scott again.

"I also know that you are an honorable man and a God-fearing Christian."

This time Scott nodded but said nothing, his handsome face maintaining a peaceful aspect which stood in striking contrast to the strained expression on Mr. McMaster's face.

"I was at church yesterday when you confronted Father James and disrupted the Holy Service."

"I didn't see you, Sir. We arrived late and sat in the back pews," reflected Scott with no hint of remorse in his voice.

"Well... hum... what I meant to say was... no... let me rephrase it as a question. What on earth caused someone as stable as you to act that way?"

"Well Sir, what Father James stated was thoughtless and cruel. The church should be a place of peaceful worship not of guilt-laden anguish. Still, I wouldn't have challenged Father James had he not invited a response. But when he did, I felt it was my honest duty to speak up." Scott talked with remarkable ease as he explained his position. Then he looked at his watch and said, "I have an appointment with a client at one o'clock, Sir."

Hardly able to maintain his composure, James looked at his own watch. Then he looked straight into Scott's eyes and with a master's voice reprimanded, "Scott, don't you think an apology is due?"

"Oh, no, Sir. Not at all, Sir. I don't need an apology. I'm not even upset at what Father James said, but it was wrong of him to preach things contrary to the teachings of Christ." Here Scott looked again at his watch; it was seven minutes till one. He quietly got up and apologetically said, "Sir, I'd like to be in my office when my client arrives. I hope you won't mind if I make a dash for it." Having said that, Scott clicked his heals and took off with long, hurried strides leaving his boss staring at the scraps in his plate with worried thoughts jostling behind his glazed eyes.

"*Whatever happened to this Thornton kid defies comprehension. He was so likable before he went to Iraq. I hate to lose him, though. He's such a good worker. Oh boy, what a mess. Doesn't even realize how inappropriate he was and still is. How can you fault someone like that and yet how can you not? Defies comprehension.*" These were Mr. McMaster's thoughts when he was startled from his reverie by the busboy wanting to clear the table.

"Are you through, Sir?"

"Oh, yes, thank you," replied James with a start.

"Would you like me to clear the table?"

"You go right ahead, son. Oh, I see; you're short on tables. I need to be going anyway. I'm sorry we took so long."

Saying that, James left the El Padre restaurant and aimlessly wandered about in downtown Oklahoma City. His feet led him past the bus station where two homeless vagabonds sat on a bench taking turns sipping from a bottle in a brown paper bag. "*Why don't they work? They seem perfectly fit. The poor wretches; they're poor enough to* be homeless but with enough money to buy booze. *Defies comprehension.*"

From there Mr. McMaster wandered past the bombing memorial, looked at the 168 empty chairs and gazed into the reflection pool at all the restless souls that crowded the place. *"What a waste. All who died were innocent. I was at my desk when the blast shattered all the bank's windows. Nineteen thousand dollars just for glass repairs. Defies comprehension."*

In Bricktown, McMaster entertained himself by surveying all the new restaurants and breweries that seemed to have sprouted all of a sudden along the riverbank. A prostitute winked at him as he sauntered. She was leaning against the wall and showing her fishnet stockings through a side split in her skirt that smiled all the way to her waist. *"What legs! She must think that I'm lonely. I was young once. I'm too old for her now."* He stole another glance at her over his shoulder and was surprised when she winked again at him, painting a wet smile with her tongue. *"Damn, she was expecting me to look back."*

Replacing his sauntering steps with purposeful strides, McMaster took refuge in a side street to escape her eyes, which burned holes in his back. *"I was fifteen years younger at the New York Catholic Convention when I had me one of those beautiful, delicious creatures. It's so much easier to become righteous when one is older. Then I couldn't but now I can effortlessly say no."*

McMaster glanced back one more time before he redirected his attention to all the renovations in what was once the deadest part of town. *"MAPS (Metropolitan Area Projects) sure did a good job. Never expected them to succeed but they sure did. Who'd have expected it? Defies comprehension indeed."*

Then, as he approached the bank, he began to feel a bit heartbroken at Scott's behavior, a bit disappointed with himself for having failed to shame Scott into an apology, a bit bewildered at Scott's genuine lack of remorse, a bit uncertain about Scott's future with the bank, and a bit squeamish about having to face Scott's father, Father

James, and Father Elias at the next church board meeting scheduled for the coming Saturday. Nonetheless, all these important thoughts failed to totally dominate James McMaster's attention as his feet managed to find their way back to the bank. His eyes were still obsessing upon the split in the prostitute's skirt that showed her fishnet hose all the way to her waist. *"Oh, boy, what legs,"* he thought as he entered the bank's lobby only to find himself face to face with Scott who was escorting his one-o'clock client out. There was a victorious gleam on Scott's face as their eyes met. Scott nodded but did not introduce his client to his boss, a calculated, courtesy move that James McMaster both understood and appreciated.

Also around noontime, but on the other side of town, Nancy finished her last morning client, went into her office at the Glamour Hair Salon, and dialed Father Elias. After five rings she got the recorded message with Father Elias's voice, "This is Father Elias. I'm unavailable at the moment. Please leave a message and I will call you back. Have a blessed day."

"Father Elias, this is Nancy Thornton. I need to talk to you about..."

Before Nancy could finish her message, Father Elias picked up the phone, "Nancy, hold on a second please."

In the background, Nancy could hear Father Elias escorting some visitors to the door. A few moments later, he was back on the line.

"I've been waiting for your call."

"I need your help Father," whispered Nancy with a voice poised at the edge of tears. She did not want anyone at her salon to hear her whimpering. So far, no one had asked her embarrassing questions but three of her clients had already called and cancelled their hair appointments without rescheduling.

"I'm in a deep mess, Father, and I don't know how to get out of it."

"We are all trapped in our lives and need God's help, my child," reassured Father Elias.

"Father, you don't understand. Scotty is not just inappropriate; he's going crazy on me. He returned from Iraq a disturbed man, a man that I no longer like, a man that I'm afraid of, a man that I don't want to be with anymore. He's not the same man I married, Father. You remember our wedding, don't you? You remember what a nice man Scotty used to be and how he saved Sara and me from..." At this point, Nancy lost her composure and began sobbing.

"Nancy, please settle down and let the Lord come to your aid. Have faith and the clouds will clear. Tell me what else is going on, child; the more I know, the more I might be able to help."

"Father, I'm scared," replied Nancy with a quivering voice. "I no longer feel safe with him, and I want out."

"Why? Has he tried to harm you?"

"No, no, he's very kind but he's also weird. I know it sounds contradictory, but he's so weird and so strong, Father. Oh, well, I worry that if he snaps, he might become uncontrollable."

"Perhaps you and Sara should stay with your folks until things return to normal," interrupted Father Elias. "Mishaps could happen, you know, and it's better to be safe than sorry."

"But Sara adores him and he tells her bedtime stories. She would never understand and it would make her very sad. Can you talk to him, Father? He will listen to you because he respects you."

"What do you think I should say to him?"

"I don't know, Father, but I was hoping you could do something to help him. Perhaps you could talk to him about his pornography, about his absent libido, and about his anti Al-Qaeda activities."

Father Elias sighed as Nancy went into the details of what had happened. She gasped between phrases, took long interrupted sighs, and sniffled as she talked.

"Why don't you have him come and see me, and I will see what I can do."

"I'll try, Father, but I doubt that he will fall for that.

You see, he doesn't think that there's anything wrong with him. But, he'll come with us to church if Sara asks him to."

"Oh God, whatever you do Nancy dear, please don't bring him to church again. He needs a doctor much more than he needs a priest. I'll pray for him, and you do whatever it takes to protect yourself and your daughter."

"But... oh well... I see... I guess it's up to me... all right then. Thank you Father. Pray for us, please."

Nancy said a polite goodbye, leaned back in her chair, and drifted into thought. *"That was a bummer of a phone call. Father Elias doesn't want anything to do with Scott. His parents and sister don't want to deal with him either. I can't stand him anymore. The only one who still likes him is Sara, and that can't last much longer. The son of a bitch is playing with my mind. I'll have to protect my sanity. I need to find me a real man. I'm pretty sexy and men still like me a lot. I'll show the pervert..."*

Nancy was startled by a knock at the door. Before she could respond, Suzie poked her head in and said, "Mrs. Cunningham is ready."

At Casady, Mr. and Mrs. Bradford had a normal day. The looks they had anticipated did not materialize, and fellow teachers did not interrogate them like they had expected. Everything seemed to go as usual with the normal hustles and bustles of a regular school day until it was time to go home. On the way to their car, they happened to run into the Headmaster, Mr. Turner, who was also a personal friend. What began as a casual chat in the hall among three friends quickly developed into a deep, convoluted discussion. The Headmaster informed them that the entire school was in the throes of gossip and that many versions of the incident were circulating. He then inquired with overflowing curiosity, "Could you please tell me what really happened?"

"It was a sad incident," answered Mr. Bradford, and after relating the details to Mr. Turner, he concluded by saying, "Scotty is a good kid. He'll be all right. He just needs time. Wars punish our souls."

On their way home, the Bradfords did not talk. Although there was nothing to say, there was much to ponder. Nancy was their only child and Sara, their only grandchild. What else could they do but wait and hope that no one would get hurt by his post-traumatic madness?

They drove slowly in the five o'clock traffic, entered the Heritage Springs Addition, turned left on Summerset, and came into direct view of their home at the end of the street. There was a police car with flashing lights parked behind Nancy's car.

"What's going on?" exclaimed Mr. Bradford.

"Oh, my God, something is wrong," said Mrs. Bradford, "The policeman is talking to Nancy."

Chapter Six
(Separation)

At the Bradford's, Nancy had a lot of explaining to do. After the policeman left, Nancy parked her car in her parent's driveway, took her suitcase out of the trunk, held Sara by the hand, and both of them walked into the house behind Peter and Frances.

"What's going on?" exclaimed Mrs. Bradford with obvious alarm. "Sara, Darling, why don't you go into the living room and play with Beaver; he's waiting for you."

"I don't want to play with Beaver. I want to go home to Daddy," pouted Sara.

"Leave her alone. She's not stupid. She knows that I left him," sighed Nancy as Sara began to cry.

"You what?" interrupted Mr. Bradford.

"I had to, Daddy. Father Elias was the one who suggested it. We talked at noon."

"Father Elias wouldn't want you to leave your husband! What did Scott do when he saw you leave with Sara?" retorted Mr. Bradford.

"He wasn't home. He coaches swimming at the YMCA on Mondays."

"You mean to tell me that he doesn't even know that you've left him?"

"No Daddy, he doesn't yet, but he'll figure it out when he gets home and finds us gone."

"Did you at least leave him a note?"

"No," answered Nancy as she held Sara in her arms and tried to calm her.

"I'll make some tea," interjected Mrs. Bradford as she scurried into the kitchen, leaving Nancy with her dad standing in the hall.

"Come into the living room and let's talk this thing over like mature adults."

Mr. Bradford led the way into the living room followed by Nancy, with Sara sniffling in her arms. As they sat quietly awaiting tea, Nancy looked at her father and, without saying another word, pantomimed that she wasn't going to say any more until after Sara had gone to sleep.

Mrs. Bradford walked in with sandwiches, tea, and a glass of milk for Sara. Time ambled as they ate and watched television in resigned quietude.

"Sara, please don't feed your sandwich to Beaver," broke in Nancy only to find out that it was too late. Obviously, Sara was not hungry but Beaver indeed was because the Bradfords, given their present befuddlement, had forgotten the routine of putting Beaver's dinner in his bowl before sitting down to eat. After the ten o'clock news, Nancy put Sara in bed and was telling her a bedtime story when the phone rang, startling everyone including Sara who started calling for her daddy to come tell her the bedtime story.

"Scott...yes...they're here," answered Mr. Bradford. "I don't think they are coming home tonight...No...I don't think that's a good idea...She's putting Sara to bed...okay, I'll have her call you when she's through."

"How does he sound?" inquired Mrs. Bradford.

"Calm but very sad. He wanted to come over but I discouraged him."

"She shouldn't have left without talking it over with him first. I don't understand what's making her run away all of a sudden. He's still a good man in spite of his problems. What other man is going to love her like he does. Kids..."

When Nancy rejoined her parents, having finally succeeded in putting Sara to sleep, Mr. Bradford said, "You'd better call him. I told him that you would. He's not taking it very well."

"Call him and say what, Daddy?" snapped Nancy, looking a bit frightened and bewildered.

"Somehow, you'll have to convince him that you're so afraid of him that you had to leave him, even though he has never tried to hurt you. Why don't you start by telling him how you left your home in such a hurry that you got a speeding ticket doing fifty in our addition?"

"That's not funny, Daddy."

"Oh! It's not? You don't find humor in what is going

on?"

Before Nancy could answer, the doorbell rang and Beaver charged the door with a barrage of high-pitched barks.

"Oh, my God! It's him, I know it," cried Nancy as she ran into the kitchen followed by her mother.

Mr. Bradford went to answer the door while the two women eavesdropped.

"Hi, Scotty."

"Hi, Mr. Bradford."

"Would you like to come in?"

"No Sir, I don't think that Nancy would like me to. But I'd like you to give her this, please. Thank you Mr. Bradford. I'd better be going now."

Mr. Bradford walked into the kitchen with a pot of yellow mums in his hand and gave it to Nancy saying, "He didn't think you wanted him to come in."

"Oh, there's a card with it. How sweet of him," purred Mrs. Bradford as she peered over Nancy's shoulder.

Nancy's eyes filled up with tears and her hands shook as Mrs. Bradford and she read the card together:

Nancy, I'm sorry Babe. I know that I'm not the same man you married, but I can't help it. I don't think that I can change back to what I was. I understand that you may not want to put up with me anymore. If you decide to leave me for good, please let's remain friends so that we can continue to do our best for Sara.

I love you, as always,

Scotty

The Bradfords sat in the living room and were quiet for a long time. Mr. Bradford was a rational man who could clearly see Scott and Nancy's differing points of view. *"There's no good solution,"* he thought as he pondered the situation. *"Scott is a good but disturbed man... Nancy needs social respectability, personal attention, and sexual*

63

satisfaction... Sara needs a daddy... Scott needs to be left alone... There's no good solution..."

Mrs. Bradford sat stunned, wondering what she would do if she were in Nancy's place. *"Oh dear, Peter and I have had such a good marriage. But I remember when we were first married how his last girlfriend, Monica, started calling me and telling me what a horrible man he was, and how he had abandoned her like he had abandoned all his other girlfriends, and that I was going to be his next victim. Whatever happened to her, I wonder? My old boyfriends never said anything to Peter because they were the ones who left me because I wouldn't go all the way. They preferred girls who were good in bed. But oh, poor Nancy! Scott won't have sex with her because he prefers pornography. I remember how hard it was not to go all the way when I was dating. So often, I came so close to doing it and I would've were it not for the fear of getting pregnant. Oh, how close I came to doing it with Johnny that one night... Gives me the shivers to think about it. I wonder who's going to be Nancy's first when she starts dating again? I bet she'll be wild, as starved as she has been. Oh, I shouldn't think these thoughts. I'd better get up and feed Beaver. Oops, Beaver? Oh, what a terrible thought—Scott is starving Nancy's Beaver! Oh, no, I shouldn't think like that. I'll get up and feed Beaver. He's been neutered, poor chap. He'll never have sex, poor poodle."*

Nancy was burning on the inside although she appeared taciturn. *"Son of a bitch, sending me flowers to make me feel guilty. I'm not going back to a weirdo. Sara will be fine. I know how to be single. I can't begin to remember how many men I dated while he was in Iraq. I had to do it in secret then, but now, I can do it openly. I'll have a different man between my thighs every night for as long as I want. I see how men look at me when they come to pick up their fat wives. I can make their wives' hair beautiful but I can do nothing about their wives' blubber. That's why those husbands look at me with wide eyes. I can feel their burning gaze between my butt cheeks. I can get any man I want. I'll choose them rich and stupid. The ones with ugly wives are always the most grateful. I'll show this weirdo of mine. I'll make him come begging when he starts missing me. No one knows that he's not Sara's father except Jane and Father Elias. They won't tell. He'll spend his life chasing Sara and me. I'll show the bastard."*

"Perhaps we should all turn in," said Mr. Bradford after the group's prolonged silence. "Tomorrow is a working day."

"Poor Beaver, he was so hungry. You should see how quickly he finished his bowl," announced Mrs. Bradford on her way back from the kitchen with a sly smile on her lips.

"Mom, I don't know about you, but I'm ready to go to bed and so is Dad. I'll sleep with Sara."

"Okay, dear, but are you sure you don't want to talk to your mom about the situation? Your dad won't mind if us girls were to have a heart-to-heart talk."

"There's nothing to talk about, Mom. I'm going to leave him. I refuse to live like that; that's all there is to it," hissed Nancy with a raised voice.

"Okay, okay, you don't have to scream. Let's all go to bed then. We'll wake up with clearer minds tomorrow."

Just as Mr. Bradford turned off the lights and got ready to follow his wife into the bedroom, the doorbell rang again and Beaver charged it with another barrage of high-pitched barks. It was close to midnight. Nancy rushed out of Sara's room half-dressed and pantomimed to her father not to open the door, whispering, "It's him again. Don't answer. He'll go away if you don't."

"But, what if..."

"Shhh," replied Nancy with finger-on-lips.

The doorbell rang again and Beaver charged it again.

"Don't open, please," insisted Nancy.

Mrs. Bradford came tiptoeing in, looking pale and whispering, "What if he breaks down the door? He's so strong you know."

"Mr. Bradford, I know that you can hear me," came Scott's voice from behind the door. "I mean no harm and you don't have to open. I just brought Sara's blanket, in case she wakes up. She won't be able to go back to sleep

65

without it. It's in a bag. I'll leave it by the door. You can pick it up after I leave. I'm sorry I bothered you. Goodnight."

From the window, the Bradfords watched Scott drive away. They waited a little while longer without making a sound. Finally, when his car lights had turned the corner and could no longer be seen, Mr. Bradford walked cautiously toward the door and looked through the peephole. Mrs. Bradford stood behind him whispering, "Do you see anything?"

Nancy, who stood a few steps behind Mrs. Bradford, came forward, held her dad by the hand, and led him back into the living room whispering, "He's still there. He probably had one of the swimmers he coaches drive the car away. Let's all go to bed. He won't break in if the door stays locked."

"But what if Sara wakes up and wants her blanket?"

"If she does, then you can open the door and get it for her."

"But, it'll be cold then."

"We'll warm it up in the microwave."

Although the Bradfords went to bed with harking ears, no other sound disturbed the night, and Beaver did not charge the door again. When Sara woke up crying, Nancy held her in her arms until she fell asleep again.

When, the next morning, Mr. Bradford went out to get the paper, he returned with Sara's blanket in a brown bag and gave it to Nancy at the breakfast table saying, "It's a bit cold. Should I warm it in the microwave?"

"Not now, Daddy," squeaked Nancy, and with obvious exasperation quickly slid the bag underneath her chair so that Sara wouldn't find out what was in it. Of course, the blanket titillated Beaver's snout. Instead of concentrating on the food in his bowl, he became obsessed with the bag, eyeing it with inconsolable yearning and faltering restraint. When his resistance was finally overwhelmed, he stole the bag from underneath the chair, dragged it into the living room, pulled the blanket out, and began chewing on it with boisterous appetite.

"Mommy, Mommy, Beaver has my blanket," cried Sara as she slid off her booster chair and dashed to save her blanket. After a brief but loud struggle, she returned to the table dragging her blanket, with Beaver snarling at its other end. When Nancy tried to wrestle the blanket out of Beaver's teeth, it tore at the corner sending Sara into a wild storm of tears.

"Dad, please do something," pleaded Nancy as she tried to calm down screaming Sara.

"None of this would have happened if you had let me open the door and bring in the damn blanket last night," barked back Mr. Bradford as he lifted Sara into his arms and walked away with her toward the bedroom.

Chapter Seven
(Intimacies)

The last five days of September passed in aloof silence. Each time Scott tried to call Nancy, she wouldn't answer. When he asked to see Sara, he was told to stop by the Bradfords after work. Nancy was never there when he visited because, allegedly, she was busy looking for an apartment. When as a courtesy Scott offered to move out and leave the house for Nancy and Sara, Mr. and Mrs. Bradford explained that Nancy would have to move to a cheaper place anyway because, given her limited income, she didn't want to be straddled with a big house payment. Of course, by default, this made Scott responsible for the entire payment as long as he had the house.

October passed with much heartache and grief as Nancy slowly moved her belongings to her parent's home while Scott was at work. Each day he would come home to find less of Nancy and Sara's things. The first to move out was Nancy's makeup and toiletries, which left the bathroom void of the delicate aromas that used to waft into the bedroom and fill Scott's nostrils with genteel innuendos. Then Sara's clothes and toys followed and Nancy's closet started to look leaner with each fleeing day. When, one day, Nancy's pillow abdicated, the bed seemed suddenly vacant on her side and, quite unconsciously, Scott began sleeping in the middle as if to mitigate the solitude of his lonesome nights.

Ever since he returned from Iraq, Scott's habit was to retire two or more hours after Nancy had gone to sleep. Nonetheless, when he would come to bed, he would always find comfort in Nancy's warm, whispering breaths, which purred down his ears and lulled him to sleep with rhythmic excursions. However, ever since she and Sara moved out, he missed the evening routine of dinner and family conversation followed by Sara's bubble bath and bedtime story. He also missed Nancy's soporific sounds that used to suffuse the bedroom with their sweet murmurings and found it harder to fall asleep without their calming tunes.

He would lie perfectly still, in utter silence, and try to recapture the muffled whimpers that, in her sleep, Nancy used to make as he lay by her side. Most nights, he would fall asleep trying—and awaken while still trying—to hear her breaths. But only in his dreams could he unleash his true feelings and parade them naked to his heart. Only in the profoundest quietude of sleep could he confess that he did not really love Nancy as a man should love a woman. He loved her, no doubt, but loved her because she was Sara's mother, because she was Jane's best friend, because she was beautiful, because she was sexy, and because she was a hard working provider. Indeed, he loved her for all the wrong reasons, more like a sister than a wife.

When pieces of furniture, kitchen utensils, family pictures, and certain accessories began to migrate, Scott was awed by the realization that Nancy had found an apartment, and that the finality of their separation had become implacable. Then, to add more pangs to his heartache, on the last day of October when Scott dropped by after work to see Sara, Mr. Bradford half-opened the door and, for the first time, did not ask Scott to come in.

"Hi Mr. Bradford. Is Sara not here?"

"No, sorry, she's with her mom."

"Well, when can I see her then?"

"I don't know, son. You'll have to work this one out with Nancy."

"But she won't talk to me when I call her. Did she tell you what her new address is?"

Here Mr. Bradford appeared a bit embarrassed as he answered, "She said that she's not going to tell anyone where she lives because she's afraid that you might find out and start going there to visit Sara whether she's ready for you or not."

"But, how am I going to see Sara then?"

"She said that you can come here after work on Tuesdays and Thursdays, and you can keep Sara with you every other Saturday and Sunday starting this coming weekend."

"Oh, and how is Sara handling it?"

"She cries sometimes, but Nancy said that she's getting used to it."

"Has Nancy seen a lawyer yet?"

"I don't know for sure."

"Well, even though today is Tuesday, I take it that I'm not going to be able to see Sara tonight. I guess I'll see her in two days then. I'm sorry about all this mess, Mr. Bradford. I know it's my fault but I can't help what I've become. I'll be back on Thursday at about the same time. Please tell Sara that I love her."

On his way to the car, Scott felt his throat tighten, making it harder to breath or swallow. He was more heartbroken than angry, however, at how the evening had turned out. All day he had dreamed of seeing Sara and could think of nothing else while hurrying through his files at work. He hadn't been able to tell her a bedtime story ever since Nancy had taken her away from him and he was so looking forward to sharing with her a new story that he had rehearsed, over and over, just for her eager, little ears.

As he got into his car, his thoughts wandered and he began to worry about how Sara's feelings might change towards him if Nancy should ever tell her the truth about her real father. He realized that Nancy did not love him and he had accepted that fact as a well-deserved consequence of his own lack of passionate love for her. And even though he strongly believed that he needed a woman's love to bring meaning to his life, he also knew deep in his soul that he could manage without that kind of love for as long as he had to. But without Sara's love he couldn't possibly survive. Sara was the bright sun that shone upon his dull, routine life and for her, he was prepared to do anything and everything.

After sitting in his car awhile under the Bradfords' watchful gaze, Scott gathered the fragments of his shattered heart, backed out of the driveway, and drove off into the vacant evening. An overwhelming sadness overcame him as he drove. He felt a desperate need to talk to someone he trusted, someone compassionate, someone wise, and someone who could help him come to terms with his inscrutable life. He had no such friends and he was not in the habit of opening his soul to his parents. The realization that he was utterly alone at this most heart-rending time of his life caused a feeling of air hunger to suddenly grip his lungs. He stopped the car, jumped out, and began gasping at the night air as if he had run out of oxygen. His overwhelming fear of choking worsened the harder he breathed. His skin began to tingle as if it were submerged in electrocuted water. He saw himself levitate above his own body and float up to the sky while his poor corpse languished down on the busy street beside his abandoned car.

As time steamed away in the upper layers of the atmosphere, his air hunger was slowly replaced by cold sweat and he slowly descended back into his body. Then, with confused trepidations, he got back into his car and drove in the direction of the Memorial Park Cemetery. He did not understand why he didn't want to go home or what he would do when he reached the cemetery but his lack of understanding did not seem to matter. When he arrived, it had gotten dark and a bit cold. The cemetery gate was locked so he parked his car along the street—by the brick-stoned wall made of deconstructed Guernica limbs and faces—and effortlessly leapt inside the necropolis. Walking on the pebbled path, he could hear his marching footsteps grind down the little, white stones as he strode towards the bench. Captain Theodore Peckford was hardly discernable to his eyes so he ran his hand over the name and then traced it with his finger from the initial C to the terminal D, sighing in the spaces between the words.

The mist obscured the stars and blurred the distant lights. Occasionally a car turning on Kelly would send parallel beams into the sky from its bright headlights. Night sounds became muffled as they penetrated the fog, reaching Scott's ears like unintelligible whispers. Motionless, he sat and carefully listened, trying to decipher the fuzzy voices of the night. His efforts, though unproductive, conjured a trance, which took him back to

Iraq, to the desert, to the oasis, to Captain Theodore Peckford, and to Captain Peckford's favorite poet, Walt Whitman.

"O Captain, My Captain, you have changed my mind, my vision, and my perceptions about most things. I no longer fit where I used to fit, nor belong where I used to belong. The world has become transparent to me so that instead of seeing and hearing people as everyone else does, I now hear their inner thoughts, scrutinize their irrational beliefs, see through their pretenses, and snicker at their unconscious delusions. Is it a curse or a blessing, My Captain, to be able to peer into the reality of things in spite of all the camouflage and makeup?

You warned me when you began teaching me, but I didn't care; I was eager to learn and couldn't have enough. You told me the story of Socrates and how he was executed because he taught people how to think for themselves and how to think with an open mind instead of allowing their cultures to do their thinking for them. You told me that once I learned how to think rationally, without my biases, that there was no going back. You warned me that I would become isolated and ostracized. Well, My Captain, it's already happening. Nancy is leaving me and taking Sara with her. She says it's because I prefer pornography to her company. How can I tell her that I hate pornography, that I do it because it makes me forget, that the real reason I can't be amorous with her is because I can't pretend about my feelings any longer? I married her because I was lonely and I loved the fact that she was pregnant. I love Sara more than life and I don't want to lose her. But it's too late now. There's no going back. O Captain, My Captain, why did you go away and where are you now when I need you most?"

Wrapped in the misty, cold night, Scott cried acid tears as he sat on the bench with head between hands gazing at his feet. As the tears dripped on his shoes, they struck a muffled beat like Whitman's sad poem that he had learned by heart in the desert, *"O Captain! My Captain! Our fearful trip is done."* He could see that he was slowly losing everything that he had ever loved, everything that he had worked hard to earn, losing everything, that is, except his soul, which is not and will never be for hire or for sale.

"I shall be true to myself, no matter the price," he thought. *"No one shall ever rob me of my dignity again. I'll be the best that I can possibly be. My soul is mine and only mine. I shall live my life like Socrates, not like Faust. I shall never pretend. O Captain, My Captain, my friend, and my teacher—you shall be proud of me; that much, I promise you."*

When Scott was ready to leave, it was close to midnight. He wiped his eyes as he took one final look at all the silent graves surrounding him, graves with buried stories that will never be told, graves with interred secrets that will never be revealed, graves of good men and good women who were trapped in lives of pretense, socially correct lives, conformist lives, lives of platitudes, lives lived with downcast eyes. *"I shall not live like them, silent, submissive, and un-heard. I shall sing my soul to the heavens with gaze uplifted not downcast. I refuse to be buried alive."*

On his way home from his pilgrimage, Scott was at peace again. He could only think of Sara, and Thursday evening, and the coming weekend. When he arrived home, he noticed that his house phone was flashing. The message was from Nancy: "Scott, I'm worried about Sara. She's not eating and Mrs. Mann says that she's not participating in play activities. The school psychologist suggested that we take her out together at least once a week. How about this coming Thursday? We could take her to McDonald's. I'll be at my folks when you come for her after work."

Scott replayed the message three times and concentrated on Nancy's tone. It carried no regret, no remorse, no concern, no tenderness, and no sorrow. It was a business-like, matter-of-fact message, a contract dictated by necessity, a desperate attempt to assuage a child's heartache at seeing her nest dismantled. He even began to wonder if Nancy ever loved Sara and remembered how forceful he had to get in order to convince her not to have an abortion.

"Boy, she was so intent on getting rid of Rick's baby, so angry at having gotten pregnant, and so infuriated when I offered to marry her instead of loaning her the money to get the abortion. It was only when I threatened to tell her mom and dad that she finally came around. I don't think that she has ever forgiven me for having replaced her playful life with a serious one."

Scott prepared a ham sandwich and a bowl of soup, sat down in front of the television, and listened to the regurgitated news bulletins: More suicide bombers and more American soldiers killed in Iraq... Saddam's trial is causing more violence...

"Oh, when will this Iraq insanity end? We can't get out without leaving a bloody civil war behind. But if we stay, we will lose more American lives and get our country deeper into debt. We're killing our country and that's what Al-Qaeda wants. That was one of Captain Peckford's deepest concerns.

It was supposed to be simple; we go in, find the weapons of mass destruction, eliminate Saddam, establish the first democracy in the history of the region, and then quickly get out. It was supposed to be Superman Simple. But nothing complex is simple. There are no simple solutions for complex problems. That's what Captain Peckford used to say."

These were Scott's thoughts as he turned off the television, went into his office, got on line, and began browsing the pornography sites. Slowly his knotted-up neck muscles began to unwind as he felt the merciful hand of relief massage his erect spine. He could feel his loins slowly rise like a long-range cannon preparing to fire. With a desperate, repetitive iron grip he tripped the trigger and felt the explosion roar throughout his body, rattling his skeleton, arching his back, and launching him into another out-of-body experience. He rose from behind his desk, took a few aimless steps, collapsed on his loveseat, and languished in steaming sweat, sad, all alone, like a smoldering volcano after the rains.

Exhausted, he lay on the couch awhile with closed

eyes and shuddering lips. *"I should get up and take a shower,"* he thought. *"I should get up right now, before I fall asleep on this couch. I should get up, take a shower, and then go to bed. If I don't get up now, I'll ruin my pants. I mustn't do any of that stuff when Sara spends the weekend with me. If I can't find a woman who can love me for what I have become, I shall spend my life reading. I love Diogenes. He was a brave man. He didn't care what others thought of him. He said that we ought to live shamelessly, like animals, with no taboos. He even took care of all his biological needs in public, defiantly, for everyone to see. I wish I were a dog. O Captain, My Captain, where are you now when I need you most?"*

Scott, curled into a fetal position, fell asleep on the loveseat in his office and did not take a shower until the next morning. The first thing he did when he woke up was to carefully wipe off the smudge inside his pants with a wet towel. He scrubbed with intense, repetitive motions until every bit of the dried-up, white residue disappeared. Then, satisfied that he had left no traces, hung the pants to dry. He hung them deep inside his closet lest Nancy should come for more of her things and happen to chance upon them. *"She sniffs at my clothes like a curious cat. She'll know if she sees my pants hanging up to dry. She'll smell them and know. She'll know immediately and not even God would be able to help me then.*

I've always done it in the guest bathroom, done it only when I was sure that she was asleep, and done it without ever leaving a trace. If she catches me now, she'll take Sara away from me, and her mean lawyer will twist the facts and report me to the DHS. Once the DHS gets on the case, I'll get branded for life and would never be trusted with Sara again. No, no one can ever find out. I can't stand to live without Sara. If they take her away from me, I would die. Sara is my life, and because of her, everything must stay pure. I need to clean up my act and gain control of my animal urges. Diogenes must not have had any children."

Chapter Eight
(Reunions)

On the second of November 2006, Thursday came sliding on wet feet. The sun tried to smile through the clouds but her eager glitters were stifled by the gray veil that shrouded the Oklahoma skies. Scott went to work with a thudding heart, which was not assuaged by the fact that he had to disapprove three of the five loans that awaited his sharp pen. They were three young families with little children who wanted to move out of apartments into homes, but they all had large credit card debts and limited incomes. His thudding heart cried for them all, but his circumspect business mind shed no tears. As he slashed their burgeoning hopes with his jagged, disapproving signature, he felt like a hired executioner performing his painful duty.

To his alarm, the image of the executioner proved too painful to sustain and, at the same time, too painful to evade. It felt like a bad burn after which the pain persevered long after one's hand had been pulled out of the fire. He tried to distract his mind with other details but the executioner's image loomed like a heavy sword over his bent neck. Exasperated, he closed the files, pushed them aside, and went for a cup of coffee. Somehow, getting up and walking away from his office caused the executioner's image to fade into oblivion. Upon returning to his desk, the sharp claws of yet another image gripped his throat.

The image of the three young families with little children who wanted to move out of apartments into homes clung to his mind like a deciduous tree with leafless branches clawing at the fall sky. He tried to work, to be productive, to appease his angst by dwelling on the two loans that he did approve but the vision of naked branches flailing in the fall sky kept intruding upon his consciousness, irking his mind, and clawing at his heart. When he tried to distract the vision by walking away from his desk for a coffee refill, the flailing branches turned into little, reaching-out hands crying with silent voices that only he could hear.

Back at his desk and still feeling bewildered, he took one big gulp from his coffee, which was so hot it startled him. Frustrated, he set the cup down and gazed at the spiraling steam while his mouth and esophagus smoldered on. The rising vapor conjured the weekend mornings when Sara would sit in his lap at the dining room table while he sipped at his coffee and read the paper. He recalled how curious Sara would become when he would get to the comics page, and how she would insist that he explain them all to her. *"My smart little Sara,"* he thought as he mused watching the rising steam swirl into the air. Then, with a sudden start, he rose, walked up to the window, gazed at the drippy sky, and mumbled to himself, *"Oh, God, yes, of course, apartment, flailing branches, apartment, reaching-out hands, apartment, silent voices crying in the night, apartment, my sweet Sara, my sweet little Sara, leaving her home to live in an apartment. No wonder I couldn't drive the image out of my mind."*

As Scott was preparing to leave, Breena walked in with two folders, which she placed at his desk without saying a word. Throughout the day, Brenda and Breena had been eyeing his restless agitation, his taciturn detachment, his refusal to go out for lunch, and his excessive coffee intake. There were several unfinished files scattered all over his desk, an unusual sight that immediately attracted Breena's attention. Silently, she reached for Scott's cup of coffee, took a slow sip, making sure that she left a red crescent of lipstick on the edge, put it back in front of Scott, and with her coy, nasal voice intoned, "Too much coffee ain't good for ya, General."

Avoiding eye contact and feeling a bit intimidated by her drone, he stared at her lip print on his cup and firmly said, "What do you need? I'm getting ready to leave."

"Boss wants you to study these two folders and tell him what you think first thing tomorrow morning."

"I can't stay. I need to go. I'll take them home with me and work on them tonight."

Smiling with red, pursed lips while wagging her finger and swaying her hips, she droned, "You know you're not allowed to do that, General. Against bank policy, remember?"

"Well, I'm pressed for time; I can't right now. I need to go." Saying that, Scott quickly browsed through the two folders, frowned back at Breena, and continued with an even firmer tone, "These will take me at least an hour to study. I just can't do that right now."

Provokingly, Breena sat in one of the chairs facing Scott's desk, coyly crossed her legs, pulled her dress a sliver above her knees, and carefully smoothed her hose starting at the ankles and massaging all the way up her lean, white thighs. Then, catching his embarrassed gaze, she groaned with wry satisfaction, "Hey, don't look at me like that. I didn't make the rules. I'm just delivering the boss's orders. You know how he is. He wants them first thing in the morning." Then, after a short pause and another tug at her dress, she continued, "What's wrong with you anyway? You've not been very friendly lately and your desk is a mess. We're all worried about you."

Looking rather bewildered, Scott scratched his head and said, "I'm sorry to be that way. I have a lot on my mind." Then, gazing at the two folders in front of him, he mumbled as if talking to himself, "Nothing can be that urgent. I don't understand the great hurry. But if I have to, I will. Okay, I'll take care of these files. When I am through, I'll leave them on his desk."

"I'll get you some more coffee before I turn off the pot."

When Breena waltzed out, Scott held his head between his hands and gazed at the files. *"The Bradfords expect me at five-thirty and I'll be lucky if I can make it by seven. I'll have to call Mr. Bradford."*

Trying to postpone his inevitable tardiness, Scott waited till five thirty and then called the Bradfords. Mrs. Bradford happened to answer.

"Hello."

"Hi, Mrs. Bradford."

"Scotty?"

"Yes ma'am. May I please speak to Nancy?"

"Ah, Nancy is not here."

"Oh, I see. And how about Sara?"

"Sara is with her."

"Did Nancy say what time they'd be coming?" "No, she didn't."

"We were supposed to take Sara out to McDonald's together. Did she change her mind?"

"You'd better talk to Peter. Please hold."

While waiting impatiently, Scott could hear unintelligible fragments of a muffled conversation going on in the background between Frances and Peter Bradford. Finally, after what seemed like a long hold, Peter Bradford picked up the phone.

"Scott."

"Yes Sir."

"They're not coming tonight. Nancy called and said that Sara is not feeling well and that she's going to keep her home and put her to bed early."

"Oh, God. Is she sick? Is something wrong?"

"No, no, there's nothing wrong. She's just not feeling well enough to go out."

"Well, what about the coming weekend?"

"She didn't say what her plans were. I'm sorry. I don't know what else to tell you."

Hearing Mr. Bradford's apologetic tone, Scott surmised that he was not being told the entire truth.

"Sir, could you please ask her to call me. It's not fair to keep me in the dark. She never answers my calls."

"I'll see what I can do, Son. I'll try my best."

Before Scott had a chance to say another word, the line went dead, which surprised Scott. *He hung up on me. He's never done that before. For some reason, he couldn't wait to get off the line.*

After that conversation, Scott felt a weight mount upon his chest and interfere with his breathing. He sighed frequently as he ruminated over the many possible reasons behind Nancy's evasiveness. He understood how deeply hurt and disillusioned she must have felt and why she decided to leave him when she did; all that seemed justifiably human to him. But he couldn't help but suspect that she was also trying to keep Sara away from him, and that made him somewhat angry. *"What if she decides to keep Sara this coming weekend?"* he wondered. *"I'm at her mercy and there isn't much I can do about it unless I get me a lawyer. But the mere idea of a legal battle is repulsive to me. She can have it all, if that's what she really wants, as long as she shares Sara with me. Sara is my one and only condition."*

When Scott finally made it home, it was close to nine. He first looked to see if the telephone was flashing and felt disappointed when it wasn't. *"She didn't even bother to leave a message?"* He then went through his e-mails hoping to find a note from Nancy, but all he found was junk. *"Not even a brief note to explain why?"*

He didn't feel hungry and there was nothing worth watching on television. Pornography was not on his mind any more, but Sara was. He went into her empty room, lay on the carpet, closed his eyes, and gave free rein to his imagination. He imagined helping her with her food at dinner, giving her a bath, telling her a bedtime story, tucking her in, kissing her goodnight, and having his morning coffee with her on his lap. He mused and mused until he fell asleep and, almost immediately, began to dream. He dreamt of Nancy's wedding to her new husband—he could see her walking down the aisle in her white dress, could hear the wedding bells ring and ring and ring until he awakened to the incessant ringing of the telephone in his office.

Startled, he glanced at his watch and ran to the phone. He could hear a faint whimpering as he held the receiver to his ear and said nothing, awaiting the other party to announce itself. As he waited, the whimpering deteriorated into loud sobs interrupted by sighing gasps, but not a word was spoken. He looked at his watch again; it was ten after midnight. *"What an ungodly hour to be* making prank calls," he thought as he contemplated hanging up the phone but didn't because he was enthralled by the sincerity of the grief coming from the other end. Still, he held his breath and waited without making a sound until the sobbing faded into deep, sighing breaths and ended with a hoarse, whispering "Hello."

"Yes," he replied and said no more.

"Scott," pleaded the harsh voice.

"Yes," he said and fell silent again, not knowing what else to say to such a strange, panting voice.

"Scotty, this is Nancy."

"Oh, my God," he screamed. "What happened to your voice? What's wrong? Are you okay? Is Sara…?"

"Scotty, please help us, please, we need you," came Nancy's stuttering plea.

"Oh, no. Is Sara okay? Are you hurt? I'll come right away. Tell me where you live."

"Building C, apartment 404, Acropolis Villas on Meridian and Sixty-third."

Scott dropped the phone, ran to his car, and darted into the night. "*Slow down, we're in a hurry,*" he kept repeating to himself as he drove. "*These were Churchill's words to his driver. Peckford told me that. A speeding ticket would delay me. I need to stay calm. That's what they taught us in Iraq. Keep your head cool in crises. Think before you act. Resist impulsive behavior. Rehearse your plans before you engage in action. No, no, nothing can happen to Sara. Nancy seems to get herself in trouble when she's on her own. I can't be left in the dark anymore. I need to stay close in order to protect them. I wish Nancy would stay and take on a lover. No one has to know. Oh, damn, I forgot my gun. Red light, come on, come on. Maybe I should run it? There's no one to see me. Slow down, we're in a hurry. Breathe deep. Keep cool. Green, it's about time. Slow down. Don't lose it. Damn, another red light. There are too many of them. They don't need a light at every intersection. Oh, here we are, Acropolis Villas. Where's C-404? No, that's A-104. Here's B-104. I'm getting close. C-104, yes, here we are, it must be right above it on the fourth floor. Good, that's Nancy at the window..."*

Scott took the stairs, three at a time, to find Nancy waiting for him at the door with finger on lips.

"Shhh... Sara is asleep. It took forever to calm her down. I had to wait till she slept before I called you."

"Nancy? Oh my God, what the hell happened to your face? Who beat you up? I'll kill the bastard..."

"Please, shhh..."

When Scott pulled Nancy into his arms, she began to shudder and gasp like an abused, abandoned puppy. He lifted her onto the green living room sofa, stroked her forehead with rhythmic, soothing motions, and at the same time surveyed the room. He recognized the furniture, arranged in good taste. The green vase looked nice sitting on the side table next to the orange lamp. The large, soft, beige chairs on each side of the window were nicely contrasted by the dark-brown rectangular table that sat in between them. On the table, arranged like a fan, were fashion magazines offset by a fresh bouquet of flowers. *"Nothing is broken, nothing seems out of order, the room is tidy, but why the fresh flowers? She never buys flowers. I'm the one who always bought them for her."* These were Scott's errant thoughts as he began his conversation with Nancy.

"Oh, Babe, you shouldn't have left. Tell me what happened. Where's Sara?"

"Shhh... she's in her bedroom, first door on the right."

Carefully, Scott tiptoed, opened the door, and peaked. The nightlight barely revealed Sara's face. *"Good, no bruises, breathing fine, uncovered, I'd better cover her..."*

"No, don't go in, she'll wake up, Scotty, come back, come back please, I need to tell you what happened."

Nancy's frantic whispers brought Scott tiptoeing back to her side. She sat up, wiped off her tears with her bare hands, wrapped her elbow around Scott's muscled arm, and laid her head on his shoulder.

"Oh, Scotty, please don't hate me. Promise me that you won't hate me after I tell you. I'm so bad..."

Scott blotted her tears, one eye at a time, just like he had done on their first date when he convinced her not to have an abortion. For some reason, this caused her to mix laughter with tears.

"You're always saving me..."

"What happened, Babe?"

"When we split up, I called Richard Straight. Remember him from high school? He was in your graduating class."

"That lecher?"

"Well, I was lonely and he'd just gotten divorced."

"Okay."

"Well, we started dating."

"Okay?"

"I fixed him dinner."

"Tonight?"

"Yes, tonight."

"Is that why you told your folks that Sara wasn't feeling well and couldn't go to McDonald's?"

"I told you I was bad."

"And?"

"After dinner, I put Sara to bed and when we thought that she was asleep, we went into the bedroom and closed the door."

Here, Nancy broke into tears again, "I told you I was bad..."

"Never mind. Go on, please."

"Well, we were making love when Sara walked in on us and started to scream."

"Oh my God. She saw you doing it? You didn't think to lock the door?"

Tears welled into Scott's eyes as he tried to keep his composure. Then, after a long, somber pause he asked, "What happened next?"

"I pushed him off me, but before I could get to Sara, he'd already pushed her out and locked the door. He could hear her scream and bang on the door but he didn't care.

He said we needed to finish what we had started and tried to get me back in bed."

Here, Nancy's tears became mixed with deep, doleful sighs. For a while, she and Scott sat silently with her head still buried into his shoulder and her elbow even more tightly wrapped around his arm. Unconsciously, in an attempt to soothe the pain of her confession, he began stroking her hand, which she clasped and held tight to her bosom as she summed up her courage and continued. "I pushed him away and tried to get to the door. He went into a rage, grabbed me by my hair, and started to slap me with all his strength while I screamed at the top of my voice, hoping that someone would hear me. With both of us screaming and crying for help, he finally came back to his senses, threw me on the floor, called me a bitch, grabbed his clothes, and, without putting them on, ran out stark naked like a mad man."

Scott stiffened up, clamped his jaws tight, and his lips became almost white. He could figure out the rest for himself. *"Sara saw it all and was frightened out of her wits. This would probably traumatize her forever. She will never trust another man with her mother. She may even have trouble dating when she grows up…"*

"That son of a bitch. I know how to find him. I'll show him…"

"Scott, promise me that you won't do anything foolish. Remember, we still have Sara to raise."

"What if he starts to stalk and pester you?"

"He won't. You know, he doesn't even scare me anymore because I know that you'll always be there when Sara or I need you."

Nancy seemed a lot calmer after her confession. Her newfound confidence even put Scott at ease; he un-stiffened as he felt his muscles unwind, his pursed lips relax, and his breaths become less rapid.

"Are you going to tell your parents?"

"Hell, no. Not my parents or yours. They'd never understand."

"What are we going to do with Sara? She's been

traumatized, you know."

"Ah, well, let's wait and see what..."

Before Nancy could finish her sentence, there was a loud knock at the door.

"It's him, I know it, he's back, he may be armed, Scotty..."

As Nancy clung tighter to Scott, a meek voice came from behind the door, "Nancy baby, please, open up, I came to apologize, I got you another bouquet of flowers, I even got something for Sara too and ..."

Scott looked at his watch; it was 1:30 am. Quietly, while the guy was still talking, Scott gave Nancy a reassuring pat on her knee, got up, walked to the door, opened it, grabbed the utterly surprised man by his neck, almost lifted him off the floor, and without saying a word, dragged him into the middle of the room. The dangling, small-built, redheaded man clung to the Walmart bouquet of flowers while struggling with his other hand to free himself from Scott's iron grip. To reward his futile, freeing efforts, Scott tightened his grip like a vise around the gasping man's neck until he began to turn gray. Seeing him in such a subdued state, Nancy began to laugh, which angered the frothing man, causing him to kick and writhe while his bulging blue eyes glared incredulously at Nancy's smug face gleaming with satisfaction.

"Mr. Richard Straight, would you like to die now or later?" came Scott's unwavering, dry voice as he loosened his grip just enough for the man to respond.

"Later, Sir, not now, please, later," and saying that, Richard Straight threw the bouquet of flowers at Nancy's feet in a desperate act of supplication and then lifted his arms above his head as if he were at gunpoint.

Scott let go of him and watched him scurry to the door with his arms still up in the air, race down the three flights of stairs with arms still high, and fade away into the night.

On the sofa, Scott and Nancy held hands in solemn silence. Indeed, there was much to be said, but the time was not right, and it was almost three.

"Scotty," pleaded Nancy. "Would you stay with us tonight? Sara would be thrilled to find you when she wakes up. It might lessen her fear and help her heal. Would you? Please."

"I have work tomorrow and all my things are at home."

"You can leave after you see Sara; you'll still have enough time to get ready."

"Okay, then, let's go to bed. It's awfully late."

In the bedroom, Scott took off his clothes but kept his undershirt and boxers on. While helping Nancy rearrange the bed and smooth the sheets, he noticed a soft, red lump wedged between the sheets and the foot of the bed.

"What's that," he asked as he pointed to the lump.

"It's nothing," replied Nancy as she quickly turned off the lights, retrieved the lump, took it to the bathroom, and threw it into the trash.

In the feeble nightlight, Scott spied Nancy's embarrassment and her hasty, furtive snatching of Richard Straight's bright-red briefs from underneath the sheets. Nevertheless, when she returned from the bathroom, she found Scott's stretched-out arm awaiting her lean, delicate body. *"Just like the good old days,"* she thought as she felt him pull her onto his chest and gently stroke her back. *"It's good to feel safe. Can't wait to see Sara's excitement when she wakes up and finds her daddy and me in bed together. If I wake up before she does, I'll pick her up and tuck her in with us."* As Nancy pondered these pleasant scenes, she molded her entire body into Scott's, wrapped her thigh around his stalwart legs, and melted away into sleep.

Chapter Nine
(Surprises)

The Friday sunrise surprised Sara when its rays climbed up to her bedroom window, stole in between the curtains, and streaked her ruddy cheek. Still in half-sleep, she tried to escape the sun's menacing fingertips by turning from one side to the other. As she did, the light startled her eyes and awakened her.

She felt breathless, hungry for air, almost paralyzed with memories of last night while certain disturbing moments flashed into her mind louder than lightning bolts across a blackened sky. She wanted to tiptoe into her mom's room and snuggle in bed with her, but she found herself too faint to move. The vision of her mom's boyfriend pushing her away and locking the door—with her mom screaming in the background—was still too hot to handle. Instead of getting up, she squeezed her pillow between both arms, turned her head away from the bedroom door, closed her eyes, and, like an opossum, feigned sleep.

For a long while she lay, afraid to move, listening to the crackling sounds of daybreak. Suddenly, a door squeaked and footsteps scraped the carpet, drew nearer, and halted outside her room. Her heart galloped, took flight, and carried both her lungs with it. Dizzy with visions, her lips went dry, her tongue stuck to the roof of her mouth, and her ears began to ring with an eerie, dissonant pitch that resounded painfully against her horrifying anguish. After a torturing, immeasurable wait, her room door creaked open, footsteps approached, and rapid, shallow breaths came closer until she felt them in her hair. Still, terror frozen, she kept her eyes shut and held her breath so long that tiny, inaudible whispers of air began to flee her throat in little bursts. The body heat from the figure kneeling beside her gave her chills, and goose bumps suddenly sprouted all over her quivering skin. But then, quite unexpectedly, a warm kiss surprised her cheek, lingered on a tender while, and gently lifted off like a soundless butterfly. In the breathless silence she heard a long, deep sigh as the footsteps retreated out and her room door clicked shut. Soon after that, the front door opened and closed, and footsteps carefully tumbled down the stairs and faded away. Still, she dared not stir until she heard her mother's busy motions in the kitchen. The soothing aromas of breakfast and coffee finally put her heart at ease and gave her the courage to get out of bed.

Scott had a long day awaiting him. He needed to finalize the file reviews before presenting them to his boss first thing in the morning, a task he failed to complete the night before. He also needed to go through the remaining files stacked on his desk and render his opinion regarding the pending loans. *"Too much work and too little time,"* he thought as he drove home to get ready for work. The road seemed a lot shorter than last night and the traffic lights were far more cooperative. Not feeling the urge to race, he let his mind meander on his favorite topic, Sara. The fresh, flushed cheek of Sara still lingered on his lips. *"Will she wake up afraid?"* he wondered. *"Will Nancy tell her that I spent the night with them? Will Nancy start taking my calls instead of ignoring them? Will she let me have Sara this weekend? Will she start accepting my dinner invitations, as the psychologist had suggested? Surely she's going to become more cooperative after last night. Surely she will let me back into their life again."* He caught himself smiling all of a sudden, something he had not done since Nancy left him and took Sara with her. His eyes glittered with good tears, tears of hope, tears of love, tears of indomitable joy.

Scott arrived to work an hour early and was able to complete last night's work on time. After his meeting with his boss, he consumed the delinquent files on his desk with rejuvenated energy. While immersed in work, Breena sauntered in, stood facing his desk, and said nothing. He saw her come in but refused to raise his head from his work, half-pretending that he was not aware of her presence. It was a short, silent stalemate interrupted only by Breena's gum-smacking slurps and Scott's paper-shuffling sounds. Finally, after one long, bleating sigh,

Breena broke the silence with, "You don't wish to notice me, General?"

"Oh, sure," began Scott, raising his head and looking at Breena with a faked startle.

"I'm sorry to interrupt your highness, but there's a postman with a letter for you."

"Postman? Letter? Oh, yes, I forgot. I did forward my military mail to my office because ... Never mind. Where is he?"

"Standing right there," Breena pointed, "in the middle of the lobby. May I usher him in, Sir?"

"That won't be necessary," replied Scott as he abruptly got up and walked towards the postman, leaving Breena standing alone at his desk. Then, a few steps away, he stopped, turned around, and surprising Breena who was poised like a curious cat at his door, reparteed with matching sarcasm, "You're dismissed, ma'am."

Scott approached the postman with controlled apprehension and meekly said, "I'm Scott Thornton."

"There is a registered letter for you. Would you sign here please?"

When Scott saw the letter, his heart began to thump. It was from the United States Army addressed to Lieutenant Scott Thornton, Hartland Bank, 4132 N. Hudson, Oklahoma City... In the middle of the lobby, Scott stood alone, staring at the letter in his hand with utter disbelief. Then, with drooping head, he slowly shuffled back to his office. Breena, seeing the expression on his face, walked away leaving him to his thoughts.

I know what they want. I gave them two years and now they want more. Reinforcements, that's all they care about. Bring in more so that Al-Qaeda can kill more. It's the safest thing, gambling with the lives of others. Damn it, I just got back my daughter and now I have to leave her again. She'll forget me if she doesn't see me for another year. I'll call her daily. But, what if Nancy won't let me talk to her? Surely, Nancy will remarry while I'm gone. Hope her new husband will treat Sara better than that dick without balls. Oh, God, I need some air. The damn files can wait and the bank can go to hell. They can't fire me now. No matter what, I'll have my job when I return. No, I'll have my job if I return. If, if, and if... There are too many ifs in my empty life, too many damn, stinking ifs."

Scott left the Hartland Bank escorted by a dozen pair of watchful eyes. With long surly strides, he leapt down the nine flights of stairs, exited on Hudson, and marched to the Survivor tree, the tree that survived the bombing, the tree that, day and night, stands guard over the bombing memorial. There, he stood at the wall under the tree and gazed at the reflection pool with its audience of 168 empty chairs arranged in terrible silence. "How many more chairs have we emptied so far and how many more will silently follow?" With that thought shrouding his mind, Scott opened the letter: "You are ordered to report to Fort Sill, Lawton, Oklahoma, on Monday, the 27th of November for two months of training before redeployment to Iraq." After reading the entire letter several times, as one does when one wishes to repudiate reality, Scott irreverently folded the letter, put it back in its envelope, slipped it into his back pocket, and redirected his moist, blurry eyes towards the 168 empty chairs poised obediently by the reflecting pool. "I could come back as an empty chair," he thought as profound furrows gripped his face, "or as an empty bench like Peckford." For some reason, the image of an empty bench instead of an empty chair stretched out his frowns into smiles as he exploded into uncontrollable, almost manic laughter intermixed with sobs and tears. Surprised by this outburst of emotion, he covered his face with both hands, rested his elbows on the wall, and tried to calm himself down. "Well, at least they gave us Thanksgiving. Can't imagine another Christmas in Iraq. I'll send Sara a gift of manna. Manna fed the Jews in the desert. Manna for Christmas? Oh, how funny is that? I'm not going back to the office. No one can fire me now. To hell with the office; I'm going home."

Before going to his car, Scott went down to the reflecting pool and like a General, surveyed the 168 empty chairs arranged by floors. All those who died on each floor were in one row and all the children who were in the nursery had their own row of little chairs. Scott saw his Sara in every little chair, gray faced with reaching arms, silent, and motionless. In the big chairs, he saw his Baghdad buddies, uniformed, stiff, with glazed eyes that followed him as he moved along the lines. By the time he reached the end, he was overcome with eerie exhaustion, which forced him to sit on the steps and support his head with both hands until he felt well enough to stand up again.

Scott marched back to the garage, got into his car, and, instead of going home as he had planned, drove obliviously—at a considerable, almost reckless speed—to the Memorial Park Cemetery. As he walked on the pebbled path toward the bench, his mind teemed with unfinished thoughts and half ideas that would briefly rise into his consciousness, flutter like a flying fish above water, and then dive back deep into his unconscious. Then, as if all time had been condensed into one doleful moment, he stood facing the empty bench. For the longest time, he gazed at the inscription *Captain Theodore Peckford* and tried to remember the cherished moments, the deep conversations, and the pedantic desert mornings of poetry and philosophy but he couldn't remember anything. All the details of his two years in Iraq had coalesced into one dusty nebula that was blowing away into the infinite interstellar spaces of the Milky Way. Exasperated, he sat down on the bench—with head between hands and elbows on knees—gazing at his black shoes turned gray with pebble dust.

The afternoon sun would have shone directly into Scott's eyes were it not for his stooped position. But with his head bent down and suspended between his hands, he avoided the sun's glare although he still absorbed its warming rays. The gentle afternoon sun had a calming effect on him. His memories of Iraq slowly returned to fill in the spaces of oblivion and his mind began to slowly rise above its dusty fog. He heard birds chatter and cars rattle in the distance. The cemetery, which was devoid of visitors at the time, gave Scott a desperately needed measure of reclusive comfort. *"I'm the only one here,"* he thought, *"the only one above ground, and the only one who can cast a shadow."* The notion that, in contrast to the living, the buried cannot cast a shadow had an enthralling impact on Scott. His mind wandered over many questions, questions of an intellectual nature, questions that Peckford would have regarded as highly philosophical. *"Oh, how funny,"* he thought as he scratched his head with admiration. *"Oh, how funny is that? I can't wait to tease my political, office friends with it. I shall ask them to define the Silent Majority and then counter by telling them that it's the dead and not the living that are the true silent majority. The living are always noisy. Only the dead are silent. What a bright idea, the dead are the only true silent majority. For every person above ground who can cast a shadow, there are thousands of shadowless dead beneath. That's another bright idea. Sitting on Peckford's bench must make me think like a philosopher. I should come here more often. I should enter these ideas on my computer as soon as I get home before I forget them.*

The thought of the shadowless dead proved short lived because, soon thereafter, Scott found himself gazing at a man's shadow standing before him. He did not want to raise his head and face the interloper who, uninvited, stood between him and the warming sunrays. *"A cemetery official, no doubt, wanting to know if I'm all right. Just because I have my head between my hands doesn't mean that I need help. So much for quiet privacy and here comes noisy life again. He's not moving away, damn it. Sooner or later, I'll have to talk to him."*

Scott pretended not to notice and kept his gaze on the ground beneath him. With his peripheral vision, however, he continued to watch the shadow, which, for the longest time, stood motionless and silent. The stance was finally broken when the shadow approached until his feet almost touched Scott's. Then Scott felt a hand reach out and touch him on the shoulder. It wasn't just a gentle tap, as one would expect from a stranger trying to arouse one's attention. No, it was a touch, soft, gentle, prolonged, and delivered with warm fingertips full of reassuring familiarity. *"I know this touch,"* thought Scott as he froze with surprise. *"But how can it be? No, I'm dreaming. No, no, it's impossible."* Overcome with trepidation, Scott cautiously raised his head and beheld the man blocking the sun.

"Hello Scotty," said the shadow with a firm, commanding tone.

Scott turned ashen white and beads of cold sweat swarmed his contorted face. He stood at attention, saluted, and the faint, stuttering words, "Oh, my God. Are you real?" barely escaped his throat. That was all he could say before his breath was cut off and the rest of his unspoken words fell back into his lungs. Unable to breathe or think, Scott began to shiver like a frightened bird that has just fallen out of its nest. Frantic tears burst out of his eyes, tumbled over his cheeks, and dripped down his chest, as he stood motionless, gazing at the interloper with terrifying disbelief.

"I'm real, Scotty," came the man's kind, reassuring voice, "as real as you are. Would you like to feel the nail holes in my hands?" Then, alarmed at Scott's ashen, deconstructed aspect, the man sat down on his own bench and commanded Scott, "At ease, my boy. We are no longer in Baghdad. Sit down please and compose yourself."

"You are real," gasped Scott when he finally regained his breath. "I never dreamed that I would ever see you again," he added, wiping his tears with his bare, sweaty palms. Then, after a long, sighing silence and with obvious, angry hesitation, he asked, "Why didn't you send me a sign that you were alive?"

Peckford scratched his head, running his fingers through his thick brown hair, took in a deep sigh, and then explained.

"I wanted to, Scotty, but I couldn't. It would have been too dangerous. I'll tell you about it later."

"How did you know to find me here?"

"I followed you from your office to the bombing memorial, to the garage, to here."

"How long have you been back?"

"I came in late yesterday."

"Where are you staying?"

"In a nearby motel under a fake name."

Scott leaned back, gazed into Peckford's deep, green eyes, and whispered with a hoarse, half-embarrassed tone, "Why don't you stay with me; Nancy left me and I have the house to myself."

"Thanks for the offer, soldier, but I need to remain invisible. Had I wanted to stay in a home, I would have stayed with my niece."

"You have a niece here?"

"My brother's daughter and a fine patriot too."

"You have a brother here?"

"It's a most delicate matter and there's a lot that you're not aware of, Scotty. It's best if you don't ask any more questions. There is more safety in ignorance, I assure you."

"I don't have much time, you know. I've received my orders. They're hauling me back to Iraq."

"I know; that's why I came."

"Oh, I guess there is a lot that I'm not aware of then. Are you going back too?"

"Perhaps."

"And what do we do in the meantime?"

"You go back to your work and I, to mine."

"You mean now?"

"Yes, Scotty, now. You leave first and after a while I will follow. Come on, soldier; get up and go. I'll be calling you later."

Scott went back to his office a changed man. He no longer cared that he was being deployed. Peckford was alive and, sooner or later, he would be reunited with his mentor. He spent the rest of the afternoon musing about Peckford and was totally unaware that he had stopped thinking about his darling, little Sara.

Chapter Ten
(Peckford)

As the remnants of that day languished into the late afternoon, Scott shuffled through his loan files like a wayward wind, intense, fast, but unfocused. His restlessness, which was apparent to all the watchful eyes, was falsely attributed to the registered letter that he had received. When he hurried out of the office soon after he had signed for the letter, conjecture and gossip busied his coworkers and irked their imaginations. Breena, the most curious of all, announced that he must have been recalled back to Iraq, basing her conclusion on the fact that she had actually seen the military envelope in the postman's hands. To make things even more blatant, Breena's inquisitiveness became uncontainable and caused her to lose all self-restraint. Holding a perfunctory file in her hand, she marched into Scott's office and, without further ado, curtly inquired: "So, what's it this time, General? Are they calling you back?"

Without lifting his head, Scott smiled and kept on working.

"Good. I thought that you had forgotten your smile in Iraq. Obviously, if you're smiling, you're not going back, so what is it then?"

Unable to hide his delight at her confusion, Scott burst into laughter as he gazed at her discombobulated face. "You're a cat, aren't you?"

Without a word, Breena sat down and crossed her legs deliberately revealing her white, succulent thighs. Unsuccessful at snaring his glance, she pulled her skirt a hand's breadth above her knee and shuffled in her seat, causing her garments to rustle into the dry silence. When even that did not attract Scott's attention, she pleaded: "Scotty, please. Could you at least show some respect and say something. We're all worried about you."

"Yes, I have been recalled," came Scott's dry, nonchalant answer.

"Why are you smiling then? I'm not a fool, Scotty.

Tell us the truth, please. We're all very concerned and we all care."

"What time is it?"

"It's almost four."

"Good, one more hour and I can leave."

"I can't believe you're being so rude to me. No one smiles at being recalled. It's a sad occasion for all of us here. Keep on smiling if you wish but, in case you hadn't noticed, none of us is smiling with you. Good-bye General. I hope you know what you're doing."

Breena left Scott's office frustrated, disillusioned, with more burning curiosity than when she had come in. Scott, on the other hand, eyed the time and darted out of the Hartland Bank as soon as five o'clock struck. Driving home, he had to restrain himself on several occasions so as not to exceed the speed limit. He needed to stop at the grocery store but he didn't. For some reason, he felt a need to get home without delay. He did not know exactly why he was in such a hurry nor did he care to explore his unconscious motives. Perhaps he thought that Peckford might pay him a visit or at least give him a call. Or he could have thought that some surprise awaited him at his door. Whatever the reason mattered not to Scott. He was simply moved to get to his empty home as fast as he possibly could.

At home, Scott paced and waited. From his living room window, he obsessively checked his street for incoming cars even though he did not have any idea what kind of car he was looking for. When darkness shrouded his view, he eyed each approaching light with anticipation and escorted it away with dismay. Like a child, he wiped his palms, moist with perspiration, onto his white shirt until it became gray with wrinkles. It was almost nine when the phone rang. He darted to his office, lifted the receiver to his ear, and held his breath.

"Hello, Scotty?"

"Nancy, what's wrong?"

"Sara is too scared to go to sleep after last night. She's crying and calling for you. Here, you talk to her."

"Daddy," came her whimpering voice, "please come. I'm scared."

"Oh, baby, don't worry, you're safe because Mommy has all the doors locked. No one can come in and bother you again."

Here, Sara's whimpers turned into sobs, became loud shrieks, and then ended with a gasping plea, "No... no... Daddy... please... come... please..."

At the same time, a car pulled into the driveway and turned its lights off but its doors stayed closed. Scott dropped the phone and darted out. As he approached the car, he saw Sara in the back seat holding her mother's cell phone to her ear and crying with doleful, exhausted eyes, "Daddy... Daddy... please..."

At that moment, Scott drowned his entire life into Sara's tears, forgot all about Peckford, leapt into the car, pulled her out of the car seat into his arms, and without another thought, nervously blurted out to Nancy, "Let's go home."

"Which home?"

"Your home."

"Your house door is wide open and the lights are on."

"Oh, well, why don't you stay here then?"

"No, no. That's not a good idea. I'll lock the door for you. Do you have your keys?"

"Oh, let me get my keys and I'll follow you in my car." Saying that, he put sobbing Sara back into her car seat and gently said to her, "Don't worry, baby; Daddy will be right behind you and mommy."

Sara's sobbing finally quieted down in Scott's large, reassuring arms as he lifted her out of her car seat and took her up to Nancy's apartment. He took her straight to bed, sat beside her, told her the bedtime story that he had rehearsed four days earlier, and stroked her hair until she finally fell asleep. A fleeting smile surprised his grim face as he listened to her delicate, rhythmic breaths purr in his ears. But, as he gazed upon her tear-smudged cheeks, a bitter pain drowned his smile and tossed him into a cerebral storm that threatened to wreck his ship on reality's unforgiving reef. *"What will this fear do to her? Will she be able to overcome it? Will she grow up to be normal?"*

In her living room, on the other side of silence, crouched Nancy on the green sofa, between frowns and tears, regurgitating last night's timorous saga with Dick Straight. *What a manic animal. How did I let myself fall prey to such a beast? Sara will never be able to sleep again in this place. Oh, what a rotten mess we're in. Perhaps, I should pack us up and return home to Scott where we would both feel safe again. I know that Sara would be able to sleep better over there. Scott wouldn't mind babysitting when I go out on dates. He wouldn't even mind keeping her on weekends if I wanted to sleep the night out."*

When Scott emerged into the living room, he looked like a withered giant. With a supplicating gesture, Nancy entreated him to sit next to her on the sofa. Standing in the middle of the room with his head in a tenebrous cloud, he mumbled, "No, no, I've got to go home before it's too late."

"Too late? Too late for what?"

"Oh, I have work to do."

"Work? This late?"

"I'm sorry, but I need to go."

"What if Sara wakes up and doesn't find you? What shall I do if she starts screaming again? I guess, I'll just pack her up in the car and bring her back to you."

"No, no, you can't do that. No, just call me and I'll come back for her."

"No, none of that nonsense. If she wakes up, we're both coming to you."

As if stunned by a stone, Scott grabbed his forehead and darted out without a word. He ran to his car and raced back home heedless of traffic rules, traffic lights, and stop signs. With mouth and brain gone dry, he was a programmed robot hurling home with babbled, unintelligible thoughts devoid of direction or clarity. Arriving safely, nevertheless, he combed the house, the rooms, the corners, the closets, the bathrooms, aimlessly looking, searching, and even sniffing. Then, exhausted, he lay on the sofa in the living room and shut his insomniac eyes.

All of a sudden, as if startled by a bright light, he dashed to the phone and was elated to find the message light flashing. Lifting the receiver with both hands, he impatiently accessed the voice box, panting as he listened. There were messages, of course, numerous messages, jargon-filled telemarketing messages, and three hang-up calls with blocked numbers, but not a word from Peckford. Disillusioned, he started pacing, unaware of time or place, mumbling with each breath, *"Come on Peckford, come on, one more ring, please, just one more ring."*

Then, as if a lightning bolt had shattered the bridge that suspended him between reality and utter confusion, he heard it. At the first ring, he grabbed the receiver and, before he put it to his ear, shouted into the mouthpiece, "What took you so long?" The answer that came back was a dial tone that droned uninterruptedly as he listened to the second ring, the third ring, and the fourth. Looking around in puzzlement, his eyes fell on the kitchen clock, which had just finished chiming. *"It's four in the morning. Oh, God, what's happening to me? I can't tell a chime from a ring. I must be hallucinating. I better get some sleep. Peckford will call tomorrow. I'm sure the hang-up calls were his. He must have called when I was with Sara. He'll call me tomorrow; surely, he will"*

Exhausted, Scott fell asleep on the living room sofa. He did not take off his clothes or his shoes nor did he try to sleep in his large, soft bed. He was a soldier on the alert, ready to mobilize in full gear at the first alarm. His dreams were snappy like an out-of-sequence slide show unintelligibly changing scenes and moods. He saw Sara falling off her horse and, when he tried to catch her, his own horse bucked and threw him to the ground. Then he saw Nancy, like Lady Godiva, riding away into the desert mirage while totally naked. Then he saw Peckford, wielding a whip, commanding a line of prisoners who were carrying water from an oasis to the camp. There was a common thread to all his dreams, a veiled connection that he was unable to discover until the Saturday morning sun caught his eyes and awakened him. *"The grunting, yes, yes, the grunting, they all were grunting, that's it, that's it,"* he thought as he rubbed his red, startled eyes. Having fallen, he and Sara lay grunting. The prisoners were grunting under the weight of forced labor in the desert sun. Peckford was grunting as he snapped his whip onto the languished prisoners. Nancy was grunting as her horse galloped uncontrollably into the desert haze. His dreams were so real, indeed, that he felt relieved when he awakened and found himself intact, without bruises or broken bones. He even had a Pavlovian surge of saliva as the kitchen clock chimed seven. *"I'll cook some eggs and wait for Peckford. This Saturday is going to be my day. I don't have to go to work. Why am I so hungry? When was my last meal? I can't even remember."*

Scott ate heartily which, in spite of his lack of sleep, made him feel rejuvenated. He was elated at the prospect of seeing Peckford again and was determined not to let anyone or anything stand in his way. He had questions to ask and much to tell. All he needed was a simple phone call, a time, and a place.

"I better tidy up the house; Peckford likes things spotless. Oh, I almost forgot, I also need to shave and shower. But, what if the phone rings when I am in the shower? I'll place the phone just outside the shower door and have my towel ready. I'm not going to miss his phone call again. And if Nancy calls, I'll just tell her that she'll have to wait. Yes, that's what I'll tell her. But, what if, like yesterday, she decides to come without calling? Oh, well, I'll just tell her to go back home. She thinks Peckford is dead. I can't let her suspect that he isn't. He'll tell me what to do tomorrow. He knows what's best."

Scott tidied up the house, shaved, took a quick shower, put on his best aftershave lotion, and donned his best suit and tie. To pass the time, he surfed the net and carefully checked out his preferred pornography sites but discovered that they couldn't distract him from his anguish. Periodically, he would lift the receiver to check the dial tone. When the kitchen clock began to chime twelve, he became restless and started to pace. It was during the chiming that he heard the phone ring. This time, in spite of his anguish, he was certain that the ring was not a chime and that the chime was not a ring. He lifted the receiver with confidence as if he were sure that Peckford were on the other side.

"Hello."

"Scotty?"

"Yes Sir."

"Get in your car and meet me at the cemetery; it's the safest place around here."

"Why don't we meet here instead?"

"Scotty, the eyes are everywhere. No one can know that I'm not dead."

"Where will you be?"

"At my bench."

"I'm on my way."

Before Scott could finish his sentence, the line went dead. Without another thought he dashed into the garage, got into his car, and drove towards the Memorial Park Cemetery. It was raining and storming, which he had failed to notice while waiting at home for Peckford's call. But now, neat and clean in his best suit and tie, he did not want to get wet. In spite of his rushed mind, he turned his car around and went back to the house to fetch his umbrella. As he entered, the phone started to ring and he could tell from the caller ID that it was Nancy. He ignored it but then, as he hurried back to his car, his cell-phone started to ring. It was Nancy again and that worried him. *"What can she want? I was just with her yesterday? I'm not answering. I'll just listen to her message later, after I meet with Peckford."*

On the way to the Memorial Park, Scott's mind was too busy with expectation to think clearly. The idea that

Sara might be in distress did not occur to him. He did not even connect the phone call from Nancy with Sara's condition. Indeed, when Peckford was on his mind, Sara was out and when Sara was on his mind, Peckford was out. He just couldn't ponder both of them at the same time nor was he aware that his brain worked like a seesaw; when one was up the other had to be down.

At the cemetery, Scott opened his umbrella, got out of the car, and careful not to muddy his shoes, trod the pebbled path to Peckford's bench. In the misty drizzle he could discern Peckford's seated figure wearing a hooded trench coat like a motionless statue patiently weathering the elements. The first thought that seized Scott's mind at that moment was that the bench was wet and that he would have to sit on it while wearing his best suit. *"I'll just stand, or else I'll invite Peckford back to my car,"* was his most pressing concern as he approached the bench. When he arrived and stood facing Peckford, his throat suddenly clamped and shut all his words in. Wordless in the rain, staring at Peckford's gleaming aspect, he clenched his toes and feigned a smile.

"Scotty, do you always dress up before coming to the cemetery?"

"Yes Sir, I mean, no Sir, I just..."

"Calm down, soldier, you're not on duty."

"It's just hard to..."

"Come, come now and have a seat. As soon as I move over, take my place; I've kept it dry for you."

Saying that, Peckford shifted to the other side and pulled Scott by the arm into his space. In the drippy silence they sat and stared at the wind as if waiting for something to appear out of the mist. In the moment's anguish, Scott's palms began to weep and his throat began to loosen up, releasing all his incarcerated words. Stormed by memories and unable to wait any longer, he began the conversation.

"Sir, I don't understand anything anymore."

"I know you don't and that's why I'm here."

"Please tell me what's going on."

"It's a long story in which you will play an important part."

"Who? Me? What? What part?"

"Hush Soldier and let me explain. You see, I had to die, disappear, and assume a new identity in order to satisfy the mission's requirements. Those who picked me up after you dropped me in the desert were secret service, women-agents of the Iraqi government."

"Women? But you were in your underwear, remember?"

"They are safer because they are seldom followed or targeted when they drive without men. They dressed and veiled me like one of them and then drove me to an underground Baghdad lab. There, they took me to the morgue, stripped me, made me up like a corpse shot in the face and chest, took pictures of me with my dog tag exposed, and, through special agents, released my photographs to the US Army full knowing that the photographs would ultimately reach the antigovernment militias and, through them, find their way into the Al-Qaeda files."

"Al-Qaeda? You mean…"

"Yes, Scotty, Al-Qaeda is everywhere. They have penetrated us here and abroad."

"And, what about us? Have we penetrated Al-Qaeda?"

"Because we hadn't yet, I remained undercover an entire year with no outside communications. Not only couldn't I call you, I couldn't call anyone else for that matter. Except for my daily Arabic lesson, I was in solitary confinement in an underground basement on the outskirts of Baghdad."

"You studied Arabic?"

"Twelve hours a day."

"Say something to me."

"*Allahu Akbar, La Ilaha Illalah.*"

"What does it mean?"

"God is great and there's no other god but God."

"Isn't that from the Koran?"

"You still remember?"

"Remember what, Sir?"

"Never mind, Soldier. Let me finish what I was about..."

"So where do I fit in all this and why are they hauling me back to Iraq?"

"You're not going back to Iraq."

"The letter said I was. Oh? You don't mean...?"

"We're all going to Beirut first."

"We're all going to... who's we... what... where...?"

"You and the others I have chosen for this mission are going to Beirut, Lebanon. I wasn't allowed to choose from the deployed troops because Al-Qaeda could easily identify them."

"And why Beirut?"

"Because you will all require new identities and a certain amount of cultural training to get you up and ready."

"Cultural training? For what? I've never been good in languages."

"You'll have to learn some Arabic, just enough to understand what is being said. You don't have to speak much but you will have to be able to say some key words."

"Key words? Key words like what?"

"Like *ahlan wa sahlan* and *shukran.*"

"What do they mean?"

"*Welcome* and *thank you.*"

"And, what's your new name?"

"You'll find out later."

"And what's the mission about?"

"About preventing terrorism."

"And what are we supposed to do?"

"We are supposed to penetrate Al-Qaeda."

Here, Scott felt his throat tighten up again, shutting in all his would-be words.

"Scotty, we need to find out in advance when Al-Qaeda is planning terrorist activities so that we can intercept them before they are implemented."

"Come on, Scotty, stop this shivering, it's

unbecoming of a soldier."

"Scotty, come now, we'll talk some more on the way to the cars."

After another complex talk with Peckford that ended with a long list of precautions, Scott found himself both anguished and exhilarated. Driving home, he felt important, heroic, and needed but he also felt frightened to the bone of what Al-Qaeda might do to them if they should be found out. His thoughts took him back to all the scenes that he had tried to forget and all the things that Peckford had taught him about humanity's violent history. Driving back in the rain, he calmed himself down by repeating in his mind one of Peckford's sayings, *"Facing death with hope is exhilarating while facing it only with courage is frightening."*

His reverie ended, however, when upon entering the house, he found the telephone message-light flashing. Since he was no longer in a hurry, he lifted the receiver and calmly retrieved his messages. There were three and they were all from Nancy inviting him to dinner at six. He looked at his watch and realized that if he were to leave right away, he would arrive on time. *"I'll call to say I'm on my way after I get in the car."* With Peckford off his mind now he got back into his car and, while still wearing his best suit and tie, proudly drove to dinner.

Chapter Eleven
(Revelations)

On the way to dinner, at the first stoplight, Scott inspected his face in the visor mirror, touched up his hair, and adjusted his necktie. Then looking around, he couldn't help but notice the young lady in the car next to him who was also touching up and smearing on her lipstick with exacting delicacy, as if she were trying out different smiles for different events.

"She must be going out on a date. It's Saturday night. Oops, she saw me looking at her." For an instant, their eyes met. The lady smiled and then, seeing that the light had turned green, took off in her red Mustang and Scott followed. *"Nice girl. Nice car. Must've been in a hurry. Funny license plate. HBDML33. Wonder what it means? Hey Baby Doll, My Linda's 33. She looks about 33. How about Happy Birthday Melinda? Or, better still, Happy Birthday My Love. That's much nicer. He could've given her the car on her 33rd birthday. Maybe her birthday is today? November 4th. Hmm, November 4th? There's something about November 4th; something that I can't remember."*

Soon, memory began to knock on Scott's head and the knocking grew louder and louder, making him restless in his seat. He shifted, flushed, sweated, and even opened the window for some cool rain air. Then, as he drove by Walmart's parking lot, it hit him in the forehead like an unexpected, flying object. *"Oh, my God. Today is Sara's birthday. She's five today. How strange. And Nancy never said a word? I bet she has a surprise party for Sara. No telling who'd be there. I'm glad I still have my best suit on. Oh, I need a gift. Walmart? It'll have to do. I'm running out of time."*

When Nancy opened the door, Scott held his hands behind his back and tiptoed in with a half-smiling, sly, malicious face. He caught Sara in mid-air as she flew into his arms screaming, "Daddy. Daddy." Then, glancing at Nancy's un-festive aspect, he began titillating Sara with a gift bag that he held just beyond her reach. Each time Sara would try to grasp it, he would pull it away whispering, "Happy Birthday. Happy Birthday, Princess." In spite of his excitement, he couldn't help but notice Nancy turn a bit pale as she hurried into the kitchen with wide-open eyes as if there was something burning on the stove. When she re-emerged a few minutes later, though better composed, she wasn't able to return the Barbie Doll's smile, which Sara held out to her face while screaming, "Mommy, see what Daddy got me for my birthday. Mommy, look in the bag and see what else I got." Nancy feigned interest as she admired the Barbie Doll with a constrained face and inspected the bag that Sara held in her other hand. There were three panties, one red, one pink, and one blue, Sara's three favorite colors. Sara stood in the middle of the room, held her breath, and waited for her mother's reaction to her exciting gifts. Nancy, who was unable to smile merely said, "How nice;" and followed it by "let's eat."

Except for Scott and Sara's bantering, no real conversation danced across the dinner table and no birthday cake followed the spaghetti and meatballs. For dessert, only Sara had milk and cookies; Scott had only cookies because there was no milk left. These minor aberrations, however, went unnoticed by Sara who, having had enough love, food, and play, was beginning to wilt in her daddy's arms as they sat together in the cushy chair facing Nancy who was curled up into a knot on the green living room sofa. Looking to Nancy for a bedtime sign, Scott found her staring into space, unaware of him or of Sara. Quietly, he carried the birthday girl into her bedroom, helped her into her pajamas, tucked her in, told her his bedtime story du jour, and stroked her hair all the way to sleep.

Nancy was still in a fixed trance when Scott tiptoed out of Sara's bedroom. Slowly, he walked towards her, hoping to attract her attention but even that failed to penetrate her silence.

"*I'll just leave her alone and go on home. She must not*

be feeling well or there's something bothering her. I bet she won't notice if I just slip away."

As Scott redirected his footsteps, stole towards the door, and tried to open it with nimble caution, he became aware of a peculiar burning sensation in the nave of his neck. When he looked back, Nancy's stare felt like a sunspot focused with a magnifier dead upon him.

"Do you think I'm in a coma?"

"Oh, no. I just thought that you might want to be alone."

"Alone? So you eat and leave, just like that?"

"Oh, I didn't mean to..."

"Scotty, we need to talk."

"Tomorrow?"

"No, now. That's why I asked you to dinner. We've a lot to talk about."

"Oh, well then, what do we have to talk about?"

"Come here Scotty; come sit next to me like you used to."

With incessant, half-commanding, half-inviting gestures Nancy motioned Scott to sit next to her on the green sofa. Avoiding Nancy's gaze, Scott fidgeted, scanned the ceiling, the walls, the floors, and even the windows. Then with sheepish, upturned lips and downcast eyes he capitulated and sat beside her.

The initial silence groaned under the weight of unarticulated thoughts as Nancy and Scott's minds spun and made preparations for what was about to follow. The ensuing awkwardness swelled by the minute, imparted a distant, vacuous gaze to Scott, and caused Nancy to blink in her stare, arrange and rearrange her dress, and tap the carpet incessantly with her hanging-down foot. This seemingly endless, wordless interaction lingered until a sudden, unexpected noise startled them both. It was the icemaker's dumping sounds that cracked the conversation ice and thawed out its frozen words. Nancy and Scott looked at each other and, seeing the ridiculous faces they both wore, relaxed and burst into hysterical laughter. It was after that thaw out that Nancy found her words and began the conversation.

"Scotty, Sara and I need you."

"You need what?"

"You heard me Scotty, Sara and I really need you."

"But you left me and wouldn't have anything to do with me and you wouldn't even answer my phone calls?"

"I'm sorry I left, Scotty."

"You mean…"

"Can you forgive me?"

"You're not thinking of…."

"Yes, Scotty, I am."

"You want to…"

"Yes, we both want to. Sara and I want to come back."

"Oh, God, you wait until now to tell me?"

"What's wrong with now?"

"I only have twenty-three days."

"Twenty-three days?"

"They're hauling me back to Iraq."

"Iraq again?"

"On November 27."

"And how long will you be gone this time?"

"I wasn't told."

When Scott said that, he fell into deep thought and was not aware of Nancy's quivering lips and held-back tears.

"Sara and I could take care of the house while you're in Iraq, fighting for our security. It's the least we could do while you risk your life for our country."

"What about your apartment?"

"We're both scared, Scotty, scared of apartments, and scared of living on our own. Bad things happen to unprotected girls and working moms who live alone. I've learned my lessons the hard way. I still love you, Scotty."

Hearing that, Scott leaned forward, supported his elbows on his knees, suspended his head between his hands, and fixed his gaze on his shoes without saying a word.

"Don't do it for me Scotty. Do it for Sara. She adores you. You love Sara, don't you?"

Nancy's sniffles became deliberately audible as she began stroking Scott's stooped back, hoping for a nod, a sign, a hoarse whisper, or a kind word. But Scott stubbornly held his downcast gaze and did not stir.

"Would you please take us back, Scotty? I'm so sorry for all the troubles I've caused you. Could you not save me one last time? Remember how you saved me when I got pregnant with Sara?"

Here, Scott rose up from his bent position, redirected his gaze into Nancy's pleading eyes, and with a big voice asked a very tiny question, "Are you sure?"

Nancy's answer inaudibly rolled down her cheeks as she nodded several times before her neck wilted and surrendered her head onto Scott's unsuspecting shoulder. Slowly, her tears softened Scott's heart and rendered it vulnerable to her supplicating pleas. As the night deepened and their dialogue ripened, Scott was transmuted from a firm negotiator to an acquiescing child. When close to midnight he got up to leave, Nancy sealed the moment with a shuddering embrace dripping with gratitude and escorted him with her tear-filled eyes all the way to his car. Little did they know that 'shadows are words outspoken in the night, to be erased when day brings in the light.'

Sleep skipped over Scott that night, leaving him open-eyed but closed-hearted. He lay in bed swaying between the two shades of darkness, the one deepening as the sun plunged into the night, the other brightening as the new day threatened to bring in the light. His thoughts were amorphous, disorganized, and strewn all over his brain without words or sounds like spilled alphabet soup.

When the kitchen clock chimed three, he woke up startled and couldn't go back to sleep. To beguile the time, he went to his computer and began surfing the net for pornography. He checked his favorite sites bubbling with spicy, sexual stews and steaming with sensual play but he could find neither peace nor distraction in what he saw.

Instead of calming him down—as they had done following myriad occasions when his heart had been tortured by malevolent reality—they rendered him more restless and pushed him over the brink of restraint. Not knowing where to turn or what else to do, he threw some warm clothes on, got into his car, and incoherently drove straight to the cemetery.

He parked his car by the locked gate, scaled the Guernica wall and scurried furtively to Peckford's bench. He wiped the rain with his bare hands, sat down on the cold marble, and occupied himself by looking at the gray, starless sky, cold and convoluted like his own brain. No bright thoughts came to him, no clever ideas, and no pacifying epiphanies. As he sat on the wet bench gazing into the silence, trying to re-collect his scattered mind, he saw in the distance the slippy shadow of a fox wandering among the dead, appearing and disappearing behind the graves like a furry-tailed ghost floating upon the night.

"I usually get my smartest thoughts on this bench," he thought. *"How come I can't come up with a bright idea now? Last time, it was here that I figured out that the dead were the silent majority. Why do I feel so trapped when I'm in this wide-open place? Why can't I come up with a good thought that makes me feel free again?"*

The night stood still and never stirred. The stillness, like a vacuum, swallowed all the slivers of noise that fell through the air. The silence and the darkness danced like young, mischievous lovers to a soundless music.

"Maybe if I start with the dead being the silent majority, I could get to a better frame of mind? Let me follow my thoughts as Peckford taught me and see where they lead me. If the dead are the silent majority then the living are the noisy minority. Well, that's a darn good idea to start with. It follows then that I'm a member of the noisy minority. Why am I silent then? I should do what Peckford taught me to do, 'speak up, make noise, be heard, and disrupt the platitudes of propriety.' That was a great Peckford saying but I wish I knew exactly what it meant."

The grave shadows groaned in the rainy wind. The

shadowless dead, too deep to be disturbed, remained unmoved by the above-earth soundless music to which the darkness and the silence danced.

"I should tell Nancy, no, I've changed my mind and you can't live with me. I don't love you and I don't desire you. You don't love me and I'm sure you don't love Sara. How can you forget the birthday of your only child? And I thought you had a surprise party for her? You only invited me to get me to take you back and you tried to bribe me with Sara. Well, I need a woman who loves me for me and not for what I can provide. There, I said it; I need a real woman's love and I also need to love a real woman. I'm so starved for love and that's why I distract my hungry soul with disgusting pornography. I am alone, so desperately alone, and except for Sara and Peckford, 'my life is a series of meaningless clichés.' Another great Peckford saying that I don't fully understand."

The night began to yawn and the soundless music suddenly stopped. The silence and the darkness left the stage and sat on the bench on each side of Scott.

"Thanks to Peckford I have come to like philosophy and have learned to question everything, especially all things sacred. Now, that's a bright idea. Yes, I should question everything, especially things sacred. So, what is sacred to me? What? What? Only one thing? No, only two things. No, three, three things, only three things are sacred to me— my country, Peckford, and Sara. Yes, only these three things are sacred to me. Now, that's a good start and, oh, I do feel less confused. Good, yes, less confused, less trapped, more free, yes, I'm going to make it after all.

My country comes first and I'm going back to Iraq to serve it again. I'll come back a hero and make everyone proud. I'm going to penetrate Al-Qaeda and stop terrorism. I'll use my hacker skills to get into the Al-Qaeda computers and discover all its secrets.

Second comes Peckford... no Sara... no Peckford... no... damn it, why can't I make up my mind? Poor Sara, her own mother doesn't love her enough to remember her birthday. That tells me a lot. She would've aborted her had I not offered to marry her instead. Sara's birthday is not Sunday, November 4, 2001. No, no, it's Sunday, March 18, 2001; that's when Nancy and I went on our first date when she was five weeks pregnant and that's when I saved Sara. I saved her before I even knew her. And now I love her because I've saved her. Poor Sara, she's being brought up by a wayward mom and a weird dad.

And Peckford did for me what I had done for Sara; he saved me from death but he also gave me a new mental identity as a free, independent thinker. He taught me that 'the bravest men are those who have the courage to be themselves and the weakest are those who're afraid to be anything except what they're expected to be.' Another great Peckford saying, oh what a great thinker, oh what a great man."

Silence and darkness got up and walked away, leaving Scott alone on the bench. The night opened its eyes. A faint gleam smiled through the mist.

"Well, I had sex with Nancy because it was expected of me and not because I really wanted to. I pretended so well that she actually believed that I liked it and that I was attracted to her. Now she wants to move in with me and sleep in my bed. She'll want sex again. She's always horny. Only this time, I don't think that I can do it with her. I'm not going to do it except with the woman I love, the woman that I have yet to find, the woman that I may never be able to find if Nancy moves in with me. Thanks to Peckford, I am what I have become and I can no longer pretend to be what I am not. I can no longer be just what I'm expected to be."

A half-gleaming halo wrapped its arms around the upper mist. The shadows faded back into the graves. The night prepared to travel to the other side of earth.

"No wonder I feel trapped. Nancy plans to move into my house this Monday while I'm at work. Hair stylists take Mondays off. How convenient. And when I leave in 22 days, Nancy's boyfriends will start sleeping in my bed and hurting Sara. And if I don't let her move in with me, they'll do it in her apartment instead and hurt Sara there just like that lecher Dick Straight did. Oh, why did I say yes to her tears?

Oh, what a mess. Oh, Peckford, Peckford, where are you now when I need you to tell me what to do?"

At the mention of Peckford, a chill climbed up Scott's spine and shuddered through his neck. He felt the moist night air spread throughout his skeleton but instead of making him cold, it caused him to become warm. He was warm with relief, the redeeming relief of having recovered his freedom on Peckford's bench.

It was almost daybreak but the sky was too thick to allow in the dawn. The furtive fox reappeared, levitating like a ghost among the graves, unaware of Scott who sat on the wet bench, poised like a stone statue among the elements.

In spite of the rainy cold, Scott would have liked to wait until the birds ushered in the sun. Peckford used to say to him whenever he would become despondent, "Scotty, have you ever seen an unhappy bird?" Now, with that good idea on his mind, Scott wanted to relearn happiness from the birds and wanted to return home in a better mood. But he felt too tired to stay any longer and his ears were beginning to throb. Getting up, he was surprised at his stiff limbs, which took walking all the way back to the Guernica wall before they limbered enough for him to jump it.

Slowly, the car heater rescued his chilled ears, re-warmed his blood, and reset his mind. By the time he arrived home, his eyes were heavy but his heart was light. Having earned back his sanity and regained his freedom, he was ready for peace, the peace that he had always found in deep, undisturbed sleep. As soon as he laid his head upon his pillow—poised in the middle of his large bed—he slipped into the profoundest layers of impenetrable slumber, blind to the slivers of light that were dripping through the sky cracks and winding up bird gossip.

Chapter Twelve
(Disappearance)

Sunday came with big bangs that shocked Scott out of his sleep. He awoke sluggish, startled, confused, and with what felt like a mean hangover. It took him awhile to gather up his wits against the barrage of incessant banging that assailed his ears. Still in half-sleep, he dreamt that he was in a boxing ring being repeatedly banged upon the head amidst loud, unintelligible cries. Like a robot, stiff and dazed, he ambled towards the frantic noise. *"Oh, someone's at the door; no I hear two talking; no three. Oh, what horrible noise."*

When Scott opened the door, Nancy's father and mother stood ghost-pale, Nancy's tear-smudged mascara covered her cheeks, and the sun was high in the sky, majestic, unconcerned. The banging three marched into the house pantomiming, babbling, screaming like a bunch of wild birds, and using muffled words that Scott could not decipher. Amidst this unexpected avalanche of chaos, however, one word kept bobbing above the noise, one word that Scott heard over and over, and it was the only word that Scott recognized. Sara, Sara, bounced up and down and flew back and forth like a ball in a racket-ball court.

"Sara? What? What happened? Where is Sara? Stop screaming. One at a time, please. Hey, hold your fire. Nancy, you talk first. What the hell happened?"

By the time the mob reached the living room, the kitchen clock began chiming and mysteriously silenced everyone. For some inapprehensible reason, all the words ceased when the chimes began and, after the eleventh chime, an eerie silence supervened. It was a heavy, throbbing silence that rendered everyone's heartbeats audible to everyone else.

"Nancy, please, what happened? Where is Sara?"

"I, I tried, I tried to call you as soon as I found out but, but you, you wouldn't, you wouldn't answer your phone."

"That's when she called us, Scotty. Frances and I

rushed to her place and we called the police. They tried to call you too but you still wouldn't pick up. As soon as the police took down Nancy's statement and searched the premises, we all rushed here."

"Will someone tell me what the hell happened," came Scott's moist, thundering voice. With Nancy's uncontrollable shuddering and Peter's sudden word block, the one who delivered the deadly blow was Frances Bradford.

"Scotty, dear, Sara has been kidnapped."

"Kidnapped? When? Where? Who? Tell me, tell me everything, all the details, everything you know." Here, Scott's voice throttled in his throat and thick saliva began to drool from in between his quivering lips.

"She was asleep and Nancy didn't want to wake her up. She just ran to the 7/11 to get a carton of milk and was gone only a short while. When she returned, the front door was open and Sara was gone."

Scott devoured Nancy with fierce eyes as she shuddered and sweated, standing in the middle of the room, with her down-cast gaze fixed on his bare feet.

"Let's all sit down and think this over. Come on Nancy. Come on Frances." Then Peter approached Scott, held him by the arm, and led him like a statue on wheels towards the big couch by the window. Scott stood there, staring at the street shadows cast by the late morning sun, robotic, unaware of time or of his own numbed surroundings. Beneath Scott's unseeing stare, the street shadows of the houses, the trees, and the cars shrank imperceptibly as they drew toward their objects. In the living room, the cautious silence hovered in the heavy air like frozen fog. Nancy and her parents sighed in stillness and stretched in their seats while Scott, unmoved, maintained his blank gaze at the shrinking street shadows.

Then, footsteps and voices could be heard approaching the front door. When the doorbell rang, Nancy jumped out of her seat with mixed hesitation and relief, opened the door, let the interlopers in, and led them into the living room.

Scott slowly turned around when he heard the officers introduce themselves.

"I'm Officer Wagner and this is Officer Cook, OSBI. Are you Mr. Scott Thornton?"

"Yes. Yes, Sir."

"Could we talk to you in private?"

"Private? Oh, sure. Let's go into my office."

Barefoot in his pajamas, Scott motioned to the officers to sit down on the small sofa as he sank into the chair behind his desk.

"Mr. Thornton, may we ask you some questions about your daughter's disappearance?"

"I, I can't, can't tell you much. I just, just found out myself."

"Could you tell us where were you at 9 am today?"

"In bed. I was asleep."

"Was anyone with you?"

"I, I was alone."

"If you were at home, why didn't you answer your phone?"

"I didn't hear it. I had a late night."

"Can you prove that you were home when your daughter disappeared at about 9 a.m. this morning?"

Scott's eyes burned and reddened as he realized what Officer Wagner was insinuating.

"Hey... Wait a minute... Am I a suspect in my own daughter's disappearance?"

"It happens all the time."

"But Nancy and my daughter were planning to move back in with me tomorrow."

"We know all that, Mr. Thornton, but it's our job to cover all possibilities."

"I wish you'd help us find her instead of suspecting me of kidnapping my own daughter the day before she was supposed to move back into my house and 22 days before I'm supposed go back to Iraq." Saying that, Scott pulled his military orders out of his desk and angrily threw them at Officer Wagner.

"You know, Mr. Thornton, we need to do this

investigation by the book even though we do not doubt your innocence. You may be asked to take a lie detector test and I would advice you to go along so as not to hinder our efforts."

It wasn't long after that before Scott apologized to the officers and agreed to do what ever was required in order to facilitate the investigation.

Scott sat in his office awhile with head between hands, listening to the unintelligible whispers in the living room and thinking. *"How can a mother leave her five-year-old daughter unattended? To lose a daughter for a carton of milk, that's only possible with Nancy. I was married to a good-looking idiot. She's not moving back here without Sara. She needs to stay in the hole she dug for herself. When I find Sara, I'm going to keep her with me and as far away from Nancy as I can. My poor Baby must have been frightened to death when she woke up and found out that she was alone in the apartment. She probably ran frantically into the street looking for her mom and somebody nabbed her, just like people nab a lost poodle. I need to remain calm. Peckford taught me never to rush when in crisis and to always slow down when in a hurry. I need to contain my anger against Nancy."*

"Nancy."

"Yes, Scotty," came Nancy's hoarse voice.

"Would you come here please?"

Nancy ran into Scott's office with wide-open eyes and stood in front of his desk like a student who had been summoned to the principal's office.

"Please, close the door and sit down."

"Scotty, I'm so sorry..."

"We have no time for that now. Just tell me what exactly happened."

"I woke up just before nine and started to get Sara's breakfast ready. I found out that I had run out of milk and you know how much she likes her cereal with milk. I would've taken her with me to get the milk but she was in such deep sleep that I decided not to bother her. It didn't take long before I was back and she was gone."

Here Nancy began to shake uncontrollably and, having trouble supporting herself, collapsed on the little office sofa. Scott, utterly unmoved by her quivering demeanor, continued his interrogation.

"Did you lock the front door when you left?"

"I didn't lock it with the key, if that's what you mean. I just shut it and took the keys with me. It locks automatically when shut."

"Go on."

"Like I said, when I came back, the front door was open and she was gone."

"Did you look in the closets and under the beds and on the veranda?"

"I looked everywhere and so did my parents and the police."

"Were there any signs of struggle?"

"No, nothing at all."

"Was the door forced open?"

"No, the police said it was opened from the inside like normal."

"And did you talk to the neighbors?"

"My parents and I walked all over the place and called her name. We even checked the playgrounds. Then the police also drove throughout the entire complex and asked around. Nothing. No one saw her leave or go anywhere."

"Are the police going to send out an Amber Alert?"

"I gave them her picture and filed a missing-person report."

"So, what do we do now?"

"They said that we should just wait and stay in touch. The officer gave me a number to call in case I should find out anything new."

"Well, I think that you should stay at the apartment the rest of today. She may be hiding because she got scared when she woke up and didn't find you. She could show up at any time."

"Will you come and stay with me awhile? I'm scared to be alone after this."

"I'll call you later. Your parents can stay with you today."

As soon as the cross-examination ended, Nancy and her parents went back to the apartment and Scott's thoughts carried him away as he examined his options. *"I'm trapped. If I go back to Iraq, they'll never find Sara. I'll have to get special permission to delay my deployment. Surely, Peckford will help me. I can't leave this town as long as Sara is missing. What a mess. I'll just sit by the phone and wait for Peckford's call. Surely, he'll call today. Surely, he will."*

To distract his worry and dilute his grief, Scott went crazy surfing the net and checking out his pornography sites. Nothing proved exciting and he couldn't concentrate on the screen. His mind was with Sara. He understood what happens to little girls when they fall into the wrong hands. His imagination ran wild, tormented him mercilessly, and he couldn't restrain it. He became more and more agitated as the minutes ticked and no soothing thoughts presented themselves to his heart. He needed to make a plan but was unable to think things through.

Something was bothering him, something beneath the obvious, some new revelation he could not exactly decipher but knew in his heart how important it was. Finally, after an hour of soul-searching turmoil, it struck him in the face and he couldn't deny it any longer. Although he felt somewhat ashamed at this sudden epiphany, he was, nevertheless, also relieved as if a burden had slid off his back. The realization that Sara was his main priority, that she was more sacred to him than his country or Peckford, and that she was currently his most pressing responsibility felt like a birthing pain, heart-rending but delicious.

That exhilaratingly selfish thought, that painfully emancipating concept, that overpoweringly binding love of a child that he had saved from embryonic jettisoning, lifted him from his suffocating mood and set him free. He leapt out of his chair bright-eyed, exuberant, clammy, and murmured to his heart, *"Yes, yes, I admit it; I love Sara more than my country, more than Peckford, more than my life, more than anything, and more than everything... I fathered her the moment I saved her and from that point on Nancy became her surrogate mother and I, her real parent. And just like I saved her before, I'll save her again. No one else can save her but me. The police have too much on their plate and Sara will never be a priority for them. She's my priority now. I need to think. I need a plan."*

Festive at his sudden relief from the situation's strangulating grip, he threw on some clothes and raced to Peckford's bench. He had no clear idea why he was hurrying back to the cemetery but something told him that it was the right thing to do. That thought felt so good to his heart that it required no further examination and he offered it no resistance. He simply obeyed its subliminal verdicts without ever wondering why.

Scott drove like a stunned bird who, having unwittingly crashed into the glass of a window, falls comatose to the ground, wakes up, shakes his head, and flies frantically away not knowing what hit him.

Chapter Thirteen
(Epiphany)

The cemetery was not empty, as Scott had expected. It had visitors, which surprised Scott until he realized that it was Sunday afternoon. "*So many visit their dead after church, but I'm here to visit the living. What a funny thought. I wish I knew exactly what it meant. Perhaps I'll find out when I get to the bench.*"

As Scott made his way on the pebbled path, he could see in the distance two boys in Sunday clothes sitting on Peckford's bench. "*They must be waiting for their parents. Surely they won't stay long. I'll just walk around until they're gone.*"

The warming sun and dying wind made Scott's walk around the cemetery a pleasant experience. He watched people solemnly standing around graves—some were holding hands, some were whispering, some were praying with bowed heads, and some others were standing lost in thought. Unlike the people he was watching, Scott became aware that his own mind was frozen and that he was pacing without thoughts while waiting for the bench to clear. Meandering about the premises, his initial pleasant feelings were gradually displaced by a dizzying restlessness as if he were trapped on an airplane endlessly circling the sky awaiting permission to land.

Finally, to his sighing relief, he saw the boys' parents motion to them to come over. As the boys ran towards their family's grave, Scott hurried towards Peckford's bench, sat in its middle, and placed his arms on each side. Only then—after settling down and composing himself, after blocking the visitors by shutting his eyes, and after securing Peckford's bench all to himself—was he able to think.

"*Why am I here? I came for a reason. What? What? I need ideas. That's it. That's why I came here. My good ideas are tied to this bench. That's why I can't think anywhere else. I came here to get ideas about finding Sara. Yes, that's what I need now. Good ideas. Just some good ideas to get me started.*

Peckford taught me that our best ideas come from our unconscious and that our unconscious is the reservoir of all lives lived. All lives lived, he insisted, and not just my life or his. My unconscious, he said, contains all the lives of humanity from the beginning of time until the present. I shall never forget his words: 'Scotty, your unconscious contains all the lives of humanity with all their emotions of joy, sadness, love, hate, shame, anger, admiration, jealousy, etc. and it's your job to stifle the bad and only allow the good emotions to surface.'

But how does all that philosophy help me find Sara? The police are too busy to give the matter their full attention. I am the only one who can devote all his time to finding Sara. But I need ideas, ideas from my unconscious, which contains all the emotions of humanity. But how can emotions help me find her? I know that I love her more than life and that kidnappings must come from the bad side of emotions. So who has bad emotions towards her? Nancy? No, Nancy is not a good mother but she can't hate Sara. But who hates Sara then? Or better still, who hates Nancy or me? We have no enemies. No? Well? Dick Straight must hate us after that night when I almost strangled him. Dick Straight? Why not? He could have been watching Nancy when the golden opportunity arose. Hard to believe but it wouldn't hurt to pay him a visit and ask him some questions. Well, at least that's a start. Good. Peckford taught me to let the facts rule but to let my unconscious be my source of intuition."

Scott tried to find better ideas in his unconscious but the only idea that kept coming at him was that Dick Straight could have done it to get back at him and Nancy. With that good idea on his mind, Scott left the bench and drove straight to Nancy's apartment. He did not have to ring the doorbell because the front door was open, as if it were awaiting Sara's return. Entering after a perfunctory knock, he found Nancy curled on the sofa with cell phone in hand staring out the window. He sat by her and gently asked, "Where are your parents? I thought that they were going to stay with you tonight?"

Her only answer was a long, stuttering sigh.

"Have the police called?"

She shook her head and said nothing.

"Has anyone called?"

She shook her head again.

"Do you know where Dick Straight lives?"

Her eyes betrayed a sudden startle as she continued to gaze out the window.

"Nancy, I need to ask Dick Straight some questions. Could you tell me where he lives?"

She got up and began to pace like a prisoner in a jail cell.

"Well? I need to start somewhere."

"He lives in a duplex on Classen and 36th."

"Do you know the address?"

"No, but I can take you there."

"Did Sara ever enter his house?"

"Only once, for a very short time."

"Was he ever alone with her?"

"He babysat for me one time when I had to see my gynecologist."

"Did Sara seem all right when you picked her up after your appointment?"

"She was fine. He didn't do it, Scotty. He doesn't have the balls."

"He had enough balls to attack you and Sara, don't you remember?" Saying that, Scott intercepted Nancy's pacing path, held her by the arm, and snapped, "Let's go."

As Scott drove towards Classen and 36th, Nancy sat next to him with arms and legs crossed, looking frightened and unsure. Not much was said during the twenty-minute car ride except on two occasions. While stopped at the Penn-and-Hefner traffic light Nancy, unable to clear her throat after several attempts, inquired with a ruffled voice, "Scotty. Are you sure this is a good idea?"

Scott nodded and drove on. At the traffic light of Classen and 50th, this time having cleared her throat, Nancy pleaded the same question. Scott did not even nod.

He just waited for the green light and drove on until they approached 36th. There, Scott asked Nancy to show him the way.

"That's the house, right there. Stop, stop, you went past it."

Scott parked three houses down the street, told Nancy to wait in the car, strode to the house, and rang the doorbell. He could hear voices and footsteps but no one came to the door. He rang again and this time he heard a little voice call, "Daddy, somebody's at the door."

"Don't open. I'll be out in a minute."

Then Scott heard a toilet flush and soon after Dick Straight cracked the door, turned instantly pale, and shut the door with a bang. From behind the door, Scott could hear him tell the kids to sit down and be quiet. After a few moments of silence, Scott banged at the door with his fist and shouted, "I just want to ask you some questions."

"I'm not talking to you. Go away or I'll call the police."

"I just want to know where you were this morning at 9 a.m."

"I was picking up my daughters from their mom's home."

"Can your ex-wife verify that?"

"Why don't you call her and find out for yourself. Her name is Trish Straight and she's in the phone book."

Scott stood at the door a while, gazed at his feet with deep reflection, and then, realizing that Nancy was right, walked back to his car. He was not aware of Dick Straight's peeping eyes, which escorted him from one window to the next until he got into his car and drove away. On the way back to the apartment, neither Nancy nor Scott said a word. By the time they arrived, the sun had set and the air was getting nippy. Scott escorted Nancy up the stairs but stopped at the door.

"Don't you want to come in?"

"No, I'd better go on home."

"Scotty, you can't leave me alone after what happened."

"I need to get home, Nancy. I have a lot to do before tomorrow."

"Let me come with you, then. I promise not to bother you."

"No, you need to stay here just in case she should come back."

"Come back?"

"Who ever kidnapped her might have second thoughts."

"And drop her back at the door just like a lost puppy?"

"Stop it, Nancy, and go in please."

"I'm not going in without you. I'm afraid, Scotty. Please, just for a few minutes."

"Good night, Nancy."

As Scott started down the stairs, Nancy tried to hold on to him but he was too quick for her. Unwilling to give up, she called to him before he reached the street.

"The movers are coming tomorrow. Did you change the locks or can I use my old key?"

"You're not moving in without Sara. Everything's on hold until we find her."

"But, you agreed…"

"Goodnight Nancy."

Nancy's siren beckoning spun down the winding stairway and followed Scott into the street all the way to the lighted parking lot. Deaf to her pleas, Scott got back into his car and faded down the street into the evening.

Driving home, Scott was hoping to talk to Peckford before the night began its Monday climb. Something in his eagerness had changed, however. Instead of wanting Peckford for himself, he wanted him for Sara. He felt certain that Peckford could help him find her and that was all he wanted to talk to him about. When he arrived, he found the message light on the house phone flashing but the numbers were blocked and there were only silent messages in the voice box. He understood that Peckford, for security reasons, would not be calling him on his cell phone. He had no choice but to wait and that's what he did.

But, instead of passing the time by visiting his pornography sites, which was his habit since Iraq, he went into his office, took out a piece of writing paper, and began writing a letter to Sara. *"I'm going to write her a letter everyday from now until I find her. And when she's old enough to understand, I'll give her the letters for her birthday. Yes, yes, letters are far better than pornography. They force me to think and bring my good feelings out. Pornography has become disgusting to me and the last few times I attempted it, I simply couldn't do it. I don't think that I'll ever do it again. No, never again. I'll write letters to Sara instead. Yes, yes, letters will help us both."* Unconsciously, it seemed, and without even noticing the significance of what he was planning, he was, in fact, preparing himself for Sara's long absence.

Letter writing proved to be a great catharsis. At about 10:30 p.m., when the phone rang, he had already written several pages and was so engrossed in his writing that he didn't lift the receiver until the third ring.

"Hello."

"Scotty?"

"Yes Sir."

"Your files are ready."

"Files Sir? Oh... You mean, you mean all the loan files we've been working on?"

"All of them."

"That was fast."

"And there's one more thing."

"One more?"

"You guessed it. I need to resume my swimming lessons."

"Where?"

"In the usual place."

"When do you want to start?"

"Tomorrow."

"Did you hear about Sara?"

"I just heard it on TV. I'm very sorry."

"What should I do in the meantime?"

"Check your mail." Click.

Scott stood up and scratched his head. *"What the hell does he mean by check your mail? There's no mail on Sunday. Oh, my e-mail."* Scott ran to his computer and began screening his e-mails. There were twenty-seven new messages but most of them were trash. There was one message in the junk box titled 'Benchmark Symmetry,' which he deleted without bothering to open. As soon as he did, the phone rang again and he could see that it was his sister calling. "The news is out," he thought, as he lifted the receiver.

"Jane?"

"No Scotty, this is Flora. Jane is asleep and I just heard. I don't want to wake her up, that's why I'm whispering. I'm in shock, Scotty. Oh, my God. Who'd do such a horrible thing?"

Scott could hear Flora's sniffles as she tried to compose herself.

"There's no need to wake Jane up. She'll find out soon enough. I haven't even told my parents and, unless some well-meaning friend disrupts their sleep tonight, they won't find out till tomorrow either."

"How's Nancy taking it?"

"She's also in shock."

"Who's staying with her?"

"No one now. I was with her earlier and so were her parents."

"Is there anything I can do?"

"It's not in our hands, Flora. Try to go to bed and we'll see what tomorrow brings. I'll try to call Jane in the morning."

When the conversation ended, Scott tried to recapture his interrupted thoughts. *"What was I thinking before Flora called? Oh, yes, I was looking at my e-mails. The one I deleted was from 'Benchmark Symmetry.' What a silly name. Who gives a damn about symmetry?"*

Scott tried to ignore his sudden preoccupation with

the word '*symmetry*' a preoccupation that became more intrusive the more he tried to suppress it. Although he did not understand this peculiar intrusion, he did feel it deeply enough that it dominated his mind. Nevertheless, even after deciding that it was nothing but a silly obsession, he couldn't resist going back to it. He clicked on the folder of deleted e-mails and retrieved the *symmetry* one: "Benchmark Symmetry offers quiet time for worship from 5:30 p.m. to 6:30 p.m. each Monday. Join the very Reverend Patrick Ford in meditation. All souls are welcome."

Scott read the e-mail over and over as if it held something deep for him, some elusive message, something he could not decipher. Then, frustrated and agitated at his bewilderment, he lay on his couch and scattered his wild thoughts to the four winds of his soul. He thought about Nancy's pregnancy and her persistent nausea and vomiting, which now he was more inclined to interpret as an unconscious, biological rejection. He remembered how he used to put his ear on Nancy's abdomen after she would fall asleep and try to hear Sara's heart beats. He remembered Sara's birth, how she came out smiling, and how he could not control his tears when he saw her face blossom out into the light. He surprised himself when his mind began to flash a five-year slide show featuring snapshots of Sara's entire life from her birth until her disappearance. His restlessness swelled under the pressure to do something when there was nothing he could do. His raison d'être had been taken away from him, leaving him with nothing to live for. He had never experienced this profound degree of hopelessness, despair, and inconsolable grief before. Sara's loss was his first painful vacuum and his first space walk into the cold, dark corridors of the unknown.

Sleep arrived with sharp teeth, bit at his earlobes, and bloodied his eyelids. A thousand insects sucked his blood and hailstorms beat him into a chill. His teeth chattered and all his muscles cramped. He tried sitting, standing, walking, stretching, and even weightlifting but without help. *"I'll go to Peckford's bench, yes, Peckford's bench will ease my mind and give me the ideas I need to find Sara. Anything is better than this. I could eat my own flesh and feel no pain. I'm going crazy. Peckford, yes, I need Peckford. I'm going back to Peckford's bench."*

Scott took off in his car without noting the time. He did notice, however, that the streets were empty and most lights were off. When he looked at his car clock, it was 3 a.m. He still drove on as if in a hurry all the way back to the cemetery where he parked his car by the locked gate, hopped over the jagged stonewall, and began his second walk du jour to Peckford's bench.

The sky was clear and the moon shone over the rows of graves, lining them with whispering shadows. This eerie spectacle stopped Scott in his tracks. He gazed at the parallel shadows and was awed by their silent symmetry as his eyes searched for the distant bench. There it stood with moonlight slits between its bars as if it were an open cage. *"Perpendicular, yes, the bench bars are lined perpendicular to the rows. Was that intentional or did it just happen? Such perfect symmetry had to be intentional. Symmetry? Bench symmetry? Benchmark Symmetry? Oh, God, the e-mail was not from Patrick Ford; it was from Peckford. "Benchmark Symmetry offers quiet time for worship from 5:30 p.m. to 6:30 p.m. each Monday. Join the very Reverend Patrick Ford in meditation. All souls are welcome."*

Scott raced to the bench, sat on it, put his head between his hands and stared at his feet. *"Peckford is meeting me here tomorrow at 5:30 p.m. He knows that I leave work at 5 and so he gave me half an hour to get here. But why is he being so secretive? It must have something to do with Sara. Yes, he must know something. Oh, God, why do I have to wait till tomorrow to find out? Tomorrow? But today is already tomorrow. Good, I don't have to wait that long then. I'd better go on home and try to get some sleep. Tomorrow is already today and today is already tomorrow. Oh, what a bright idea this is. I do get my best ideas here, on Peckford's bench. Enough. Enough thinking for now. It's time to go home. Time to go back to Sara."*

Chapter Fourteen
(Discoveries)

Scott slept well during the few remaining hours before daybreak. His sleep would not have been peaceful, however, were it not for his dream work. As soon as he closed his eyes, he fell into a REM state with a newspaper in his hands. On the front page, *'Kidnapped Girl Found Un-Harmed,'* was featured in large, eye-catching letters. He tried to read the text but it went blurry. He flipped nervously through the pages until his eyes fell on the obituaries. At the end of the list of deceased, he found his e-mail: *'Benchmark Symmetry offers quiet time for worship from 5:30 p.m. to 6:30 p.m. each Monday. Join the very Reverend Patrick Ford in meditation. All souls are welcome.'* And displayed next to the e-mail there was a picture of his little Sara, smiling.

Seeing Sara's smiling face next to Peckford's e-mail gave him great peace of mind and allowed him a measure of restorative sleep. Oddly enough, the fact that she was in the obituaries did not seem to matter and was mercifully disregarded. He awakened at sunrise full of vigor and abounding with alacrity. He wanted to make sure he got his office work done and finished before five o'clock and so he arrived at the Hartland Bank at 7 a.m. He worked obliviously until his attention was usurped by his fellow employees, who came in at eight and seemed surprised to find him already at his desk. Several of them came close to his office and, assuming a solemn stance, gently tapped the door and inquired with myriad doleful phrases about Sara. He did not invite anyone in but merely appeased them with, "Thanks for your concern. The police are on the case. We hope to find her soon."

But Breena was different. She waited until all the rest had expressed their concerns and then she marched in without knocking and stood, restless legged, by his desk. Although she maintained silence, there was no way to ignore her exothermic presence. Her posture was angry, evocative, reproachful, teetering at the edge of tears, and quivering with implacable grief. When Scott looked up at her face, he was taken aback by her bulging red-eyes, which fixed him with a penetrating gaze. The encounter proved dumbfounding as neither of them could break the focused glare. This staring duel went on for a long, disconcerting while and was only broken when Mr. James McMaster, Scott's boss, walked in and without acknowledging Breena began talking to Scott.

"I didn't think you would be working today. Aren't you needed at home?"

"No Sir, actually, I've nothing to do at home and work keeps me from going insane."

"Any news?"

"No Sir, all we know is that she walked out when Nancy dashed to the store to get some milk. There was no sign of struggle and nothing was stolen. The police think that she panicked when she woke up and didn't find her mother in the house. They figure that she ran out looking for her mom and someone, who happened to be passing by, picked her up and took her away."

"But, you have no idea who that person might be?"

"Nancy and I can't think of anyone we know who would do this to us."

"And the police?"

"They're not saying much. They promised to call us whenever they find out anything and asked us to stay close to home."

"And why aren't you home then?"

"This is close enough, Sir. They have all my numbers and I check my home messages every hour."

"Is there anything I can do?

"I don't know what it could be, Sir, but thanks for being there for us."

All this was said with polite reverence on Scott's part but without visible emotion. This, of course, did not escape Breena who gazed with consternation at Scott's vacuous face. She could not comprehend his tacit calm vis-a-vis her conspicuous anxiety. Nonetheless, she realized from Scott's demeanor that she would have to start the conversation if there were to be any.

"May I sit down?"

"You just heard it all."

"Why didn't you call me?"

"Why should I call you?"

"You shouldn't be alone at times like these."

"I'm okay."

"You have no idea how much I care about you, Scott. I'd like to help if you'd let me."

Here Breena's tears began to flow, dripping on the floor in front of Scott's desk but she refused to wipe her eyes when Scott handed her a tissue paper. She just clenched the tissue in her fist and stubbornly maintained her stance until Scott asked her to sit down. She sat without protesting and immediately crossed her legs, flashing her white, succulent thighs at Scott's dry sockets.

"Breena. There's nothing anyone can do now except wait."

"I didn't mean that I wanted to help you find Sara. I just wanted to help you by being with you at this difficult time."

"Oh, I see."

"Well?"

"Why don't you let me call you when I need you. I don't feel alone at the moment because I've so much to keep me busy."

"You promise?"

"Yes."

Breena got up and pranced away to her desk, hoping that Scott's eyes were following her. When she turned around to sit in her chair, she glanced and was disappointed to find Scott's eyes already occupied with the papers in front of him.

The rest of the day passed in relative quietude as a solemn air dominated the office. Scott did not even take a lunch break and worked diligently without ever leaving his desk until the hour struck five. Before anyone could engage him in compassionate conversation, he dashed out of the office with unconcealed urgency, got into his car, and drove straight to the cemetery. On the way, he felt a strange peace come over him, which reinforced his unusual calm in spite of the gravity of the situation. He remembered his dream with the newspaper headline: '*Kidnapped Girl Found Un-Harmed*,' remembered Sara's smiling picture poised next to Peckford's e-mail, did not recall that she was in the obituaries, and profoundly believed that after his meeting with Peckford the headline in the dream would have to come true.

Exiting the Broadway Extension, he turned south on Kelly and was about to enter Memorial Park Cemetery when he noticed that the silver Mercedes, which had driven behind him up the Broadway Extension, was still following him as he drove down Kelly. Instead of entering the cemetery, he drove further south, entered the Toyota dealership, parked his 2002 Camry, and walked into the showroom. From behind the glass, he saw the silver Mercedes enter and park a few car spaces beyond his. James, one of the salesmen that Scott knew, approached and began talking to him. The time was 5:25 p.m. and he did not want to be late for Peckford. His mind sparked. He asked the salesman to come see his car and out they walked together. Approaching the silver Mercedes, he took a good look at the woman behind the wheel who, when she saw them approaching, turned her head the other way but not before Scott recognized her. It was Breena.

"James, do me a favor, will you."

"Sure, Scotty."

"I really came to introduce you to a friend of mine so you can help her find the car she needs."

"Sure, Scotty."

"Just tell her that Scotty sent you."

"Sure, Scotty."

"She's shy, you know. Just walk up to her, tap on her window, and tell her that I sent you. She's the blond in that silver Mercedes and her name is Breena Birdsong."

"Sure, Scotty."

As James Palmer walked toward Breena's car, Scott

got into his Camry and drove to the cemetery. There were some wilted Sunday flowers on some graves and the pebbled path was sputtered with wrinkled rose petals but Scott passed through these scenes without a thought and plowed his way straight to the bench. It was a cloudless day and the sun, which was about to bid the sky goodnight, splashed long, dusky shadows behind the graves. Peckford, wearing a light brown jacket over his khaki shirt and pants, blended well with the fall colors and was barely noticeable in the distance. When Scott approached and was greeted by Peckford's silent, sallow face, he became alarmed and his mouth went dry. That look, which Scott had become acquainted with in Baghdad, always portended something worrisome.

After exchanging curt, polite greetings Peckford and Scott sat in silence. No bright ideas came to Scott nor could he muster enough courage to voice his questions. He felt suspended like a solitary cloud, hovering between sky and earth, awaiting rain that was not forthcoming. This relative inertia endured until Peckford broke the wall of silence with a short, simple question, "How are you doing, Soldier?"

With his words unlocked, Scott took in a deep sigh and breathed out his burning question, "Sir, why Sara?"

Without replying, Peckford reached into his pocket, produced a Barbie doll, and handed it to Scott. Scott's eyes bulged and froze in their gaze while his head began to wobble as if it were about to fall off his neck.

"Was this Sara's?" asked Peckford with a calm but assertive voice.

Scott could not shatter his stunned state. He was in a sort of sleep paralysis where he could hear and feel but could not move.

"Was this Sara's?" repeated Peckford but with a harsh, commanding voice.

Scott, still frozen in his trance, could not mount an answer and started to look glazed. Peckford, becoming alarmed, shook him by the shoulder and shouted in his ear as through he were too far to hear normal speech, "Was this

Sara's?"

The sheer volume of Peckford's voice shattered Scott's iceberg and thawed out his words. Slowly and hesitantly, he glared at Peckford with softened eyes and whispered, "I gave, gave it to her, two days ago, for her birthday. I, I bought it, bought it from Walmart. Nancy forgot her birthday. Where, where did you, where did you find it, Sir?"

"It found me."

"What, what found, who found what, Sir?"

"I found it lying on my bed when I returned to my hotel this afternoon."

There followed a long pause peppered with sighs and tears that remained un-wiped in reverence to form and decorum. Then, as the tears dried out in the wind, Scott lost his stammer and became more assertive.

"Who knew to bring it to you?"

"Nothing escapes them, Scotty."

"Escapes whom, Sir?"

"Al-Qaeda."

"Al-Qaeda in Oklahoma City, Sir? Why? What for?"

"They're everywhere, Scotty, and they know a lot more about us than we know about them."

"But, why us? Why Sara? What have we done?"

"They must know about our mission and they have not forgotten how you managed to hack into their Baghdad computers when you were there. Thanks to you, we intercepted and aborted so many of their operations before they caught on. They have a long memory, Scotty, and we should not underestimate them."

"That's why they kidnapped Sara?"

"They've neutralized us, Scotty, haven't they? You won't go back to Iraq as long as your daughter is missing, will you?"

"But, why us? There are thousands of targets all over the country. Why you? Why me? Why Sara?"

They're changing strategy, shifting from egregious terrorism to tacit disruption. They've organized micro cells all over the US and Europe and their orders are to disrupt social harmony and spread fear. They're starting fires, polluting waters, and supplying local gangs with drugs. Their aim is to sicken our society and, in time, render us defenseless. They're planning far, far ahead."

"And what about you, Sir?"

"I can no longer play dead."

"What're you going to do?"

"Await my new orders."

There was another long pause as Scott thought out the implications behind Peckford's words. The scope of what Peckford had articulated proved too vast and too profound for his anguished mind. Being more adept at obeying than thinking, he needed specific answers and detailed instructions but instead, he found himself lost in a whirlwind of concepts that he could not fathom. There was one particularly desperate question on his mind, however, which he needed answered but was too afraid to ask. It took all his courage and several failed attempts before he voiced it.

"What, what will, what will they do, do to Sara?"

"It's not in their interest to harm her."

"Oh? No? Are you sure? What should I, what should we do then?"

"Let's sleep on it and we'll meet again tomorrow, same time, same place."

"Do you think that they're following us?"

"If they are, they'll risk exposing themselves. Our local whereabouts are not important to them."

"So, you're saying that we should do nothing?"

"Scotty, calm down. All I'm saying is that they've found a way to circumvent our military might. Now, our mission is to outsmart them but not to alert them. You'll receive your orders through me. Meanwhile, keep your lips pursed and behave like a bereaved father."

Scott drove home, his mind resounding with unintelligible echoes. In a way, he could make enough sense of Peckford's words to settle down his mind but, in spite of his spurious calm, he was incapable of any kind of focused thinking. He drifted like a ship without a rudder caught in a storm too far away from shore to see any landmarks. When he got home, the telephone was flashing and there were many messages, all of them from his mom, dad, Nancy, and Jane. There was nothing from the police, however, which after Peckford's briefing did not surprise him at all. His mobile phone, which he had silenced when he was with Peckford, had two frantic messages from Nancy begging him to call her. When he tried her home phone and she did not answer he called her mobile, which she answered at the third ring.

"Nancy, what's going on? Have you heard anything? Why aren't you home?"

"I've been home all day. Some neighbors brought food and some of my friends called; nothing else happened. Then Jane and Flora dropped by and took me with them to your parents' home."

"Is that where you are now?"

"Yes, Scotty, and there are lots of people here too."

"Where?"

"At your parents' home."

"How are they doing?"

"Who? The people?"

"No, my parents."

"Not so well. I wish you'd come and spend some time with them."

"Was that why you called me?"

"Yes, Scotty."

"Oh, I see. Well, tell them I'm on my way."

There were cars in the Thornton's driveway and on both sides of the street but the house was conspicuously quiet, devoid of the usual hum that people tend to generate when they get together. There were people in both living rooms sitting solemnly amidst hushed conversations and bewildered looks. Occasionally one person would lean over to whisper something into another's ear, provoking a resigned nod or a rueful expression. Other faces wore blank stares, their eyes mechanically focused upon inanimate objects that chanced to intercept their gaze. This subdued animation changed when Scott walked in and was abruptly replaced by a babbling tumult, which caused Jill and Howard to rush into the foyer, grapple Scott into their shaky arms, and audibly sob and gasp as if he had just returned from war.

After Scott's arrival, a sense of relief slowly suffused the house and the visitors, having served their turn, began to leave. One by one on their way out they would give a hovering hug to Jill, a curt embrace to Howard, and a handshake to Scott. By the time the last visitor had left, it was close to eight and Scott found himself at the dinner table surrounded by his extended family. Flora and Nancy sat on each side of Jane, a triptych that faced Scott who towered between his mom and dad. Unlike a wake, a despairingly sympathetic love tether held the group together as they lit up hopes and snuffed out worries, leaving most of the food unconsumed. It was as though Sara's disappearance had caused a mellowing of hearts and conjured a meekness of spirits that held the night together like a prayer holds all the bowed heads in its gentle palm.

When the time came for the ensemble to scatter, Scott found it hard to leave without saying a few words in private to Nancy. He did not know what he was going to say but that did not seem to bother him. He knew in his heart that the right words would come to him at the right moment. A feeling of inner restlessness was spurring him to action as if he were on the verge of emanating some grand idea or experiencing some profound epiphany. A sudden largess overcame his soul, a noble exhilaration, a generosity of spirit that overwhelmed his senses and moved him to run toward Nancy, calling her at the top of his voice as she got into her car.

She, having heard his call, stayed in her seat, held her door open against the hissing, cold-night-air, and waited for him with a shiver in her soul. Panting, he placed his hands on the car top, bent forward, looked into her red eyes, hesitated, redirected his gaze onto her moist cheeks, her blue lips, her white hand clutching the ignition key, her skirt flapping up her thighs, her bobbing breasts buoyant with anguish, and after a gap of gasping silence blurted to her face, "Nancy, ah. Would you, ah. Would you like to, ah. Nancy, would you please come home with me?"

As if suddenly aware of his beckoning gaze, Nancy released the ignition key and tried to pull down her unruly dress with one hand while she covered her cleavage with the other. Having occupied herself with such seemingly purposeful motions, she tranced into the night as if she were in suspended animation and said nothing.

"Nancy? Nancy dear, wake up. Nancy, where are you? Nancy, please..."

Scott's words, swept by the wind, remained unheard. He tried to speak louder, almost shouting into her ear, but nothing penetrated her levitated trance. Stumped by her impenetrable distance, Scott felt his heart swell in his chest, gallop at exhausting speed, and then stop, breathless, at her feet. At that very instant the wind, the night, the hand-gripped moment, the white noise of the unsaid, the steaming soup of memories welling out of his unconscious, the mélange of nerve and verve that frothed within his brain, his mutating truths forcing themselves upon his immutable yearnings, and all the dark clouds of chaos thundering in his soul—all of these formidable, feuding forces seemed to suddenly collapse into a peaceful calm and hand him the key with which to unlock Nancy's reverie.

As if moved by a redeeming, kindly force, he began wiping Nancy's cheeks, soothing her lips, and stroking her chin with his fingertips. This fragile moment cracked with every tremulous touch until it almost snapped. Slowly, her chin began to quiver, her wet lips gasped a breath, and she began to murmur in fervent prayer. Then, having inaudibly lipped a Hail Mary, she let go of her dress, raised Scott's salty hand to her lips, and pasted a moist, supplicating kiss deep into the wet womb of his palm.

Chapter Fifteen
(Forbidden Liaison)

Scott, steaming with confusion, drove behind Nancy into the cold November night. Unconsciously, he was torn between the dissonant emotions of intransigent reality and implacable grief, and between the opposing needs of fortified reason and fearful despair. This sustained, subliminal tension created an overwhelming desire for catharsis. Unaware of these feuding forces within his unconscious, Scott felt an ineluctable urge to discharge his anguished mind and defuse his heavy-laden soul. But, in his confusion, he could not see through the thick fog of the moment what was soon to take place underneath the tenebrous cloak of night.

In this precarious mental state, he waited at Nancy's apartment while she collected her things and then drove behind her to his home. Holding hands, they tiptoed into the empty house like two furtive teenagers, closed the door, and stood in the half-lit foyer word locked and panting as if stunned by the moment's timorous heft. The silent unsaid convulsed like a gravid uterus in the crescendo of labor, relentlessly thrusting and wielding more and more tension with each mounting contraction. There was no escape from the tolling clock of reality, no means to silence the drumming of hearts, no force to halt the swirling of thoughts, no ice to temper the swelling of loins, and no water to quench the smokeless, raging fire that was about to consume them.

When minds cannot think, instincts rise to the rescue. In one deft, sweeping scoop Scott gathered Nancy into his leonine arms and carried her through the silent hall into his den. In the middle of the unlit bedroom, curled within Scott's arms, Nancy's memories flashed back to the last and only time they had sex in this very room after Scott's return from Iraq. It happened on his first night back and that was when she realized that something dreadful had changed her man. She shuddered when she recalled how he slowly undressed her, stood her naked in the middle of the room, took her while she was bent over, and then tossed her on the bed like a used rag, turned his back to her, and fell asleep.

"Scotty."

"What is it, Babe?"

"Would you be kind this time?"

"What do you mean, this time?"

"You know..."

"Are you afraid?"

"A bit."

"What's wrong, Babe?"

"I don't want it to be like the last time."

"What about the last time?"

"You know...on your first night back..."

"Back from where?"

"Back from Iraq."

"So, what happened?"

"You don't remember?"

"Did it have to do with Sara?"

"Oh, Scotty, please put me down. We need to talk."

No lights were lit as Scott laid Nancy on his bed, lay beside her, pulled her onto his chest, and began to unzip her dress.

"Scotty..."

His lips intercepted hers in mid-word and began whispering moist, ambrosial longings. Then they meandered onto her flushed cheeks, her swooned eyes, her doughy earlobes, her sighing neck, and her half-nude shoulders redolent with all the aromas that waft through her stylist salon.

"Scotty, let me take off my dress before you rip it."

"Oh, yes, your dress. Stand up and let me help you. Ah, your bra, that needs to go, too. Your panties, oh how tiny, they're hardly worth it."

As Nancy stood naked by the bed, Scott turned on the side lamp and devoured her with his hungry eyes.

"Scotty, stop staring at me like that. You're frightening me."

"Oh, I'm sorry. What do you mean, frightening you?"

"It's that same look, Scotty."

Nancy's mind was still shrouded by memories from their first night after Iraq. She never forgot that dissonant look, full of angry passion, full of need and rejection, full of longing and disgust, full of lust and repulsion, full of post-traumatic confusion bordering on mania.

"What look are you talking about? I'm looking at you because you're beautiful, because you have the figure of a dancer and the skin of a teenager. I'm looking at you because I love what I see."

"You still love me after all I have done, after filing for divorce, after losing Sara?"

"I still love what I see."

"Do you love me more than you love your pornography?"

"What pornography?"

"Scotty, you don't remember all the hours..."

Oblivious to her plea and unaware of her astonishment at his new mindset, Scott pulled Nancy into his famished arms and took her breath away with a smothering kiss. She could taste his tears seeping into her mouth and dripping down her neck. When she was able to look into his eyes, she found them soft, buoyant, gleaming with gratitude, and brimming with kindness. The look that she had feared for so long was gone, effaced by the night, replaced by a long-suffering gaze like a drizzle of rain in midsummer or the eyes of an icon gleaming with mercy. She no longer had any reason to question, to fear, to inquire, to doubt, or even to understand. Her Scott was back, back like a remission after a long battle with cancer, like a prodigal son, like a resurrection, back with undamaged soul, back whole from Iraq. Her eyes blurred as she began to untie his necktie, unbutton his shirt, unbuckle his belt, and unzip his fly while Scott lay motionless, like a silent colossus, complacent, yielding, submissive, resigned. Then, as if awakened from an out-of-body trance or a dream-smothered sleep, he abruptly blurted, "What, what do you think, what do you think you're doing?"

"Darling, how can we make love with me totally naked and you fully dressed?"

"Oh, yes, I'm fully dressed."

"And you still have your shoes on."

"Oh, I still have my shoes on?"

"Come back from wherever you are, Darling, and pay attention to me for a change."

It was a fecund night, inexhaustible, insatiable, inextinguishable, and inexorable like ocean waves that come rhythmically, come synchronously, come with a swashing beat to break repeatedly at shore without fatigue. Time waltzed as it warmed its cheeks upon their flames, smiled as it sprinkled them with a few more precious moments from its holy essence, and then, as if embarrassed that it had gazed too long, took off in a huff and let the morning in. When Nancy felt the Tuesday morning rays creep and nibble at her cheeks, Scott was already awake gazing at her with a smile on his face. Without a word, as if not to disturb the morning quietude, he began stroking her arms, smoothing her hair, and kissing her fingertips, one by one, like a bee in a jasmine tree.

"Have you been awake all night, Darling?"

"Awake? I don't remember."

"So what do you remember then?"

"Every moment, every sound, every breath, everything."

"Everything? No one remembers everything."

"Everything from the time the wind lifted up your dress in the car till now. I remember the rattle of the ignition key when you released it to hold down your unruly dress. I remember your kiss burning my palm. I remember every move, every moan, every groan of your liquid body, your mouth that tasted like honeysuckle, and your boisterous spasms that split the night."

"Scotty, you're embarrassing me. Where did all this poetry come from?"

"Poetry?"

"Oh, never mind, who's hungry?"

"Hungry?"

"Scotty, you have to be hungry..."

"I'll be the cook then."

"No, I'll be the cook."

"Well, let's cook together then."

Breakfast was rife with circumferential trivia and tacit with denial of Sara's looming vacuum. No heavy-hearted conversation sauntered among the scrambled eggs, the toast, and the tea. It was as though the two lovers had dreamfully found each other, honeymooned their first night together, and awakened with embarrassed smiles that glistened upon their bruised lips. Nevertheless, when it was time to go to work, they comported themselves in perfect harmony as if they had been living together for years. Their absolute oblivion of Sara's kidnapping and their new fascination with each other felt like a delicious reverie, a welcome respite from the spiteful fact that they would, sooner or later, have to face together and apart. Meanwhile, still clinging to their spurious renaissance, Scott walked Nancy to her car and kissed her goodbye underneath the shy morning sun. It was not a perfunctory kiss like one would give his partner before going to work; rather, it was a famished kiss, a welcoming kiss, and an insatiable kiss that one would give his soul mate after a heart-rending separation.

On her way to work, Nancy was quickening with joy, shivering with serendipity, and shaking with her rock-and-roll tunes that beat out of her car radio. She couldn't wait to call Jane and tell her about last night. She couldn't wait for the day to pass and her work to end. She couldn't wait to be home with Scott again. Her mind began to spin a thousand plans as her future grew more secure by the minute. She and Scott would get back together because Scotty was back, back to what he used to be before he went to Iraq. *"Oh, well, if we can't find Sara, we'll make another one or two or three,"* she thought.

The Glamour Hair Salon was the gossip broadcasting station of the region. Located in the northeast corner of May and Britton, it drew on clients from all the prestigious neighborhoods. Although Nancy was the sole proprietor and had her own loyal clientele, she also leased space to several other stylists, both men and women, who drew their own clients from other neighborhoods. When Nancy parked the car and pulled out the ignition key, her rock-and-roll mood floated away into the sudden silence, leaving her in a pensive state, bewildered and confused at Scott's unforeseen conversion. Her thoughts were flighty, unfocused, thrashing in sundry directions, and meandering over a maze of un-trodden mental landscapes with no exit in sight. At that moment of recognition, she felt happy and sad, secure and insecure, real and unreal, sane and insane, and all these disparate emotions collided in her heart, bouncing off each other with great clamor. She wanted to believe that Scott was hers again, that he wanted her again, and that he loved her again. She wanted to believe that Scott was attracted to her because of her alone and not because of Sara.

Throughout the past five years, she was haunted by her competition with Sara but was never brave enough to share this obsession with anyone, even her best friend, Jane. *"Would Scott have proposed to me were I not pregnant with Sara? Would he have loved me if I were not Sara's mother? Was our life together only for Sara's sake? And what would happen if we were never to find Sara? Would he cling to me more because I am Sara's mother, or would he reject me because I was the one who lost her?"* These were not comforting thoughts; they were bitter cogitations that resurrected disturbing questions. She found herself sighing repeatedly while walking to her salon, gasping as if she were air hungry, wiping her tears with fingers irreverent of mascara, and frantically rubbing her ears hoping to drown these noisy thoughts. But, no matter how hard she tried, one questing thought screamed louder than noise. *"Will he ever love me for me alone or will Sara always stand between us?*"

Nancy walked into her shop with smudged cheeks and a sweaty neck. Two of the stylists were already working and didn't pay attention to her coming in. The other two had not arrived yet, which allowed her to have the break room all to herself. She had just enough time to tidy up before her first client arrived. It was Barbara Martin, who came every five weeks for a heavy blond weave. She was a cheerful Latina divorcée who had changed her name from Martinez to Martin as part of her divorce resolve, and as part of her alimony she managed an allowance of a $100/month for hair styling. She always greeted Nancy with an affable smile followed by, "My ex is *steell* paying to keep me beautiful and we don't want to disappoint *heem*, do we?" This monthly leitmotif was usually followed by a shared laugh that heralded the tedious process of hairstyling. Only this time, Barbara did the laughing alone while Nancy maintained a detached, un-participating stance.

"Nancy, you don't laugh with me no more; what *ees* wrong?

"Oh, you haven't heard?"

"Heard?"

"That Sara was kidnapped."

"But you don't say; you're *keedding*; tell me the truth now; I'm your friend, no?"

"It's the truth, Barbara."

"No *keedding*?"

"No kidding."

"You *wont* to tell me all about *eet* or you *wont* me to *com* back another time?"

"I don't mind telling you. The whole world knows, anyway..."

There were tears in Barbara's eyes by the time Nancy finished her story. A brief moment of silence floated while Nancy worked on Barb's hair. Then, all of a sudden, Barbara popped the awkward question, "*Dose* he blame you for Sara's *keednapping*?"

"He doesn't seem to, anymore."

"Anymore?"

"Well, he was quite angry with me at first, but yesterday we made up."

"Made *op*? *Wot* do you mean? You're already divorced; so *wot's* there to make *op*?"

"Well, he asked me to go home with him last night."

"But you don't say? *Jost* like that, he *ask* you to go home with *heem* and you *deed*?"

"I've been wanting to for a while and he was okay with it when Sara was with us. But, after Sara's disappearance, he changed his mind and then he changed it again. It's real confusing..."

"Do you still *lov heem*?"

"I don't know anymore, but I do need him. He makes me feel secure."

"And *dos* he *lov* you?"

"I don't know. He must need me, too."

"Well, what did he say to you after you went home with *heem*?"

"We didn't talk much."

"What *deed* you do?"

"We made love all night."

"All night? Is he superman?"

"Yeah, he is."

"Would you *lon* him to me when you're done with *heem*?"

"Why? Don't you have a boyfriend?"

"I have three, but none of them is as *goode* as that. *Goode* men don't *wont* women like *os*; they want younger and educated, you don't *theenk*?"

"You can say that again."

"I'll never get *marreed* again; will you?"

"To Scotty, yes. Having lost Sara, no decent man would ever want me as his wife."

Nancy had smaller conversations with subsequent clients. She began feeling more tired as the day went on and started to yawn from lack of sleep. Her feelings of happy confusion were slowly replaced by deep feelings of sadness. She worked automatically with solemn detachment devoid of alacrity. Those who noticed blamed it on the kidnapping and showed their respect by avoiding the topic. By the time her day ended and it was time to go home, Nancy found herself sitting among piles of questions that had no answers.

It was her habit, before locking up the place, to sit in the break room with her feet elevated, review the day's accounts, and glance over the next day's appointments. That day, however, she found herself incapable of such organized activities. Instead of elevating her tired feet she paced the workroom, and instead of studying the accounts she gazed at the empty client chairs in the waiting room, and instead of glancing at the next day's appointments she stared at her many faces as they faded in and out of the panoramic salon mirrors. She felt terribly alone except for the ebb and flow of her myriad reflections, which in their coming and going seemed to keep her company.

Marching to her car, she clenched the ignition key as memories of yesterday's evening wafted underneath her skirt, lifted it to the wind, and began to ask some embarrassing questions. *"Which home do I go to now, mine or Scott's? Why didn't he call me and why didn't I think to call him? Why didn't we make arrangements this morning before we left for work? Why do I feel as if we had a one-night stand? Reminds me of the many ones I had when he was in Iraq. I hardly remember their faces. One-night-stand men are my type of men; after we do it, I never call them back and they never call me. It takes one look for me to seize the moment. I don't hesitate. Just like yesterday, seized the moment and didn't hesitate. What the hell."*

Nancy drove with all these issues stirring beside her. She made up her mind to go back to her apartment and call Scott from there. She didn't want to use her cell phone because she didn't want him to assume, not even for one second, that she was on her way back to him. No, she wanted him to know that she was already at her apartment so that if he still wanted her to join him, he would have to invite her again. That was her plan as she ascended the stairs to her apartment. Leaning against the door of Apartment 404, Building C, Acropolis Villas was a brown paper bag.

Staring at the bag, Nancy hesitated awhile, went back into the street, looked around, went upstairs again, sat on the last step facing her door, and glared at the brown paper bag as if it were capable of telling her what next to do. For reasons that were not clear to her she was afraid to open it even though she realized that sooner or later she would have to. While trying to overcome her fear, she divined several ways to delay and procrastinate. *"Perhaps I should call Scotty and let him come and open it. Perhaps I should call the police instead. I don't have to open it to get into the apartment. What if it had something poisonous or explosive or dirty? What if it belongs to someone else and was placed here by mistake? What if it has a body part in it?"*

Unable to muster enough courage to overcome her paper-bag fear, unable to make a deft decision with her free-falling mind, and unable to override her tumbling emotions she decided to open her apartment door, walk in, and leave the bag outside. *"I'll go in and have a beer. Yeah, I need beer and music. I need to quiet down my mind. I need to forget all about the damn bag. I bet it's empty and full of nothing but air. I bet Dick Straight put it there just to taunt me. He just can't get over me. What an asshole."*

Chapter Sixteen
(Tacit Assignments)

On his way to work, Scott had no thoughts of Sara or Peckford. This suspending of reality lived on, accompanied him all the way to his office, and stayed with him as he negotiated through his workmates' inquisitive greetings and wry glances. At lunch break, he took off and without knowing why found himself under the Survivor Tree at the bombing memorial. He gazed at the 168 empty chairs, gazed into the reflection pool, gazed into the 168 startled faces that inhabited the place, and began to count the children among them. He counted 20 frightened, little faces but only 19 small, empty chairs. *"Where did the extra face come from?"* he wondered.

He tried to study the features of each child but found them indistinct. Each time he would focus on a face it would blur away, leaving blue fear in the empty eye sockets. When he gazed at the last face, the 20th face, it did not blur and the eye sockets were not empty; they were filled with fateful tears that flowed down her dirty cheeks. Her azure eyes were barely discernable behind the tears, and her features were stunned by fright but her golden locks of hair glowed like a halo around her timorous face. It took a while before Scott recognized the un-blurred 20th face. At the moment he did, he felt a lightning bolt strike him in the head and emerge from his feet, leaving him steaming in his shoes. He began jumping like a barefoot madman on hot coals, reaching for the halo with supplicating hands, and resounding at the top of his inner voice, *"Oh, my God, this is Sara, my little Sara, my kidnapped Sara."*

Visitors around the Survivor Tree became alarmed at Scott's spectacle. Not privy to his state of mind, all they could see was a tall, agile, well-dressed man repeatedly jumping towards the lowest branches of the Survivor Tree, which seemed to recede away from him the closer he got to them. A history teacher with a flock of high-school students who happened to be visiting at the time took advantage of the scene to expound on the myth of Tantalus from which the word tantalize derives. However, unlike Tantalus, when Scott became too exhausted to continue his desperate attempts at reaching Sara's halo, he leaned his face against the wall and like a child cried out all of his tears...

Scott returned from the 'wailing wall' looking pale and clammy. He went straight to his desk, put his head between his hands, and closed his eyes. He wanted to see Sara's face again, the face that he saw under the Survivor Tree, the face surrounded by a halo of golden locks of hair. He tried to conjure her face, her features, her aspect, her smile, her stance, and was astonished at his inability to recall any of it. *"What's wrong with me? Why can't I recall my own daughter's face? I must be going blind in the mind. Blind in the mind? Did I just think that? That's a deep thought that needs to be written down before I forget it. That's my best thought ever, better than the Silent Majority or any other thought I had conceived at Peckford's bench. Peckford's bench? Peckford? Oh, I almost forgot that he's going to be waiting for me at 5:30 today. Oh, what's happening to my mind? Blind in the mind with eyes that can't even see my little Sara's face?"*

Scott reached for his wallet, pulled out a picture of Sara, held it before his eyes, and began to study her face. He could clearly see her features but still couldn't recall them. He felt as though he had never seen them before and that caused him to become even more alarmed. *"What's wrong with my brain? I can't recall my daughter's face even when I'm looking at it? I must be going mad..."*

"Sorry to disturb you, General, but I'm worried about you."

"Ah?"

"You don't look too hot, you know, and you're still as pale and clammy as when you first walked in. And that trick you played on me yesterday was very naughty. It took me quite a while to shake off that Toyota James fellow; he just wouldn't take no for an answer because of what you said to him. You'd have to be dumb to trade a Mercedes for a Toyota. I can't believe you did such a thing when all I wanted was to be with you at this trying time."

"Breena, please, I don't feel so well at the moment and..."

"I wouldn't be here if I thought you felt well. You need a friend, Scotty. Would you please stop avoiding me for a change; I've never done anything to hurt your..."

"I can't recall Sara's features."

"What the heck do you mean by that?"

"I'm looking at her picture but I still can't recall how she looked. It's like her memory has been erased from my mind."

"Excuse me, but that's a bunch of baloney. Get hold of yourself, General. Let's have dinner tonight and I'll make you feel better. You need me Scotty and I'm here for you to..."

"Do you know what *blind in the mind* means?"

"Blind in what mind?"

"What does it mean to you, Breena Birdsong?"

"It means that you need a friend whose mind is clear because your mind is murky."

"And what else does it mean?"

"What else could it mean?"

"What else does it mean to you personally?"

"I think that it means that you need to get laid."

"I got laid yesterday and that didn't help a bit."

"You have a girlfriend?"

"Sort of."

"Sort of? Who is she? Do I know her?"

"She's my ex."

"Nancy? Oh, God, you're disgusting. Why would anyone sleep with his ex? Don't you think there are other women around?"

Breena left Scott's office in a huff and went into hers without looking back to see if Scott was eyeing her. Scott, on the other hand, tried to do his work but found that he couldn't. He ended up staring at Sara's picture until the clock struck five. Startled by the chime, he put the picture back into his wallet and hurried away without tidying up his desk. There was so much chaos in his brain that he needed to organize. He needed to talk to Peckford and hoped that Peckford would be able to help him understand what was going on in his blind mind. He needed to know how come he could make love to Nancy—the woman he didn't love, the mother who wasn't a mother, the neglectful mom who managed to lose her own daughter—and still enjoy every second of it. He needed to come to terms with his intrusive, disturbed feelings. And, most urgently, he needed solid reassurances that his little Sara was going to be returned to him unharmed.

On his way to the cemetery, Scott's exhausted mind froze and became a mental iceberg laced with deep blue echoes. He could not think and didn't even care to thaw out his mental block. He just drove on as though he were a horse pulling a carriage down the road. When he arrived at the necropolis he scurried down the pebbled path with robotic feet without looking ahead, without looking for the bench, and without looking for Peckford. Before he knew it he found himself standing before his mentor, tongue-tied and dumbfounded.

"Won't you sit down, Soldier?"

"Oh, it's my cell phone."

"Why don't you answer it then?"

"Babe? What? Where? Are you sure? Oh, my God. I should've known when I couldn't see her face even with her picture in my hand. I know you don't understand. I'll explain later. No, you come to the house. No, I didn't change the locks. I'll be home in an hour or so."

"Scotty, you've turned pale all of a sudden."

"Well, Sir, it's bad news."

"Is it about Sara?"

"Yes, Sir."

"And what did Nancy have to say?"

"She found a brown paper bag at her apartment door."

"And what was in the bag? Scotty, come now, you've always been strong. Soldiers don't cry. Start talking and you'll feel better. What was in the bag, Soldier?"

"Sara's hair."

"Just a lock of two?"

"No, Sir. Nancy said that it looked like they had shaved her entire head and put it all in the bag."

"Was there a note?"

"No Sir, just her hair."

"Scotty, stop crying. This is very good news."

"Good news? How do you suppose, Sir? What's so good about someone shaving my daughter's head?"

"Scotty, wake up from your ice-blue despair and think. It's good news because it means that they don't intend to harm her."

"How do you know that, Sir?"

"They could have put in a finger, a toe, or an earlobe pinned to a ransom note, and they didn't."

"Oh, so why are they doing it then?"

"To taunt us, to neutralize us, to tell us that they know all about us, and to make sure we understand that if they choose to they could harm us all."

"And why us, Sir, why Sara?"

"There are thousands of similar cells all over the country, Scotty. We were chosen as victims because we had plotted against them and had aborted several of their operations. Their plan is to stop us in our tracks with tactics that are far superior to our military power. When I contacted the Homeland Security to report Sara's kidnapping they told me that they already knew about it from the police reports. All local police departments have been alerted to report any malevolent harm incurred by active or discharged military personnel or their families. The Homeland Security is studying their new modus operandi by putting together patterns from intelligence reports taken from myriad sources."

"Have they harmed any of their victims yet?"

"No and they won't because they prefer to hold us hostage."

"How long is this going to go on, Sir?"

"It's a long-term battle, Scotty. Instead of one big iron curtain, we now have thousands of small, invisible, house curtains. Instead of blatant, bloody, international terrorism, we now have tacit, frightful, domestic disruption. They are moving their operations from armed training camps in foreign lands to unarmed training cells right in our midst. Cells are recruited by personal contacts and receive their orders verbally; nothing is written, e-mailed, or telephoned, and the cells are kept isolated and independent of each other. Cell contacts use pseudonyms and the same person never contacts the same cell twice. They call their cells *Bacteria* and their effort *Operation Plague.* Just like biological warfare, they plant their *Bacteria* in vulnerable locations and watch them spread their *Plague.*"

"Oh, Sir, this sounds terribly evil."

"Evil, ingenious, and hard to intercept, Scotty."

"And how did they get so smart?"

"We made them so by defeating their military tactics and squeezing them out of their enclaves."

"So, what's going to happen next?'

"You mean to Sara or to our country?"

"To both, Sir."

"In the long run, terrorism kills itself because it lacks a noble ideology that can sustain it. In the annals of history, terrorism has always lost and those targeted by it have always prevailed. Suppression and subterfuge are short-lived. New terrorist generations become repulsed by their disruptive actions partly because they see that they could never win and partly because their collective conscientiousness ultimately rebels against the injustice inflicted upon innocent people."

"And how about in the short run? How about Sara?"

"The Homeland Security, in collaboration with the local police, thinks that they will be able to locate the cell that kidnapped Sara. If they find it, they will choose their time, close in, and rescue her."

"And what do we do in the meantime?"

"We live, Scotty. We live a life as normal as possible. We live for joy and love. We live to show them that they cannot disrupt our noble fabric with their misanthropic *Operation Plague.*"

"Why do they hate us so much, Sir?"

"Too many reasons but they all have to do with the excesses, contrasts, and injustices inherent in maintaining a superpower. The same story repeats itself throughout history and we're no different."

"But what about Sara, Sir? I cannot live for love and joy without her. Inside of me there's a profound sadness that I'll never get over unless she returns. My feelings are changing Sir, changing about everything, and I no longer understand them."

"Feelings change whenever they wish and we can't control them, Scotty. In most situations, they control us and we need to learn how to deal with them."

"Oh, Sir, I feel lost and have so many questions on my mind. I'm so glad you are here to explain them to me."

"I won't be here very long, Scotty. I've already received my orders and I'm going back to Iraq. Homeland Security, however, is going to revoke your orders because they want you on site."

"But I'd feel lost without you, Sir. Perhaps, if I go back to Iraq, I could forget my pain."

"You can't go back Scotty. If you go back they'll kill Sara."

"What?"

"They will, Scotty."

"So, you're going back and I'm staying here. Is that it?"

"I'm afraid so, Soldier."

"And we can't communicate as long as you're gone, right?"

"But we can when I return."

"But what if I need you in the meantime, Sir?"

"Soldier, sooner or later, you'll have to become the captain of your own ship. What better time to begin than when your captain is gone."

"But, what if I end up making the wrong decision?"

"If one learns from one's mistakes one should not be afraid to make them. Nature always wins, my boy. Follow your natural instincts, be true to yourself, and let your heart lead you. Don't be afraid to attempt the impossible if you think it's the right thing to do."

"Would you like for me to attempt the impossible, Sir? If that's what you're trying to tell me, give me the order and I'll risk everything for Sara's sake."

"Whatever you decide to do, Soldier, do it quickly and don't tell anyone what you're doing. Your chances of succeeding are much better if you work alone:

> *'If you can force your nerve and heart and sinew*
> *To serve your turn long after they are gone*
> *And so hold on when there is nothing in you*
> *Except the will which says to them hold on.'"*

"Who said that, Sir?"

"Kipling."

"And what does it mean?"

"It means one should never give up."

"Is that an order, Sir?"

"Al-Qaeda is everywhere."

"Is this the last time I'll see you, Sir?"

"I'll call you when I return. In the meantime, Special Agent Smedlund of the OSBI will be your contact and if I need to contact you, I'll do it through my niece."

"What's her name, Sir and may I contact her if I need to contact you?"

"Let's leave her nameless for now, Soldier. There's a time for everything."

Peckford stood up, smiled, and walked away, leaving Scott alone on the bench. Scott watched him fade away down the pebbled path, his brown jacket and khaki pants blending with the fall colors and his form slowly diminishing into the evening mist like that of a movie star before *The End* appears upon the screen.

Scott's mental iceberg slowly thawed out as he sat among the warm quietude of graves. Slowly, he realized that Peckford had answered none of his urgent questions. On the contrary, he had given him more questions to ponder and new feats to accomplish. Instead of helping him he had ordered him to help himself, become his own captain, and assume total control of his own emotions.

That Peckford-bench encounter pierced Scott's heart like a poisoned arrow because he realized, deep in his soul, what it really meant. With Peckford out of sight, it suddenly dawned on him that Peckford had tacitly entrusted him with the grave responsibility of outsmarting Al-Qaeda and rescuing Sara. Without saying it, Peckford had implied that Sara's best chances lay with Scott and not with the OSBI or the Homeland Security.

"I must be strong and careful. I must act alone. I must become invisible. It's all up to me. Oh, my God? How can I fight Al-Qaeda alone? But that's what Peckford seemed to order me to do. There was a sense of urgency in his words. He must think there's little time left. I must use every moment.

I need to get hold of myself and start doing some serious thinking. I need to save my little Sara now. Otherwise it'll be too late. That's what Peckford meant when he said, 'Whatever you decide to do, Soldier, do it quickly and don't tell anyone you're doing it. Your chances of succeeding are much better if you work alone.' I need to be brave. My orders are to never give up. I feel so overwhelmed. Oh, how confusing."

Chapter Seventeen
(Confusion)

When Scott, in his confused state, arrived at his home, Nancy's car was in his driveway. Thinking he was at Nancy's apartment, he walked up to the door and instead of using his key he rang the doorbell. When after a while no one came he rang again, let out a perfunctory cough, and began to whistle. But in spite of all these subtle announcements he heard no sound and no footsteps approached. *"Why doesn't she open her door? I know she's in her apartment because her car is in the driveway. I wonder if she's napping? Oh, of course she's napping because I kept her awake all last night. I think I'll just go on to my home and wait for her to call me when she wakes up."*

Scott, still confused, got back into his car and drove off. At the first stop sign, his mind began to cloud as he pondered which way to turn and couldn't decide. With his foot on the brake he hesitated, read the street names, read them again, tried to discern which way was north, which way was east, and where did the sun set today. Meanwhile, while deliberating all these complex, directional issues a line of cars was growing behind him. Finally, a loud honk startled him, forcing him to leap into the crossing at the same time another car was passing through. Angry honks and screeching tires added clamor to the dumbfounding chaos but coincidence was merciful and it all ended safely without incident.

Scott parked his car at a gas station, got out, and tried to calm himself down. He looked around and carefully studied the corner shops. Although inspecting his surroundings helped him regain some sense of direction he was, nevertheless, still unaware that he had actually left his home in order to go home. Standing by his car and slowly recovering his bearings, he couldn't help but feel confounded because he couldn't make up his mind what he should do next.

Awaiting his mind to clear, there was one decision that he could make while still mired in this mental marshland of his. He got back into his car, drove it to the pump, pulled out his credit card, and started fueling. As the gallon and dollar numbers began to scroll past his eyes his gaze became fuzzy and, feeling a bit vertiginous, he got back into his car and sat down while his tank filled up.

His mind, a blank slate at the time, was suddenly jolted by the pump thud, which indicated that his tank was full. Something about the finality of that thud spun his mind into a state of alarm and piqued his senses. Something about that thudding sound resurrected buried echoes from the catacombs of Baghdad, echoes that assailed his unsuspecting ears and incarnated into the sharp chop of a butcher or the bounce-less drop of a severed head. He got out of the car, looked around with circumspect paranoia, cautiously re-pouched the gas nozzle, and then drove straight home.

On the way back, a feeling of déjà vu unclenched his jaws, loosened up his grip on the steering wheel, and smoothed out his frowns. Then when he saw Nancy's car in the driveway, a sense of familiarity overcame him and grew more and more intense as he approached his front door, reached for the doorbell with his key, but stopped short of ringing. Mesmerized in the evening hue with key pointing at his doorbell he was startled out of his confusion by Nancy's whimsical remark when she surprised him by opening the door, "Have you lost your keys, Darling?"

"Oh, no, here they are."

"So, why didn't you use them?"

"I was about to when you opened."

Nancy, seeing Scott's confusion, pulled him in, closed the door, and led him by the hand into the living room. Poised on the sofa was the brown paper bag with Sara's hair in it. For a while they stood motionless, gazing at the bag with trepidation as if it held Sara's head. All of a sudden Scott put both hands to his ears and repeated at the top of his voice, "No, not again, not again, no please, not again."

"What is it, Darling? What are you screaming about?"

"I heard it again."

"It? What the hell is it? What did you hear, Darling?"

"The thud."

"Thud? What thud? There was no thud. Honey, are you okay?"

"I don't know. I'm fading, fainting. I better sit down."

When Scott collapsed on the sofa he was beaded with cold perspiration and his eyes were rolled back in a fixed gaze. His appearance frightened Nancy, causing her to run to the kitchen for a wet towel. When she returned she found him shivering uncontrollably and gasping for air as if he were choking. She thought about calling 911 but as she approached the phone he stopped shivering, his eyes mellowed, and his breathing settled down. She ran to his side and began wiping the sweat off his face. The cool, fresh feel of her wet towel relaxed his constrained expression and slowly helped him regain his composure.

"Nancy, what happened?"

"You scared me."

"What did I do?"

"You fainted when you saw the bag."

"Oh, the bag, where, where is it?

"It's right here beside you."

Scott sat up awkwardly and with uncertain, cautious fingers reached for the bag and peeked. A scent of old memory wafted from within and held him hostage to its siren call. In disbelief, he glared at Nancy who was watching him with gaping eyes, dipped his nose into the bag, and sniffed. His face began to contort and his eyes reddened as he sent a hesitating hand into the bag, pulled out a fistful of blond, curly hair, and cuddled the locks to his cheek.

"What is it, Scotty?"

"Do you smell it?"

"Smell what? What? What are you talking about?"

"Here, take a whiff."

Saying that, Scott reverently placed the fistful of hair

under Nancy's nose.

"What is it?"

"You can't tell?"

"Well, it reminds me of church."

"So what is it then?"

"I feel that I know it but I can't name it."

"It's incense."

"Incense? What does that mean? Surely, she's not being locked up in a church."

"A church? I wish."

"Scotty, could you please tell me in plain words what the hell do you mean."

"If she were locked up in a church, she would be real easy to find."

"Scotty, please come down to my level."

"In Iraq, incense is used to aromatize homes and rich Bedouins use it to aromatize themselves by fanning its fumes underneath their gallabiyas."

"Gallabiyas?"

"The long, loose cloaks they wear."

"You can't be serious. You mean some Bedouins came all the way from Iraq to kidnap Sara? What the hell did you do to these people, Scotty?"

Scott's mind, stung by Nancy's mordant question, began to feel cornered and overwhelmed again. What he had tried to suppress was suddenly brought into sharp focus and flashed back onto his mental screen. Drained of all his kindness he snapped back at Nancy with uncharacteristic acrimony.

"I don't want to talk about it. I never want to talk about it. These memories need to stay six feet under."

Startled by his acrid answer Nancy broke down and, mixing smiles with sobs, buried her tear-smudged face into Scott's shoulder. Feeling suddenly redeemed by the realization that Sara's kidnapping was not an unfortunate consequence of maternal neglect but rather a malevolent act engineered by vengeful Bedouins, she cried tears of relief rather than grief. Scott, misinterpreting Nancy's tears, was ruefully touched by her display of emotion.

Calmly, he smoothed her hair, stroked her back, wiped her cheeks, but said nothing. His mind was far away in Baghdad, collecting clues from long-buried memories, from six-foot-deep memories, from the decayed skeletons of memories interred a long time ago beneath his conscious mind.

Under the spell of Scott's soothing strokes, Nancy fell into an exhausted sleep and remained so until the phone startled her. Scott jumped at the first ring and, seeing that it was a local number, lifted the receiver.

"Hello."

"Mr. Scott Thornton?"

"Speaking."

"This is Special Agent Smedlund of the OSBI. May I visit with you for a minute?"

"Oh, yes Sir, please."

"We need to examine Sara's Barbie doll that we know is in your possession. Could you possibly drop it at my office on your way to work tomorrow?"

"Oh, yes Sir, I'd be glad to."

"You know where our offices are?"

"Oh, yes Sir, north of 63rd on Harvey."

"Good then."

"Is that all, Sir?"

"For now, yes. I'll call you again whenever I have something else to say and you can call me anytime on this number."

"Is that your office number, Sir?"

"No, it's my private cell phone."

When Scott returned to the sofa, Nancy's eyes were teeming with questions.

"Who was it?"

"The police."

"What did they want?"

"They want me to stop by on my way to work to answer some more questions."

"Should I go with you?"

"No. They want me alone. Something to do with my

going back to Iraq, I presume."

"Oh, you think that you might not have to go back?"

"I'd rather not as long as Sara's missing."

"Oh, God. I don't think that I can make it without you, Scotty..."

In a burst of emotion Nancy flung her arms around Scott's neck and nestled her face into his chest. Scott intuitively reciprocated by holding her tight, patting her on the back, and kissing her head, which was poised beneath his chin. For some inscrutable reason, Nancy's purring on Scott's chest caused him to feel hungry. Realizing that he had not eaten all day he whispered into her ear, "Aren't you hungry? Let's cook something. It's getting late, you know."

At dinner, solemn silence was the entrée as Nancy and Scott wrestled with forbidden thoughts. Nancy, still incredulous of Scott's sudden conversion to normalcy, was wondering if he would after a certain period revert back to ignoring her in favor of Internet pornography. *I wonder if he'll make love to me tonight. If he does, it means that he really wants me. If he doesn't, it means that last night was just another one-night-stand.* To some extent, Sara was also on her mind. Although she felt relieved of the guilt of having lost her, her main worry at the time was that she might lose Scott if Sara were not found. Sara was the bond that held the family together and kept Scott reined in. *I don't think that he'll keep me if Sara doesn't return. I'll never forget the words he shouted back at me as he went down the stairs of my apartment: 'You're not moving in without Sara. Everything's on hold until we find her.' This man loves only Sara and tolerates me just because of her.*

Scott, on the other hand, was concerned that the Homeland Security and the OSBI might not be able to find Sara in time. His worry stemmed from knowing that Sara was only one among thousands of victims who needed attention and there was no reason to give her priority over all others. *Perhaps it's time I take matters into my own hands. I'll appoint myself the detective on the case. That's what Peckford wanted me to do. I do have a clue that no one else knows about. I can smell incense in her hair and that gives me a lead. I wonder if the Barbie doll smells of incense too. I left it in my car and I can't show it to Nancy because she can't know about Peckford or about Al-Qaeda."*

After dinner, awkwardness supervened as Scott and Nancy cleaned up the kitchen and put away the dishes. Then, when the teamwork ended, they found themselves standing face-to-face in the middle of the kitchen not knowing what else to do. During their five years of marriage their routine after putting Sara to bed was for Nancy to retire to the bedroom to watch some nighttime television and for Scott to work on his computer. But because of the divorce and without Sara at home their time-honored routine proved hard to recapture. While Nancy hoped that Scott would scoop her up into his arms and whisk her into the bedroom like he did the day before, Scott hoped to carve some computer time for himself because he wanted to Google the incense clue and search out the Oklahoma dealers. That divisive moment lingered as the awkward couple stood wordless under the bright kitchen lights.

"Babe, you must be tired after last night. Wouldn't you like to go to bed early?"

"Well, I was tired but I took a nap when I returned from work. You're the one who should be tired and it isn't that early. It's close to ten, Darling, and we both have full days tomorrow."

"Oh, I see, I had no idea. I guess my research will have to wait till later."

"What research?"

"Incense research."

"You mean..."

"It's a good clue."

"Come on, Honey, let's go to bed now and you can work on your clue tomorrow."

Nancy held Scott by the hand and led him into the bedroom. There was no obvious display of emotion as they got ready for bed, no sexual innuendos, and no conversation. But when the lights went off Scott whispered into the darkness as if talking to himself, "I'm going to be the one who finds Sara; you wait and see."

"I'm glad you found me first, Darling."

"What do you mean by that?"

"Well, don't you remember the day I walked into your bedroom by mistake and started screaming?"

"And I carried you back into Jane's bedroom?"

"You sure did."

"You were having a nightmare, weren't you?"

"Sort of..."

"Sort of?"

"Do you really want to know why I was screaming?"

"Yes."

"Are you sure?"

"Stop teasing."

"I was frightened because Jane made a pass at me."

"Oh, no, and I carried you back into her bedroom. Oh, how funny."

"Is that all you have to say?"

"What else is there to say? You're still friends and that was a long time ago."

Here, Scott turned his back to Nancy and drifted into his own thoughts. He did not touch her or kiss her goodnight, as was his habit. Nancy reached for his back and stroked it gently, hoping to regain his attention. When he did not respond, she cajoled, "Where are you, Darling?"

"Here."

"I meant where's your mind?"

"In the bag."

"What bag?"

"The bag that has Sara's hair."

"Are you going to think about it all night?"

"Yes."

"Well, goodnight then."

"Night."

Chapter Eighteen
(A Clue)

On Wednesday, November 8, 2006 Nancy and Scott awakened on different sides of the bed. At no point during their morning routine did they mention Sara or acknowledge the brown paper bag poised on the living room sofa. It was as though Sara's disappearance had rendered them taciturn to a reality that was too painful to confront that early in the morning.

At breakfast, they talked about the weather and work stress but avoided Nancy's contemplated move back in with Scott. Then, having made plans to meet at Scott's home after work, they took off on their separate ways, Nancy to the Glamour Salon and Scott to the OSBI.

In the OSBI parking lot, Scott opened his trunk, retrieved the Barbie doll, and held it to his nose. As he sniffed, swirls of November wind wafted up his nostrils, diluting the Barbie's scent. He tried turning his back to the wind and even putting his head inside the open trunk but the intruding eddies found their way into his nostrils regardless of position. Exasperated, he got back into his car, closed the door, and took a deep sniff. The misty morning wind hissing against his windshield and billowing around his windows proved most distracting to his olfactory faculties, causing him, after several failed sniffs, to give up the effort and march into the building with Barbie in his hand.

In the middle of the foyer, unmindful of his surroundings, he shut his eyes, held the doll to his nose, and took in a slow, concentrated sniff. His tall, stiff, commanding hulk—posted underneath the brass chandelier in the center of the lobby with eyes closed and Barbie doll to his nose—alarmed the receptionist, causing her to stand up and address him with a firm, loud voice, "Sir, could you please tell me what you think you're doing?"

"It's incense, I can smell it now, and tobacco..."

"Sir, you need to tell me what you're doing here or else you need to leave the premises." Saying that, she pushed a concealed alarm button and, almost immediately, two undercover officers emerged to her rescue. Surveying the scene and discerning the apprehension in the receptionist's eyes left no doubt in their minds that this well-dressed Barbie-doll man, poised like a closed-eyed colossus, was emotionally disturbed. Quickly, they flanked him, held him by the arms, and escorted him out. He offered no resistance until the howling wind shocked him out of his aromatic trance just outside the OSBI door.

"I'm here to see Special Agent Smedlund. He's expecting me. He wants the Barbie doll."

"And what makes you think that our grownup chief wants your little Barbie doll, Sir?" said one of the officers with a smirk.

"I'm Sara's dad, the girl who was kidnapped on Sunday..."

"Could we see your driver's license, please?"

"I'm Lieutenant Scott Thornton..."

Special Agent Smedlund was a short, stocky, ruddy-faced man of kind, affable manners. He greeted Scott warmly, asked him to please sit down, and dismissed the two officers who escorted him in.

"Thanks for dropping by, Mr. Thornton. The Homeland Security thinks that the doll might help them; they want their forensic division to take a careful look at it."

"Will they be keeping it?"

"I doubt it; they usually return such items after they have been examined unless they constitute important evidence."

"And if the doll proves to be important, how long would they keep it?"

"They'll keep it only if they need to use it as a court exhibit. You don't need to worry; sooner or later you'll get it back."

"It means a lot to me, Sir. I hate to part with it."

Scott took one last forlorn sniff before he handed the doll to Special Agent Smedlund who examined it carefully but, unlike Scott, did not bother to smell it, assuming that

Scott's sniffing was nothing but a grieving father's emotional act at surrendering his daughter's doll.

On his way out, Scott did not forget to smile when he went past the receptionist who had pushed the alarm button. She, of course, returned his smile with a headshake, went back to her computer screen, and never gave him a second look.

On his way to work, Scott's mind ruminated over Sara's Barbie doll. His canine-like olfactory memory recalled and pondered the scents as he drove to the Hartland Bank. *"I wonder why the incense scent was faint while the odor of stale tobacco was strong. Could the kidnappers have taunted Sara by blowing smoke at her doll? How cruel. Oh, how horrible. I wonder if they are torturing her? Oh, God forbid. Oh, how frightened she must be. But Peckford said that it's not in their interest to harm her. So who gives her a bath then? Surely, not a man? Surely, they would assign a woman to be her caregiver. Terrorists can't know much about children; they spend their time learning to kill not to nurture. Oh, it all makes sense now; the woman who's taking care of Sara must be a smoker and smokers do need incense to deodorize their homes. I can't think of her in the hands of abusing strangers. Oh, God, please help us. Soldiers shouldn't cry... I can't help it... I need to rescue Sara before they harm her and before I go crazy."*

At his desk Scott found a pile of work that needed attention. He tried to concentrate, to be productive, to pretend that he was in control, to stop the flow of his inner tears, but all to no avail. Giving the doll to Special Agent Smedlund broke his heart, set his imagination ablaze, and made him feel as if he were surrendering Sara's body to forensics. *"What if they sexually molest her? What if they torture her or starve her or keep her in a dark room all by herself? Dark room, all alone, thirsty, starved, that would cause Sara to lose her mind. She'd never recover, never be the same. Like the ones we rescued from the bombed buildings of Baghdad, no water, no food, no light, no company; they never recovered, oh, how horrible. I have to find her. If I wait, she'll die a skeleton like the prisoners of* war. *'If you desperately want something done, do it yourself,'* said Peckford. *I'll have to do it alone. Yes, do it all alone."*

Scott was noticeably restless to his coworkers but no one dared to approach him. They watched him pace in his office like a mad man, babbling as he walked back and forth in his tiny quarters like a caged leopard. Then he surprised everyone when he darted out of his office, went straight into Breena's, asked her to Google incense, and gave her no further explanation.

She stood at attention in response to his surprise visit, waited until his speech was over, then walked up to him and led him by the hand to a chair where he collapsed without resistance. She then went to her computer and before long produced some sheets of paper that she handed to him. With eyes surveying the papers he walked up to her, gave her an absent-minded hug, and went back to his office.

At his desk he pushed the piled loan files aside and began to highlight certain addresses. *"Most of the incense is sold in candle shops. Terrorists don't buy candles. No, no, there has to be other outlets. Where do kidnappers buy their incense from? They could have brought it with them from Iraq but then they would risk custom investigations at the ports of entry. No, there is a source here but where is it? Peckford taught me that if I am willing to think, I could outsmart terrorists. Well, I'm thinking and I can't come up with anything worthwhile. I can't use my own computers here or at home; it's too risky because I know that I'm being watched... Peckford used to say that computers are open windows with lights on; they advertise us to the world instead of hide us from it. I'll have to find them with my own mind and let Breena to do the computing. She's not being watched by Al-Qaeda. Oh, Peckford, Peckford, why did you leave me?"*

At noon break Scott surprised Breena by asking her out to lunch. She tried to hide her smile but said yes without hesitation. They left the office together escorted by many sets of curious eyes and marched towards the lobby.

"Where are we going, General?"

"Let's go into the tunnel; there are plenty of places there."

"Why underground? Do you have a migraine?"

"It's safer that way."

"Safer? Are you all right?"

"I'm paranoid but I have my reasons."

"Whatever you say, General."

In Billy's Deli, Scott chose a corner spot and sat with his back to the human river flowing in the tunnel. While Breena ate her sandwich, Scott stared at his and said nothing. The silence cast its shroud over the ambient noise and drowned it but still Scott said nothing. While his unseeing eyes gazed at the untouched sandwich before him his mind meandered the incense maze that ramified throughout his imagination. After Breena finished her sandwich and with the skimpy paper napkin skillfully blotted the angles of her mouth, she looked coyly at Scott and whispered, "Where are you, General?"

"Oh, I was just thinking."

"Your sandwich and I are waiting."

"Waiting? Who's waiting?"

"Wake up, Honey, take a bite, and talk to me. You don't ask a girl out and ignore her."

"I'm sorry; I was in incense land."

"And what's this incense chase you're on?"

"It's a clue, but that's all I can say."

"You mean..."

"You don't need to know any more, Breena. It can get dangerous and I don't want you to get hurt."

"Me? Who's gonna hurt me?"

"The less you know the safer you will be and that's all I can say now."

"I don't understand but I guess I'll go along if that's what you want."

"Thanks, Breena, I need a good helper."

"So, what is it that you need me to do?"

"The papers you printed gave me hundreds of candle stores that sell incense. What I'm looking for are other kinds of stores and incense dealers. I know how to do the research but I'm afraid to use my own computers because they could be tapped. If you could research it for me from your home computer it would be best."

"So, what is it exactly that you want me to research?"

"Why don't you Google perfume stores and incense and see what you can find. In Iraq, that's where incense is sold."

"Iraq? What does incense have to do with Iraq?"

"Breena, just think of yourself as a soldier and obey your orders without asking why."

"Aye, aye, General. Aren't you going to eat?"

"Let's go back. My stomach is in knots."

On their way back through the underground tunnel not much was said but Breena noticed that Scott was surveying his surroundings, stopping here and there as if window-shopping, and glancing about with circumspect eyes. At the office they parted casually and his last words to her were, "Thanks for agreeing to help. I'll check with you tomorrow."

Feeling reassured after his meeting with Breena, Scott was able to concentrate on his work and went through several pending files with reasonable efficiency. But as the afternoon sighed and stretched its tedious arms he became restless and his mind began to spin, scattering his thoughts in sundry directions. Using his office phone instead of his cell phone he called Nancy and asked her to pick him up at work.

"What's wrong with your car?"

"I'll tell you later."

"So, you just want me to finish my work and come pick you up?"

"Yeah, just call me so I can meet you downstairs."

"It'll be around five-thirty; is that okay?"

"Sure, I'll just work until you call."

At five o'clock, on her way out, Breena stopped at Scott's office.

"Are you staying?"

"Yeah, I'm behind; look at all these files."

"Well don't forget to go home and eat something."

"And don't you forget to do your research."

"I'll do my part, General."

Breena waltzed out, waving goodbye like a pageant queen, leaving Scott with his delinquent files. As she exited the office, she did not glance back to see if Scott was eyeing her. What mattered now was that he needed her and that opened the door for all sorts of encounters that she looked forward to.

Nancy picked up Scott at the Hartland Bank entrance with unconcealed excitement. Eager to resume her wifely role, she met him with a smile, gave him a kiss, and asked about his day. Then, being careful not to press him with questions and giving him all the time he needed to open up, she merely inquired, "Where to, Darling?"

"Ah, let's just drive to 63rd and May."

"What are you looking for?"

"There's an organic food and vitamin store on the northwest corner that I need to check out."

"Is your car in the garage?"

"Yeah, we'll get it later."

"How was your day, Darling?"

"Busy."

"So was mine."

Nothing else was said until Nancy parked her car in front of the Organo-Vite store. Scott took a cautious look at his surroundings, surveyed the store entrance awhile, then sank into his seat and whispered, "Nancy babe, could you please go into the store and ask if they carry incense?"

"Incense? Oh, I see. And if they have it, would you like me to buy some?"

"No, if they do, I'll go in and check out their supply."

Waiting for Nancy to return, Scott sat low and busied his mind with technical questions. He knew from his experience in Iraq that there were many grades of incense and that the price depended on quality. He was not sure, however, that his nose could discern between the different varieties. *"I have to try. I have to train my nose as one would train a police dog. If I can learn to discriminate between the different varieties, I might be able to identify the incense on Sara's hair."* Lost in these musings, he was startled when Nancy opened the car door and got in.

"Did you find anything?"

"They don't carry it."

"Well, let's go up May then; there are many other stores on that street that might sell it."

Driving north on May they made several stops but Nancy came back empty-handed every time. They even tried grocery stores but to no avail. Finally, when it had gotten late and they were both worn out, Scott tapped Nancy's hand and said, "If you'll take me back to my car, I'll take you out to dinner."

"You would? It has been so long since we've gone out together."

"It's good to scout the town for clues."

"Clues?"

"You never know. Each time we eat out, we might see something, hear something, or smell something that might bring us closer to Sara."

"Oh, yes, I see, one never knows when a clue might pop up." There was tacit disappointment in Nancy's voice as she realized that Scott wanted to take her out on a clue hunt. She would have preferred the more romantic motives but, nevertheless, she played along with a smile and feigned eagerness. Going back, she took the same route driving south on May to 63rd. Suddenly, Scott held her by the shoulder and asked her to turn toward a used car dealership on their left.

"But, what's in a used car dealership, Darling?"

"It's not the dealership; take a look at the store next door."

"Oh, the one that says International Foods?"

"You got it."

This time, Nancy scurried back from the store with a triumphant expression, opened the door, and blurted, "They've got it. I talked to the storeowner. He said that they have several varieties but that the best is the Arabian incense that comes from Yemen."

"Great, let's go in and check it out."

"You can't today; they've already closed the counters."

"Oh, what luck."

"They open at ten and close at six everyday except Sunday. We can come by tomorrow, after work."

"Or we can meet here at noon break."

"Whatever suits you, Darling."

"What did he look like?"

"Who?"

"The owner."

"He was, he was tall, dark, with white hair and he had an accent."

"Was his English okay?"

"Okay? He spoke with a perfect British accent."

"British? Are you sure?"

"That's how he sounded to me."

Hearing that, Scott smiled and scratched his head. He knew that Iraq came under British mandate after the First World War and that educated Iraqis spoke British English. Looking at Nancy with gratitude he whispered as if they were not alone in the car, "You did very well today. Where would you like to go for dinner?"

Chapter Nineteen
(Incense)

Throughout the night Scott's dreams were suffused with incense. Periodically, he would wake up, go to the brown paper bag, sniff Sara's hair, and return to bed. He found it harder to go back to sleep each time he sniffed the bag but he never considered bringing the bag into the bedroom and leaving it by his side. For reasons that he could not fathom something about the bag, poised on the living room sofa, pacified his mind and gave him a more propitious view of Sara's destiny. The bag was both away and within reach, just like Sara, and that symbolism stormed silently into Scott's desperate, dream work.

Perhaps, deep in his unconscious, he associated living rooms with civil behavior and bedrooms with animal passions. Perhaps, he might have recalled how frightened Sara must have felt when Dick Straight pushed her out of her mother's bedroom and closed the door. Perhaps, he could have remembered stroking Sara's hair as he put her to bed on her birthday night, the day before she was kidnapped. Perhaps, he could have recalled certain censored memories from his first night back from Iraq when, standing in the middle of their bedroom, he took Nancy while she was bent over with her hair dangling from her head. Or, perhaps, it could have been the beheadings, which he intimately witnessed while incarcerated in the catacombs of Baghdad and the heads, which he watched role down the rocky slope, splashing their bloody hair into the tenebrous air. Scott's unconscious was rife with such forbidden scenes and verboten memories, which kept him from bringing Sara's hair into the bedroom.

Nancy, on the other hand, slept undisturbed and was never aware of Scott's tumult. Having been treated to an elegant dinner with wine and dessert caused her to fall into profound slumber and filled her dreams with courtship dates and dinners that she and Scott had had while she was pregnant with Sara. Those were happy times because she felt secure, loved, needed, and these feelings grew as

Sara grew inside of her. For Nancy something about a full tummy was blithe, reassuring, and soporific perhaps because, were it not for her pregnancy, she would not have experienced the security of a good life with a good husband. And now, with her good husband back and her tummy full again, she floated effortlessly down the sleep river, unmindful of the tumult on its banks.

Irked by fractured sleep, Scott got up early, made coffee, and brought it to Nancy.

"It's still dark; what time is it?"

"It's six-thirty."

"You're already dressed?"

"I'm behind in my work."

"You didn't sleep well, did you?"

"Not as well as you did, but I feel fine."

"You're coming home after work?"

"Sure. I'll see you then."

Scott left unperturbed at Nancy's half-closed eyes, which shut before he could finish his last sentence. Her stuporous oblivion of their planned mid-day rendezvous with incense at the International Foods store was understandable given the hour. As he drove to work, many exigencies occupied his mind but Nancy was not one of them. Thinking ahead, he wanted to get to the Hartland Bank an hour earlier so that he could take two hours for lunch. Intuitively, he preferred to explore the incense clue alone and was rather relieved when Nancy did not seem to recall last night's plans of meeting him at noon.

As he worked on his loan files, his mind meandered and weaved an intricate web of intrigue around Sara's abductors. He no longer thought of them simply as kidnappers because they were not after a ransom. Rather, they were after revenge, which made them much more evil and made him far angrier. Irked by his rage he planned for all the possible situations that might mire his quest and was especially prepared to tackle Al-Qaeda single-handedly regardless of consequences. This delusional sense of confidence imparted by his rage gave him momentary relief and allowed him to better concentrate on the backed-up loan files piled on his desk.

When fellow employees began to trickle in a little before eight, he hardly noticed them. He even forgot that he had commissioned Breena to research incense on her home computer. His focused mind rendered him impenetrable to his surroundings almost to the point of oblivion. That was his mental state when Breena walked into his office with a shuffle of papers in her hand.

"This is a hard topic to research, General."

"What did you find?"

"Not much. Not much at all. Many sell it but no one seems to specialize in it except aroma therapy salons, which have been coming into fashion lately."

"That's no help."

"Well, that's all I could find."

Exasperated at Scott's ingratitude, Breena shoved the papers under his nose, sat down, crossed her white legs, and waited. Scott studied the papers carefully with a highlighter in his hand but ended up highlighting nothing. Without raising his head, he arranged the papers into a neat bundle, handed them back to Breena, and said, "Thanks, but this information is not useful."

"Not useful? You know how many hours I have spent looking up this mess?"

"I'm sorry. I didn't know I was giving you an impossible task."

"You could at least say *thank you*."

"Oh, yes, of course, thank you; thank you so much, Breena."

"What else would you like me to do?"

"Let me think about it and we'll talk later."

Breena left Scott's office feeling rather useless and a bit offended by his change of attitude. Scott, on the other hand, managed to forget all about Breena as soon as she walked out of his office. He returned to his loan files but kept his eyes on the clock, which was slowly ambling towards eleven.

The International Foods store on May and 63rd was busy with myriad nationalities mulling through the isles when Scott walked in. As he looked around he heard different languages and saw a variety of ethnic attires, African, Indian, Arab, etc. The shelves were rife with strange and colorful goods from exotic lands. There were several big, open-mouthed barrels full of varieties of olives from which a tall, white-haired man was ladling samples for customers to taste. An array of massive cheese drums could be seen inside a walk-in refrigerator each time the door was opened by one of the employees. A frail young woman was wielding a huge curved knife with handles on both ends to cut a chunk out of a large Parmesan cheese drum. Lebanese sweets, Iraqi manna, Syrian raisins, Turkish pistachios, and dried Arabian dates were seductively displayed beside the counter in clear-faced boxes.

After surveying all the aisles in search of incense, Scott approached the checker and asked to see the owner. Without saying a word, she pointed to the tall, grey-haired man ladling olives into quart containers for a queue of olive lovers. While Scott waited his turn, he studied the owner's impressive features. In his mid-sixties with darker skin, sparkling blue eyes, and white hair thick with curls he stood remarkably firm at about six-foot-three. He had an affable aura about him and seemed to derive great joy from matching his customers' personalities with the right variety of olives. When Scott's turn came, the owner smiled, made a polite bow, and asked him with a most proper British accent, "And, how may I help you, Sir?"

"I'm looking for incense?"

"Incense? Oh, you must be the other half of that fair lady who came in last night after we had closed. I believe her name was Nancy, wasn't it?"

"You have a very good memory," smiled Scott.

"Well, let me get someone to handle the olive queue while I help you with the incense."

The owner disappeared into a side room and returned with a young man who took over the ladling task.

He then motioned for Scott to follow him as he led the way to the spice aisle.

"It is most uncommon for an American to ask for incense. May I ask how you intend to use it?"

"I want to aromatize our home with it before our guests arrive to dinner."

"Indeed, it creates a most amiable ambiance and is especially good at masking cooking odors. What might you be cooking for your guests?"

"My wife is preparing a leg of lamb."

"Gigot? It's my favorite meat. Where did you learn to like lamb?"

"In Baghdad."

"You don't say. That was my home city before we fled. My father came with the British missions after the Second World War, married my mother, stayed, and died in Iraq. We fled in the summer of 1990, just before Saddam invaded Kuwait, because we could tell that war was imminent."

"I was deployed in the summer of 2004 and stayed two years."

"How was Baghdad when you left it?"

"A lot of destruction."

"I wish I could visit but..."

Rueful tears welled in the owner's eyes, drowned his words, and erected a temporary wall of silence between the two tall men. Scott, touched by the owner's pain, put out a friendly hand and said, "I'm Scott Thornton."

"Jolly to meet you, Sir," said the owner as he shook Scott's hand. "My name is Hedrick Lester."

Even though the place was busy, Hedrick took time to show Scott the different kinds of incense he carried and where they came from. He had incense from India, Africa, China, and Arabia but the best he had came from Yemen and it was also the most expensive. It came in little plastic bags adorned with Arabic writings. Scott held a bag in his hand, sniffed it, and remarked with wonder, "I can't smell anything."

"Indeed, Sir. You'll have to burn it first."

"What do the writings say?"

"*Bachchour al Yamen,* or Incense of Yemen and the name of the importer, *Abdul Bassit Ahmadi* and sons."

"You have quite a variety which tells me that there must be enough demand."

"Indeed, Sir. Many nationalities use it but the Saudis are by far my best customers."

"I didn't realize we had a lot of Saudis in Oklahoma."

"They're mostly students, Sir, and most of them go to OCU. They come usually on Saturdays and buy Arabic foods, Persian Tumbac for their water pipes, and incense."

Scott left the International Foods store with a small sack of Yemeni incense and a package of Persian Tumbac, the two odors he had discerned in Sara's shaved hair. Without thinking, he drove straight to OCU and started to comb the streets where students lived. He even opened his window and periodically sniffed the air, hoping for a scent of incense to reach his nostrils. Then he parked his car, went into the cafeteria, stood in line, carried his food tray to a central table, and sat down. As he ate, his eyes and ears went all over the place in search of clues. Conversation noise dominated the air as students weaved laughter, screams, and culinary sounds into a colorful bouquet bustling with youthful vigor. It reminded him of the army mess halls around Baghdad and that memory took him back to Iraq. After a brief, reflective trance, and realizing that there were no clues to be found in the clamor of this college beehive, he returned his half-eaten tray and drove back to work.

Many thoughts assailed his mind as he drove but the most urgent was that he had to find Sara before it was too late. He knew that if he could not find her within one week from her disappearance date, November 5th, his chances of ever finding her would become meager. *"She was kidnapped on Sunday and today is Thursday. I only have two days. I need a plan. I need to act. No time to waste. I'll take tomorrow off. I wish I had a dog that could sniff for incense. I'm better than a dog. Must go to work. I need a plan. I need to act. No time to waste."*

Scott's afternoon work was disturbed by the two-day ultimatum he had set for himself. He did automatic work but found himself incapable of creative or analytical thinking. Multiple visions of Sara surfaced in every file he opened. Her face—at times smiling, at times pleading, and at times smudged with helpless tears— would suddenly appear like a pop-up on a computer screen. After an hour's struggle against the demons of distraction and inefficiency, he arranged his files into three neat heaps: finished, unfinished, and untouched. Then he got up and marched to Mr. McMaster's office.

Mr. McMaster, who always left his office door open when he was in, was on his computer when he heard Scott's announcing cough and welcomed him in with a reassuring smile.

"Have a seat, Scott, and tell me what's on your mind."

"Well, Sir, I'm having a hard time getting my work done."

"Any new developments?"

"That's the problem, Sir; five days have passed and nothing has happened."

"You mean the police have not made any progress?"

"Not at all, Sir."

"Do you have any plans?"

"Could I take the rest of today and Friday off, Sir? I have a certain clue that might lead to something."

"Take off then and don't look behind. Work can wait but your little daughter can't."

Scott found himself driving back to the Oklahoma City University. He had no idea what he was going to do when he arrived; nevertheless, he did feel a strong compulsion to return to the area. With open windows, he started his search at 23rd Street and moved north, combing the student housing areas one by one, surveying all the discernable details with his paranoid vision. There were dogs, cars, bicycles, walkers, cyclists, and rowdy youth groups among the many street scenes that Scott eyed with utmost suspicion. But against that backdrop of animated student life there was a conspicuous absence of children and incense.

It wasn't long before the scenes began to repeat and blend together, causing Scott to feel dizzy and disoriented. Not willing to capitulate to fatigue, he parked his car and began an aimless walk that lasted until dark and proved equally unproductive. Feeling defeated and overwhelmed, he tried to find his car but couldn't, which caused him to become even more frantic. He began running over lawns from one street corner to another, his search becoming more and more blurred with the deepening darkness. That was his state of mind when he chanced upon a small, bald head shimmering through an old house window on a certain street corner.

Overwhelmed with hurried confusion, he did not even realize the serendipity of what he had seen until he was on the other side of the street. Then, as if stunned by a high voltage charge, he felt his entrails crawl and his muscles writhe with pangs of terrifying anticipation. As he ran back for a second look, a hurried hand pulled the window curtains shut and turned off the light.

Utterly exhausted with a thousand burning thoughts flaming in his mind, he could not decide what next to do. He did not even consider calling Special Agent Smedlund or noting the house address. Time was hissing by like wind and he felt an overwhelming urge to act, to charge the guns like he once did in Baghdad with thoughtless disregard to safety and consequences.

An eerie battle cry burst out of his throat as he charged the window with all his momentum, catapulted himself into the air like a massive wrecker ball, and crashed into the room amidst an explosion of shattered wood and glass. A woman howled from the next room like a wounded hyena and a child screamed her lungs out with petrifying fear. Unaware of his wounds and bruises, Scott sprang to his feet and broke into the next room like a rabid animal frothing at the mouth. Curled into the corner was a dark-skinned woman holding Sara down and smothering her cries with her hand. With lightning might, Scott tore the woman off Sara with one arm, picked Sara up with the other, and hurled out of the shattered window back into the cold night.

With Sara in his arms, he ran like a wild horse without knowing where he was going, without noticing the cell-phoning crowd gathering at the scene, and without feeling Sara's choking arms around his neck. He ran until he found himself at a well-lit gas station on Pennsylvania and only when he entered the station's convenience store did he stop running and call Nancy.

"Nancy, you need to come and get us right away."

"Where've you been all this time?"

"Nancy, please, come and get us right now."

"What's wrong Darling?"

"Nancy, please, hurry up and come."

"What happened to your car?"

"I can't find it."

"Where are you?"

"We're in the gas station at the corner of Penn and 30th."

"Who's with you?

"Sara."

"Oh, Darling, you're not making sense. Sara is gone and you must be hallucinating..."

"Just come and get us, please. I'll explain later."

"Have you contacted the police about your car?"

"I'll call Special Agent Smedlund as soon as you hang up."

"Why Special Agent Smedlund?"

"Never mind, please, hurry; Sara doesn't look too good."

Chapter Twenty
(Sara)

On her way to the gas station Nancy was in a mental storm of alarmed confusion. She had never witnessed Scott exhibit such desperate helplessness or sound so lost and perturbed. Something had gone awry and threw him out of control but she was not sure what. *"Could he be having a nervous breakdown and hallucinating about Sara? He seemed convinced that she's actually with him. Ever since he returned from Iraq, he hasn't been right. May God help me if we don't find Sara and may God help me if we do."*

When Nancy arrived at the gas station, there was no one within sight. In fact, Scott had taken refuge inside the convenience store because Sara was wet with cold sweat and shivering out of control. Waiting for Nancy, he tried to reassure Sara by telling her that she was safe, that he loved her, that everything was going to be fine, and that they would never ever leave her alone again. All that and more had no effect upon her drowning arms, which gripped his neck in a noose. As if she had been shipwrecked and rescued from arctic waters during a violent storm, she seemed frozen in a state of petrified alarm whose main external manifestation was intractable shuddering.

Upon seeing Nancy's car through the large glass window Scott dashed out with Sara clinging to his neck, an apparition that shocked Nancy to the bone. Trembling with surprise, she fumbled trying to unlock the passenger door while Scott and Sara cringed in the cold night wind. After what seemed too long a while and seeing that Nancy's confusion had reached a point of alarmed disorientation Scott ran to her side, opened her door against the hissing wind, and shouted in her ear to move over. As she did, the car started to move forward and almost ran into the gas pump before Scott could get his foot on the brake. All this while, Nancy was babbling unintelligibly at the top of her voice, "Oh, no, brake, gas pump, watch, no, stop the car..."

"Here, Nancy, hold Sara so I can drive."

"Eh, yes, come baby, come to Mommy."

"Sara baby, it's okay, you're safe, go to Mom so I can drive us home."

No amount of pleading could pry Sara away from her dad's neck; the more he tried, the tighter her noose clamped and all this without ever shedding a tear or uttering a word. Realizing that there was more power in her little arms than in his, Scott got out of the driver's seat with Sara hanging from his neck, quickly jumped into the back seat, and called at Nancy to get hold of herself and drive them home. While all this transpired the night's white noise was becoming audibly replaced by police sirens that were racing toward the little corner house with the demolished window.

At home, Sara remained frozen and wouldn't let go of her father's neck. Together they sat on the living room sofa beside the bag containing Sara's hair while Nancy sat on the other side of the bag, gazing into nothingness. Like a leaky faucet the silence grew louder until it became deafening, drowning all thoughts into the puddle of its dripping moments. No motion, no action, no desire, and no pain could scale the mighty walls of inertia that sealed off the Thornton world. It was as though the brown paper bag like a black hole had devoured the battle cries of the past four days and replaced them with icy exhaustion.

Suddenly, the doorbell startled everyone and for the first time since her rescue Sara began to scream uncontrollably just like she did when her father catapulted himself into her captives' window. Scott knew better than to open the door with Sara screaming around his neck. Amidst her frightened screams he motioned to Nancy to open the door while he held her tightly with both arms and paced the room, hoping to calm her down. The toll of the bell must have struck a nerve deep in her little brain, releasing a sudden avalanche of fear.

When Special Agent Smedlund and his assistants walked in, the screaming had reached such a pitch that it caused them to stand still, lower their heads, and pause as if in prayer. Then, after hastily surveying the scene, they turned around and quietly walked away. At the door Smedlund whispered an apology to Nancy, suggested that Scott and Sara should seek medical attention, said that he would call in the morning, and left without another word.

Sara's eerie shrieks took a long time to subside, raising everyone's exhaustion to a new peak. No words of reassurance could assuage the dread in her eyes or cause her to unshackle her father's neck. Scott remained a prisoner of her tetanic arms until she finally fell asleep upon his chest. Cautiously, he laid her in his bed and lay beside her fully dressed, motionless, almost breathless, and fell asleep. Meanwhile, to escape Sara's loud screaming, Nancy had taken refuge in the kitchen. When she walked into the bedroom to tell the couple that dinner was ready she found the pair asleep in each other's arms.

Tiptoeing back to the kitchen, she sat down alone to eat. It was close to midnight when she started to put up the dishes, working quietly and hardly emitting a sound, when a fork fell out of her hand and hit the aluminum sink with a clank. That was all it took for the screaming to resume but this time it sounded doubly loud and dreadful. When Nancy darted into the bedroom and turned on the light both Sara and Scott were clinging to each other and screaming incoherently at the tops of their voices.

Feeling contaminated by their fear and not knowing what else to do, she ran back into the kitchen, picked up the fork from the sink, placed it on the kitchen table, and sat down staring at it. Awaiting the screams to subside she found herself becoming befuddled and getting angrier by the minute. Paradoxically, instead of feeling more secure with Scott she began to feel more threatened and wished she could return to her own apartment where she felt at home. *"I don't belong here anymore. I need to move away and leave them alone. They belong together and all of a sudden I feel like an intruder. This is no longer my home. My home is my apartment."*

The night proved torturous as alarming dreams nipped at both Sara and Scott. Whenever a plume of sleep endeavored to escape from in between their gnawing nightmares it was invariably snuffed by the light from a passing car or the chatter of the heating vent coming on and off at un-timed intervals. That Thursday night—November 9, 2006—was the herald of a long chain of nights that felled Sara and Scott's sleep but hardly affected Nancy's, who took refuge in the guest bedroom away from their noisy dream works.

The morning proved more merciful than the night. Whatever darkness had brought about was washed away with light. Nancy awoke, got dressed, left a note, and went to work while the sleep-deprived couple enjoyed a dreamless interlude. It was close to noon when the phone rang, startling both Sara and Scott. They sprang out of bed and ran in opposite directions without a moment's thought of what they were doing. But before Sara could resume her eerie falsetto Scott held her high in his arms and with her raced to the phone. Thankfully, this time Special Agent Smedlund did not hear Sara's piercing shrill and Scott had no trouble finding his voice.

"Mr. Thornton, we're dying to talk to you and Sara; is this a better time or would you like one more day to recover?"

"Ah, we just woke up. Could you just give us an hour or two to get ready?"

"Why don't I come by this afternoon then. Would four o'clock give you enough time?"

"Ah, sure, we should be okay by then."

"I wouldn't leave the house, if I were you. The reporters have already gotten wind of the situation and I'd rather be the one to talk to you first."

"I wasn't planning on going anywhere. Besides, it's too soon for Sara to leave the house."

"Well then, keep your door locked and don't answer the phone."

"What if it's my family or my boss?'

"It's best to talk to no one now, not even your wife who's already at work."

"Oh, Nancy's not home?"

"She's at work like I told you. Don't worry; we've taken all the necessary precautions and our eyes are everywhere."

"Did you apprehend the bastards?"

"We did and I'll tell you more when I see you."

After hanging up the phone Scott sat down and took a deep look into Sara's wide-open eyes as she quietly sat in his lap. They were glacial-cold with a blue, mesmerizing stare and her face was gelled in a white, expressionless mask. Her stone-like stillness proved more disconcerting to Scott than last night's piercing screams. Not knowing what to say, he tried to calm her down by stroking her hair, as was his habit before putting her to sleep. Startled from his unawareness by her unyielding bristles, he quickly pulled back his hand and mumbled apologetically, "Oh, I'm sorry, Princess." Without a word, Sara took his hand, put it back on her head, and as she moved it back and forth a faint gleam warmed up her frozen face. Encouraged by her thawing, Scott pulled her onto his chest and ventured into their first conversation.

"Princess, you must be hungry, aren't you?"

Sara's response was to put his hand back on her head and move it back and forth.

"Sara, wouldn't you like to help me make breakfast for the two of us."

Her face betrayed a faint, Mona Lisa smile but she said nothing.

"Sara, have you lost your tongue? Won't you talk to your dad? Sara, Honey, please..."

This one-sided conversation went on a long while without evoking a single word from Sara and caused Scott to become increasingly worried. Nothing that he said or did could entice her to speak and the harder he tried the more contorted became her face. "*I better not get her anymore upset than she already is. She'll talk when she's ready. I'd better take her into the kitchen and start some eggs. What if she had refused to eat all the while she was kidnapped? She could be starved. She can eat without speaking. I know she'd love some cereal.*" As these thoughts were troubling Scott's mind, the phone rang, startling them both and causing Sara to clutch her father's neck with fierce, trembling arms.

It was Nancy who was calling but Scott, remembering Special Agent Smedlund's orders, did not answer. Soon after, his cell phone, which was still in his pocket, began to ring with Nancy's calls. Thereafter followed numerous telephone calls from family and friends, which Scott did not answer and each ring brought about a greater startled reaction from Sara. Finally, Scott muted all phones and dedicated all his energies to feeding Sara.

With Sara still hanging from his neck, he went into the kitchen, prepared a bowl of cereal, sat down at the kitchen table, and held a spoonful to Sara's pursed lips. After a cautious pause her lips parted, gulped the spoonful, and like a hungry nest bird opened wide her eager mouth and squeaked. Scott could not feed her fast enough and, when the first bowl was consumed, did not bother to inquire if she wanted more. In a few minutes a second bowl was consumed followed by a third, plus a glass of milk. Only then, when her hunger and thirst were satisfied, did Sara's eyes fill up with tears as she uttered her first words, "Daddy, you're bleeding."

Scott carried Sara to the bathroom, turned on the light, stood in front of the mirror, and gasped. Dried blood filled the scratches on his face and bloodstains spattered his torn sleeves and pants. Sara's clean-shaven head stood in sharp contrast to her dingy pajamas, which had become stained with Scott's blood. There was a gray ring of matted dirt around her neck, her hands were as dark as her soles, her nails were coalminer black, and her face looked like a chimney sweep's.

"What have they done to my beautiful little Sara? She looks like a homeless girl who has been sleeping in the streets and begging for food. How come I didn't notice all that last night? I shouldn't have let her go to bed dirty. And Nancy? Why didn't she say something? How strange."

After a sighing gaze at her disheveled spectacle, Scott

sat Sara down on the counter top and whispered playfully, "How about a bubble bath, Precious?"

Chapter Twenty-One
(Dialogues)

Scott and Sara spent a quiet afternoon at home while reporters, neighbors, and other onlookers busied the street with their comings and goings. Sara said very little after her bath, was content with playing at her dad's feet, and hopped into his lap at the slightest noise. Scott was afraid to leave her alone long enough to take a shower and clean up, postponing all that till after Nancy arrived from work.

Awaiting Special Agent Smedlund, time ambled slowly relative to Scott's burning curiosity, which kept pace with his galloping thoughts. He had so many questions about Al-Qaeda, the kidnappers, and his car that he left behind. He wondered if he was going to be deployed back to Iraq and if Peckford had been informed of the recent happenings. All these questions hissed in his mind while he sat with Sara and ignored the mounting commotion outside. Suddenly, a thought overcame him that he could not resist. *"What if, in retaliation, a suicide bomber should blow up his home? What would happen to Sara if, now that the word is out, officious reporters should begin assailing the house and banging at the door?"*

Consumed by these thoughts he carried Sara in his arms, went to the living room window, and cracked the curtains. There was a police car in the driveway and many more cars in the street. Groups of people were gathered and several reporters with their cameramen were on standby. A few well-wishers were carrying posters:

Welcome Home Sara & Go Home Al-Qaeda

Kidnapped Children's Hero Is Everyone's Hero

Send Foreigners Home & Bring Soldiers Back

Scott Thornton: War Hero—Home Hero.

It took Scott awhile to assimilate what he saw. The fact that Sara's rescue had impassioned the public mind and made him a hero was not something he was prepared to handle. Being innately reticent, he preferred the taciturn corners of private life to the noisy fireworks of notoriety. Even Sara's tongue became temporarily un-tethered at the sight, "What're all these people doing here, Daddy?"

"They are happy for us, Princess."

"They make me afraid."

"What makes you afraid?"

"People."

"All people?"

"Yes."

"How about the police?"

"They make lots of noise."

"Does noise scare you?"

"Yes."

Closing the curtains, Scott carried Sara back to her play spot and hid the bag containing her hair underneath the sofa lest she should ask what was in it. He was even afraid to turn the television on for fear that it might agitate her. Waiting, they spent the rest of the afternoon in amicable quietude, exchanging very little conversation. Twice, Scott asked if she were hungry and twice she nodded no. When Scott mentioned that Nancy would soon be home, Sara did not even nod and kept on playing at his feet with some toys that he had saved for her. All of a sudden the street became noisier and soon after, the doorbell rang, causing Sara to spring into her dad's lap and cling to his neck. When he tried to carry her to the door, she began screaming and clawed his already lacerated neck with her dirty, untrimmed fingernails. Nothing that he said mattered and her agitation grew fiercer the closer he got to the door. When he reached to open it, she pleaded with a piercing "Nooooooo..." that deafened his ears and those of Special Agent Smedlund on the other side of the door. Amidst the screams, Scott shouted with his mouth pressed to the door, "I'm sorry, Sir, but I don't think that I should open the door just yet." Then, he carried Sara back into the living room where she nested in his lap and refused to leave his neck.

After her gasping sobs had quieted down into sighing sniffles and her exhausted arms had fallen off his neck, Scott laid Sara on the sofa and stroked her back until she fell asleep. Quietly, he reached for his cell phone and whispered into Special Agent Smedlund's ear, "Sara has just fallen asleep and Nancy should be home soon. You can come in with her but please be extremely quiet."

Having seen enough traumatized children during his long career as an OSBI officer, Special Agent Smedlund was quick to understand and quick to act. Awaiting Nancy's coming, he cleared the street of supporters, reporters, well-wishers, and onlookers and did it all with gentle persuasion. All those who understood the heightened awareness of traumatized children left amiably. The few who refused to leave were intransigent reporters who considered it their solemn duty to inform the public of such a newsworthy saga. These were the ones who swarmed Nancy as she got out of her car and before she could close the garage door. The only way Special Agent Smedlund was able to get them off her back was to remind them that they were trespassing.

Nancy was most grateful to rid herself of the reporters again, having been first assailed by them upon leaving the Glamour Hair Salon. Special Agent Smedlund, who had visited Nancy earlier at her salon, updated her on Sara's situation, explained that he had asked Scott not to answer the phone for security reasons, and tiptoed with her through the garage door into the house.

On the living room sofa sat Scott with Sara sleeping by his side. He motioned to Nancy and Special Agent Smedlund to go to his office while he eased himself off the sofa and followed them. Leaving the office door open and in full view of Sara, Scott whispered, "I'm sorry I still look so bad but I couldn't leave Sara long enough to shower and tidy up."

"I'm glad you're alive," whispered Smedlund. "We found firearms and explosives when we searched the premises and had you not surprised them with your stunning entry they would have surely shot you."

"I only saw the woman; were there others in the house?"

"They were having a secret meeting in the attic, all four of them. By the time they came down and figured out what had happened, you were gone, some of their neighbors had already called the police to report the incident, and a few other neighbors were at their door offering to help. When you called me and I alerted the police chief, it was all over for them. Of course, they're still clinging to the story that they don't know anything about Sara and that whoever broke in must have been a drug addict desperate for money."

"Bastards; I hope you're not gonna let them out on bail."

"All we need is your testimony and for you to identify the woman and they'll all be handed to the Feds."

"Are they denying their Al-Qaeda connection?"

"Of course, but they won't get away with it. Homeland Security and Military Intelligence have already determined that all four men and the woman have fake passports with fake names and they're almost sure that they are Saudis who were trained in Afghanistan."

"Can you photo ID them from your files?"

"No, but the Feds can and the Saudi Arabian Ambassador is most eager to help us with their true identities."

"Do you think that they'll give us the names of other Al-Qaeda ring leaders operating in the US?"

"We can make them talk but I doubt that they have any useful information. All their contacts use fake names and no person ever contacts them more than once."

"So Peckford was right, wasn't he."

"He's always right when it comes to Al-Qaeda operations."

"Peckford? I thought you said that he had died," blurted out Nancy in utter shock.

Scott and Smedlund looked at one another awhile

and then Scott mumbled with downcast eyes, "Sorry Babe, it's a MI secret and no one is supposed to know. I'm sorry I slipped but you mustn't tell a soul."

"Oh, I see," retorted Nancy with obvious sarcasm. "Well then, what the heck does MI mean? Am I allowed to know that much, at least?"

"Military Intelligence, and it needs to remain that way, you understand?'

"Well, I think that you two need to finish talking alone. I'm not sure I need to hear any more about this kind of bullshit."

After Nancy left the room Smedlund asked Scott his most pressing question, "How the hell did you know how to find her? You have outdone the MI, Homeland Security, and OSBI and made us look pretty sorry. We'd like to know who gave you your clue and why you didn't share it with us. We'd also like the name of your informant."

Smedlund spoke with a firm, distressed voice and was obviously worried about the answers partly because of the Feds and partly because of the media. When Scott did not answer he started to look worried and pleaded with a fatherly voice, "Scott, we just don't want to be made fools of. This is not a good time for the nation to lose confidence in its protectors. If the media gets wind of this and blows it out of proportion, we'll have a lot of trouble on our hands. All we need are some answers so that we'll know how to handle this rather delicate situation; I'm speaking on behalf of both, the Homeland Security and the OSBI."

"My clue, Sir, was incense."

"Who's this Incense? Does he have a surname?"

"No, Sir."

"Where the hell did you find him, or did he find you?"

"I could smell it in Sara's hair and on her Barbie doll."

"Smell it? Smell what? You're not making any sense, Lieutenant. Are you sure you're alright?"

"Sir, I could smell incense in Sara's shaved hair which was left at Nancy's door in a brown paper bag and I could also smell it on her doll." Saying that, Scott stole into the living room, retrieved the bag from underneath the sofa, and put it under Smedlund's nose. "Can you smell it, Sir?"

With obvious consternation, Smedlund sniffed the bag, stared into Scott's face towering over him, and with obvious relief remarked, "I can smell it but I don't understand how this was enough of a clue for you to find Sara. Moreover, why didn't you alert us about the hair?"

"Because I was afraid that forensics would want it and I didn't want to part with it like I parted with the doll. That was all I had left of my little girl."

"And how did this incense help you find Sara?"

"It didn't Sir, but it got me started in the right direction. It was Sara's bald head that gave me the real clue and caused me to act on the spur of the moment."

To Smedlund's incredulous ears and glaring eyes, Scott related the intricacies of his inquisition, which Smedlund had a hard time believing were it not for Scott's sincere demeanor and the myriad discoveries of his sundry investigations. After all was told and after Smedlund had fully accepted the reality that it was serendipity rather than Scott's detective genius that had solved the case he got up, shook Scott's hand, and whispered, "Wait till I tell the Feds how you found her."

"What do you mean, Sir?"

"Well, they'll have a hard time believing your story but they'll have to because it's the truth, the whole truth, and nothing but the truth."

"They won't be upset with me, will they?"

"Oh no, on the contrary, they'll commend you for your fearless bravery and untiring perseverance."

"You think that they'll change their mind and send me back to Iraq, now that Sara is home."

"I doubt it. Sara needs you now more than ever and it'll take you a long time to get her over her fears."

"And what about Peckford? Will I ever see him again?"

"I'm sure you will when he returns. But in the meantime I wouldn't mention his name to a soul and I'd also make sure that Nancy doesn't. I saw the look on her face when she found out that he wasn't dead. She's liable to talk unless you convince her of how serious the consequences would be to our investigations of Al-Qaeda activities on U.S. soil."

"Do you know where my car is, Sir? I can't remember where I left it."

"It's on 30th just north of OCU. You got ticketed for illegal parking."

"And Sara's Barbie doll?"

"Oh, the Feds have it. We don't need it anymore, do we?"

"Well, Sara needs it, Sir; it'll make her feel comfortable."

"I'll bring it to you as soon as I get it back. I'll have to put in a request for it from forensics. Was there anything else that you smelled on the Barbie doll that I need to tell forensics about?"

"Well, unlike Sara's hair, the doll had a strong stench of tobacco that overpowered the incense odor and made it harder to detect."

"Tobacco? How does that tie in?"

"Well, it was the kind of tobacco that is smoked in water pipes. Her kidnappers must have smoked their water pipes and blown the smoke into the doll just to taunt Sara."

"What else are you going to teach us, Son?"

"What do you mean, Sir?"

"Well, we found water pipes in the house but we couldn't find any drugs, which made us wonder what the hell did they use them for. It seems that you've also solved that one for us, Lieutenant."

"And what about the media, Sir? I know that they're going to hound Nancy and me so what do we say to them?"

"Just tell them the truth."

"The whole truth, Sir?"

"Yep, and nothing but the truth, so help you God."

"One last request, Sir. Are they going to take Sara to the hospital? It would frighten her out of her mind."

"It's procedure, Son. Don't you want to know if she's been molested?"

"No, Sir. I don't and she doesn't need to be reminded."

"Well, I see your point, and given that this has become a federal case, let me see if we can do it with a specially trained child psychologist who can visit her at home instead."

Chapter Twenty-Two
(Fear)

After Special Agent Smedlund left, Scott took his place by Sara on the living room sofa while Nancy remained in the bedroom. The setting sun was absconding with the lingering remnants of light and the street had become vacant of interlopers. Scott was in a dilemma because he needed to retrieve his car but, at the same time, did not wish to leave Sara's side. Of course, Nancy could do her part and, anyway, it was time for the two to have a talk. Leaving Sara to her peaceful sleep, Scott tiptoed into the bedroom to find Nancy lying on the unmade bed staring at the ceiling. Scott sat next to her, and said nothing. He looked at her blond hair, blue eyes, lean tall figure, and graceful curves and felt nothing. *"What don't I like about her? I wonder why I have no feelings for her. She's beautiful and sexy but I'm not attracted to her. I can pretend to love her and I'm happy to take care of her if she'd just be a good mother to Sara. I wonder why Peckford said to me, 'We live for joy and love.' How could he have known that I have no feelings for Nancy, no love for her, and no joy with her? Am I that transparent?"*

The silence continued, grew heavier by the breath, and finally cracked, forcing a deep, stuttering sigh out of Nancy and softening her surly eyes with warm tears. Scott wiped her cheeks with his dirty fingers, coughed, repositioned himself to be in direct view of her face, and began the fateful conversation.

"Nancy, what's wrong?"

"Nothing."

"Nothing, and you're crying instead of celebrating?"

"I just feel overwhelmed."

"Overwhelmed? I thought you'd feel relieved."

"Maybe I just feel left out."

"I don't understand."

"Well, you found Sara without my help, you rescued her without my help, and now you're taking care of her without my help. I have no idea how you managed to find her and she hasn't said a word to me since she's been back."

"Well, I..."

"Oh, let's face it Scotty, you don't need me; you just need your Sara and now that you've found her I feel left out and alone."

"But Baby, you're her mother..."

"Don't Baby me please; I know when I'm wanted and I know when I'm not."

"Of course you're wanted. What kind of talk is that?"

"Well, if I'm so damn wanted, what do you plan to do with me now?'

"Do with you now? What do you mean?"

"I mean what do you plan to do with me now that you have found your Sara."

"My Sara?"

"What do you plan to do with me, Scotty? That's all I want to know right now."

"We can live together here, as we had planned before she was kidnapped."

"Live together? Would that be good for Sara? What would she tell her friends? My parents live together but they're not..."

The un-uttered word was followed by a prolonged, hissing silence as Scott and Nancy gazed evasively at opposite sides of the room. The suffocating stillness stretched and yawned like mountain fog and wrapped its gray scarf around their throats. Their un-aired cries, dry and hoarse with anguish, finally found their voices when Scott hesitantly popped the half question.

"Would you?"

"Yes."

"You would?"

"I would."

"But you were the one who divorced me and wouldn't let me see my daughter."

Nancy gulped, her heart began to race, and her lips began to quiver with half words and stuttered phrases.

"It wwwould... it wwwould be best... be best for... for

Sara?"

"And how about us, Babe?"

"Us?"

"It should be best for us too, shouldn't it?"

"Oh, yes, us, sure..."

"Are you really sure, Nancy?"

"Sure? Oh, yes."

"You want to marry the same man you had divorced?"

"I shouldn't have... I mean, I should've... should've waited."

"Waited? Waited for what?"

"Waited for you to come back to your senses."

Scott pulled away, got up, walked to the middle of the room, and stood in the exact spot where he had taken Nancy on his first night back from Iraq. He gazed at the carpet as if it were holding the ghost of a distant memory that had been transmuted into unintelligible, haunting echoes, echoes which he could hear but could not decipher. Like an Alzheimer victim—though no longer able to recognize his own life, continues to gaze at it with stubborn consternation—he stood on that very spot unaware of his surroundings or himself.

Nancy saw and understood with her intuitive mind that something had overcome him, something grave that should not be disturbed. She even suspected that it was her last phrase that precipitated it all but did not have the courage to shake the moment for an answer. Quiet stillness gripped the bedroom as fateful moments dripped from the leaky faucet of time and trickled down the great unknown. Not a breath, not a sigh, not a motion rattled the solemn silence until the shattering scream brought down the house.

Shaken out of his trance Scott flew to Sara's side to find her sitting, wide-eyed with hands on head, shredding the room with her timorous voice. Against her flailing limbs, he lifted her into his arms, folded her against his chest, and with a choked voice paced the living room. Amidst this fitful pacing and unearthly screaming, Nancy walked in, stood away from Scott's marching path, and glared at the spectacle with cold sweat dripping from her face. At Nancy's sight the screams took on an even higher pitch, causing Scott to motion to Nancy to return to the bedroom. Still, the screams persisted with unrelenting force until, overcome by strained exhaustion, they subsided into gasping moans.

Cautiously, Scott walked into his office, sat down in his leather chair, and held Sara's tears to his chest. Suspecting that she might have had a nightmare, he whispered into her ear, "Did you have a bad dream, Precious?'

"Uh-huh."

"What was it about?"

"Mommy was trying to shave my hair."

"What was she using?"

"A buzzing razor."

"Is that what they used when they shaved your head?"

"Uh-huh."

"Who did it?"

"The woman."

"What did she look like?"

"Like Mommy."

"You mean she was blond?"

"No."

"What was she like?"

"I don't know?"

"How did she remind you of Mommy?"

"She frowned."

"But Mommy loves you."

"Uh-huh."

"Sure she does. You're just upset now because of that bad dream."

"I'm scared."

"Scared of what, Baby?"

"Scared of Mommy."

"But Mommy loves you."

"Uh-huh."

"What is it, Baby?"

"I want to stay with you."

"All the time?"

"All the time."

"What will you do when I go to work?"

"I'll go with you."

Behind them Scott could hear Nancy's sighs as she stood in the office door. She must have heard part of the conversation because when Scott turned and looked at her she was wearing a forlorn frown over her face. Before he could soften her aspect with some reassuring remark the doorbell rang, re-startling Sara who resumed her eerie screaming with renewed vigor.

When Nancy opened the door, the Thorntons stood in the cold darkness, motionless, petrified by Sara's penetrating screams. Mr. Thornton was quick to suggest that they leave and return the next day. But Nancy, having invited them earlier, insisted that they come in.

"She'll calm down when she sees you."

"Are you sure?" replied Mr. Thornton.

"She's easy to agitate but she'll have to get used to being with us again."

Nancy led the Thornton duet into the living room and motioned for them to sit down. While quietly awaiting Sara's screams to die down, the doorbell rang again, treating the Bradford ears to a second surge of wild cries that was followed by a third when Jane and Flora arrived. To insulate Sara, Scott closed his office door and left it to Nancy to entertain the riddled family. Unlike Nancy, he did not feel that the time was right to overwhelm Sara with visitors and was intent on keeping her in his arms until they had all left.

When after a while the waiting had become awkward, Nancy tapped gently on Scott's door and whispered, "They wanted me to ask you if there was anything that they could do to help out."

"Yes," whispered Scott, "let them help you bring my car back."

"Where is it?"

"On 30th, just north of OCU."

"Okay, I'll go with Jane and get it."

Within a few minutes, Sara and Scott had the house to themselves. By then Sara had calmed down again and, in her father's arms, was relishing the newfound quietude. It was during this delicate hiatus that Scott began his cautious interrogation of Sara.

"Sara Baby, you like it when the house is quiet, don't you?"

"Uh-huh."

"And it scares you to hear the phone or the doorbell ring, doesn't it?"

"Uh-huh."

"What did they do to you in that house when the doorbell rang."

"They locked me up in the dark closet."

"Was the closet clean and empty?"

"It was full of clothes."

"Was there enough room for you?"

"The box was empty."

"What box?"

"The box in the closet."

"Is that where they locked you up each time the doorbell rang?"

"Uh-huh."

"How big was the box?"

"It was dark and I couldn't move."

"Could you breathe okay?"

"My throat hurt."

"Why?"

"I don't know."

Scott's heart began to drum in his ears and a suffocating sensation gripped its long fingers around his throat.

"Baby, would you like to take a walk outside?"

"Where outside?"

"In the backyard."

"Are there stars?"

"I think we can find a few."

Scott wrapped Sara in a thick blanket and walked out with her into the cold, dark backyard. The sky was fringed with a haze of city lights but the dome was an adorned cupola with winking stars flickering with life. On Scott's arms, Sara lay flat, gazing, pointing, and taking in deep sighs of cold night air. Scott did not ask any more questions. He was enthralled with watching Sara, oblivious of her closed-in fears, aloft upon his arms, merrymaking with the stars, and being reborn as a five-year old girl. Under the stars, her face assumed a peaceful aura and her eyes twinkled with sparkles of joy. The starlight had washed away, at least for that little while, all the fears that had gripped her baby face.

While Sara was preoccupied with her star toys, Scott was pondering more mundane issues such as Sara's seeing her grandparents, Sara's going back to school, and his going back to work. He suspected that life, as they had known it, would not simply resume just because Sara was back. In their wake, however, Sara's crying fears resurrected some of his own fears that he thought had long been buried in Iraq. Memories of the many scenes he had witnessed un-scrolled in front of his mind like a war movie. Being a two-year veteran of fear he had learned not to underestimate this formidable enemy of inner peace. On the contrary, he considered it with grave awe and recoiled from it with insurmountable dread.

While Sara sky-gazed in the cold darkness, memories when he and his three Humvee buddies lost their way in the chaos of an explosion welled up into his conscious mind. Memories, un-welcomed and uninvited, froze his eyes in a vacuous, seeing stare. Scenes interred underneath his consciousness resurrected themselves, forcing him to re-view the sinister details of how they were captured and taken to the catacombs of Baghdad, how they were chained in a dark hole, and how they were kept there till after the evening prayer when the tall man arrived.

He was a redhead in his forties with a handsome, shaven face and ice-blue eyes like nails, pinned with focus. In spite of his penetrating aspect, they remained hopeful because his attitude was dignified and calm, his motions poised and slow, and he interrogated them in regal English. They remained hopeful until he found out that they were in communications and motioned to his men to bring the sword. Johnny was held down first with neck over the butcher's block and, before he could even say his prayers, his head rolled off into the gutter while his neck splashed red puddles onto the ground.

Then Tim, wailing, was pulled to the block and held down by his hair. He kept trying to look back at Scott and Frank until his screams were chopped in two.

With blurring eyes Frank and Scott looked at each other but before they found out who would be next, grenades surprised the scene and in a flash their captors were gunned down into the blood-spattered ground before they could muster any resistance.

Scott and Frank hit the dirt and wouldn't look up until they heard Peckford's voice.

"Thanks for planting the chip in your boot, Scotty. Without it, we wouldn't have found you."

Securing the scene after the battle, picking up the two beheaded soldiers, and inspecting the premises for firearms and explosives, Scott and Frank worked together, bonded by their near-beheading experience. What they said to each other they said with their eyes without ever a whisper as if fear had temporarily tied their tongues into violet knots. It did not escape them, however, that the tall redhead was not among the dead but at the time they were too afraid to talk about it. Inside their shaken brains the specter of the tall, blue-eyed executioner burned too hot for words and they tried to obliterate it by denying it voice.

Memories when Scott and his three Humvee buddies lost their way in the chaos of an explosion have haunted all his days and nights since. These tenebrous memories deepened further into noir loneliness when Frank was killed by a sniper's bullet two days later, leaving Scott with no one to bond with against the relentless raids of his recalling mind. Indeed, it was these relentless memories that had become the cornerstones of Scott's soul and the building blocks of his mind.

While still holding Sara in his arms, Peckford's words after that rescue resonated with his pulse. "Once fear conquers your heart, the only means to overthrow it is to hurl yourself back into it, over and over, until it runs away from you instead of you from it. Waste no time reasoning with fear, Scotty; its only antidotes are reckless courage and blind faith."

All these suppressed thoughts clamored in Scott's mind, making inaudible, high-pitched noises that polluted his peace. Even though he did not wish to disturb Sara's stargazing respite he, nevertheless, was at a loss because he did not know what to do to suppress his own white noise. He even tried to distract himself by following Sara's example but stargazing caused his neck to go into painful spasms, rekindling Johnny & Tim's catacomb scenes and causing him to restrict his gaze thereafter to the horizontal dimension.

With fiery thoughts still flashing images from Johnny and Tim's executions, Scott began to walk slowly towards the house. *"What a turn of events,"* he thought. *"The same stars that have given Sara respite from her fears have set mine ablaze. Life is a two-faced coin but instead of heads and tails, there is joy and fear. The coin of the poor is copper, of the middle class is silver, and that of the rich is gold. But, rich or poor, it still is a two-faced coin with joy on one side and fear on the other. Yes, we are tossed into life like coins and wherever and however we land becomes our destiny. Oh, what a bright idea this is. I must go in and write it down before I forget it. Peckford would be proud of me for thinking it."*

Scott walked back into the house with a rejuvenated Sara in his arms. He took her into his office, sat her on the couch, and began to write down his thoughts. As he wrote about his fears he gained more insight into his weird mental states and could see why they had evolved the way they did. Sara's fears had not only strengthened the bond of love between him and her, they had also given him another chance to understand and confront his own fears.

If all he needed were blind faith and reckless courage, then Sara's rescue had provided him with both. He felt stronger, more hopeful, more balanced, and more eager to fulfill his destiny as a devoted father. Eyeing Sara as she quietly sat on the office couch and gazed at him with adoring eyes, he took one look at his clothes and gasped.

"Oh, *I still haven't had a shower and I can't till Nancy returns. Oh, but what if Sara won't stay with Nancy while I take my shower? Well, I'll have to wait till she falls asleep and then take it. I have to clean up before going to bed tonight. I look like a hobo and I don't want Sara to see me like that when she wakes up in the morning. I hope I don't have catacomb nightmares tonight. Oh, what a horrible thing is fear.*"

Chapter Twenty-Three
(Family Affairs)

On their way to OCU, Nancy and Jane had a heart-to-heart talk about the new life situation, which Sara's return presented. Having heard Scott and Sara's office conversation, Nancy had become alarmed and shared her worry with Jane.

"Do you think that Sara blames me for her kidnapping?"

"Oh, Nancy, get over it; Sara is too young to blame anyone, let alone her own mother."

"But I heard her tell Scott that she was afraid of me."

"This is fear talk; I wouldn't make much of it."

"But what if she continues to reject me? You and I know that if she doesn't come around soon, Scott will end up rejecting me too."

"Don't be silly, Nancy, my brother won't reject you no matter what happens. He adores you, remember?"

"I don't think he can love me if Sara stops loving me."

"If he had doubts, he wouldn't have asked you to remarry him."

"It wasn't as spontaneous as you think; I had to manipulate the proposal out of him."

"Manipulate?"

"You know, I made him feel sorry for me."

"Sorry for what?"

"I pouted and told him that I felt left out."

"You didn't. Tell me you're kidding."

"Well, I was desperate for his attention and that was the only way I could get it. He's just too preoccupied with Sara to notice me."

"But that's expected. For God's sake girl, be patient. Sara will eventually calm down and he'll come around; it's just a matter of time."

"And what if she doesn't?"

"What do you mean, doesn't?"

"What if she doesn't calm down?"

"It may take time, but surely she will. Quit worrying

so much."

"The way I see it is that if Sara stays frightened, Scott will devote all his time to her and none to me, and if she won't let me come near her, Scott will not come near me."

"You know, Nancy, you make it sound like you're the step mother and he's the real dad. When did this role reversal take place? You're worried instead of being overjoyed at the return of your only child? How the hell did this happen?"

"You're just taking your brother's side. Nobody wants to see it my way, not even my best friend."

Tears in Nancy and Jane's eyes choked their conversation from that point on and silence supervened until they found Scott's car. They parted without a thank-you or a goodbye and went on their separate ways into the night.

As Nancy drove back home, her mind hummed with the new family dynamics. *"Jane wasn't much help,"* she thought. *"She didn't seem sympathetic to my position. No one seems to care about me since Sara's return. Even my parents are on Scott and Sara's side and now I find out that Jane is too. I am alone and I am left out. I'll have to take care of myself from now on. Oh, there's a SUBWAY. I'd better get something to eat. There hasn't been much food in the house since Sara's return."*

When Nancy arrived, there was not a light in the house. *"I guess this means that I should be extremely quiet because they're already asleep. Alone and left out, that's how it's going to be from now on, alone and left out."*

Entering through the garage she tiptoed in, turned the kitchen lights on, and did not even bother to check the bedroom. Instead, she sat down at the kitchen table, ate her sandwich, and glared at the walls. She was too restless to sleep, too tired to read, and too afraid to watch TV lest it should wake up Sara. Feeling trapped inside her new state, she went into the second bedroom, lay on the bed without taking her clothes off, and tried to sleep. Even though she would have liked to look in on Sara and Scott she resisted that urge and stubbornly forced her thoughts to wander elsewhere. All this, of course, interfered with slumber's long smooth fingers, causing them to clench into a white fist.

As Nancy's insomnia amplified her fatigue, and midnight wrapped its cold arms around the house, nightmares began to sprout in the master bedroom. First Sara awakened screaming and then Scott, taking turns in alarming each other until the early sunrays absconded with their dreams and served them a potion of uninterrupted sleep. Meanwhile, Nancy, who was growing more perturbed with each scream, decided to take refuge in her apartment instead. Acting on her urge and not bothering to leave a note she snuck into her car and drove off to her own bed.

Returning to her apartment gave her an unfettered sense of peace, which empowered her and crimsoned her pale spirits. Surprised by these redeeming feelings she stepped outside her apartment door, stood on the exact spot where she had found the brown paper bag, clenched her fist, and with blanched knuckles rang her own doorbell thrice. She then turned on the living room TV and lights, walked into her bedroom, slid into her nightgown, and relishing all the bright lights and television noise, promptly fell asleep.

Her night was alight with dreams. She flew with albatross wings across oceans, above clouds, around the moon, and away from storms. She flew for days without ever landing, ever resting, and ever sighting shore. Like a hot air balloon, she levitated undisturbed throughout the night until her cell phone woke her up at eight.

"Where are you, Babe?"

"At my apartment."

"Have you been there all night?"

"I left at two. I just couldn't go to sleep at your place."

"I thought it had become our place."

"Well..."

"Sara needs some clothes. Can you drop them by on your way to work?"

"You know how hectic my Saturdays are. Why don't you and Sara come and get them."

"I don't think Sara is ready to leave the house yet. Besides, it's not wise to bring her back near the place where she was kidnapped."

"How about if I bring them with me after work?"

"She's been in the same jammies for a week now. I washed them yesterday while she had her bath. She should be able to wear her regular clothes during the day."

"Okay, I'll pack some clothes and drop them at your front door on my way to work."

"You're not coming in?"

"There's no time. I'll see you after work."

Scott did not quite understand Nancy's behavior but was too preoccupied with Sara to think of anything else. Sara awakened while he was talking to Nancy but did not scream as she had done all through the night. Instead she sat in bed with a smile on her face and did not say a word until he hung up.

"I'm glad Mommy is not going to come in."

"Glad? What are you glad about, Baby?"

"I'm glad because with you, I don't feel scared."

"But Mommy loves you."

"Uh-huh."

"And you love her, right?"

"Uh-huh."

"Wouldn't you like to surprise her with a hug when she drops by with your clothes?"

"I don't need clothes."

"You want to stay in your jammies all day long?

"Uh-huh."

"Don't you want to get dressed and go for a ride?"

"No."

"What would you like to do then?"

"Play."

"And what am I going to do while you play?"

"Clean up."

"You won't be afraid if I leave you alone while I

shower?"

"No."

"Wouldn't you rather be with Mommy while I'm in the shower?"

Sara did not answer. Instead she jumped into Scott's lap and snuggled as he wrapped his arms around her. After a few minutes of this quiet bonding Scott carried Sara into the kitchen and began preparing breakfast while his ears listened for Nancy. He knew that she would not ring the doorbell but hoped that she would at least pop in to say good morning and give Sara a hug before going to work.

After breakfast when no one had come in Scott opened the front door and froze. Facing him was an open-mouthed, brown paper bag with Sara's clothes in it. Before he picked it up he looked around, listened for furtive feet, and sniffed the air. A feeling of déjà vu crawled under his skin, causing him to pace the living room with long, restless strides. Sara, feeling ignored, stepped into his path and, smiling, lifted her arms for him to pick her up. When he continued to pace without noticing her she broke into tears, which promptly delivered him from his absent-minded consternation.

Seating Sara in his lap, he wiped her tears, calmed her down, and then asked his desperate question.

"Baby, why did you leave the apartment on the morning you were stolen?"

"I didn't leave. I just opened the door thinking it was Mommy."

"You mean someone rang the door bell?"

"Yes."

"And who was it?"

"The woman."

"What did she tell you?"

"She said that Mommy was downstairs waiting for me."

"And what did you do?"

"I held her hand and went down with her."

"And then?"

"There was a car waiting."

"And who was in the car?"

"The two men."

"And how did she get you into the car?"

"She opened the door, pushed me in, and they took off."

"And where was Mommy?"

"She wasn't downstairs like the woman said."

Here all questions ceased as Sara buried her contorted, whimpering face into Scott's chest. Scott pressed his lips onto Sara's shaven head and gave his imagination the freedom to recreate Sara's captivity. He could imagine how they might have treated his little girl and how frightened she must have felt having no understanding of what was happening to her. In Iraq, at least, he knew what he was up against but his poor Sara had no clue. His thoughts scaled new heights of insight as he, with lips still pressed to Sara's bald head, pondered the situation.

"My innocent, unsuspecting, little girl—abducted from her own familiar world and hurled into an alien prison that shrank to a dark, tiny box inside a closet at the toll of a bell— has already been to hell. Can anyone bring back a child from hell? How does one un-hell a soul and teach it to trust the world that had betrayed it? My own horror is mild compared to hers. When I went to Iraq, I went prepared for my own baptism by fear and it still shudders me to think and not to think about it. To think and to try not to think equally take away my breath. If I cannot recover from my own visit to hell how can I expect it of my frail, little Sara? Fear, hell's devil, has invaded us both and I neither have the faith nor the courage to overthrow it. Oh, Peckford, how right you were when you said: "Waste no time reasoning with fear, Scotty; its only antidotes are reckless courage and blind faith."

Scott and Sara spent Saturday at home because Scott could not convince Sara to go for a car ride. The mere mention of leaving the house frightened her and any sudden noise or ring caused her to cling to her dad's neck with drowning arms. When he asked her if she would like to see her grandparents or her aunt, she shook her head and withdrew into her shell. When he asked her if she would like to see her Mommy, a blank look overtook her face and swallowed her words. When he asked her if she was eager to go back to school, her entire body quaked violently as she covered her bald head with both hands. It was then that Scott understood why she did not wish to be seen.

He felt a need to talk to someone, someone he could trust, someone close, someone like Peckford. Telling Sara that he was ready to take his shower, he put her in the bedroom and, leaving the door open, went into the bathroom and called Jane who was so happy to hear his voice. After answering her incessant questions and relating to her the rescue story, he opened his heart and poured out his concerns: "How can I go back to work when she won't leave my side? How can I make her trust Nancy again? If I wait till her hair grows back, school will be over. She doesn't want anyone to see her shaven head. What are we to do?"

Jane, who had no experience with children, could not come up with any worthwhile ideas. She had a friend, she said, who worked for DHS and knew a lot about such matters but she was afraid to ask for her help because she didn't want the DHS to get involved in Sara's case. But she did give Scott a rather good suggestion: "Why don't you talk to Mother? She has raised both of us and knows a lot more about children than me."

"Is she at the office?"

"She's in the next room talking to a buyer."

"Well, don't interrupt her. I'll take a quick shower and then I'll call her on her cell phone. How's the Thornton Real Estate Agency doing? If I should get fired from the Hartland Bank on account of Sara, I might have to join the family business."

"Oh, Silly. They'll never fire you because you are too good."

"They will if I had to stay home with Sara."

"Well, in that case, we'd love to have you here and you can bring Sara with you to work."

"How's Dad doing?"

"He'd like to see you but from what you've just said I doubt that Sara is ready to see anyone yet."

"Let me work on her and I'll let you know."

"Oh, wait. I think Mom has just gotten off the phone."

Scott had an emotional conversation with Jill who did more listening than talking. She had never cared for a fear-shocked child given that both Scott and Jane had relatively normal childhoods. The only shock she and Howard had to face was Jane's sexuality, which they learned to countenance but never quite understood. Her only good idea was Frances. She reminded Scott that Frances Bradford was a first grade teacher at Casady.

"Surely, Scotty, having taught for so many years she would have had to deal with many a disturbed child. Besides, she's also Sara's grandmother, which would make it easier for Sara to trust her."

"Have you talked to her?"

"Of course I've talked to her. We talked yesterday while at your place."

"Yesterday?"

"While you and Sara sat in your office and the rest of us waited in the living room."

"Who let you in?"

"Nancy, of course... Are you okay Scotty?"

"I just don't remember you all coming in."

"Well, you were preoccupied with Sara. The Bradfords don't teach on Saturday. Give them a call; I'm sure they'd like to hear from you."

While taking his shower, Scott's mind tried to fathom the magnitude of Sara's problem. Hers was not a simple fear that she could outgrow with time. No, it was an indelible fear that was capable of devastating the rest of their lives, a fear that had already neutralized him and rendered him dysfunctional. He realized that he needed help but did not know where to turn. Frances Bradford was a good place to start especially since Nancy would have already filled her in on all the details, and so he resolved to call Frances as soon as he got dressed.

Sara, while her father was in the bathroom, was busy at play on his bed. When Scott emerged freshly shaven and neatly dressed she was quick to remark that it was time for her to get dressed too and having said that, she ran into the living room to fetch the brown paper bag. It was at this very moment that the doorbell rang, causing her to drop the bag and run screaming into her father's lap. Amidst her screams the doorbell rang again and again but Scott knew not to answer it. Instead, he carried Sara in his arms and paced the bedroom trying to calm her down. Soon the rings turned into loud knocks and unintelligible voices could be heard, which caused Sara to scream even louder and become uncontrollable, gasping as if she were being choked. Scott would have liked to answer the door, silence the interlopers, and deactivate the doorbell but being locked into Sara's drowning arms he could do nothing but pace.

When the voices died down Sara was listless, drenched with sweat, and the brown paper bag lay on the floor with her clothes strewn around it. Scott put her to bed and lay next to her with a thousand thoughts vying for his attention. He wanted to call Frances but did not want Sara to hear the conversation nor could he leave her side as long as she was awake. Mercifully, exhaustion came to his rescue when Sara's gasping sighs became rhythmical purrs and a peaceful aspect smoothed her contorted face. It was then that he stole back into the bathroom and called Frances.

Frances, having listened to Scott's story, gave her suggestions like a methodical teacher would.

"Well, Scotty, my heart cries out for Sara and, after what you have told me, I am not surprised at her behavior. The frightened children I have had to deal with are usually abused and we have a school psychologist who helps us out with them. But what happened to Sara is beyond ordinary fear and no one here would know what to do."

"What am I to do come Monday? Should I insist that she go to school?"

"Oh, no, do not make this child do anything she's not ready for. She needs time and a lot of it before she can learn to trust again."

"What am I to do about her fear of Nancy?"

"That worries me sick because it's a well-deserved fear. Nancy had no business leaving Sara alone. I couldn't believe it when I heard it. We never left Nancy alone when she was growing up."

"Well, she must have acted on an impulse without thinking."

"Don't make excuses for her, Scotty. If she's reported to DHS, she'll get in big trouble for child neglect."

"Oh, what would they do?"

"They may not allow her to keep Sara until a judge hears her case and decides."

"Who's going to report her?"

"Who knows, the police, some well-meaning neighbor, Sara's teacher, or anyone else who hears the story?"

"Do you know any doctors who specialize in frightened children?"

"Our school psychologist refers difficult cases to Dr. Alma Adams, a well-thought-of child psychiatrist."

"That's good to know. I may have to take Sara to her if she doesn't improve."

"Peter and I would love to baby-sit if she'd let us."

"Well, let me see how she feels about all that and I'll let you know."

"How's Nancy handling all of this?"

"She keeps her distance."

"What?"

"Well, I think that she's afraid to do anything because everything seems to alarm Sara."

"I hate hearing that. A mother's place is with her child. Surely, she sleeps with her at night."

"Well, yesterday she slept in her apartment and the day before, in the guest bedroom."

"No way!"

"She said that she couldn't sleep because of Sara's nightmares."

"Oh, Scotty, this is so wrong. A frightened child needs her mother. I'll have to have a talk with this daughter of mine."

"She'll come around, I'm sure. Don't hound her, please. She is probably feeling both afraid and guilty and doesn't know how to deal with the situation."

"Well, you're kinder than I am. I'll try not to interfere. Please let us know when we can be of help."

Talking with Frances Bradford left Scott with more questions than answers. It made him realize, however, that he had to make some important decisions and that he had to make them all alone. *"No one can help me help Sara. I was the one who saved her and I'm the one who will have to save her again. I wish Peckford were here. I wish I could visit the bench; I seem to get my best ideas at the cemetery. Oh, what a mess. We are one fear-riddled bunch. I never understood it till I talked with Frances but Nancy is just as afraid as Sara and me. She's afraid of being found out... I wonder if she has a lot more to hide than anyone knows about. Even her own mother is appalled at her behavior. Oh, Peckford, Peckford, where are you now?"*

Chapter Twenty-Four
(Complications)

Scott's mind was in disarray as it tried to sift through the realities of his new life. The more he pondered his situation the more forgetful he seemed to get until finally, his brain blanked out and shut down. He could not remember past or present nor could he even cast his gaze toward the future. Trapped within his frozen intellect he found himself gazing at the front door with unseeing concentration devoid of any meaning. Then, slowly, as if his brain was beginning to thaw he could remember something about the front door, something recent, something perhaps important, but he could not recall what.

In his frustration he walked up to the door and stood staring at it as if it held the key to the remainder of his life. Standing there no ideas came to him, no thoughts spurred him to action, and no pacifying epiphany descended upon his discombobulated soul. As he turned around and began to walk away a question quartet played before his eyes and flickered as if begging for answers. *"Who rang the doorbell? Why did they bang at the door? Why the loud voices? What was all that commotion about?"*

Obsessed by these taunting questions he turned back, walked up to the door, reached for the handle, opened a crack, and cautiously peeped. There was no one waiting, no brown paper bag, no note hanging on the doorknob, and no sign that anyone had ever been there. Encouraged, he cracked the door a bit wider and stuck his head out. Hidden in the right corner stood a handsome bouquet of flowers with a note clipped to it. Seeing the flowers disarmed his spirits and surprised his eyes with grateful tears. As he gazed at these colorful smiles of nature his lost thoughts, like a waft of little birds, alighted back in a flurry upon his vacant mind and flooded it with birdsong.

As these good feelings overcame his suspended intellect and returned to him his lost courage, he jettisoned his caution, darted at the bouquet, and, without examining it, took it straight into the living room and opened the envelope. It was from his coworkers at the Hartland Bank congratulating him and wishing him well. The smallest signature was Mr. McMaster's and the largest, the most ornate, was Breena Birdsong's. Relieved, he laid the card by the bouquet and went in to check on Sara.

"Baby, you're awake?"

"I'm hungry."

"How about if we go out for a ride and get something wholesome to eat."

"Go out?"

"The sun is up and it's a nice day."

"But."

"But what, Baby? What are you afraid of?"

"The trunk."

"What trunk?"

"The trunk of the car."

"What about it?"

"I'm scared of trunks."

"But why?"

"Because they put me in one."

"What? Who? Oh, Baby. Is that why you're afraid of cars?"

"Uh-huh."

"Oh no. No one will ever hurt you again because Daddy will always be with you from now on."

"Always?"

"Always."

"You promise?"

"I promise."

"Can we go to McDonald's?"

"Only if you get dressed. They won't serve you at McDonald's if you're in your jammies."

Helping Sara dress, Scott felt a sudden flush of overwhelming joy that fluttered in his heart and beaded his skin with warm sweat. *"Now I understand what my mother meant by hot flashes,"* he thought. For a flapping moment, he gazed into Sara's frightened yet eager eyes, wiped the sweat off his brow, took in a deep sigh, and wondered: *"What else have they done to my Baby? I'm not going to ask. She'll tell me when she's ready. Bit by bit, she'll tell me. Yes, bit-by-bit, that's all I can stand anyway. Bit-by-bit won't kill me. That's the best way to get accustomed to poison, bit-by-bit."*

Hand in hand, Scott walked with Sara to the garage, helped her into her car seat, and drove off on their first voyage together since her captivity. As he drove he kept an eye on her face, which seemed to change expressions with the change of scenery. Back in her own little world her eyes would open wide at the sight of children in other passing cars and she would raise her hand as if to wave hello but would not complete the gesture till after the cars had long passed. This fascination with other kids intrigued Scott and begged an explanation. Only after a while did it occur to him that depriving a child of the company of other children is tantamount to taking them away from their own little world and throwing them into a world inhabited by giants. *"Children need children to make up their world and Sara has not seen a child since her last school day, eight days ago. No wonder she was willing to venture to McDonald's in spite of her fear of leaving the house."*

Scott took Sara to the McDonald's that had an indoor playground. Her eyes were already busy roaming while they stood in line. When they sat down to eat Sara took one perfunctory bite of her hamburger, took off her shoes, jumped into the pool of frolicking kids, and was lost among the giggles and play screams that bustled in the hive. Scott watched with relief as Sara interacted with joy, totally oblivious of the bitten-once hamburger that was growing cold awaiting her return. Then, as if from another dimension, an eerie cry rattled the place and caused great alarm among the awaiting parents. While others agonized with long necks and gaping eyes, Scott knew it was Sara and rushed in to investigate. Behind the slide Sara had trapped herself into a moonwalk cage and was unable to get out because the jumping kids around her were hindering her from reaching the exit. As soon as she saw her dad she held her helpless arms to him and continued to scream until he pulled her out. Sobbing uncontrollably, she held on to his neck and with her doleful eyes begged him to take her home.

On the way back, her eyes did not venture out as they had before; she merely occupied herself with looking at her hands and examining her little fingers. Nothing was said as Scott drove on but his mind was getting more and more alarmed as he was coming to grips with the reality that any small cue could set Sara off and hurl her back into a phobic state. *"How can I send her back to school when any reminder of her captivity throws her back into a fear storm?"*

As Scott drove up to the house, he noticed a silver Camry parked by his mailbox and saw a woman ringing his doorbell. Not recognizing the car or the woman, he became a bit perturbed. *"Could she be one of those officious neighbors who could end up agitating Sara?"* But as he pulled into his driveway he saw that she was carrying a thin black briefcase and that caused him to become even more worried. Quickly, he helped Sara out of her car seat, lifted her into his arms, and walked slowly towards the front door, all the while hoping that she would not decompensate at the sight of this stranger. Standing at the porch was an obviously professional woman in her early-thirties, brown-haired, green-eyed, elegantly dressed in a dark gray suit, awaiting them with a smile and an extended hand.

"Hello, I am Debbie Hunt, a CPS worker from the DHS."

Scott was struck by something familiar but had no time to unravel it. From the median between awkwardness and surprise, he extended his hand.

"Hi, I'm Scott and this is my daughter, Sara. What can we do for you, Ma'am?"

"I'm here to interview Sara."

"Did you call?"

"No, we're not supposed to call before we come."

"You just show up?"

"That's right."

"I suppose you'd like to come in."

"Yes, please."

As Scott opened the door with Sara still on his arm, he caught Sara staring at Debbie Hunt with a curious gleam in her eyes, totally devoid of apprehension.

"I'm familiar with DHS but what does CPS stand for?"

"Child Protective Services. We are a part of the Child Welfare Program."

"Oh, good, please come in then."

In the house, Scott sat Sara in his lap and whispered in her ear that the lady is just here to ask her some questions. He was intrigued when Sara showed no signs of alarm and seemed eager to cooperate. Sara and Scott watched as Ms. Hunt pulled some forms out of her briefcase and with pen in hand began her interview.

"Sara, I'm your friend and I'm here to help you."

"Uh-huh."

"Now, in order to help you, we need to have a little talk."

"Uh-huh."

"Has your mama ever left you alone except that one time when you were taken away by strangers?"

"Uh-huh."

"Where does she go when she leaves you alone?"

"To the store."

"And how long does she stay gone?"

"A long time."

"And how often has that happened?"

"A lot."

"What does she tell you before she leaves?"

"Not to open the door and to call her if I need her."

"Do you know her number?"

"No."

"How can you call it then?"

"I just push one button."

"Oh, she must have programmed her number for

you."

"Uh-huh."

"Are you afraid to be alone?"

"Uh-huh."

"Why didn't your mama take you with her?"

"I don't know."

"Do you love your mama?"

"Uh-huh."

"Do you think she loves you?"

"Uh-huh."

"Can you tell me what you're afraid of now?"

"Uh-huh."

"What are you afraid of, Sara?"

"My mommy."

"But you just said that your mama loves you."

"Uh-huh."

"Why are you afraid of your mama?"

"She locks me up in my bedroom whenever she has boyfriends."

"Have any of her men friends tried to hurt you?"

"Uh-huh."

"What did they do?"

"The one pushed me out and closed the bedroom door."

"What else did they do?"

"They made me go to my bedroom when I didn't want to."

"Did you hear anything from your bedroom?"

"Uh-huh."

"What did you hear?"

"Noise."

"What else besides noise?"

"Squeaking."

"Have any of your mom's friends tried to undress you?"

"No."

"Were you with any of them alone, without your mama?"

"No."

"Would you like to go back to your mama?"

"No."

"Where would you like to stay?"

"Here with my daddy."

"Does your daddy take good care of you?"

"Uh-huh."

"Are you afraid when you're with your daddy?

"No."

"Are you afraid when you are with both daddy and mama?"

"No."

"Are you afraid when you're alone with your mama?"

"Uh-huh."

"Where did you sleep the last two nights?"

"With my daddy."

"Where was mama?"

"I don't know."

"One last request and I'll leave you alone, Princess. Would you please take me around and show me the house?"

"Uh-huh."

As Sara held Ms. Hunt's hand and showed her the house, Scott sank into the living room sofa with his head between his hands and gazed at his black shoes. He was not prepared to hear what he had just heard nor was he eager to confront Nancy's neglect of Sara at this time of crisis. He was lost in the chaos of this new information that the CPS worker so skillfully extracted out of Sara, information that toppled his world and shredded his feelings for Nancy beyond repair.

Before Ms. Hunt left, Scott inquired if her report was going be detrimental to Nancy's maternal rights. Ms. Hunt's answer was very professional. She said that her CW (Child Welfare) supervisor would evaluate the report and decide whether to file it with the district attorney or to consider the evidence insufficient to bring the charge of maternal neglect against Nancy. But, until this issue gets decided, she asked Scott to keep Sara at his home and be her primary guardian or, using the DHS lingo, be her PRFC

(Person Responsible For the Child).

At the door, while Sara played in the living room, Scott whispered to Ms. Hunt his final question.

"Is anyone going to talk to Nancy and hear her side of the story? Some of the things that Sara said may not be true."

"Don't worry. I'll be interviewing Nancy next."

"Will she know that you are coming?"

"As I told you before, Mr. Thornton, we don't call; we just knock, come in, look around, and start asking questions."

"When will you be going?"

"I'm not allowed to say."

"Do you know where to find her?"

"We know where she works."

"Are you going there now?"

"I'm not allowed to say."

"But, I need to know how to deal with her when she comes home tonight. I don't want her to get mad at us while Sara is still so jittery."

Debbie Hunt smiled as she looked into Scott's inquisitive eyes and with a wry expression humored him with, "Surely, Mr. Thornton, you'll be able to handle the situation without much trouble. After all, you have survived Iraq, have snatched Sara out of her kidnappers' grip, and have outdone the OSBI and Homeland Security. Certainly, a hero of your caliber has enough courage to conquer his own domestic troubles."

"Oh, I see," mumbled Scott awkwardly while still peering at Debbie Hunt with déjà vu enthrallment, "but I'm not really worried about me; I'm only worried about Sara."

"I can only tell you that your first priority is to protect Sara and I'm confident that you'll do it well."

Chapter Twenty-Five
(Dénouement)

Debbie Hunt left in her wake a playful Sara and a pensive Scott. Something about Debbie Hunt was eerily familiar. No matter where he looked, her features lingered in his eyes like an old, indelible memory. Something about her short brown hair, her profound green eyes, and her confident professional demeanor pierced his soul and titillated his intrigue. He wished he could be with Nancy during the interview, not to provide reassurance or to help her explain, but rather to observe how Debbie Hunt was going to conduct the interrogation and to be privy to the secrets that he felt certain she was going to uncover.

As his mind thrashed about, he found himself getting restless to the point of agitation. While Sara played, he paced the living room with unseeing eyes blinded by storms of tortured visions. Unable to restrain his imagination, which took off like a startled bird, he found his mind beckoning Peckford for relief. *"What would you tell me if you were here? Oh, Captain, why have you left me when I need you most? I need to go to the bench. Yes. I get my best ideas at the bench. To the bench, to the bench, that's where you would want me to go."* Looking at Sara sitting by the sofa with eyes closed, arms floating in the air, and lips smiling as if breathing something magical he sat by her, stroked her head, and feeling the bristles quickly pulled his hand back and inquired.

"What're you doing, Baby?"

"I'm playing blindfold."

"What game is that?"

"I just close my eyes and imagine myself flying."

"And where are you flying to?"

"To the sun."

"And why is that?"

"Because it never gets dark when the sun is up."

"Well, how about a car ride in the sun then. It's a sunny day."

"Uh-huh"

"Well, how about it?"

"Will you bring me home before dark?"

"Sure, Princess."

Sara opened her eyes, lowered her wings, stood up, looked her dad in the eye, and whispered, "You promise you'll bring me home before dark?"

On the way to the cemetery, Scott was too preoccupied with his own tumbling thoughts to notice Sara. Repeatedly, his mind tried to focus and repeatedly it failed. His brain was so chaotic that he even forgot what he was stressing about. All he could recall was that seeing Debbie Hunt titillated his curiosity and caused him to become so unsettled that he felt an urgent need to go to the bench. Meanwhile, Sara sat quietly in her car seat and looked out the window with fascination as if she had never seen this world before. With the sun now listing westward, it cast short shadows along the roadside and caused the tall trees in the Memorial Park Cemetery to throw oval shades all along the entrance to the parking lot.

Scott and Sara walked silently on the pebbled path leading to the bench. The gravestones were exceptionally brilliant under the westing sun, which animated the air with a numinous light. Unlike her dad, Sara seemed entertained by the stone angels along the pebbled path and skipped merrily without apprehension. Scott, on the other hand, oblivious of the sacred majesty of the place and of the still finality that groaned under his feet, plowed on with heavy breaths and vacuous eyes. As he neared the bench he paused, lifted Sara into his arms, and looked about with circumspect suspicion as if to ensure that no interloper lurked behind the shadows. When he was satisfied that they were alone he cautiously approached the bench, sat in its middle, and put Sara down to play beside him.

Slowly, a sense of orderly peace soothed his agitated chaos as he regained his ability to think. *"What am I doing here anyway? I must have come for a reason but I cannot recall why. How strange to become so forgetful at my young age.*

Oh, now I recall. Yes, I think I came here to think about Nancy and Debbie Hunt. I need to be ready for her when she returns from work. I need to say the right things and contain her anger, which no doubt she will bring home with her. This woman has no love in her.

Oh, why did I think that? Can't be true. No, can't be true. But why am I still thinking it then and starting to believe that Nancy doesn't know how to love?

Here, I said it again! Nancy doesn't know how to love. And there is more. I also think that she doesn't know how to be loved. That's it, yes, that's it, and now I understand; I understand her very well now. I also understand what this means. I hate to admit it but it has to be true. If Nancy cannot love it must mean that I have never been loved by a woman? Oh, how horrible not to have ever felt a woman's love. But, what does that have to do with Debbie Hunt and why am I still preoccupied with her?

Peckford would be proud. I do get my best ideas here on his bench. He was the one who told me that those who do not know how to receive love also don't know how to give it. I guess Nancy is one of those loveless people. It sure took me several years to figure it out. But now I know and that will help me know what to do next."

Scott's thoughts settled down after his epiphany. He let his eyes meander among the graves as he took in slow chestfuls of fresh fall air and sighed them out with steaming relief. Meanwhile, Sara skipped around him unaware, her lips piping rhythmically as if singing a lullaby. The sun, still hovering above the horizon, was beginning to impart a subtle blush to the suspended clouds. Reluctant to disturb the celestial calm, Scott got up cautiously, held Sara's hand, and whispered, "It's getting cold and it'll soon be dark. Come on, Baby; let's go back home."

When Scott and Sara arrived, Nancy's car was not in the garage. Scott glanced at Sara but instead of dismay her face gleamed with peace. As they walked in, he found himself thinking about dinner rather than wondering about Nancy who should have arrived by then or at least called. With Sara playing at a safe distance, he reached for the phone to call Nancy and twice his fingers refused to dial. A cold sweat erupted upon his chest, causing him to sigh repeatedly. His prior restlessness slowly returned to his limbs and confusion began to creep back into his head. In an act of reckless courage he dialed Nancy's cell phone, got her recording, hesitated, but did not leave a message. He then dialed her apartment number and after several rings she came on the line with a harsh, loud voice.

"What the hell do you want from me?"

"I was just wondering when you're coming home."

"I am home and so are you."

"But, don't you want to be with us?"

"Not after what that child welfare bitch did."

"What did she do?"

"She asked me all these personal questions and made me feel like I was a horrible mom."

"Is that why you're upset?"

"She came to my salon without being invited and waited until I could talk to her."

"So what's wrong with her trying to do her job?"

"All these questions which I had to answer and she wrote everything down as if I were a criminal."

"And what did she tell you?"

"She told me nothing. She just filled out her damn form and left."

"Did she say anything before she left?"

"Just that her child welfare boss was going to look at the file and then decide if it should go to the district attorney."

"Was she polite?"

"Yes but she made me feel like a tramp with all her questions."

"What did she ask?"

"Never mind. She knew too much about me. She knew things no one should know. It took me a while to figure out that she had to have talked to you and Sara. The bitch must have visited you first but when I asked her if she had, she just said that she was not allowed to say. Why did Sara tell her all that stuff? Whose side is she on anyway? I feel like I've been betrayed by my own daughter and by you too."

"I never said a word about you, Babe. She just interviewed Sara."

"Yeah, but you let her in and you didn't have to. You both betrayed me."

"Babe, why don't you bring some clothes, come over, and we'll talk about it."

"I never want to talk about it ever again."

"And how about Sara?"

"How about that little traitor?"

"Traitor? She's only five for God's sake and she needs you."

"I'm not sure anymore. You're the one she needs. She's afraid of me and, after that visit by the bitch, I'm also afraid of her."

"Calm down and tell me what would you like for dinner?"

"What dinner?"

"Dinner, with us tonight."

"I've already eaten. You and Sara have your dinner together. Good bye Scotty."

By the end of the conversation, Scott turned pale and had to sit down. He was surprised to find Sara standing behind him and feared that she might have heard the entire exchange. He pulled her onto his lap and said nothing. They both sat huddled together in the dim light without a sound or motion. Scott's thoughts carried him far away into a dark cave from which the only light he could discern was a bluish blur at the cave's mouth. He felt desperately alone and straddled with a grave responsibility. The more he tried to understand Nancy's position, the more his compassion oozed out of him, leaving him stiff with unwelcome anger. He glanced at Sara's bald head resting upon his chest, rhythmically rocking up and down, and became disturbed when he realized that it was actually bouncing with his heartbeats. This creepy realization slowly filled him with livid fear and distorted his features to such a degree that it alarmed Sara. Cautiously, she sat up, held Scott's face with both her hands, and said, "I love you, Daddy."

Could this five-year-old child have sensed her father's loneliness and tried to temper it with love? Could she have realized that her own mother had no love left within her? Can children be that insightful? These were Scott's thoughts as he looked down at Sara's moist eyes and wondered if his little girl knew enough about love to suffer its absence. He felt that he had to do something but his mind did not come to his rescue. Then, as if out of thin air, Sara blurted out the question to his face, "Why don't you invite Ms. Debbie for dinner?"

"Oh, no, that would not be proper."

"She gave you her cell phone number and said that you can call her anytime."

"Oh, no Baby, this wouldn't be right."

"I liked Ms. Debbie."

"I liked her too."

"She's pretty."

"Oh, you noticed?"

"I think she liked me."

"Oh, sure Baby, everyone likes you."

"My mommy doesn't."

"You shouldn't talk like that."

"You know what Ms. Debbie said to me when I was showing her the house?"

"What?"

"She said that you were a hero."

"Hero? Do you know what that means?"

"Can I call her? We can play a game after dinner. You can marry her. She'll be a good mommy."

Scott was stung by Sara's assertion. After a moment's reflection, he chose a strategy of distraction and denial.

"No, Baby, calling Ms. Debbie wouldn't be proper. Let's cook dinner together and then we'll call Mom again and see if she has changed her mind."

"But you don't love Mommy."

"Sara?"

"And Mommy doesn't love us."

"Oh, Baby, don't talk like that. We're a family and we love each other."

"I don't love Mommy."

"Sara, I just asked you not to talk like that."

"But Mommy scares me."

"No Baby, you're just afraid of too many things right now."

"Uh-huh."

Cooking together, Scott and Sara said very little but were happy and content just to be together. Chopping onions with tearful eyes Scott's mind wandered among the pasta and tomato sauce, among the spices and boiling water, and among the fragments of a conversation that lingered in his ears. He tried to find an explanation for Sara's precocious intuition and the only thing he could come up with was fear shock. *"Could it be that her fear might have sparked her sudden insight? Could fear make a child become acutely aware of love's presence and love's absence? Could fear make a child suddenly grow up? Why did she want to fix me up with a woman I hardly knew? Could she have sensed that I was enthralled by her? Has she given up on her mom and me? What does her little mind see that I cannot see? She has never exhibited such tendencies before. I can't believe how assertive she was. Could it all be because she feels betrayed by Nancy? Or could her hidden fears be playing a part in all of this? How could she have become so insightful at her age? She speaks like a psychic who sees the souls of people through their faces. What a surprising little child."*

The apparition of Sara—consumed in her sparkling, little world, pretending to cook with her little bald head shimmering under the kitchen lamps—gave him an unexpected chill. Soon, he began to feel overjoyed but did not understand why until his wondering eyes fixed their

236

gaze again upon Sara's shimmering head. This vague intimation caused him to stop chopping, take in a deep sigh, and pause in thought. He felt as though he was surprised by a rainstorm after a long drought, a storm that soaked him to the bone. He could feel joy trickling through his clothes and stroking his skin with child-like fingertips. Still, no matter how hard he tried, he could not decipher why Sara's bald head would conjure such a blithe feeling inside of him.

Then a lightning bolt struck him between the eyes and took him to a time five years before. He remembered their wedding night when Nancy slowly took off her clothes and stood naked in the lamplight by the bed. Her little abdomen with Sara inside of it shimmered like a full moon quickening with dreams. He remembered holding it with both hands, putting his lips to the navel, and whispering into Sara's unborn ears, "Welcome back baby."

The joy of the memory mingled with the joy of the moment overwhelmed his heart with the realization that he had twice rescued Sara's life from the ruthless fangs of fate. Having never experienced such overwhelming joy before he had to admit to himself that he had loved Nancy not for her self but merely as one would love a surrogate mother. He had, however, and for a very long time harbored an attraction for Nancy and found her seductive. Perhaps that was why their life seemed so perfect before Iraq; Sara filled the house with love, Nancy filled it with sensuality, and vacillating between these two fierce natural forces he was content.

He tried to remember how he felt when he found out that he was going to Iraq. He remembered the letter that carried his orders and his extreme grief when he realized that he had to leave Sara for two years. He did not remember grieving for Nancy or longing for her when he was away. All he thought about was Sara. And when he thought that his neck was next on the chopping block, all he wanted was to see Sara one more time before his head rolled. That was when Peckford came to his rescue and that was when the gratitude he felt for Peckford was so overpowering that it caused him to idolize Peckford from that point on. Peckford became his savior, mentor, friend, and demiurge. The more he knew him the more he admired and loved him. Peckford's intellect with its vast repertoire of knowledge fascinated Scott and made him realize how unenlightened he would have remained had he not been saved by Peckford.

It was no longer hard to understand why when he returned to Nancy he could no longer make love to her. After his frightening, near death experience and his Peckford experience, he could feel the livid loneliness between Nancy and him resonate with loveless echoes that had lost their sensuality. He agonized to discover what was missing and never quite understood that it was the contrast between his renaissance and her primitive mind that had made sex with her unthinkable. It was, indeed, his rebirth after his baptism by fear that had made it strikingly difficult for him to have sex with a beautiful woman that he did not love.

And the pornography—his long-abandoned refuge, his distasteful distraction from his conjugal duties—kept them conveniently apart and caused Nancy to become disgusted with him, which suited him well. He wanted Peckford's mind and soul in Nancy's body and that proved to be an impossible transmutation. Starved for a woman's love almost to the point of insanity, he still was unable see it until his assertive Sara pointed it out to him today: "Can I call her? We can play a game after dinner. You could marry her. She'd be a good mommy." *"What else is this little bald head going to teach me?"* he thought.

His eyes filled up with grateful tears as he and Sara sat down to eat. Before they broke bread he held her hand, lifted it high above her head, and said, "Would you like me to say a prayer?"

"A prayer?"

"Yes, Baby, a prayer of thanks for you."

"Uh-huh."

"Close your eyes, raise your other hand to the air, and imagine that you are flying towards the sun where it never gets dark."

"Uh-huh."

"And imagine that God is waiting for you to heal you of your fears."

"Uh-huh."

"And ask him with all your heart to heal both of us today because only courage and faith can heal fear."

"Uh-huh."

"Now, keep your eyes closed and get ready for the trip."

"Uh-huh."

"Dear Lord. Please heal Sara's fears and mine today and give us back our lives. And heal Nancy's heart from anger and fill it with love. Fill all our lives with so much love so that we will not do foolish things from the lack of it. And hold us together in your arms so that we'd never stray again. We ask all this in Jesus' name. Amen."

When Scott finished, Sara still had her eyes closed and her wings up in the air. Her sweet face had an angelic gleam and her lips quivered with unaired words that Scott fully understood.

Chapter Twenty-Six
(Untidy Details)

After dinner, Sara began to look tired but would not hear of going to bed alone. She wanted Scott to tuck her in and the emotion promise not to leave her side till morning. Scott, who had a healthy respect for fear and understood the seriousness of, obliged Sara with a long bedtime story that sent her unafraid into a dreamful sleep. When he was certain that she was in deep sleep he tiptoed out of the bedroom and went to his office to check his e-mails.

Sitting in his chair, waiting for his computer to boot up, he was piqued by a strange sense of apprehension that surprised his heart and took over his purposeful thoughts. Instead of checking his e-mails he found himself focused on trying to explain this uncanny feeling. He first attributed it to Nancy and Sara's rejection of one another, then to the numberless unknowns that lay ahead, then to his Monday plans should Sara refuse to go to school, and then to all the untidy details that begged for order as a result of their new life situation. In spite of all these plausible explanations he wasn't satisfied and continued to thrash about for a better reason for his strange apprehension. But wherever his mind traveled on this quest it met a wall, which it couldn't scale.

Frustrated, he clicked his e-mail link and busied himself with deleting the scores of intrusive, meaningless messages that greeted his tired eyes. There were, however, e-mails from his parents, his sister, Nancy's parents, his boss, and Breena Birdsong, all well wishing and gratulant, which he answered with sincere gratitude. Then, when he was about to log out, a new e-mail popped on his screen from Patrick Ford. His heart galloped with adrenalin as he rubbed his eyes and double-checked the name. It was from Patrick Ford, the very Reverend Patrick Ford, which meant that it was from Peckford.

Hesitantly, he opened the e-mail not knowing whether to expect good or bad news. His eyes bulged at the message: "Benchmark Symmetry offers quiet time for worship from 5:30 p.m. to 6:30 p.m. each Sunday. Join the very Reverend Patrick Ford in meditation. Adults only; no children please."

Tomorrow was Sunday, which meant that tomorrow he would be seeing Peckford. His excitement and curiosity peaked as he began to imagine what tomorrow's meeting might bring. He got up from his chair and began pacing the living room with mind ablaze. His thoughts took him back to Iraq and burnished all the dusty details of his Peckford days. But Peckford's message clearly excluded children. What was he to do with Sara? He went back to his screen, read and re-read the message and was pleased and reassured when it did not change. "Benchmark Symmetry offers quiet time for worship from 5:30 p.m. to 6:30 p.m. each Sunday. Join the very Reverend Patrick Ford in meditation. Adults only; no children please."

Scott would have slept well were it not for this unearthly message. With his hyperbolic angst, he lay wide-eyed, listening to Sara's breaths, at times sonorous, at times restless, and at times groaning with fear. Three times she awakened and three times he lulled her back to sleep by stroking her back and telling her that he would never leave her side. When the sun began its climb up the eastern horizon, Scott was still awake with dry, staring eyes gaping with anxiety.

At breakfast, he gently inquired from Sara if she would like to visit her Aunt Jane or her grandparents. He did not have to wait for an answer because Sara's eyes said it all before she uttered a word.

"Sara, Baby, wouldn't you like to visit Grandma Bradford or Grandma Thornton?"

"No."

"How about Aunt Jane and her friend Flora?"

"No."

"What would you like to do today?"

"Stay with you."

"Would you like to go somewhere?"

"No."

"It's Sunday and the sky is all bright and ready for

you. Is there any one you'd like to see today?"

"No."

"Wouldn't you like to see Mom? How about if we take her out to lunch?"

"I'm scared of Mom."

"But Mommy loves you."

"Uh-huh."

"Oh, by the way, Monday you get to go back to school and see all your friends. Are you excited about it?

"Uh-huh."

Scott, though unhappy about Sara's fear of Nancy, was relieved that she was at least willing to go back to school, which would allow him to return to work. But, he was in a quandary as to what to do with Sara at 5:30 p.m. There had to be a way out of this siege but he couldn't find it. He thought of returning to the bench for a good idea but changed his mind when he remembered that on Sunday the cemetery would be full of visitors. Staying in the house was beginning to make him nervous but he could tell that Sara was not eager to go out yet. For lack of a better idea, he called Nancy.

"Good morning. How was your night?"

"I slept well because it's quiet here."

"Oh, I see. Well, would you like to join us for lunch somewhere?"

"I'm not sure."

"But, Nancy, you'll have to get with Sara sooner or later. Why not get started today? We all need to get over our fears and Sunday is a good day for fellowship."

"I'm not ready, Scotty, not after what happened yesterday."

"Nothing happened yesterday."

"Have you already forgotten the humiliating interrogation I suffered at my salon? That DHS bitch did a number on me that I will never forget."

"She was just doing her job. She has nothing personal against you."

"Oh, shut up Scotty. I can't get her out of my mind. What if the district attorney orders me to attend six months of child neglect classes before I am deemed safe to be alone with Sara?"

"Child neglect classes? What are you talking about?"

"I'm not as dumb as you think. I made a few calls to some of my clients who had had encounters with DHS and they assured me that I'll most likely be ordered to go to child neglect classes."

"I had no idea."

"What do you care? You are a hero now and I'm just a neglectful tramp."

Before Scott could counter, Nancy hung up, leaving him with more questions than he could manage. There was no one that Sara was willing to be with and without a sitter he wouldn't be able to go to the bench. That was Scott's quandary when his brain stormed and handed him the saving idea. He walked up to Sara who was entertaining herself in the living room with her blindfold game and whispered in her ear, "Baby, would you stay with Ms. Debbie for an hour while Daddy goes on an errand this evening?"

"Uh-huh."

"You wouldn't mind?"

"I like Ms. Debbie."

"How come?"

"She likes me."

"Are you sure she likes you?"

"Uh-huh."

"How do you know that?"

"She was nice to me."

Scott called Ms. Hunt's cell phone. The time was about 11 a.m. When she didn't answer, he hung up without leaving a message. *"She could be in church,"* he thought. *"I should have left a message. Why am I shaking? Why is my mouth dry? I'll wait a while and call again. I don't know anything about her. She could be married with kids of her own. How can I ask her such a favor? I must be mad. I better call again and leave her a detailed message. If she can't do it, then she won't call back. Good. That'll give her time to decide. I'd better call now before she gets out of church."*

When Scott called again, Debbie Hunt answered.

"Ms. Hunt?"

"Yes."

"This is Scott Thornton."

"Oh, hi. Is Sara all right?"

"Yes, yes, she's fine."

"Anything wrong?"

"No, not really."

"Well, is there anything I could help you with?"

"Well, I was hoping you could if you don't think it's improper."

"I don't think that heroes do improper things."

"You're too kind. I need, I need a baby, I mean I need a babysitter today from 5:30 till 6:30."

"I see. Would you like me to help you find one?"

"I don't think Sara's ready to be with a stranger. She's still very frightened."

"How about relatives?"

"I have already tried; she won't even consider her grandparents or my sister."

"Why not?"

"She's ashamed of her bald head and doesn't want them to see it."

"I see your problem. Have you asked her if there's anyone she doesn't mind being with?"

"Uh-huh."

"Well. What did she say?'

"She wants you."

"Me?"

"Only you."

"Oh, let me see. Ah, you caught me by surprise now. Well, I don't have plans this evening. Oh, no, I do have something but it can wait. For Sara's sake, I'll be happy to do it. What time would you like me to show up?"

"Could you come at about five? I promise, it won't take long."

"Glad to do it, Mr. Thornton. I'll be there at five."

When Scott hung up, Sara was eyeing him with a

wry smile, much too adult for her baby face. Her expression so took him by surprise and caused him to return a feigned smile from underneath his frowning brow. He must have appeared comical to Sara judging by her hearty giggles, which accompanied her as she skipped out of the room.

"Does this child know something I'm not aware of? Why is she so tickled at me? And why am I getting nervous as if I'm about to go on my first date? This strange situation has gotten out of hand but I have no choice; I have to go to the bench and Ms. Hunt is the only babysitter acceptable to Sara. Why? Because she was nice to her? I wonder if that meant that Nancy was not as nice? Oh, what a tormented life we all seem to lead."

The time till Ms. Hunt's arrival snailed. Scott tried to fill it with meaningful activities such as going out for a car ride or for lunch but Sara declined, saying that she was happy to stay home. They talked, played games, and then Scott had a good idea that he cunningly executed.

"Baby."

"Uh-huh."

"Don't you want to visit your grandmas and grandpas? They miss you and they'd love to see you."

Sara did not answer and her face became visibly distressed.

"What is it, Baby?"

Sara put her hands over her bald head and whispered, "I don't, I don't want them to see me like this."

"I see. If you could visit them without being seen, would that be okay?"

"Daddy, you're silly."

"But if you could, would you?"

"Uh-huh."

Without a word, Scott dialed his parents' home.

"Good morning Mom."

"Oh, Scotty, so good to hear from you. How is Sara?"

"She's fine, Mom, and she'd like to talk to you."

When Scott handed the phone to Sara, she did not demur. Instead, she gleamed as she took the phone and began a charming conversation with Jill Thornton, who was overjoyed to visit with her granddaughter before she gave the phone to Howard. The conversation with Grandpa was equally nurturing, leaving Scott much relieved at having reconnected Sara with her grandparents.

When this experiment proved successful, Scott repeated it with Peter and Francis Bradford with an equally joyful exchange. The last call to Aunt Jane proved a bit awkward. Flora was the one who answered and, with a hesitant voice, said that Jane was not available at the moment. When Scott inquired as to her whereabouts Flora began to cry and told Scott that they had had an argument and were most likely going to split up after more than 12 years of being together. When astonished Scott asked why, Flora mumbled that Jane had been having an affair for a while and that it had finally come to a head yesterday when she confronted Jane.

"Oh, Flora, I'm so sorry to hear that. I think of you as my sister."

"And I think of you as my brother, Scotty."

"Have you ever met the other woman?"

"No but Jane told me a little about her yesterday."

"Oh, that breaks my heart to hear."

"She's in her thirties and I guess she's pretty."

"Prettier than you?"

"She's not fat; I'm certain about that."

"What does that have to do with anything?"

"You know how Jane is. She has a perfect figure and I think that I was starting to embarrass her."

"What does that lady do?"

"She works for the DHS."

"Oh?"

"And her name is Debbie."

"Oh, really?"

"I'm sorry Scotty, all this talk and I've not even asked you about Sara."

"Sara is fine and getting better day by day. She just talked to her grandparents and I was wanting her to talk to her aunt."

"Jane has her cell phone and she'd love to talk to Sara."

"Do you think she's in church?"

"No. She told me she was meeting Debbie for lunch."

"What Debbie?"

"Debbie Hunt, her secret lover."

Scott did not call Jane's cell phone. His mind was busy reassembling the facts. *"No wonder she seemed so comfortable with Sara and me and acted like she already knew us. Jane must have told her a lot about us. Now I understand why she accepted to baby-sit without much hesitation and didn't mind working Sara's case on Saturday. It all makes sense now."*

Sara, who had heard the conversation, had a few questions of her own about Aunt Jane, which Scott settled tactfully. Then he thought that they might surprise Nancy by just showing up at her apartment and taking her out to lunch anyway.

"Baby. How about if we surprise Mom, pick her up, and take her out to lunch."

"No."

"Oh, come on Baby. Let's do it and see if it works."

"No."

"But why?"

"I'm afraid of that place."

"What place? Oh, I see. Well, what if we ask her to meet us somewhere?"

"No."

"But she's your mother. You can't avoid her forever."

"Uh-huh."

"Let's call her and see if she's changed her mind."

"No."

"Well what is it that you'd like to do then?"

"Stay home."

"Now, Baby, you need to conquer your fears and you can't do that by staying home."

"Uh-huh."

"So, how about lunch at a nice place?"

"With lots of people around?"

"Yes. Lots of people."

"And you'll be with me all the time?"

"All the time."

"Okay, I'll go."

Chapter Twenty-Seven
(Back To Iraq)

Scott and Sara spent a nice afternoon having lunch, driving about, and talking. They even talked about her hair and how long it would take to grow back. Then Scott suggested that she might want to don a hat until her hair grows back. The idea struck a nerve in Sara because her eyes quickened and she became suddenly animated.

"What is it, Baby?"

Sara put her hands on her head and said nothing.

"Would you like us to go hat shopping?"

"Uh-huh."

"I happen to know that the children's section at Dillard's has a nice hat selection. How about it?"

"Uh-huh."

On their way to Dillard's, Scott drove in front of Sara's school and without saying a word slowed down and keenly observed her face. With hands back on her head, she tranced as she gazed at the large steel gate with *St. Helena* emblazoned on it. Her blinking eyes peered into the schoolyard with a mélange of eagerness and trepidation. It reminded Scott of the stage-fright look that wears the faces of first-time actors in a school play. After the car drove past *St. Helena* Sara's hands slowly dropped back into her lap as she inquired with a sighing, almost woeful whisper, "Would they let me wear my hat at school?"

"You would be the most elegant preschooler the school has ever known."

"Elegant?"

"Everyone loves a girl with a hat."

"Really?"

"Oh, yes, my little darling. You'll be the talk of the school."

"And they won't make fun of me?"

"No way. They'll envy you. You might even start a school fashion."

"You mean like a model?"

249

"Just like a model, Baby. Like a lovely model out of a fashion magazine."

Sara walked out of Dillard's wearing her hat, sat in the car wearing her hat, went into the house wearing her hat, and went to bed wearing her hat. The confidence imparted by the hat was discernable in her sudden, carefree attitude, her twinkling eyes scouting for flattery, and her rejuvenated eagerness to explore rather than withdraw. Her meek voice became assertive, her play dynamic, her motions brisk, and her recluse shyness was transmuted into exuberant alacrity. The metamorphosis was so rapid that it took Scott by storm and whirled his mind into a dervish state. He felt uplifted, grateful, and mystified. *"How could a hat do all of that? Reminds me of Samson's tale. Take her hair away and her powers are gone. Cover her head and her powers are back. Could God be telling me something? There's a strong message here for me to heed. What is it, though? Dear God, what does all this mean?*

Without being aware of it, Scott began to pray. His lips mumbled unintelligibly and his numinous vision gleamed a reality incredible to the unfaithful. He did not even attempt to understand this new dimension that he was guiltlessly traversing because it had warmed up his heart with its unearthly bliss. To understand is to have one's questions answered but since no one questions Godly feelings, no one seeks to understand them either. They are welcomed gifts that descend upon us from a holy height and we adopt them wholeheartedly with awe and gratitude.

A feeling of subdued elation suffused the house as Scott and Sara afternooned in huddled quietude among whispering conversations and frivolous activities. Together, oblivious of the external world around, they played in peaceful harmony as if they were age mates magically poised somewhere between childhood and adulthood. That was Sara and Scott's state of mind when they were startled from their tranquil reverie by the intrusive tolling of the doorbell. Furtive time, unnoticed, had sped and brought at five o'clock sharp Ms. Debbie Hunt to their front door.

This time, Sara did not scream when she heard the doorbell ring. Instead, she just froze behind her gaping eyes as she watched Scott scurry to the door and usher Debbie Hunt in. At Ms. Hunt's sight, Sara quickly thawed out, her eyes softened, and her face took on a warm, welcoming blush. Unlike their formal first encounter, this time Ms. Hunt came in wearing jeans and a baseball cap and instead of the briefcase she was holding a basket-full of children's books in her hand. It took little introduction and no time for the hatted girls to sit together on the living room sofa and begin reading. No grieving goodbyes were exchanged before Scott left, no lingering embraces detained him at the door, and no last words of instruction were whispered in Ms. Hunt's ears. In fact, when Scott left he was scarcely noticed by the merry couple who carried on unaware of the surprised look that straddled his face all the way to his car.

On his way to the Memorial Park Cemetery Scott briefly reflected on the welcome change that Ms. Hunt had brought to Sara's world. Their anachronistic camaraderie fascinated him and occupied his mind, a welcomed distraction from the heavy-hearted feelings that assailed him as he drove to his bench rendezvous. *"What did Ms. Hunt do to win Sara's heart?"* he wondered. *"She's kind, gentle, attentive, graceful, and loving. But does that imply that Nancy was not? Does that mean that Sara was hungry for such attention because she never got it from her own mother? Could it be that Nancy treated Sara well only when I was around and that, during my two-year sojourn in Iraq, she failed to nurture Sara with enough love? Could it be that Nancy never really loved Sara because she was her un-wanted child, the child that she wished to abort but was bribed into having by my promise of marriage?"*

These were Scott's preoccupying thoughts as he parked his car and walked towards the bench with a cottonmouth and a fluttering heart. Subliminally, during his long excogitation in the car, a restless voice from within nagged at him to guess the reason behind his rendezvous with Peckford. As a soldier, however, it was more instinctive for him to obey and go to where he was summoned rather than wonder why. Nevertheless, in spite of his unwillingness to explore the reasons, he knew that deep inside his fluttering heart there lurked a dormant fear that was about to be awakened. This heavy realization accompanied him like a shadow as he hesitantly trod the pebbled path towards the bench.

In the distance, half-concealed by the waning autumn light, he could see the sitting figure of a man wearing a light brown jacket over a khaki shirt and pants. The poise and calm of the sitting form became unmistakably clear to Scott's blinking eyes as he neared the bench.

"Sit down, Scotty. So good to see you my boy."

"I thought, I thought you were in Beirut."

"I was but had to return."

"Trouble, Sir?"

"Big trouble, Scotty."

"Oh, it's that serious?"

"It is, my boy, and we need your help again."

"Me? What can I do?"

"We need you to just look around and see if you can identify someone for us."

"Identify someone? Where Sir?"

"In Baghdad."

"Oh. You mean I've got to go back to Iraq?"

"I'll have to take you back Scotty, but just for a few days."

Shocked at what he had just heard, Scott looked into Peckford's deep-green eyes and was mesmerized by their ominous, fixating gaze.

"But Sir..."

"We have been infiltrated by Al-Qaeda and we think that the infiltration is from within the US/Iraqi Transition Committee. It's a high-level infiltration that is stifling our efforts to train the Iraqi police force and transfer power to the Iraqi government. Al-Qaeda has been too successful lately in its hits on the Iraqi forces."

"And you think that I can help, Sir?"

"You're the only one who can, my boy."

"The only one, Sir?"

"You are the only survivor of the catacomb massacre. Johnny, Tim, and Frank were all killed and you're the only living soul who saw their killers' faces."

"But all the killers are dead, Sir."

"Not all of them, Scotty. Do I need to remind you that there were six and we only found five? We have reason to believe that the one who escaped is a member of the Committee and we need you to attend the upcoming meeting and identify him for us. As soon as you do that you can go back to Sara."

"Do you think that's why they kidnapped Sara?"

"You got it, Soldier. Communications always sits in on the Transition Committee meetings and Al-Qaeda didn't want you back because they knew that you might recognize him as soon as you saw him."

"What if he doesn't show up for the meeting?"

"He will if they think that you're still here and he won't if they get wind that you're back. That's why no one should know."

"You think that my life is in danger, Sir?"

Peckford sighed and looked away to hide his face. The moments droned while Scott stared at his shoes and Peckford breathed into the shadows of a conversation that had gone awry. Then after a cough, when Peckford turned back to face Scott, his eyes were almost dry but his expression was still an ineffable mixture of sternness and pain.

"You are a hero, Scotty. You have saved Sara when we couldn't do it and exposed one Al-Qaeda cell that we would have never discovered. Because of you, we have arrested four men and one woman and they're talking..."

"Talking, Sir?"

"They're giving us vital information Scotty, information that will lead to the dismantling of almost all the Al-Qaeda cells in the US."

"Oh, really Sir, and all that because I happened to

find Sara."

"Really, my boy."

Saying that, Peckford patted Scott's shoulder, cleared his throat, and with a dry voice continued.

"You have such bountiful humility, Scotty, that you misestimate your worth. Single-handedly you have broken the chain that we couldn't break and for that we are forever grateful and most proud that you're one of us."

"I had no idea, Sir. I was just trying to find Sara."

"I know what you mean, my boy, but do you really understand what I mean?"

"Not exactly, Sir."

Peckford breathed an exasperated sigh and, looking straight into Scott's face, explained.

"In saving Sara and exposing this Al-Qaeda cell you have become a national hero. You are on your way to fame and you don't even realize it. Just wait and you'll see what will happen when you return from Iraq this time."

Not knowing what to say and not sure that he really understood Peckford's concept of heroism, Scott became restless and without further thought blurted out the question, "When do we leave, Sir?'

"Tomorrow morning."

"But what about Sara?"

"The Committee meets on Tuesday morning. You have to be there a few hours before to be briefed and readied. They'll be changing your appearance to make you unrecognizable and your nametag will carry your operational name, James Belford. You'll be sitting in the background as a US reporter."

"But what about Sara, Sir?"

"Ms. Hunt will keep Sara while you're gone."

"You know about Ms. Hunt?"

"She's one of us, Scotty and she's already been to Iraq. She's one of our bilingual social workers who helped organize the Iraqi Women's League."

"She speaks Arabic?"

"Her mother is Iraqi; she came here as a student and married one of our Tinker Air Force men, a Captain."

"You mean…"

"We were the ones who assigned Debbie to your case."

"Oh…"

Bedazzled, Scott scratched his head and rubbed his eyes. Too much information had been suddenly downloaded into his brain and he needed time to internalize the facts. Peckford, realizing that, waited until Scott was partially recovered before he continued.

"We leave at 8 a.m. from Tinker Air Force Base. Park your car outside tonight for all to see. Ms. Hunt will drive her car into your garage tomorrow morning. Close the garage door before you transfer your duffle bag into her trunk. She will then drive you and Sara to her home, park her car in the garage, and close the garage door before you get out with your duffle bag. She then will tell you how to get to Tinker's Gate 5 without being noticed and we'll pick you up from there. You only have to prepare Sara. Debbie Hunt, as your CW worker, will handle all the rest. Not a soul should know, Scotty, not even Nancy or your parents. While you're gone, Sara will not be going to school and her teacher will be told that you took her away on a one-week vacation. Mr. McMaster and your coworkers will be told the same story and so will Jane, Flora, Nancy, and all the grandparents."

"You know about Flora? Sir, this is quite overwhelming."

"We cannot allow Al-Qaeda to infiltrate us, Scotty, and you're the man who can put an end to it."

"And you want me to pose as a reporter? I'm a soldier, Sir. I know nothing about reporting."

"You'll be briefed and outfitted en route and you'll be in role by the time we arrive."

"I'm both sad and happy, Sir. Is that possible?"

"I'm sad and happy too, Scotty. I'm happy to see you and happy that you've found Sara."

"And what are you sad about, Sir?"

"I'm sad because I'm taking you back to Iraq and away from your daughter when she most needs you.

Baghdad is a dangerous place, Scotty, but I'll have to suffer it until my job is done. Nothing gold can stay."

"What does that mean, Sir?"

"It's a poem by Robert Frost that reminds us that the golden moments of life are very transient."

Hearing that, Scott rubbed his eyes again and lowered his head.

"Come now, Scotty. Soldiers don't cry."

"Would you please say it Sir?"

"Say what, my boy?"

"The poem about golden moments."

"It'll make you more sad to hear it."

"How can I be more sad, Sir?'

"I may not be able to recall it."

"Oh, you know it, Sir. You know it like you know all these other Greek and Latin proverbs that you taught me. I'd like to hear it, Sir. Can you please say it?"

Peckford hesitated, cleared his throat, and with a moist voice whispered into the harking, graveyard air:

> *"Nature's first green is gold*
> *Her hardest hue to hold*
> *Her early leaf is a flower*
> *But only so an hour*
> *Then leaf subsides to leaf*
> *As heaven sank to grief*
> *As dawn goes down to day*
> *Nothing gold can stay."*

After the poem, silence eased the evening into the night and sent the patriots on their ways home. When Scott arrived, Sara and Ms. Hunt were still at play, oblivious of time and place. He sat next to them on the sofa, took the book from Ms. Hunt's hands, and announced to Sara that he was going to tell her a magical story, a story that was so new that it had not even been written. Then, looking into Ms. Hunt's all-knowing, deep-green eyes, he began: "There was once a golden country that needed the help of one of her very special soldiers because it was slowly turning green and he was the only one who could turn it back into gold..."

When, the story ended, Sara looked into her dad's eyes and with a resigned face asked, "Are you going back to Iraq, Daddy?"

"Oh, no my princess. I'm through with Iraq. I just need to go away on a small business trip. I'm representing the Hartland Bank at a financial meeting in Washington, DC. I'll be back within a week and then we'll never be separated ever again."

Sara's face became contorted with fear at the news and her blinking eyes looked pleadingly to Ms. Hunt.

"Sara, would you like to stay with me while your dad is away? We'll have such a good time together and I won't have to go to work because my vacation starts tomorrow."

Sara suddenly lit up as she looked to her dad for approval. "Please, Daddy, can I stay with Ms. Debbie while you're gone?"

"Well, don't you think that we should give your mom the first choice?"

Sara's eyes brimmed instantly and she violently shook her head, sprinkling her tears all over the sofa. Scott pulled her into his lap and as she pouted whispered into her ear, "You can stay with Ms. Debbie and since she's on vacation, you can be on vacation too."

"You mean that I don't have to go back to school all of next week?"

"All of next week, my love."

"Will that be enough time for my hair to grow back?"

"If you eat and sleep well, it just might grow that fast."

Smiles quickly replaced tears as Sara listened to Debbie and Scott make Monday's plans. Debbie would pick them up at six and take them to her place. Scott would sneak out from Debbie's backdoor onto a back street where a taxi would be waiting to take him to the airport.

That night, Sara slept but Scott's eyes never shut. Peckford's words—*Baghdad is a dangerous place, Scotty, but I'll have to suffer it until my job is done. Nothing gold can stay*—played doleful music for his dreamless soul. His imagination burned with acid fear as he contemplated all the possible risks awaiting Peckford and him. A frequent Peckford quote popped into his mind, gave him encouragement, and kept him company because it was coined by Helen Keller, a deaf-blind American woman who refused to surrender her life to doom and despair, "Security in nature is a superstition. Life is either a daring adventure or nothing."

Chapter Twenty-Eight
(Dread)

The City Of Peace was its official name when in 762 Al-Mansour built it on the west bank of the Tigris. He employed a hundred thousand architects, craftsmen, and laborers and completed it in four years. The site was chosen because of its strategic location between the Tigris and Euphrates, and was actually the location of an old Sasanid village, *Baghdad*, meaning *given by God*. The ancient ruins of the adjacent Sasanid capital Ctesiphon provided Baghdad with stones. In that same valley, which had furnished sites for some of the mightiest capitals of the ancient world such as Babylon, Nineveh, and Ur, thrived the new city. In a few years—given the reaches of the Tigris to China and the Euphrates to the Mediterranean—it became an international center of great political and commercial importance, its degree of splendor and prestige rivaled only by the mighty Constantinople.

The old *City Of Peace*, capital of the Abbasid Caliph Al-Mansour, site of Shahrazad's legendary adventures, *The Thousand and One Nights,* was the city of war to Scott's dreamful mind. That Sunday night, while Sara slept with her vacation dreams Scott slept with his Baghdad nightmares. Too much had happened too quickly and his mind was busy putting things in order with its laborious dream work. On several occasions Scott found himself sitting at the edge of his bed, holding his head between both hands, staring at his feet, and wondering if he would be able to recognize the infiltrator. The trauma of the beheadings had cauterized certain regions of his brain, charred some ugly details, and rendered certain facts irretrievable by interring them beyond the reaches of memory.

Sara woke up early before sunrise because her mind was teeming with new excitement. She, being used to her dad preceding her in rising, felt especially privy to find him still asleep and decided to entertain herself by counting his breaths. As her clandestine activity progressed she noted that his breathing was becoming rapid and interrupted by choking sounds. Feeling scared she reached for her dad's throat as if to un-choke it. This well-meant, gentle act triggered a violent cry out of Scott as he gripped Sara's hand, shoved her away, and sat up gasping for breath.

Sara's tears could not be assuaged nor her fear appeased. In a desperate act of self-defense she locked herself in the bathroom and would not come out. Scott, having quickly recovered from his violent confusion, tried to reassure his fear-locked Sara by using his entire repertoire of fatherly skills. But, regardless of his persuasive efforts, her irrational mind prevailed, rendering her impenetrable to her father's pleas. This was the state of affairs when Scott, still in his pajamas, opened the door for Ms. Hunt.

"You forgot to open the garage door. It's six o'clock."

"Come in, please, we have a crisis."

"Oh?"

"Sara has locked herself in the bathroom."

"Why? What happened?"

"She put her hand on my throat when I was having a nightmare. I thought I was being beheaded so I let out a shout, grabbed her hand, and shoved her away. This must have frightened her beyond reason because she's no longer responding to me."

"Oh, poor girl. Shoving her must have rekindled bad memories. She must've been shoved a time or two before; otherwise she wouldn't have acted that way. Let me see what I can do."

Ms. Hunt walked behind Scott into the bedroom, stood by the bathroom door, and with a sweet, playful voice began talking to Sara.

"It's time for us girls to start our vacation. Are you getting yourself ready?"

"No."

"Would you like me to help you get ready?"

"Uh-huh."

"Well, how do I get in?"

"Through the door."

"But the door is locked."

"Uh-huh."

"Would you like me to open it?"

"Uh-huh."

Scott was ready with a clothes-hanger wire, which he used to probe the door. As the door popped open, he saw Sara's shadow crouched in the bathroom corner like a chicken before a fox. While he waited in the bedroom Debbie walked in with some of Sara's clothes in her hand and, as if nothing had happened, proceeded to help Sara get dressed while cheerfully talking about the vacation week awaiting them. As Sara mellowed down Debbie became more animated and, when the two emerged from the bathroom, Sara had her clothes on and wore a shaky smile over her worried face.

While Scott hurriedly dressed, Debbie parked her car inside the garage, closed the door, and put Sara's suitcase in the trunk. Within ten minutes, all packed and ready, they left in Debbie's car according to plan and arrived at Debbie's home at six-thirty a.m. During the ride, many a furtive glance was exchanged between Debbie and Scott while Sara sat quietly in her car seat looking out the window. As soon as they walked into Debbie's living room, and before anyone could sit down, Debbie motioned to Scott to take his leave. He knelt by Sara, put her hand on his throat, and said, "I'll miss you baby but when I return I'll have some nice surprises for you. Washington is full of goodies."

"Uh-huh."

"Will you miss me?"

"Uh-huh."

"I love you."

"Uh-huh."

With duffle bag in hand Scott gazed one more time into Debbie's deep-green eyes as one would gaze at a lush, familiar landscape before leaving it. Then, with a querying mind, he disappeared through the back door. Sara and

Debbie wasted no time. They collaborated on preparing breakfast and began to plan their vacation week together. They planned to go out every day, shop, read books, tell bedtime stories, and play all sorts of games.

Their first day passed effortlessly, without much turmoil, and at no time did Sara mention her mom or her dad. She behaved as though Debbie was her only parent and was quite content to be alone with her. It did not escape Debbie, a social worker trained in child abuse, that Scott's startled shove of Sara was all that it took to add him to her fear list. The very one who had risked his life to save hers had become, by the nightmarish devices of his own fears, the fomenter of hers.

It was futile of Debbie to try to exorcise Sara's sudden dread of her dad. She already knew that fear possessed an eerie logic of its own, a delusional ideology that did not respond to the reassuring finger-strokes of reason. Knowingly, she played along, not mentioning Scott to Sara, and hoping that by the time he returned she would have forgotten that single, frightening incident that had shattered their détente. Shoving must have sparked a powerful cue in Sara's flammable mind, a cue that set her old fears ablaze and sent her newfound security up in smoke.

There was work to be done, skillful, tacit work to un-ruffle the unconscious storms that mercilessly hurled their lightning bolts onto Sara's unsuspecting mind. Debbie Hunt, who saw her week with Sara as a chance to redeem the little girl's mind from the fray of fear, spent the first night half-awake with Sara's case albatrossed around her neck. Scott was Sara's only chance at a normal life and if she did not let go of her fear of him she would end up with no life to live and no home. Debbie agonized over Sara's predicament with a heart made soft by all the wretched children she had seen and was unable to help. Sara, on the other hand, was salvageable and it was up to Debbie to do the saving. There had to be a way, a method, some psychological ploy by which to help this fallen robin unto her nest again. The words of Emily Dickinson resonated with her heartbeats, as she lay deep in thought after her first full day with Sara:

> *"If I can stop one heart from breaking*
> *I shall not live in vain*
> *If I can ease one life the aching*
> *Or cool one pain*
> *Or help one fainting robin*
> *Unto his nest again,*
> *I shall not live in vain."*

The study of fear had been a life-long interest of Debbie Hunt ever since her college days. It all began when her professor of psychology, Dr. Kosbine, assigned the class a list of topics to choose from as titles for their course papers. When none of the suggested topics appealed to her, she went back to the professor and asked him if she could write her paper on fear. The idea so astonished Dr. Kosbine that he asked her to explain the reason behind such a peculiar choice. Standing at his desk like a guilty child before a father, she suddenly became dumbfounded, began to shake, and her contorted face teetered on the brink of tears. Seeing her sudden surge of transference, the professor asked her to sit down, folded his arms, lowered his eyes, and patiently awaited her explanation.

A long silence loomed as she tried to compose herself and reorganize her thoughts. While he waited, her mouth went dry, she fidgeted, clenched her sweaty palms, and made several attempts to swallow but without success. Noting her dysphagia, the professor brought her a glass of water and that gentle act of kindness was all it took for her to break down in a torrent of tears. Still, Dr. Kosbine neither cleared his throat nor spoke; he simply sat behind his desk with folded arms, a doleful expression upon his face, and patiently awaited her catharsis.

When she was able to speak, she began by telling him that he was going to be the first person to hear her story, a story that no other living soul had ever heard. Then, in the quivering quietude of his office, she told him of her date rape. It was her first date. She was fourteen and the boy had just gotten his driver's license. They went to his parents' lake cabin and drank beer. He was drunker than she was when he raped her in spite of her violent protestations and desperate pleadings. On the way home with torn clothes and bruised faces, they hit a deer, swerved off the road, and fell into a deep creek. The boy was instantly killed and she never had to explain her torn clothes or bruised face to anybody. Because of that doubly traumatic incident, she developed a fearful mistrust of men, never went out on a date again, and never drank.

The catharsis from having unveiled her adolescent fear for the first time granted her an emancipating sense of relief. When the kind professor walked her to the door the only words he said were, "You do need to write about fear, my dear, and I can't wait to read your paper." Later on, she learned that the professor had added fear to his list of suggested topics and that in subsequent classes more students chose to write about fear than any other subject. What she neither told her professor, nor anyone else for that matter, was that it was her fear of men that caused her to prefer the non-threatening company of women.

Given her experiences, it was not surprising that Debbie Hunt chose fear as the subject of her Master of Arts thesis. She entitled her paper *On Fear*, and subtitled it *The Backache of the Post Traumatic Stress Disorder Syndrome*. While writing her manuscript, she was struck by the inadequacy of fear terminology and the poverty of fear research. This reinforced her belief that fear, the most pernicious force within the human psyche, had not been deemed worthy of scholarly study by the academic psychology departments of the day. In her efforts to reverse this tacit curfew and bring fear research under the lights of academic theaters, she consulted the medical terminology texts, which derive their nomenclatures from Greek and Latin roots. There, in the Greco-Roman alcoves of the Medical Sciences Library, she found her needed terms.

To describe the fear explosion that can be sparked by the most menial of cues, she borrowed the word *anaphylaxis*. This compound word derives from the Greek *an* "without" and *phylaxis* "protection". It was coined by the French physiologist Charles Richet to indicate the exaggerated reaction of an organism to foreign protein. This malapropism suited her needs far better than the banal term, *panic attack*, and from its root she borrowed two other sorely needed terms. She used the term *tachyphylaxis* from the Greek *tachys* "rapid" to indicate that repetitive exposure to cues can cause a reduction in fear and considered the epithet more apropos than the common variety term, *exposure therapy*. The term *prophylaxis* from the exact Greek word meaning "an advance guard" she used to indicate that the avoidance of cues, given enough time, could also reduce fear through memory erosion.

After graduation, Ms. Hunt's interest in fear was instrumental in directing her career. Her first job as a social worker was at the VA hospital in Oklahoma City. It came about when one of her professors suggested that she might continue her study of fear by working with the war-shocked veterans returning from Afghanistan and Iraq. Being a Vietnam War veteran himself with myriad good connections, he wrote a letter of recommendation to the VA Chief of Staff who interviewed and hired her two weeks later. Her hiring, however, was contingent on her spending one year in Iraq because there was greater need for her kind of work in Baghdad than in Oklahoma City. It was in Baghdad that she collaborated with Captain Theodore Peckford and, through him, helped train the Iraqi Women Volunteers to take care of Baghdad's orphaned, war-shocked children.

She was especially effective because she taught in Arabic and her lectures had a profound and lasting impact. In the syllabus, which she prepared especially for the Iraqi Women Volunteers, there were chapters on Fear Shock, Fear Dynamics, Fear Recognition, Fear Therapy, and Fear Prevention. By the time she left, she had a sizable following and was direly missed by all who knew her, especially Captain Peckford with whom she had had many a deep, psychological discussion.

When she returned to the VA Hospital she became involved in several child abuse cases committed by some of the shell-shocked veterans that she was working with. It was during that brief period that she became convinced that child abuse is a chain reaction whereby the powerless abused of today became the powerful abusers of tomorrow. Influenced by her own experiences and by Karl Menninger's proverbial observation that "What we do to our children, they will do to society," her calling gradually shifted from working with traumatized veterans to working with traumatized children. After much soul searching, she resigned her position at the VA Hospital and went to work for the DHS in the Child Welfare section.

Her eventful background coupled with her passionate dedication to abused children made her quickly stand out among her DHS peers. It was not surprising then, given her professional assets, that Peckford inclined her superiors to assign her to Sara Thornton's case without her knowing that he had anything to do with it. Other ramifications such as her devout friendship with Scott's sister Jane and her hero worship of Scott and Peckford were conveniently coincidental and proved most useful for Debbie Hunt's powerful bonding with the Thornton family.

After her first day with Sara, Debbie Hunt, the inveterate student of fear, sat in deep contemplation by Sara's side. Over and over, she rehearsed the details of how she planned to exorcise fear out of Sara's heart, especially her sudden-onset fear of her father. As a veteran student-and-victim of fear, she had great respect for the fierce, life-altering forces that fear could wield upon its victims. She was also well aware that at Sara's impressionable age, such forces might prove stubbornly implacable. Nevertheless, although she had thus far lost her own battles against fear, she was determined not to lose Sara's and toward this end she set her mind to work.

All the time she had at her disposal to affect a change in this innocent child's besieged mind was one miserly week. Entangled in this fear triangle were Sara,

Scott, and herself. But she was the triangle's right angle, the only one who really understood the fierce forces of fear and was qualified to manipulate them. The task at hand was to un-program Sara's fear circuits and to rewire her brain with a new set of connections that were immune to fear. But how to do that, how to conquer the mighty fear giant with a slingshot was the overwhelming question that nagged on Debbie Hunt's mind.

Gazing at Sara's angelic face and listening to her soporific, rhythmic respirations presented an idyllic scene of peaceful serenity to Debbie Hunt's tearless, staring eyes. But what flighty bats clung upside down inside the ventricles of Sara's little brain and how many spark-ready dynamite sticks hid underneath her placid consciousness were deep concerns that piqued Debbie Hunt's insomniac mind. She recalled a discussion that she had had with Peckford in Baghdad on how easy it was to infect the brain with fear and how difficult it was to disinfect it. Peckford likened it to herpes because it took one exposure to acquire it and from that point on it lived off the victim's life, forever residing in his mind. And like herpes it could through contagion linger on beyond the victim's death by infecting others and others ad infinitum...

As evidence, Peckford cited multiple examples of national and cultural fears that had swayed humanity throughout its history such as the Inquisition, which was created in the early thirteenth century, gripped Europe for six-hundred years, crossed over to us in the seventeenth century in the Salem witch-hunt, and continues to tacitly sway mass feeling until today. "Entire cultures," he explained, "are still afraid of many imaginary things and we are no different. Our post-war fear of communism and the insanity of McCarthyism that ensued are but one example of mass hysteria that can infest an entire nation and shake it in its roots."

The realization that fear could be assuaged but might not be expunged created a desperate feeling in Debbie Hunt's heart, a feeling that swelled inside her chest, rendered her air hungry, and caused her to sigh repeatedly but without satisfaction. Petronius's adage, *"Primus in orbe deos fecit timor,"* flickered in front of Debbie's eyes like multi-colored police lights. *"If it were fear in the world that first made gods,"* she thought, *"then let the gods come to my aid and unmake this little girl's fears now."*

Her tearless, staring eyes softened at the realization that she needed her faith in God to help her calm Sara's stormy seas. Instead of bowing her head in prayer she bowed her head until her lips touched Sara's pink, little hand. There upon this soft altar of innocent childhood she gave permission to her tears. She gave permission without ever knowing why—as one would give permission to a horse to gallop off for no other reason than because it wants to. She only came to understand her tears when, before sleep came to her rescue, the last thought that bobbed on her choppy brain waves was, *"Were it not for my fear of men, I could have had a little daughter of my own."*

Chapter Twenty-Nine
(Baghdad)

Scott paid the taxi and walked into Tinker Air Force Base through Gate 5 to find Peckford waiting for him at the guard station. After presenting his papers, a Humvee whisked them to a hanger next to the airport runway. The drive, which could not have taken more than five minutes, seemed like a long, endurance ride through a blistering desert. An intentional silence prevailed throughout the short ride so that the driver would not be privy to any conversation. Peckford, who sat in the front, hardly acknowledged Scott's presence. Scott, on the other hand, was undergoing a violent physical transformation. His heart and breaths were rapid, his skin was sweating profusely, and his mind was vertiginous, swirling underneath a tidal wave of undercurrents. It did not occur to him to think about or explain this sudden transformation; he merely endured its havoc as if it were a well-deserved consequence of some fatal sin that he had committed unaware.

When the Humvee stopped and let its passengers out, Peckford was alarmed at Scott's pallid, soggy skin and drenched clothes. His first thought was that Scott was cowering at the prospect of going back to Iraq but his words of reassurance, "Scotty, no need to worry, you're not going back as a soldier," though penetrated Scott's ears and echoed within his skull, failed to alight upon his consciousness. Scott seemed suspended in a surreal, unearthly halo hovering over but utterly detached from his own body. When they walked into the hangar, Peckford led the way, carrying Scott's duffle bag while Scott tailed behind with blank eyes and stilted limbs.

Peckford remained silent until they entered the airplane and sat down on two adjoining chairs with the duffle bag at their feet. There, he began the conversation with, "Scotty, you're going to be briefed after take off and your identity is going to be temporarily changed from Scott

Thornton to that of a USINN reporter by the name of James Belford."

Scott, from his recluse state of being, did not respond, which alarmed Peckford. He held Scott by the shoulder, shook him violently, and shouted into his ear, "Scotty, come down from wherever you are."

"Uh-huh?"

"Scotty, where are you?"

"Uh-huh?"

"Scotty, are you... Oh, I'm so sorry. Forgive me, please. I didn't even think about it. Oh, how insensitive of me."

"Sorry about what, Sir?"

"About the Humvee."

"Oh, what Humvee, Sir?"

"It brought back bad memories, didn't it?"

"You mean..."

"No more Humvees for you Scotty boy. They carry within them scary mementos from the beheadings."

"Oh, is that it, Sir?"

"That's all it is, my boy. A bad flashback from a time you and I would rather forget."

"But, it was so long ago, Sir."

"Not long enough, my boy. Not long enough. I'm so sorry. I should have paid more attention."

It was merciful that the briefings did not commence right after takeoff because it took Scott another 45 minutes before he finally regained his composure. By the time the special officers began the briefings he was, nevertheless, calm and ready to absorb the information pertaining to his new role as a USINN reporter. And when at last the tedious briefings were over, Scott Thornton reclined in his seat, closed his eyes, and tried to rehearse his new identity as James Belford of New York. It was not unexpected, however, given the previous night's insomnia and the morning's Humvee anaphylaxis that he soon fell into a profound sleep from which he did not awaken until they landed in Baghdad early Tuesday morning.

It was 3 a.m. when they disembarked at Al-

Mansour's war-torn City of Peace and were taken to their respective quarters at the American camp on the outskirts of the city. While Peckford slept, Scott lay awake with fear stabbing at his mind. The Humvee ride exhumed in a flash all his interred memories from the beheadings. That, plus having slept most of the way from Oklahoma City to Baghdad, barred merciful sleep from closing his ajar eyes until the early morning call-to-prayer cracked the shell of dawn and filled the auburn sky with *"Allahu Akbar. La Ilaha Illallah."* The sound of those soothing Koranic chants, those soporific signatures of Islamic cities, tempered his fear and eased his alarm. He did not understand why those echoing, siren calls-for-prayer resounding from the minarets of Baghdad's skyline should have such a tranquilizing effect upon him but he accepted the imparted calm with sincere gratitude. It was during this vouchsafed state of peace that he heard a gentle tapping at his door.

It was Peckford, dressed and ready for the day.

"It's about time, Scotty. The meeting begins at 9 a.m. and you'll have to be there before they start arriving." Having said that with a half-commanding, half-apprehensive tone he handed Scott his reporter's badge with (**James Belford**/**USINN**) boldfaced on it and said, "I can't be seen with you from here on. Agent Leforge will be here soon to make you up with your new disguise so that you won't be recognizable to anyone who might have seen you before. You'll just walk in and take your seat with the other reporters. If they ask you questions, you answer them as you had been instructed during your briefing. Do not volunteer any information and try to be as invisible as possible. Here are your papers and fake ID."

"And what do I do if I should recognize one of the killers?"

"You will do nothing and pretend that you have seen nothing."

"Then how do I tell you so that you can apprehend him?"

"We're not going to apprehend him."

"What?"

"He would be more valuable to us if we do not let Al-Qaeda know that we know."

"So, you want me to identify him and then you're not going to punish him for all that he did?"

"Would you rather punish one man and expose our soldiers to more Al-Qaeda hits? It is far better for us to feed them information that would reduce their effectiveness as a whole and render them more vulnerable to our counter-terrorism efforts."

"Oh, I see. You just want me to identify him and go on as if nothing had happened."

"Indeed, my boy."

"So, how do I inform you when I recognize him?"

"We have cameras everywhere. When you return to camp, you will get to identify him on the screen."

"And what if he doesn't show up for the meeting?"

"It's a very important meeting and we have leaked word that some counter-Al-Qaeda measures will be decided upon after the reporters have been dismissed. Basically, we have let them know that they cannot afford to miss the meeting."

"And after I identify him?"

"After that, my boy, you'll be flown back to Oklahoma City without delay."

"Well, Sir. I think I've got it."

"Go then, Soldier, and do your country one more favor."

The meeting was held at Dar Al-Salam, a high security complex on the outskirts of Baghdad used by Iraqi and American officials for joint meetings. Its outer circles were guarded by uniformed American forces but within its complex, most of the security officers were not uniformed and posed as gardeners, janitors, clerks, and facilitators. Delegates entering the complex had to show their identification badges at the first, second, and third guard stations and had to wear them at all times when they were within the complex. Helicopters guarded the place from the air as cars, from myriad directions, lined up before the first guard station.

Baghdad's November sun was merciful and some earlier rains had turned the arid landscape into green pastureland. There were birds fluttering among the flowers and, with the car windows wide open, birdsong sputtered the air with musical blossoms that belied the subliminal tensions in the atmosphere. The dissonance between nature's music and war's reality struck Scott as a cruel anachronism. A bright idea flashed upon his mind and kept him company throughout the drive from the military camp to the meeting place. *"Only birds are free,"* he mused, *"and none of the flying creatures can be herded by humans. Humans can herd anything else they wish to herd, including other humans, but they cannot herd wild birds. What a grand idea. I must share it with Peckford. Surely, he would agree with me that only birds are free."*

Scott as James Belford, accompanied by two security officers dressed as reporters, entered the complex in an old Toyota SUV, showed their badges at all three guard stations, parked in the designated spaces reserved for reporters, and walked into the building. At the entrance, there was another security checkpoint with metal detectors, just like the ones in airports, followed by a mandatory body search. Shoes had to come off and computers had to be pulled out of their cases. After the search, badges and ID cards were checked one last time before entrance into the meeting room was granted. The entire process was obligatory and applied to all attendees without exception.

The meeting room was underground because Al-Qaeda possessed missiles and could possibly sabotage the meeting with close hits. Scott and his two escorts sat in the space reserved for reporters along the east wall of the room. However, once the escorts had made sure that he was well-situated with a good view of the entire area, they took their leave and disappeared into the incoming crowd. Other reporters trickled in, took their place along the east wall, and commenced to interact among each other with hushed voices. Iraqi, American, British, and French military delegates began to take their designated places around the central table. The atmosphere was solemn and the air was heavy with expectation. Still, among this eclectic hum of men, Scott's scanning eyes saw no one they recognized.

Peculiarly enough, the seat on Scott's right remained vacant while the seat on his left was occupied by an Iraqi reporter who said very little after a hushed exchange of perfunctory greetings. It was when the meeting was called to order by General Jason Arms that Scott, for no discernable reason, began to feel eerie. There was going to be a preliminary meeting delving into generalities followed by a closed-in meeting where reporters would not be allowed. At the end of the preliminary meeting, and before the closed-in meeting was to begin, there would be fifteen minutes allotted for questions.

Scott, who already felt alone in that strange crowd, found himself getting more and more uncomfortable by the minute. He had no one to turn to for reassurance and his uncanny sense of helplessness grew overwhelmingly threatening. As his ears harked for cues and his eyes roamed the room for faces, his heart steadily gripped his chest from within, causing a choking sensation to rise into his already dry throat. Without knowing it, he turned pale and began to hyperventilate. The reticent Iraqi reporter to his left noticed his distress and almost said something to him but refrained because, at that very moment, a tardy reporter furtively entered the room and sank into the place on Scott's right.

As the meeting proceeded, Scott's sense of suffocation reached an alarm level, causing him to begin gasping for air. Oblivious of the fact that the meeting was being held underground, his air-hungry eyes began to surf the room for windows and when he couldn't find any his sense of asphyxiation escalated, making his distressed breathing audible to those around him. The tardy reporter on his right got out of his seat, grabbed a bottle of water from the main table, and handed it to him without saying a word. It was a most welcome balsam to his parched throat, which began to relax its grip as soon as it was moistened by the first swallow. Scott's initial, noisy gulp was followed by subdued swallows and ended in polite, inaudible sips. Grateful at having his voice back, he turned to the tardy reporter on his right to thank him.

He was a tall, handsome man in his thirties with red hair, blue, piercing eyes, a well-trimmed handlebar mustache, and a goatee. His tag carried the name, (**Jonathan Brighton/BBC**). With his pale, sweaty face, Scott must have looked like a ghost when he faced Jonathan Brighton and whispered, "Thanks, Mr. Brighton, I really needed that drink."

"Quite all right, old chap." quipped Jonathan with a heavy British drawl. "Hope you're not falling ill. Baghdad isn't for every bloke, you know."

"I'm finding that out."

"Indeed, it takes a while to get used to it. But, don't worry, you will."

As that short interlocution ended, Scott nodded, feigned a smile, and turned his attention back to the tedious meeting. As he took notes and tried to show interest, his mind had already returned to Oklahoma. He thought of Sara and Debbie Hunt's deep-green eyes, of his colleagues at the Hartland Bank, of Jane and Flora's impending breakup, of Breena Birdsong's white succulent thighs flashing upon his eyes, and of Nancy's un-motherly behavior toward Sara. His entire trip seemed a waste of time because there was no one in the room that he recognized. While these thoughts assailed his turbulent mind the open meeting ended and General Jason Arms, after answering some questions, asked the reporters to leave.

On their way out, as they passed the security checkpoint and were about to disperse, Jonathan Brighton turned to Scott to say goodbye. He was a most gracious man with dignified attitude, slow, calm, poised, and articulate. His demeanor and British accent reminded Scott of Hedrick Lester at the International Foods store. As they shook hands and their eyes met, Scott had a feeling of déjà vu. Something about the voice, the accent, the poise, the blue eyes, reminded him of someone he knew. All he could think of was Hedrick Lester and it might have ended there but for a minor coincidence that piqued his memory.

Walking back toward the old Toyota SUV, the two security officers dressed as reporters joined him as he reached the car. Only this time, instead of sitting by the driver's side, he was asked to sit in the backseat. Sitting alone in the back made Scott feel a bit odd but he surmised that it was a calculated move because the tinted windows made him less visible. As the car bounced its way over the bumpy road back to camp, he became aware that there was a prickly object underneath his left thigh. Feeling under his leg, he found a small, bluish nail, which he picked up and was about to throw out of the window when the strange feeling of déjà vu came back to him. Something about Hedrick Lester, Jonathan Brighton, and a bluish nail pricking him in the thigh intrigued his unconscious but the ensemble made no sense to his conscious mind. Whatever the connection was between the two British-sounding men and the nail, he could not decipher, but it did cause him to put the nail into his pocket instead of throwing it out.

No engaging interlocution transpired during the drive back. The security officers hardly spoke and Scott, who had nothing to say, passed the time by playing mind games. Attempting to find a common thread between Lester, Brighton, and the blue nail proved most amusing. Lester and Brighton both had British accents. Lester had been and Brighton is in Iraq. Both were tall and handsome men. All that was fine and easy to see. But the blue nail, how did it tie into the ensemble? Scott held on to that thought until it finally dawned on him that both men had blue eyes. It was at that very moment, when the Toyota pulled into the camp, that his mind flashed the sword onto his reluctant consciousness.

"Sir, we're here," said one of the officers as he opened the door for Scott. "We have arrived, Sir. Sir? Are you okay? Oh, no, no, don't try to get up, you need to lie down, Sir, just for a few minutes, you're looking awful pale."

Saying that, the officer pushed Scott onto the seat as his eyes rolled back and he fainted. Not knowing what else to do, one of the security officers ran into the camp while the other stayed with Scott until the gurney with two medics arrived. At the clinic, the PA found Scott's blood pressure and heart rate in the normal range and when he asked him to try to stand up, he did without any trouble. When the PA questioned him further, Scott merely said that he was feeling much better and would rather go back to his room than stay under observation. When he got to his room, and before he could close the door, lie down, and try to recollect his thoughts, Peckford came rushing in.

"Scotty, you need some food. That's why you fainted. You've had no food since you left Oklahoma City. Let's go to the officer's mess hall."

"We need to talk, Sir."

"We can talk there."

"No, Sir, we need to talk here. I don't feel like eating."

"I was watching you on the screen. You looked pretty shaken. You must have recognized him."

"I did, Sir, but only after I was on my way back."

"Back in the car? Why did you look so shaken during the meeting, then?"

"That's another story, Sir. I'm not as brave as I thought I was."

"You can't mean that."

"I do, Sir. The closed room underground reminded me of the catacombs and that's all it took for my heart to sink."

"Oh, I see. I didn't think to warn you that these meetings are always held underground."

"I have no control on when I explode, Sir. The slightest cue can do it. It's very frightening."

"I need to keep you away from Baghdad, Soldier. Why don't you tell me what you saw and you can go back tonight on the redeye flight."

"Well, Sir, it was this nail that put it all together for me."

As he said that, Scott pulled the little blue nail out of his pocket and surrendered it, as if it were an object of great military value, to Peckford's incredulous fingers. Holding the nail close to his eyes and inspecting it carefully, Peckford inquired with amazed disbelief, "This silly blue nail put it all together for you?"

"Yes, Sir, it did."

"And how's that, Son?"

"The man who beheaded Johnny and Tim had blue, piercing eyes, Sir, eyes like blue nails and pinned with focus, Sir, and he was a redhead. I didn't recognize him until the nail pricked me in the thigh on the way back. He had grown a handlebar mustache and a goatee. He was the one sitting next to me, Sir. His name is Jonathan Brighton."

"Are you sure, Scotty? Jonathan is one of us and his older brother, Jim, sits on the committee. If you're wrong, we stand to make a terrible mistake. We don't want to offend our British allies."

"I am sure Sir. Sure because he had the same voice, same height, same gentle manners, and same British accent as the one who interrogated us before he decided to execute us."

"Scotty, if you're right, this is a most horribly unsettling truth."

"Sir, have you checked if his mother is Iraqi?"

"Why do you say that?"

"Because he may look like his British father but may have Al-Qaeda loyalties through his mother."

"Where did you get this wild idea from?"

"From Hedrick Lester and Debbie Hunt, Sir. Both have Iraqi mothers."

"And who is Hedrick Lester?"

"The owner of the International Foods store, the one who told me that the Saudis buy incense from him, and that's how I stumbled upon Sara."

"Scotty, you're either hallucinating or else you're smarter than all the rest of us here. Come along with me."

Scott followed Peckford into the operations room and watched him give orders to the one in charge of communications. After some minutes on the computer, the communications guy showed Peckford the screen. Peckford's face blanched as he lowered his head, walked toward Scott, put his hand on his shoulder, and said, "Thanks, Scotty. We shall be forever in your debt."

"Did he have an Iraqi mother, Sir?"

"You are much smarter than all the rest of us here, my boy. You had to come all the way from Oklahoma City to Baghdad to teach us how to think. Indeed, he does have an Iraqi mother, the daughter of a radical cleric who was a devout supporter of Saddam, and she still lives here in Baghdad."

Hearing that, Scott's eyes filled up with peace and a veil of gratitude smoothed his features, replacing the deep furrows with serene smiles. His fisted hands dropped to his sides and opened up like pink hibiscus blooms after a rain. His throat loosened its fist and his saliva flowed into his dry mouth like a cool waterfall. Astonished at his unexpected catharsis, he gazed into Peckford's deep-green eyes and exclaimed with a moist voice throttled with tears, "Oh, Sir, all of a sudden, I'm no longer afraid."

Peckford's furrowed forehead, pondering the magnitude of Scott's discovery, neither heard nor understood the inner meaning of what Scott had just uttered. Speaking loud enough for Scott to hear him, but mostly talking to himself, he murmured, "No wonder, Al-Qaeda knew all of our moves."

"Sir, did you hear what I just said?"

"What did you just say, Soldier?"

"I think, Sir, that my fear has just left me."

"What on earth do you mean by that, Son?"

"What I mean, Sir, is that now, Sir, because we can pay them back, Sir, I'm no longer afraid of being underground, or of having my neck grabbed, or of seeing a sword hang over my head in dreams."

"Oh, I see. Please forgive me. I should have had a deeper understanding of what you were going through. But worry no more, Lieutenant. We'll pay them back in kind. We'll pay them back so that they'll become even more frightened than they already are."

"I thought that they were fearless, Sir. That's how everybody thinks."

"Remember the proverbial words of Epicurus: *'It is impossible for the one who instills fear to remain free from it.'* I've quoted that one to you before, haven't I?"

"I don't remember it, Sir. I wish I had because it would have helped me. Who is Epicurus, Sir?"

"Never mind about Greek philosophy now. You have a daughter waiting for you in Oklahoma City and that's where your mind needs to be."

"I feel hungry, Sir. I think I can eat now."

Late that evening, as Scott was packing his duffle bag, Peckford dropped by to say bon voyage. In his hand he carried a beige scroll, which he presented to Scott.

"This is for you, Soldier."

"What is it, Sir?"

"A small gift from all of us here."

Scott, feeling overwhelmed, un-scrolled the gift not knowing what to expect. Seeing that it was a painting, he laid it on his bed under the light and stood gazing at it with blinking eyes.

"Do you like it, Scotty?"

"Yes, Sir, but I don't understand it."

"It's an oil painting of Baghdad in 1919 done by an English officer who must have been stationed here at the beginning of the British mandate. I bought it at a flea market from one of the locals."

"Baghdad was so beautiful then, Sir, so much more beautiful than Baghdad now. Is the artist famous?"

"I think he was just an amateur painter. I even asked some of our British colleagues and they couldn't identify him either. We could barely decipher his signature because it had faded out but the year, 1919 is still legible. His name was Captain Olen Willis."

"I don't deserve this painting, Sir. I wish you would keep it."

"It belongs to you, Scotty, because one day it will bring great significance into your life."

"How's that, Sir?"

"We live dangerously here, Son. It needs to be in a safer place, where beauty is truth and truth, beauty."

"What does that mean, Sir?"

"It's a famous Keats quote."

"I've heard of Keats, Sir. We studied him in high school."

"He's an English poet who died very young. The quote comes from a poem, *Ode To A Grecian Urn*, that addresses the immortalized men and maidens carved on a marble vase."

"Would you please quote it for me, Sir?"

"Instead of focusing his deep-green eyes on Scott, Peckford gazed at the Baghdad painting, traveled back in time to the year 1919, and recited the last stanza, which frames the quote:

> When old age shall this generation waste,
>   Thou shalt remain, in midst of other woe
> Than ours, a friend to man, to whom thou say'st,
>   "Beauty is truth, truth beauty"—that is all
> Ye know on earth, and all ye need to know."

"I don't understand it, Sir. Truth is often ugly as in Sara's case and beauty is often untruthful as in Nancy's case. So how come he says they are one and the same?"

"He's not talking about life, Son. He's only talking about art. Only in art, Scotty, beauty is truth and truth is beauty. A work of art has to be beautiful to be truthful and has to be truthful to be beautiful."

"Is that why you want me to carry it to a safer and a more peaceful place, Sir?"

"Indeed, Lieutenant, indeed. War is reckless; it destroys indiscriminately, destroys everything in its way including art."

"But that's a very sad thought, Sir."

"Baghdad is a very sad place, my boy, sad for those who are staying and sad for those who are leaving. Where there's no art, there's no joy. Save yourself and the painting, Son, and leave us to our woes."

"When will I see you again, Sir?"

"Better say goodbye now, Soldier. In Baghdad, we never make promises."

"But, Sir?"

"When you get to Tinker, you'll find Sara's Barbie doll waiting for you."

"What?"

"And you do not have to go identify the woman who kept Sara. And Sara will not have to undergo a medical examination. It's all been taken care of. Goodbye, Soldier."

Saying that, Peckford shook Scott's hand and hurriedly marched out before Scott could see his brimming eyes. Reverently, Scott rolled up the painting, threw his duffle bag over his shoulder, held back his tears, and ambled towards the Humvee waiting to take him to the airplane. No timorous tempests erupted from his unconscious mind as he entered the Humvee, and when he boarded the airplane he did not turn back for one last look at all the fears he had left behind. Peckford's metaphors ensconced in the Baghdad painting and the Barbie doll did not occur to him until after he was airborne far and high into the Mesopotamian sky. There, in the cloistered altitudes of the midnight darkness, he un-scrolled the painting and let his gaze meander through its river gardens and saunter among the minarets that obelisked its horizon.

"What a lovely piece of truth and beauty," he thought. *"I wonder why Peckford chose this very painting as my goodbye gift. Why did the man who knew all the words of the world choose to use this painting as his last testament? Everything this man ever implies has at least two meanings, the obvious and the hidden. Besides truth and beauty, what other obvious meanings are there? Perhaps, by carrying the beautiful Baghdad back home, I'm in fact saying goodbye to the war-torn Baghdad forever? Perhaps, by taking back only the good memories, I'm actually leaving the bad ones behind? Or perhaps, by returning to peace, I'm indeed saying goodbye to war? Yes, all these are obvious meanings and I see them clearly in the peaceful lay of this ancient city."*

Scott closed his eyes awhile, reopened them, and looked anew at the painting. This time his gaze hissed through its lonesome palm trees, its cobblestone streets, and its serpentine alleys. *"What meanings lie concealed among these somber scenes?"* he worried. *"That I belong with peace, truth, and beauty while he belongs with war, falsehood, and ugliness? That by giving me back my life, he was giving away his in return? That just like the two Baghdad's will never meet again, he and I will never see each other again? That by exchanging my fear for hope, he was actually taking on my fear and giving up his hope? Or that by giving me this gift and reuniting me with Sara's Barbie doll, Peckford was in fact saying goodbye to me forever?"*

Pondering these meanings, Scott's eyes got heavy and his heart began to gallop, spurred by nostalgic feelings that were too hot to touch and too sharp to hold. The Peckford goodbye was deeper than silence and heftier than thoughts. It reeked of an ominous finality that smothered Scott's heavy eyes with acerbic tears and drowned his exhausted mind into the swirling undercurrents of restless sleep. It was only when he awakened refreshed—several hours later—that the folly of these morbid thoughts became clear to him and brought a reassuring smile to his lips.

The engines groaned against the night. The airplane scratched the sky in flight. The darkness glowed; the stardust snowed. Then close to home they turned to light.

Chapter Thirty
(Domestic Developments)

On Tuesday, November 14, Lieutenant Scott Thornton left reporter James Belford in Baghdad and on Wednesday, November 15, he was back in Oklahoma City. The same taxi was waiting for him outside Gate 5 and it dropped him where it had picked him up two days earlier, in the back street behind Debbie Hunt's home. Scott did not have to knock because he found the backdoor open. Walking in with duffle bag in hand, he found Sara and Debbie at the dinner table waiting for him. When Sara saw him, she shrieked, jumped into his arms, and wrapped her hands around his neck. This time, Scott did not shove her back. Instead, he held her tight to his heart and whispered in her ear, "I missed you, Pumpkin. Guess what I brought you back from Washington."

Sara didn't answer but held on like a vise to Scott's neck and wouldn't let go.

"Wouldn't you like to see what I have in my duffle bag for you?"

"No."

"Not even if I have a Barbie doll?"

"Barbie doll?"

"Yes, a Barbie doll."

"The same Barbie doll that the woman took away from me and blew her smoke on?"

"The very same one I gave you for your birthday."

Debbie's eyes gleamed as she watched Sara necklace Scott with no hint of apprehension. There was no room for words as eyes filled up with joy and dialogued in clamorous silence. Scott's gratitude shone through his face like a halo as he gazed at Debbie Hunt with giddy astonishment. Having managed to exorcise Sara's fear of him made her his heroine. He did not care to know how she did it just as he did not care to understand how his own fear took leave of him in Baghdad. His un-inquisitive mind preferred the awe of mysteries to the detail of analyses.

As they sat down to eat, his eyes kept oscillating between Sara and Debbie as if he were beholding some numinous apparition never seen before. He saw Sara as twice kidnapped, once by Al-Qaeda and once by fear. He saw himself and Debbie as Sara's rescuers and that new perception suggested to his mind that they had just formed a united anti-fear front.

Debbie, who was also eyeing Scott, was having remarkably similar feelings. It thrilled her to see Scott and Sara reunited under a fearless sky but it surprised her to feel so overjoyed at Scott's gratitude towards her. She also did not dare to understand why she was feeling that way and, like Scott, preferred to accept the mystery without explanation.

Of course, as far as Sara's case was concerned, Debbie realized that there was more work to be done and that it had to be accomplished more carefully and at a much slower pace. Meanwhile, Sara had her father's heart to grow up in and that was all that Debbie Hunt required in order to help Sara overcome the rest of her fears.

Under the cover of night, Debbie Hunt took Scott and Sara back home. She parked her car in the Thornton garage, unloaded the couple's gear, said good night, and was about to take leave when Scott, as an afterthought, inquired, "Did you get to talk to Nancy?"

"I called her to say that you had taken Sara away on a short vacation to calm her down and that you'd be in touch with her as soon as you returned."

"And what was her response?"

Debbie answered Scott's question by redirecting her gaze to Sara while pursing her lips. With that simple gesture she managed to tell Scott that the rest of the conversation was not for Sara's ears. Standing in the garage with Sara by his side, Scott nodded and did not press the issue further. Instead, he waited until after Debbie gave Sara her goodbye hug and then asked, "Are we going to see you tomorrow, perhaps?"

"Well, I do have the rest of the week off."

"I take it they don't expect me at work this week either."

"Mr. McMaster doesn't expect you back till next Monday."

"And how about Sara?"

"I took care of her school too."

"Well then, how about lunch? We could all meet at Johnny's at noon."

"That will be fine. Don't forget to call Nancy and the rest of your family. They're all a bit worried."

After Debbie left and Scott put Sara to bed, he found himself getting restless because too many unfinished thoughts were pecking at his mind. His most urgent problem was Nancy who had estranged herself from Sara as if she were no longer the mother. He could not understand how any mother, no matter what the circumstances, could estrange herself so heartlessly from her very own child. It was time to have a confrontation and so, without hesitation, he called Nancy's home. It took her a long while to answer and when she did her opening statement was, "What do you want from me, Scott Thornton? I'm no longer your wife and now that you have your daughter back you need to leave me and my life alone."

"But Babe, isn't she your daughter too?"

"Not anymore, Scotty, not anymore. She's afraid of me and I'm not good for her."

"But, we can work on her fear together. For a while she was afraid of me too."

"Scotty Thornton, I never wanted her and I still don't. I wanted to abort her and you were the one who wouldn't let me. Well, you can have her all to yourself now. I'll sign the papers and give you full custody."

"But, Babe, how about us? I thought we were getting back together for Sara's sake."

"I thought so too, but after what happened I have realized that it won't work."

"And why won't it work?"

"Because I don't love you and I have never loved you."

"But I thought..."

"Let's face it, Scotty, we just fell in together because of Sara. You have no idea how many times I wished I had not listened to you."

"What do you mean by listened to me?"

"I mean that I should have had an abortion in spite of you."

Here Nancy's voice broke down as she began to sob like a forlorn child. Then, after a few gasps, as if the time had finally come for her to empty out her coffers once and for all, she continued on with her confessional while Scott listened with incredulous ears.

"There's so much more that you don't know, Scotty. When you were in Iraq, I cheated on you with several men. I invited them to the house because I couldn't leave Sara with anyone without them suspecting that I was fooling around. We had to lock her in her bedroom because she wouldn't leave us alone and because she wanted to crawl into bed with us. She was old enough to know what was going on and some of the men roughed her up a bit when she kept on screaming and wouldn't shut up. I'm not real proud of all that, Scotty, but I don't love you and I don't want to be a mother and we'd all be happier if you'd keep Sara and leave me alone. I'm not a mother, Scotty, and have never been. I hear other women talk about their children with passions that I've never ever experienced.

Oh, Scotty, there is so much more you don't know that you do need to know. I didn't have a one-night stand with Rick. His name was Ricardo Chavez and we had wild sex, night after night, for months and months. We had orgies, ménage a trios, did drugs in bed, got ourselves so drunk we couldn't even remember what we did and with whom. I slept with all of Rick's friends and they all liked me until I got pregnant. Then they wanted nothing to do with me. I have no idea who Sara's father is. Didn't you ever wonder why Sara lagged a bit behind her peers, why she was developmentally late, why she acted younger than her age? Sara was a drug baby, Scotty, and she still drags because of it. I was wild, Scotty, and I still have a wild streak in me. All I wanted was men and more men. I never had enough, Scotty, and I couldn't be with any one man very long. I changed them like I changed shoes, cheated on them, dumped them, and got dumped by them. That was my life before Sara and I liked it that way and I still do.

I only married you for security but now that my business is good, I'm fine without you. I never wanted to be a mother and I still don't. I resented having had Sara and I still do. There's not a day that I don't regret having her around my neck. Scotty, are you listening? I like being single and I like to date lots of men. I've never been faithful to any one man and I don't think that I can ever be. I'm different than other women, Scotty. You and Sara deserve better. I'll pack the rest of Sara's clothes tomorrow and leave them outside my door. Tell her whatever you want; I don't care. She needs to live with you because you are the better parent. Give me back my life, please, and take Sara away. How about it, Scotty?"

Scott, mesmerized by Nancy's honesty barrage, lost all his words. As Nancy asked him repeatedly if he was listening, he just sighed and his tears dried up in their sockets. The truth, the whole truth, and nothing but the truth exploded inside his brain like a bomb. He made several attempts to say something in return, to utter even one single word, or to formulate one clear thought but he couldn't. His mind, under the merciless salvo of truths, was shell-shocked into a blank slate and all his preexisting thoughts were temporarily wiped off.

"Scotty, please, are you listening?"

"Scotty, please say something."

"Scotty, Scotty, oh, never mind..."

Finally, among tears, sobs, sniffles, and long stuttering sighs, Nancy mumbled a remorseful goodnight and hung up the phone, leaving Scott alone in a desert full of dry sand, hissing wind, and vast, empty spaces.

He wanted to tell Nancy that he understood that she was different just like he understood that he also was different. He wanted to tell her that he wasn't any better than she was, that it was better to accept what we are than pretend to be what we are not, and that they should continue to be friends for Sara's sake. He even wanted to confess that he was just as much to blame for their loveless breakup as she was. He wanted to say anything he could think of to make her feel better about herself but such thoughts did not sprout in his shell-shocked brain till much later, long after Nancy had hung up the phone, and long after midnight.

Merciful sleep that night was mercilessly shattered by Nancy's confessional, which left Scott with the double responsibility of being both Sara's mother and father. Overwhelmed by these torrents of concern he floated out of control in a stream of confusion down the lonely alleys of night with not a light in sight.

When the morning began creeping into the gaping windows, it found Scott on the living room sofa still staring down the forsaken alleys of a night that was no longer there.   His thoughts, and he had many, remained unarticulated, unheard, and unrecalled. His trance was deeper than abandonment, deeper than despair, deeper than love, and deeper than life. Without his thoughts, he could no longer recognize who he was. He needed his thoughts to return to him so that he could become Scott Thornton again, so that he could reclaim his lost identity, so that he could re-find his soul among life's rubble, and so that he could become Sara's father and mother again. His only anchor, the only compass point from which he could calculate his position on this vast ocean of living, was love. There were only two facts he was certain about—that he loved Sara and that Sara loved him. All that he had to help him navigate his way back to a meaningful life were these two stable points, these two shining stars across a black sky, these two guiding lights that were going to lead him back to the cradle of safety. Such was his state of mind when Sara awakened and rushed into his lap.

There was no fear in her eyes, her face was awash

with joy, and her demeanor was frivolous like birds. To his fatigued, sleep-deprived body, Sara was a garden bustling with morning glory and ready for frolicsome glee. *"How can children make us forget our troubled world?"* asked Scott as he bounced Sara on his knees. Her sunny presence quickly uplifted his spirits, buoyed him out of his dreary state of mind, and gave him wings with which to tame the sky. *"How can such a powerless creature have such powers of transformation?"* thought Scott as his lost thoughts alighted back onto his mind and reintroduced him to the world. And thus, with his state of mind reinstated, Scott waltzed Sara through the rest of the morning without one flat note and at noon, the well-dressed couple found themselves at Johnny's awaiting Debbie Hunt.

While waiting, Scott at first entertained Sara, then he checked his cell phone for messages, and then he looked out the window at the cars coming into the parking lot. He understood that Debbie would have called him if she were going to be late but when half an hour had passed he reached for his cell phone and called her instead. She sounded perturbed, hurried, detached, and even asked him what was he calling her about.

"We were supposed to have lunch at Johnny's at noon."

"Oh, I'm so sorry, I totally forgot. I had a crisis this morning and I'm still a bit shaken. You don't mind eating without me, do you?"

"Oh, not if you're busy. I had some ideas I wanted to bounce off you, ideas about Sara, but they can wait."

"Oh, let me have a rain check today and we can plan something for tomorrow."

"Ah, I know that Sara and I have more time on our hands than you do. I only needed you to sit with Sara while I got the rest of her clothes from her mom's house. Nancy was going to leave them in a suitcase by her apartment door. I don't want to take Sara there with me. It would remind her of the kidnapping."

"Oh, I see now. Why don't you go ahead and eat and I'll come to your house later this afternoon."

"Everyone else is at work, you know, and she won't let anyone else baby-sit her except you. I'm sorry to be such a bother but too much has happened since I've returned."

"I know, Mr. Thornton, and I'll be there for you as soon as I can. I just can't give you an exact time."

On the way back to the house, Scott began to rehearse the details of his new life. *"Nancy wants out and I've got Sara all to myself now. Sara won't let anyone else baby-sit her except Debbie. I don't even know if she'll be able to go to school with her bald head and frightened mental state. Who's going to pick her up from school, now that she won't let her grandparents do it? I can drop her at school on my way to the office but she'll have to stay with someone until I get back from work. Debbie Hunt has already done enough for us and I can't keep asking her to do more and more. Besides, she has her work and her own troubled love life, which seems about to cause Jane and Flora to break up after so many years of being together. I don't know what I'm going to do. I can't even talk to Peckford. Oh, what a lonesome mess."*

Awaiting Debbie's call, Scott and Sara passed a quiet afternoon at home. Scott was starting to feel exhausted but his mind would not let him take even a short sofa nap. He called his mom and dad at the Thornton Realty but could not speak to Jane because she was with a client. He felt so isolated that he even called Breena Birdsong at the Hartland Bank and had an amiable chat with her. He tried not to tell her too much but when she found out that he needed help with Sara, she immediately volunteered. He promised that he would call her if he couldn't get anyone else to baby-sit. And for some unconscious reason he felt too uncomfortable to tell her about Debbie Hunt because he was afraid that she might misconstrue what that relationship was all about. Of course, he never said a word about his trip to Baghdad and certainly did not tell her that he thought about her white, succulent thighs during the underground security meeting.

All these thoughts and feelings were slowly taking charge of his life, causing him to feel trapped, and not offering him a safe harbor to resort to. It seemed as though his entire life orbited around Sara and her daily requirements with total disregard to his own private needs. Having lost Nancy's support was a major blow and there was no substitute in sight. He recalled the story of Breena Birdsong's pioneer forefather who came for the Oklahoma Land Rush of 1889 and whose wife died of cholera while they sailed across the Atlantic from England. They buried her at sea and he had to marry another woman on the ship so that she could take care of his three children. His new wife treated his children so poorly that they left home as soon as they could and never returned, leaving him to die unfulfilled and alone. He was afraid that the same thing would happen to him, that he would have to marry a woman out of need, a woman that he did not love, a woman who might end up mistreating Sara, and that he would end up alone. Heavy-hearted, he waited and mused until Debbie, at about five p.m., finally showed up.

Debbie seemed upset and was most apologetic about her late arrival. Scott, on the other hand, seemed tired and overwhelmed by his own pessimistic thoughts. What saved face was Sara's alacrity and jovial welcome of Debbie. This little, chirpy girl brought smiles unto the faces, swept away the gray frowns that threatened to dim the room, and turned all the lights back on. It was a tacit lesson in life taught by a child to her adult caregivers. Not to disturb the newfound cheer, no further questions were asked and no knowing glances were exchanged between the two adults before Scott left on his short excursion to Nancy's apartment.

On the way, some of his feelings for Nancy resurfaced and teased his mind. He didn't love her but loved some things about her, felt sorry for her but at the same time he liked being with her, found her attractive but was no longer attracted to her, found her beautiful but was no longer moved by her body, and thought of her as a libertine but he also envied her for it. He wished he could be a bit of a libertine himself but he was always too serious, too conservative, too shy, and too inhibited. The only time he ever threw caution to the wind and surrendered to his inner whims was when he asked Nancy to marry him in order to save Sara. The few other women he had dated before Nancy all ended up leaving him because he could not get serious about any of them. *"I'm thirty-six and I've not fallen in love with a woman yet,"* thought Scott as he approached the Acropolis Villas.

When Scott climbed the stairs to Nancy's apartment there was no suitcase waiting by her door. Scott rechecked his bearings—Acropolis Villas, Building C, Apartment 404, but there was no suitcase in sight. He hesitated, listened, paced, and finally rang the doorbell. Hurried footsteps came, stopped, looked through the peephole, and then opened the door.

"Hi, Scotty. Come in."

"Ah, you, you're dressed up! You look like you're going somewhere."

"Hot date. A banker like you but loaded. His wife is a client."

"You're dating a married man?"

"Oh, grow up Scotty."

"Well, what does his wife think about it?"

"She doesn't know, silly, not yet anyway."

"Nancy, are you sure this is a good idea at this time?"

"Here's the suitcase, Darling. Everything's in it. You'll have to come back for her bedroom furniture some other time. Perhaps this weekend if he takes me to Vegas. I'll leave the key under the mat so you can move her things back to your house."

"Don't you want to know how Sara is doing?"

"Good-bye, Scotty. I need to finish putting on my makeup. He's taking me to Mahogany and I've been dying to go to that restaurant. Many of my clients rave about it and I've been ashamed to tell them that I've never been. Tonight is going to be my night. I'll catch up with you later."

Scott put Sara's suitcase in the trunk of his car and drove off with a profound feeling of loss sitting like a ghost in the passenger seat beside him. The feeling was so real, so incarnate, that he almost asked it to fasten its seatbelt. He had never experienced such a corporeal reverie before or seen an image so virtual yet so tangible he could almost run his hand over its belly. As he drove into his garage the image of a fetus being pulled out of its uterus materialized in front of his eyes. It was at that moment of reckoning that the reality of what had just happened flashed into his eyes like a distorting aura. Feeling defeated, he surrendered his head to the car seat and closed his eyes, hoping to obliterate the disturbing vision of the infant being pulled by force out of its uterus. It did not work and the vision persisted like a migraine aura on a pitch-black screen. When, after a few minutes, the vision passed out of his sight, it left him with a pounding headache and the unmistakable realization that Nancy finally got the abortion that she had wanted five years and nine months before.

Scott walked into the house carrying Sara's suitcase in his right hand and holding his head with his left. His appearance so alarmed Debbie that she rushed to his aid, tore the suitcase out of his clutched grip, helped him into the living room, and watched him drop his body like a dead weight onto the sofa. Sara, who had witnessed the entire scene, became frightened and started to cry but without screaming. Sensing her distress, Scott pulled her onto his chest, covered her ears with both his hands, and then sighed his rhetorical questions into Debbie's startled eyes.

"Can a mother abort herself? Can a mother abort herself of her only child? Can a mother abort herself of her only child five years after her child was born?"

Chapter Thirty-One
(The Bond)

Debbie Hunt stood dumbfounded as she looked at Scott stretched on the living room sofa with Sara's head cuddled upon his chest. To her unfulfilled maternal instincts, this was the ultimate love scene. Unconsciously, she had a strong craving to complete this love triangle and a subliminal desire to become the missing arm that connects its two loose sides. The longer she stood, the more intense grew her urge to join love's communion and the greater the pain of un-belonging cried within her chest. Furthermore, Scott's rhetorical questions had so taken her by surprise that she began to feel weak in the knees while she ruminated over his preposterous anachronism: "Can a mother abort herself of her only child five years after her child was born?"

Torn between being a childless woman with suppressed instincts and an androphobic woman with denied desires, her legs shook harder the longer she gazed and finally buckled, causing her to fall to her knees by Sara's side. Unnoticed by the cuddling couple but wanting so much to join them, she started to stroke Sara's back with her right hand while she held on to the sofa with her left. When Scott—with closed eyes and still deeply submerged in his psychic pain—began to shiver, Debbie Hunt, as if moved by some numinous force, slid her left hand onto his forehead and wiped off the cold sweat with her bare palm. The compassion of this simple gesture did not escape Sara who slanted her eyes toward Debbie's hand with a gleam of gratitude. Even at her inexperienced age, she could discern with her childhood instincts how desperately her dad had needed the sincere touch of a kind woman.

There was never a moment during Scott's entire life when a touch conjured so many rich emotions. With his eyes still closed, he was overcome by tears that flowed down both corners of his eyes onto his temples. The noise of the unsaid reached deafening heights as the silent three struggled with the many meanings of kindness, each one from his different level of deprivation and despair. Scott, who was starved for a woman's sincere attention, was touched the more deeply knowing that there were no ulterior motives to Debbie's stroking hand. Sara, who saw Debbie as the selfless, loving mother she never had, was moved to see her attend to her father's forehead with so gentle a touch. Debbie, who hungered for a child's love and a man's un-sensual attention, was surprised by a shivering wave that spread upstream between her kneeling knees.

Life's precious moments being always ephemeral makes them all the more formative. That instant, which cemented the bond of kindness among Debbie, Sara, and Scott, was a deft example. By the time Scott recovered and Sara recuperated, Debbie had become burnished with a fiery flush that crimsoned her cheeks and blotched her pulsating neck. It would have been embarrassing for the group to sustain that moment any longer than they did and even more embarrassing to deliberately dismantle it. The only other way out was to pretend that it never happened, much like an accidental kiss on the lips that was half-intended for the cheek. To that purpose, Debbie rose and sheepishly sighed that it was time for her to leave in order to attend to some urgent business that awaited her.

When Friday morning rolled in, Scott felt a yearning need to call Jane. Unaware of his own inquisitiveness towards Debbie, most likely because of unconscious repression, he merely wanted to reconnect with his sister after his frightening reconnaissance in Baghdad. He even entertained the idea of having a heart-to-heart talk with her regarding Nancy's unforeseen metamorphosis and hoped that Sara would not protest to a lunch with her aunt. He was thrilled when she answered the phone.

"Thornton Realty, how may I help you?"

"Ah, I'm looking for someone to have lunch with Sara and me and I was told that your agency provides such escorts for Iraqi veterans?"

"Oh, Scotty, I'm so glad to see that your sense of humor is back. Wow, so you really think that Sara is ready to have lunch with her aunt?"

"I haven't asked her and don't plan to. You're just going to happen upon the scene."

"Oh, Scotty, are you sure that will be okay?"

"Nope, not sure yet, but if you'll say yes, we'll find out for sure."

"You and your word play."

"Well, how about it, Sis?"

"Well, I was going to have lunch with a friend who seems to be having relationship problems but I bet she wouldn't mind rescheduling, especially if I tell her that I'm having lunch with my hero brother and his recently rescued daughter."

"So, how 'bout The Olive Garden at noon?"

"Hmm, how about Panera at one?"

"Good. Can't wait to see my little sister."

Panera was buzzing with business when Scott, holding Sara's hand, strolled into the joint. It was hard to find a table for three and while Scott was peering, Sara was busy rearranging her Dillard's hat, a brown French beret with a golden button on top. Even though she did not know that Aunt Jane was about to walk in on them, she was self-conscious enough not to leave home without her beret, her own fashion defense against all the emboldened looks and inquisitive eyes. With her repertoire of newly arrived suitcase clothes, she had enjoyed selecting her own attire and matching it to the planned activities of that day. Such innocent activities pleased Scott to no end because they indicated that Sara was moving closer to normal and farther away from fear.

When a window table cleared Scott seized it, which caused Sara to remind him that he had not ordered yet. Having been to Panera before, she knew the routine of first standing in line, ordering, and then finding a table. This prescient warning from his little girl surprised him as he struggled for a plausible answer. When he couldn't find any, he decided to tell her the truth and observe her reaction.

"Baby, we'll order after Aunt Jane joins us. It would not be polite to let her pay for her own food when you and I were the ones who invited her here."

"Uh-huh."

"Are you afraid of Aunt Jane?"

"Uh-huh."

"But she loves you. You're her only niece, remember?"

"Uh-huh."

"Is it your hair?"

"It didn't grow back like you said it would."

"And why is that?"

"Because you came home too soon."

"Well, it's going to grow much faster now."

"Why?"

"Because of Aunt Jane. You see, every time I have lunch with Aunt Jane I end up getting a haircut a week later. I've known that about her for a long time and that's why I've asked her to have lunch with us."

"Really?"

"Really, Honey, but you must pretend that you don't know and so must I; otherwise her magic won't work."

"Oh?"

"You see, Aunt Jane doesn't know that she has that gift and I haven't told anyone but you. If her friends and clients find out they'd start avoiding having lunch with her because haircuts are quite expensive."

Sara's eyes lit up as she rearranged her beret one more time in anticipation of Aunt Jane's magic. When after a few minutes Jane showed up at the door, Sara ran into her arms without hesitation, surprising both her dad and her aunt. It was after this remarkably successful subterfuge that Scott felt free to leave Sara and Jane together at the table while he stood in line to order.

With Sara around, Jane and Scott said more with their eyes than with their words. The conversation meandered through comfortable topics and sauntered about pleasantries while waiting for Sara to finish her food. Then, as if stung by a bee, Sara let out a sudden shriek, jumped out of her seat, ran to the door, and leapt into Debbie Hunt's arms as she walked in. Apparently, she had seen her coming in with Aunt Flora through the big glass window while Jane and Scott were preoccupied with table talk.

It took a few awkward moments before everyone realized what had happened. It was not coincidence that had contrived to convene all parties at Panera at the same time; it was, in fact, serendipity. Apparently, Jane had wanted Flora and Debbie to have a talk so as to help Flora get over her obsession that she and Debbie were having an affair. She had planned to get them together at noon at The Olive Garden where they could all talk openly about the matter. But, when Scott called and asked her to meet Sara and him for lunch, she was so excited that she decided to take a rain check and let the two hash it out without her. It just happened that The Olive Garden was so busy at noon that the waiting time was going to be about 45 minutes. To avoid the awkwardness of waiting together, Flora and Debbie agreed to try other restaurants but the ones they tried were equally busy. After much driving around, each in her separate car, they ended up at Panera.

Of course, based on his telephone conversation with Flora, Scott was still in the mindset that Jane and Debbie were having an affair and that Flora and Jane were in the process of breaking up. Consequently, among the five, Scott's face appeared to be the one most riddled with surprise as Debbie and Flora approached to say hi. He became even more surprised when, surveying the other four faces, he did not find reflections of his own anxiety in anyone else's eyes. Even Sara seemed at ease with Aunt Flora and appeared to no longer mind being the center of attention. And thanks to this centripetal attraction, any initial awkwardness was quickly dissipated and replaced with songs of praise for Sara's attire, beret, and mature manners. The only one who really understood Scott's obvious astonishment was Flora who, having told no one of her conversation with Scott, knew why he was stunned and realized what he was thinking.

When the perfunctory group remarks finally died down, and Debbie and Flora felt free to proceed to the ordering line, Sara wouldn't let go of Debbie's hand and accompanied them to the queue. It was during these few precious minutes in line, while Sara was with Flora and Debbie, that Jane was able to tell Scott the entire story.

Apparently, Jane had become acquainted with Debbie Hunt when, as a realtor, she had helped Debbie find her current home almost a year ago. Jane was so impressed with Debbie's confidence, clear mind, and patriotic spirit that they fell into a lunch friendship. They not only enjoyed each other's company; they also became each other's confidants and held soul-to-soul talks about their lives and their sexual preferences. While Jane was a homosexual from birth, Debbie was heterosexual by inclination but after her date rape at fourteen she developed such a pronounced fear of men that she became an absolute androphobe. Unable to shake off her fear of men, and frustrated by her own sexual inadequacy, she turned her energies to helping abused women and children so that they would not end up like her.

In the process of working with these abused children and women, Debbie filled her spiritual void with religion and became a devout Catholic. Considering herself still a virgin, since she had never consented to having sex with any man, she identified deeply with the Virgin Mary's Immaculate Conception and made the Virgin her patron saint. Debbie's new faith filled her soul with joy and sustained her through many a personal crisis. In her heart of hearts she sincerely believed that the Lord had directed her to a life dedicated to helping abused women and children. With this calling in her heart, she had no trouble resisting men's advances or suppressing her own sexual urges. Her faith, besides bringing her peace and fulfillment, gave her life a noble meaning and granted it a sanctified purpose. She saw herself as a nun without a habit in God's selfless service.

What Debbie's faith did not do, however, was rid her of her fear of men. Short of that, it was a perfect answer to her spiritual needs and a strong equivocator of her sexual urges. She felt no need to conquer her androphobia because she had no need for men and was quite content living as a confirmed virgin doing the Lord's good work. There were moments of faltering, of course, when she felt an irresistible attraction to certain members of the opposite sex. To combat such weaknesses, she would go into her bedroom, kneel in front of the statue of the Virgin on her dresser, and pray feverishly until the urge had passed. Prayer provided her a way out of difficulties and lighted her path when she had to venture into unfamiliar situations and unknown territories. Consequently, during her sojourn in Iraq, and on her numerous confrontations as a child welfare worker, Debbie Hunt functioned as an absolutely fearless angel of mercy.

Jane became an avid admirer of Debbie and as their friendship blossomed, she found herself spending less time with Flora. When Flora confronted her, she openly confessed that she and Debbie had developed a strong friendship that she was unwilling to end just to appease Flora. This caused Flora to become suspicious and obsessive about the relationship, thinking of it in sexual terms when it really wasn't. In spite of repeated reassurances from Jane, Flora continued to feel betrayed and that was when Jane suggested that the three of them should meet to discuss the matter openly. Debbie, who knew of Flora's suspicions, offered to suspend her friendship with Jane but Jane refused, insisting that one cannot right someone's wrong impressions by suspending a love as sublime and pure as the one that bound their friendship.

That was the state of affairs that characterized the Panera lunch ensemble on Friday, November 17, 2006—a date of great international and domestic significance. On that very same day on the international front, the newspapers reported that President George W. Bush and Prime Minister of Australia John Howard discussed Iraq strategy over lunch at an Asia-Pacific Economic Cooperation meeting in Hanoi. Meanwhile, in an interview, the British Prime Minister Tony Blair said that Iraq "is pretty much a disaster." But, unlike the international scene, by the time the Panera lunch ensemble had dismantled, a lot had been achieved and all toward a good and peaceful end.

Flora, after lunching with Debbie, was left with no doubt that Jane's relationship with Debbie Hunt was a platonic one indeed. She apologized to both Debbie and Jane for having doubted their integrity and asked that she be invited occasionally to their tête à tête retreats, a request that was granted with reciprocal joy.

Debbie became more comfortable with Sara and Scott and felt more at liberty to become a part of their family unit at a more personal rather than professional level. Her newfound ease would prove instrumental in conquering Sara's repertoire of fears as she began to tackle school and all the cruelties that children tend to wield upon those who are different.

Jane had a rejuvenated sense of relief after she was exonerated by Flora and allowed to maintain her open bond with Debbie. She especially admired Debbie's cultured mind and was looking forward to more in-depth discussions regarding the current plights of humanity and the infinite vicissitudes of human nature.

Scott, who so far had been the most emotionally disturbed, began to see personal peace arising from the horizon. His issues with patriotism, heroism, Peckford, Nancy's abandonment, Sara's fears, and his own tantalizing mirage of noble sentiments that had hitherto eluded his reach, seemed as though they were going to get tidied up with Debbie Hunt's help. He even felt a slight flush rise into his cheeks as he unleashed his thoughts toward certain unspeakable possibilities that the future might bring to his heart if serendipity continued to treat him as mercifully as it had.

There was one issue, however, which maintained a painful void within his chest. Deep in his soul, he missed

Peckford's friendship, missed it bitterly, missed it painfully, thought about it with every vanishing moment, and wanted it to be part of his daily life as was Jane's friendship with Debbie. But what he was really and unconsciously wishing for was one of nature's absolute impossibilities. He was wishing for Peckford's intellect and soul but wanted them— somehow, he knew not how—to hail from inside a woman. With that impossible quest upon his mind, Scott said goodbye to the Panera lunch ensemble and drove Sara back home with more wonder in his heart and more awe in his spirit than he could ever comprehend.

Chapter Thirty-Two
(The Crib)

The rest of that Friday afternoon proved most eventful for the unsuspecting Thornton couple. Indeed, it held surprises for both Scott and Sara, surprises that neither of them could anticipate because instead of coming at them from without, they actually arose from within their convalescing souls and jolted their brains like high-voltage electric bolts.

Nothing seemed ill at ease when Scott and Sara took their leave from the Panera lunch ensemble. Indeed, the group as a whole had scattered after a most amiable dénouement and everyone seemed happy and hopeful as they said their goodbyes. As usual, Sara and Scott drove up to the house but this time their approach was impeded by an unforeseen development. Sara, who had been quiet while enjoying the November afternoon sun, surprised her dad with, "I don't want to go home."

She said that at about the time Scott was approaching their driveway. Stunned by her assertiveness, he stopped the car at the curb, turned the engine off, and not wanting to reveal his surprise, patiently waited for her to explain. During these few silent moments, Sara fidgeted, took off her beret, nervously passed her hand over her stubbled head, and said nothing. As Scott continued to observe her, he realized that a serious transformation was taking place. Sara, who had left Panera calm and chipper, was transmuting into a different person right before his eyes. As she tried to hold back her tears, her face contorted into a frightful, tortured look, her knees clamped together like a vise, and her lips began to quiver.

"What is it, Princess?"

"Nothing."

"I'll take you wherever you want to go if you'll just tell me where."

Sara did not answer. She merely stared dead ahead, ignoring her tears as they dripped, un-wiped, over her frowns. Scott did not know whether to press her for an answer or to wait for her to open up when she was ready. Waiting, he patiently wiped off her tears as she maintained her blank stare, totally ignoring him. Then, acting out of fatherly intuition, he reached for the beret, which lay in her lap, placed it over his own head, and began to arrange and rearrange it while looking at himself in the visor mirror. It did not take long before she snatched back her beret with a suppressed giggle that she could only hold for a brief moment before breaking out into loud laughter.

Without saying a word, Scott restarted the engine and, pretending to be a taxi driver, looked at Sara and inquired, "Where may I drive you ma'am?"

"Somewhere."

"Do you know the address, ma'am?"

"No."

"What kind of place is it, ma'am? I have a detailed map of the city and can look it up for you."

"It's a bed place."

"You mean furniture place?"

"Uh-huh."

"Are you looking for a bed, ma'am?"

"Uh-huh."

"What kind of bed?"

"A bed to sleep in."

"But there are many kinds of beds, ma'am, and different stores specialize in different kinds."

"Uh-huh."

"Well, are you looking for a water bed or a sofa bed or a..."

"I just want a bed with a fence."

Scott's head swirled as the weight of her words shattered his playful mood and pulled him back to reality. It reassured him to know that Sara was ready to sleep in her own bed—even though he did not quite understand what a fenced bed meant nor what it was that had brought about Sara's sudden burst of resolve.

"Well, Princess, your mom said that we can pick up your bedroom furniture any time we want."

"I don't want it."

"You don't want what?"

"I don't want it, I don't want it, I don't want it."

As Sara demurred, her voice crescendoed from an assertive rejection to a barking outrage and, after the third protestation, she exploded into bitter sobs. Scott turned off the engine again and held his breath. Something was happening to his daughter, something profoundly painful, something reeking of bitter memories that, for reasons yet unrevealed, had suddenly surfaced into her little mind. All he could think of was Debbie Hunt. He wished Debbie were with them to help him decipher Sara's massive eruption of underground emotions. He felt profoundly at a loss and all he knew to do was to hold her hand and wait.

Slowly, the storm passed, leaving Sara drenched with red, swollen eyes, smudged cheeks, and blue-bitten lips. Her stubbled, bald head haloed defiantly in bold contrast to her washed-out visage. Still, Scott could think of nothing intelligent to say and, fearful of saying the wrong thing and sparking yet another explosion, he remained solemn. His mind, however, was awash with disturbing thoughts that were making him feel angry and out of control, especially because he did not know how to turn them off. *"Why doesn't she want her own bed? Most kids would love to sleep in their own beds. Whatever happened to make her hate her bed with such violent anger? Maybe I don't need to know. But, maybe it would help her to tell me."*

"Princess, what happened in your bed to make you stop liking it?"

Sara lowered her eyes, clamped her knees together again, and did not respond. Her expression, however, turned from defiant to doleful, letting Scott know that she was not ready to talk about it. There was nothing else to do but start the car and drive towards Kiddy City, a furniture store on May and 50th. On the way, Sara asked no questions and he volunteered no information. He simply drove on while his mind was being assailed by heinous thoughts that ran wild and refused to become harnessed.

In the parking lot of Kiddy City, Scott put Sara's

beret back on her head and said, as he opened the door, "Let's find you a nice bedroom set, Princess." As the couple browsed their way around the store, Sara's face began to regain its excited tempo and her manner changed from submissive to assertive. Observing her, Scott thought it odd that of all the beds they looked at, she only showed interest in the cribs that had high rails.

"These are cribs, Princess, for one or two year old children. You're a lady now and you need a lady's bed. How about something like that pink suite over there?"

"I want a crib."

"But Princess, you're too old for that kind of bed."

"I want a crib."

Under her dad's persistence, Sara's face began to regain its doleful expression as she became passive and disinterested. It was not a negotiable situation. She wanted a crib or else she wanted nothing and Scott did not know what to do. His only saving notion was to ask for Debbie Hunt's help but he did not want to call her with Sara by his side. Fortunately, there was a small coffee shop with a play station attached to it at the other end of the store. He walked Sara towards that station without saying much, ordered a cup of coffee for himself, a milk shake for Sara, and sat down. There were some children at play, which, he hoped, would tempt Sara to join them. After a few sips from her milkshake, and to her father's sighing relief, Sara cautiously approached the playful gang and, bit by bit, eased herself into the action. It was during that long-awaited respite that Scott called Debbie Hunt and related Sara's sudden developments to her. Then, after telling his tale, Scott asked his burning question, "Do you have any idea what happened to bring her bed to mind? She couldn't have heard us when Nancy told me that I could come for her bedroom suite this weekend."

"It must be her suitcase of clothes, then."

"How's that?"

"It must have signified a permanent separation from the mother who not only did not want her but had also hurt her."

"And how's that related to her bed?"

"The clothes signify freedom from hurt because while she was dressed, she felt secure. The bed, on the other hand, is where she doesn't have her clothes on, and where she must have been hurt..."

The moment of silence that ensued after Debbie's ominous analysis was shattered by a fierce sense of rage as Scott's loud, eerie reproach echoed across cyberspace into Debbie's ear.

"You're not suggesting that..."

"Scott. I don't live far from where you are. Let me come and have coffee with you."

"No, I don't want to wait. I want you to tell me right now what you're suggesting."

"Hang on, Mr. Thornton. Hang on for just a few more moments. I'm on my way."

As Scott awaited Debbie's arrival, his thoughts became a pack of wild hyenas. Although he did not want to face them, they were determined to stare him straight in the face and taunt him mercilessly. The confrontation proved too painful to endure, causing Scott to cover his ears with both hands, a desperately helpless attempt to subdue the clamor inside his brain. While Sara played, Scott watched with flaming eyes, unaware of the cup of coffee cooling by his side. His ideas became unfocused, unnatural, and un-collated. His painful realization that one can escape from any situation by blocking it out of his mind—except when that situation is in one's own mind—had a near-manic effect upon him and flung him into a hallucinatory mode.

"That's such a good idea. We cannot escape our minds. That's a great idea. I need to write it down and share it with Peckford. We cannot escape our minds because we are our minds. That's even a better idea. Yes, oh yes, we are indeed our minds. We are what we think. We are our thoughts. Oh, I'm sounding just like a real philosopher now. Peckford would be so proud of me. I'm proud of me. But, oh, dear God, if that is true then Sara's thoughts are also who Sara is? Oh, how horrible it is to be Sara then, because I can

tell that Sara's thoughts are painful thoughts, bad thoughts, ugly thoughts, even dirty thoughts, and she cannot escape them because they are who she is. Oh, I shouldn't have developed this great idea. It's a horrible idea. It forces me to listen for Sara's thoughts and to hear them crying out from her fear-riddled brain. Oh, may God have mercy on us all."

It was while Scott was in this deep hallucinatory state of mind that Debbie Hunt walked in and took a seat opposite him at the table. His face, pallid and distant with roaming eyes and mumbling lips, looked like a ghostly apparition from a Shakespearean play. Even though she sat facing him, he looked through her without noticing her presence. Sara, who seemed quite busy at play with the other kids, did not notice Debbie either. After observing Scott's mannerisms awhile, Debbie gently tapped on the table and asked with a kind but high-pitched voice, "I thought you wanted me to join you for coffee."

Scott, as if awakened from somnambulism, shivered a bit, greeted her with a sigh, and then remorsefully whispered, "I'm sorry I raised my voice to you and thank you for coming again to our rescue."

"Glad to be here for you and Sara."

"So what do I do now?"

"You mean about the crib?"

"Yeah, the silly crib."

"You buy it for her and pretend it's okay."

"You're kidding, of course."

"I don't kid in serious matters."

"So why do you think that I should buy it? Wouldn't that teach her that it's okay not to grow up?"

"You buy it for her because you don't want to force her out of the security of regression, not now when she is making a good recovery."

"Regression?"

"When reality is too painful, children regress back to a more secure period of their lives. Sara was happiest when she was in her crib, living with you and Nancy before you went to Iraq."

"But that was a long time ago."

"That's where she wants to be right now and you should let her."

"So, tell me the real reasons why she's rejecting her own bed then. You insinuated a lot but said nothing specific and that set my imagination on fire."

"Let's not talk about that now."

"Why? You don't think I can handle it?"

"You can but you shouldn't."

"And why's that?"

"Because the less you know the better you'll behave with Sara."

"I don't understand."

"Knowing changes your behavior and Sara will pick up on it."

"So, you're saying that I should go on as if everything's all right. As if letting Sara sleep in a crib is all right?"

"Yes, Mr. Thornton. For the time being, that's what I'm recommending."

Scott had nothing else to say and would have remained dazed were it not for Sara who, having noticed Debbie Hunt, ran into her lap with the cheerful look of play still on her face. It was at this propitious moment that Debbie looked at Scott and said, "What are you waiting for, Daddy? Let Sara choose her own bed and go buy it for her."

Startled from his reflective daze, Scott looked at Debbie and Sara with vague eyes. Sara giggled when she saw his expression and pulled him by his coat as if to awaken him. When after a few gentle tugs he still seemed distant, Debbie reached across the table, gave his hand a firm squeeze, and whispered to his disconsolate face, "Come on Mr. Thornton. Sara needs her bed."

"Huh?"

"Sara needs a bed. Get going and buy it for her."

"Will you come along, please?"

"If you want me to."

Sara walked back to choose her bed holding hands with Debbie and Scott. That same afternoon, a new set of bedroom furniture was delivered to the Thornton home including a crib, which was assembled in Sara's room without much fanfare and positioned in the corner at the furthest point away from the window. Even though the crib's position was aesthetically unappealing, it was, nevertheless, positioned where Sara wanted it to be. And for the first time since her rescue, Sara Thornton curled into a fetal position and went to sleep all alone in her own little bed-with-a-fence.

Chapter Thirty-Three
(Intrusion, Regression, and Rescue)

Saturday morning begged the night to stay as Sara and Scott slept in their separate, dreamful beds and resisted the intrusions of light. But, at about eight o'clock, Scott's cell phone rang.

"How about donuts for breakfast?"

"Who's this?"

"You don't say?"

"You must have the wrong number, ma'am."

"No, I don't, Sir. You're Scott Thornton and your daughter is Sara."

"And whom am I talking to?"

"It has only been a week and you've already forgotten my voice?"

"Who are you, please?"

"Wouldn't you like to guess?"

"It's too early for this, ma'am. Goodbye."

Scott buried his eyes into the pillow but before he could loosen his jaws, the phone rang again, and again, and again...

"Donuts for breakfast on their way, Sir."

"Who are you, woman?"

"Breena Birdsong, your lonesome coworker."

"Oh, God, Breena, what're you doing up so early?"

"May I bring you donuts, General?"

"If you insist. But you don't even know where I live."

"You want to bet?"

"Oh, I forgot, everyone knows where I live since I found Sara."

Scott rubbed his eyes, sat up in bed, and the first words out of his mind were, "*Sara might love a donut for breakfast.*" But, after that thought, he suddenly awakened to the reality of the intrusion. Breena and he were on amiable terms but their relationship had always been strictly professional and had never stepped outside the

Hartland Bank. What does she really want and what is she really after were the two alluring questions that danced before his eyes. But his mind, which craved more sleep and less analysis, pulled him back to his pillow without a thought as to when Breena would show up or what would happen if she were to ring the doorbell and frighten Sara.

As soon as he fell asleep, his dreams took over his ship's rudder and furtively steered him toward the sunset with the sunrise in pursuit. But, no matter how fast he sailed, the sunrise sped still faster until it caught up with him just before he was about to disappear into the horizon. At the very moment when his ship was captured by the morning sun, the doorbell rang, startled him out of sleep, and scattered his dream over the blue waters. He jumped, but instead of running to the door, he ran to Sara's room and was relieved to find her still asleep.

Before Breena could ring again, he opened. She wore an alacritous smile over a black jump suit and her eyes twinkled with egregious novelty. Her hair, arranged in swirls of gold, bounced off her shoulders as she swaggered and swayed before his somnolent eyes. Concealed behind her back she coyly held a small box of donuts. That posture, with both her arms stretched behind her back, exaggerated her bosom, making it protrude like a promontory.

"I'm sorry. I fell back to sleep after you called."

"Well, this is the first time I've seen you without your clothes on, I mean without your suit."

"Oh, I'm still in my..."

"May I come in?"

"Oh, sure, please. Make yourself at home while I go get my robe."

As Scott turned to let Breena in, he felt a small hand curl up into his. Immediately, he turned his attention to Sara who was standing beside him and apologetically explained that his friend, Breena, had brought them donuts. Sara did not respond but continued to tightly hold on to her dad's pajamas as he ushered Breena into the living room. Although he became tongue-tied with Sara at his flank, his mind did not fail to notice that Sara not only managed to sleep through the doorbell ring but that also she did not seem frightened by this intrusive stranger.

When Scott asked Breena to excuse them so that they could go change into more proper clothes, she took the hint and immediately remonstrated that she had not come to stay but rather to give them the donuts and be on her way. Scott did not offer a rejoinder as he followed Breena back to the door. At the door, however, while out of Sara's sight, Breena surprised Scott's arm by stroking it rhythmically with the backs of her fingers as one would stroke the under-jaw of a cat. And then, while still continuing with her rhythmic motions, she looked into his wide-open eyes and whispered, "Call me any time, General. I'm not doing anything this weekend."

Encouraged by Sara's indifference to Breena, Scott returned to the living room and, offering Sara a chocolate donut, pleaded with a hint of humor, "Wouldn't you like to visit your grandparents today? They miss you and are dying to see you."

"Uh-huh."

"Is that a yes, Princess?"

"Uh-huh." Saying that, Sara placed the chocolate donut back into the box and wiped her fingers on the boxes edge.

"What's the matter, Baby? You don't like donuts anymore?"

Sara looked straight into her dad's eyes and with unprecedented sharpness declared, "I don't like her."

"Which her?"

"The one who brought the donuts."

"And how come you don't like her? All she did was bring us donuts."

"I don't like her because she likes you."

"Oh, and what's wrong with that?"

"Because if you start liking her, you'll stop liking Ms. Debbie."

Scott swallowed the surprise with admirable calm and, lifting Sara into his lap, inquired, "And why can't I like them both?"

"Can you call Ms. Debbie? Can you call her now, please? Please, call her, Daddy. She might like to have donuts with us."

"But, Baby, Ms. Debbie has her own life, you know. And I don't think we should bother her anytime we feel like it."

"I'm not hungry anymore."

"Well, would you like to watch cartoons on TV?"

"No."

"What would you like to do then?"

"I'd like to go back to my bed. Will you help me get back in it?"

Scott lifted Sara back into her fenced bed and watched her shrink into a fetal position, close her eyes, put her thumb into her mouth, and drift away. Another regression was taking place and that worried him because school was coming up on Monday and he only had two days to bring her back into the world. The only one he knew to turn to was Debbie but he didn't want to bother her that early in the day. To pass the time, he brought the donut box into the kitchen, made coffee, and unleashed his thoughts. He tried to think of what Debbie would do if she were to find out that Sara had regressed again. But, while trying to hold that thought, his mind slipped and began to puzzle upon Sara's attitude towards Breena. However, before he had a chance to examine Sara's sharp rejection, his mind slipped again and this time it landed on Breena's lips. His hairs stood on end as he felt Breena's fingers stroking his arm and his mouth salivated as he rehearsed her words, *"Call me any time, General. I'm not doing anything this weekend."*

Each time he tried to pin his mind on Debbie and Sara, it slipped back to Breena's wanton lips and buxom frame standing before his door. As he tried to overcome this neurotic fixation on Breena, his loins started to throb and his heartbeats became painful as they pounded like ritual drums into his ears. To distract his mind from this most vexing reverie, he opened the donut box and escaped into voracious oral satisfaction until all six donuts were gone. His temporary stress release, however, ended with the last donut and, as he pecked on the debris, his mind had already relapsed back to Breena. He began to feel trapped by his Breena obsession and realized that he was not going to be able to resist it much longer. A fecund seed had been implanted into his mind and he knew that he was not capable of suppressing its sun-hungry buds for long.

He could not divine any other method out of this mental trap except by calling Debbie. He went to his cell phone, still charging next to his bed, and with automatic fingers placed the call. It was nine a.m.

"Hello, tiger. What a pleasant surprise."

"Debbie?"

"Stop it. I don't tease well this early in the morning."

"Oh, no, I'm sorry, wrong number."

"Stop it, General. The donuts must have gotten to your head. Did you eat them all in one sitting?"

"Breena?"

"Yes, my General. Your Breena awaits your command."

"Ah, I meant to call Debbie."

"Stop it, please. It's okay to be human on weekends."

"Ah, I don't know what happened, but I wasn't trying to call you. Besides, Sara is asleep and I can't leave her."

"She won't stay with her grandparents awhile?"

"We haven't tried yet."

"Surely you could escape for an hour or two."

"I don't know if it's going to be possible."

"Will you try, at least?"

"Ah, let me see what I can do. Too much has happened too soon. I can't promise anything. I'll try."

As if driven by some indomitable force, Scott began to pace incoherently. He could feel his insides, as if drawn by some mighty magnet, pull him mercilessly toward Breena. The image of her white thighs, beckoning him each time she crossed her legs in his office, fixed itself upon his inner eye and moved like a floater with his roaming gaze. For reasons that he did not try to understand, he wanted to fly to Breena and consume her body like he did her six donuts. His urge was but a raging fire that neither he nor anyone else could extinguish and only two ways to put out that fire lay un-trodden before his reddened eyes. He could either let this conflagration consume his body and reduce it to ashes or else he could consume Breena and by doing so, re-introduce a Nancy-like dissonance between him and his Sara.

Once his mind reached that focal point of decision making, he suddenly thawed and like a boneless hulk wilted onto the living room sofa. He was never going to subject his Sara to more dissonance. If Sara disliked someone, he was going to avoid that someone for Sara's sake regardless of his own preferences. With Sara's welfare on his mind, Scott found a third way to put out the fire. Thinking of Sara—curled into a fetal position and sucking her thumb deep inside her fenced bed—was all it took to silence his obsessive yearnings for Breena and to remove her seductive image permanently out of his mind. Relieved at having won this internal battle between his instinctive drives and his selfless reason and careful not to make another Freudian dial, he took in a long sighing breath and very meticulously dialed Debbie Hunt's mobile phone. It was ten a.m.

Debbie's voice was full of eager undertones when she answered on the second ring, having obviously pre-programmed Scott's cell phone number into hers.

"Mr. Thornton? Is Sara okay?"

"Oh, yes, thank you, but she has regressed again, and I'm so sorry to keep bothering you, but I have no idea what to do, you see, well it's a long story and you may not have the time, but you see she's sucking her thumb, oh, it's so hard to explain..."

"Mr. Thornton, it's okay, just calm down a bit and then tell me slowly what really happened."

Scott was able after some coaching to relate to Debbie what had transpired from the time Breena rang the doorbell till his Freudian call. Debbie listened carefully and then asked one question, "Has Sara ever known about Breena?"

"There's nothing to know. I've never seen Breena outside the office and I've never mentioned her name to Sara. She's just a coworker and nothing more."

"I think it would be best if I came over then."

"Oh, thank you, thank you so much. Sara would be delighted to see you."

"I'll be at your door in half an hour."

Hastily, Scott jumped into the shower, got dressed, tidied up the house, made coffee, and then sat on the couch by the window. He cracked the curtains just enough to see the street, leaned forward in his seat, and positioned his face right behind the curtains so that he could see without being seen. Awaiting Debbie, he made several attempts at relaxing his taut neck and back muscles but his one-track mind would not grant him release from his frozen posture. All he could do was to fixate his mindless gaze upon the street and, like a hunter lurking behind a blind, await the sudden appearance of his prey.

When Debbie's silver Camry made its appearance, his heart flipped and skipped, giving him a lump in the throat that he could not swallow. He found himself staring at the car as it neared his driveway and then eyeing Debbie's movements as she got out of her car and walked towards his front door. In a flash, his mind took him back to the first time he saw her standing at his door as Sara and he drove in. He even remembered her thin black briefcase, her elegant dark gray suit, her professional demeanor, her confident smile, and her extended hand as she introduced herself with, *"Hello, I am Debbie Hunt, a CPS worker from the DHS."*

Why all these details rushed into his consciousness was a mystery to Scott as deep as why, all of a sudden, he had become fascinated by the details of Debbie's appearance as if he were seeing her for the very first time. Mesmerized in his window seat, he felt a child-like thrill as he watched Debbie approach and secretly admired her vibrant figure marching with elegant strides towards his front porch. She wore black jeans, a black turtleneck, and a white blazer that contrasted admirably with her brunette skin, short-brown hair, and deep-green eyes. For the first time ever, Scott gasped as he realized what a beautiful woman Debbie Hunt was. Lost in this very thought and pondering how come he had never noticed her beauty before, he was alerted by a gentle tapping at his door.

Startled, he jumped out of his seat, opened the door, and whispered, "Thanks for remembering not to ring the doorbell."

"Is she still asleep?"

"Yes, oh, please, come in, and, oh, thank you for coming. I really hated to impose but I didn't know what else to do. Please, have a seat. I made coffee. Would you like a cup?"

"Sure, Mr. Thornton, a cup of coffee would be fine."

When Scott returned with coffee, Debbie had left the living room and was standing by Sara's door. Not wanting to bother her, he sat on the living room sofa, placed the two cups on the coffee table, and waited for her to join him. The coffee was almost cold by the time Debbie returned and took her place on the other side of Scott. Even though Debbie's face wore a worried look that Scott found unsettling, nothing was said as they sipped on their lukewarm coffee and avoided each other's eyes. Periodically, Scott would look at Debbie and she would return his look with an enfeebled smile that belied her concern. He knew that she would say something when she was ready and he also knew not to rush her with questions while she was still thinking.

After tipping the coffee cup to take the last sip, Debbie broke the silence with, "She's still deep in sleep."

"Should we wake her up?"

"No, let her rest."

"Is she still sucking on her thumb?"

"No but it is still in her mouth and she is still curled up like a fetus."

"What do you think happened to cause her to regress so fast?"

Debbie repositioned herself so that she was looking straight at Scott before she asked, "Does Breena carry any resemblance to Nancy?"

Scott, taken aback, coughed, struggled for words, lowered his eyes, and after a short pause, whispered, "Well, now that you said it, she sure does. Oh, God. She not only looks like Nancy but she also acts like her."

"Well, it all makes sense then."

"What do you mean?"

"Sara is not only afraid of Nancy, she's afraid of anyone that reminds her of Nancy. In psychology, this is known as transference."

"Transference? You mean that seeing Breena transferred Sara back to her life with Nancy?"

"You're very close. Seeing Breena evoked deeply buried emotions of fear that were accrued while Sara lived with Nancy. These painful, frightening emotions were then projected onto Breena, causing Sara to reject Breena because she personified the threat to Sara's life with you."

"So, she escapes her emotions by going to sleep?"

"That's what traumatized children do. When they feel threatened, they regress into an earlier, safer stage of their lives and hibernate in it."

"And how long will she stay asleep?"

"She's afraid to wake up, Mr. Thornton, afraid to wake up to a new reality that threatens her newfound sense of security and peace with you."

"And so, we just let her sleep?"

"Yes, we just let her sleep until she's ready to wake up."

"And then, after she wakes up, what do we do?"

"We get rid of her transference."

"And how do we do that?"

"We're already doing it."

"We are?"

"When she wakes up and sees that you're with me instead of Breena, she will settle down and learn to feel secure again."

"But, what if you were not here when she wakes up?"

"I have no plans to go anywhere."

"But, we have no right to take away all your personal time. You have done more than enough for the Thorntons."

Debbie's eyes slowly gleamed with delicate moisture as she lowered her gaze, hoping that Scott would not notice. But her tears surprised Scott, whose detached demeanor belied his enthrallment. Not knowing how else to respond, he lowered his eyes and fixed them on her fingers instead. During this silent interlude, her fingers fumbled for a position and then became fisted as if they were holding some valuable secret. While each of them tried to think of something to say, the stillness between them stretched and yawned until it became too awkward to sustain.

The first to emit a polite cough was Scott. Debbie responded by un-fisting her hands and rubbing her sweaty palms onto her jeans. Then, as if that motion was her first word, she continued, "You see, Mr. Thornton, I know a lot more about you than you care to know about yourself."

"Oh?"

"Well, I've been in communication with Captain Peckford via a special Internet Iraq Line and I also meet with him each time he comes to Oklahoma. He feeds me, among other things, the social reports pertaining to the conditions of women and children all over Iraq and I also translate for him certain Baghdad newspapers that carry pertinent articles about the Iraqi people, their ideas, and their perceptions of our US military efforts. Then, I use this information to update the monthly pamphlets that get incorporated into the syllabus, which I had written for the Iraqi Women Volunteers when I was in Baghdad. I've been doing this ever since I came back from Iraq last year. No one here is supposed to know and no one really does except you, now."

Scott's eyes went wild with surprise and enthrallment. He cocked his head as he smiled at Debbie with unconcealed admiration and fascination.

"And all this time, I thought you were just a DHS

worker."

"Well, I am that too. But it is because of my Peckford connection that I happen to know what you've done for our country both here and in Iraq and how well you've served our anti-terrorism cause. Mr. Thornton, you may not know it, but you are a national hero. However, for your own safety and because of certain Al-Qaeda cells that are still operating in the US, your name has been kept secret and your planned decorations have been temporarily suspended."

Scott was overtaken with embarrassment as he mumbled, "I don't think that I did all that much really, and I sure don't feel like a hero should feel."

"And how should a hero feel, Mr. Thornton?"

"I don't know. Perhaps a hero should feel important or significant or at least special and I don't feel any of these things."

"But that's what makes you a true hero. Your sincere humility, Mr. Thornton, is indeed your crown."

Here, Debbie's expression changed from an admirer to a supplicant as she took leave of the moment and quoted: "You give but little when you give of your possessions. It is when you give of your self that you truly give."

Scott's eyes opened wide and he cried, "Who said that?"

"Kahlil Gibran in *The Prophet*."

Scott was so taken by Debbie's quote that he craved more. Something about her ability to quote so poignantly reminded him of Peckford and Peckford's erudite excogitations. Without a tint of embarrassment, he confessed, "I've never heard of him but I like how he says things. What else did this prophet say?"

Debbie was thrilled at being asked to say more about Gibran. After introducing *The Man From Lebanon* to Scott and telling him that he was one of her favored spiritual writers, she quenched Scott's thirst with one more of Gibran's sayings about giving: "There are those who give with joy, and that joy is their reward. And there are those who give in pain, and that pain is their baptism. And there are those who give and know not pain in giving, nor do they seek joy, nor give with mindfulness of virtue. They give as in yonder valley the myrtle breathes its fragrance into space. Through the hands of such as these God speaks, and from behind their eyes He smiles upon the earth."

Scott was so deeply moved and overcome with emotion that he reached for Debbie's hand lying flat on the sofa between them and began stroking it with his fingertips. Debbie, who had not allowed a man to touch her ever since her rape, froze underneath Scott's soothing fingers and for some inscrutable reason did not withdraw her hand. Instead, she surprised herself and Scott by clasping Scott's hand with a famished grip, pursing her lips, and holding her breath. The stunning language expressed by a man's touch felt so foreign to Debbie's heart, so uncultivated, so unnatural that it held her spellbound and spiraled her thoughts into burning swirls of disbelief. Transfixed by the moment, she held her breath as long as she could endure but when she at length breathed out, her sigh droned like a pastoral oboe crying for love among the hills.

Scott waited for Debbie's pallid lips to stop mumbling but they didn't nor did her crimson blush recede from her face. She seemed suspended by some numinous force somewhere between reality and the ether. He tried to listen to her mumblings but the only words he could decipher were "the moving finger," which she incoherently repeated over and over. Reluctant to intrude but unable to control his need to rescue her from wherever she was mired, he leaned over, lifted her compliant hand to his lips, and whispered into her clasping fingers, "What did the moving finger say?"

Shocked by his warm, moist breath, she pulled back her hand, put it in her lap, repositioned herself, and with downcast eyes replied, "Oh, it's just a quote from Khayyam."

"And who is Khayyam?"

"An eleventh century Persian poet."

"And what did he say about the moving finger?"

"He wrote a quatrain about it."

"What's a quatrain?"

"It's a group of four lines of verse."

Scott, noting Debbie's reticence, moved closer to her, held her hand again, and pleaded, "What did this moving finger say?"

Without lifting her eyes or taking back her hand, Debbie recited Khayyam's quatrain:

"The moving finger writes and having writ
 Moves on, nor all thy piety or whit
 Shall lure it back to cancel half a line
 Nor all thy tears wash out a word of it."

When she finished, Scott for the first time saw her tears, which she carefully wiped with her free hand. Then, after a polite pause, he looked at her as if he were seeing her for the first time as a real woman and with gleaming eyes confided, "You're starting to sound just like Peckford. You know how to use big words with deep meanings and they sound good the way you say them. You even have his deep-green and profound eyes. Now I understand why you've always seemed familiar to me."

Debbie chuckled at Scott's unexpected remark and asserted, "He must have rubbed off on me just as much as he rubbed off on you."

"And I'm sure glad he did."

Here, Debbie found a way out of this awkward situation. Grasping the moment, she pulled back her hand and redirected the conversation towards Peckford and Scott.

"What a remarkable man, Peckford. In his last communiqué, he told me that, thanks to your recent ID, they had successfully deluded Al-Qaeda on several occasions and have been able to abort several of its planned operations. He also said that this has made Al-Qaeda furious and that he fears they might throw all their powers into some desperately reckless retaliation just to show us how powerful they still are."

Scott nodded approvingly and added, "I sure know how mean they can get when they're angry."

"Well, they're very angry here too because, contrary to all expectations, the cell you uncovered when you rescued Sara has been talking and has given us valuable information about the structures and functions of other US cells. With this major breakthrough, which took the Homeland Security by surprise, you have done your country another great favor, Mr. Thornton, and that's why we all feel indebted to you. Giving my time and attention when you and Sara need me is but a very small payment on the debt we all owe you."

"Don't talk like that please. It makes me feel very uncomfortable."

"Well, tell me then how you'd like me to talk, and I'll be happy to change."

"I'd like you to talk to me like a real woman talks to a real man and I'd like you to stop calling me Mr. Thornton and start calling me Scott instead."

Debbie, grasping the significance of Scott's remark, blushed, stood up as if at attention, hid her restless hands behind her back, sat down again, and then exclaimed with newfound wonder, "Oh, dear, I'm going to have a hard time calling you Scott and even a harder time treating you like a real man when I hold you in such high regard."

"Oh, come on, it can't be that hard. You're already a member of the Thornton family and Sara loves you like a child should love a mother."

Debbie, like Peter, for the third time denied as she proclaimed, "But, oh, no, I'm not sure I'm ready for all that. I will need time, lots of time before I stop seeing you as a hero and begin seeing you as a real down-to-earth man."

Scott's face suddenly took on a firm, piercing look and he addressed Debbie in the very same manner in which Peckford used to address him under similar conditions. Unaware, his voice became cuttingly sharp, commanding, and slow as he rejoindered, "Debbie Hunt. Sooner or later you'll have to stand up to your own fear just like I stood up to mine. You can't keep running away from the part of life that makes you a real woman."

Debbie, stunned by Scott's frank confrontation, fell silent as she fumbled for an answer. Then, when no real answer came to her mind, she took refuge in simple denial and pretending not to understand what truth Scott was alluding to, exclaimed with much surprise, "What fear are you talking about? I'm not afraid. I've done more with my life so far than most women my age and I'm very content with what I have become."

Scott's face did not waver and his voice became even more assertive as he, in an authoritative manner that Debbie was unaccustomed to, reiterated the same sentence that Peckford had said to him on multiple occasions after the catacomb beheadings, "Debbie Hunt. Denial is not the way of the brave."

"Oh, Sara! Good morning, Princess. Come here to me. Oh, how much I've missed you."

It was with saving grace that Sara appeared when she did and, glowing with gladness at finding her dad sitting very close to Debbie on the living room sofa, flung herself with a loud giggle into Debbie's wide-open arms.

Chapter Thirty-Four
(The Bells)

Saturday passed in poised harmony as Sara and Debbie, who seemed to have become inseparable, directed Scott's activities. It was all done, however, in the name of rehabilitation. Whatever was deemed good for Sara was done with a teaspoon of humor and a tablespoon of hope. Thus, the three had lunch at McDonald's, loitered in the Quail Springs Mall, saw an animated movie in the afternoon, and hastily drove home before dark.

By the time they walked out of the movie theater, the sky had darkened and the clouds wore a tenebrous frown. Sara took one look at the sky dome and the first words out of her mouth were, "I want to go home."

Debbie and Scott watched her cheerful little face lose its smile and become contorted with fearful furrows. Without saying a word Scott lifted Sara into his arms, hurried to the car, and motioned to Debbie to sit next to Sara in the backseat. On the way home, Debbie held Sara's hand and asked, "Did you like the movie?"

"Uh-huh."

"Do you have a tummy ache?'

"No."

"Do you like it when the sky gets dark?"

"No."

"What does it remind you of?"

"The box."

"What box?"

"The box in the closet."

"And what else does the dark sky remind you of?"

"The trunk."

"What trunk?"

"The trunk of the car."

Debbie reached for the inside car light, turned it on, and while still holding Sara's hand whispered in her ear, "Was there anyone with you in the box or in the trunk?"

"No."

"Were you all alone in these dark places?"

"Uh-huh."

"But now, the lights are on, right?"

"Uh-huh."

"And both your dad and I are with you, right?"

"Uh-huh."

"So then you're not alone and it's not dark anymore, right?"

"Uh-huh."

After the last uh-huh, Sara's furrows began to relax, leaving an exhausted face in their wake. During the remainder of the car ride home, nothing else was uttered as Debbie, still holding Sara's hand, watched her close her tired eyes and slowly capitulate to sleep. At home Scott carried Sara off to her fenced bed where she curled into a fetal position, put her thumb in her mouth, and began to suck on it.

In the living room, Scott turned to Debbie and inquired, "How did you know about the box and the trunk?"

"I didn't."

"That was an amazing piece of detective work then."

"I recognize transference when I see it."

"Why did you suspect it?"

"Whenever a small thing causes a big emotion, it's transference. When the dark sky brought great fear to Sara's face, I knew that the closed-in darkness had to be a cue."

"I didn't even suspect the connection even though I knew about it. The bastards used to lock her in a box inside a closet whenever they had company and used to put her in the trunk of their car when they had to leave home."

Debbie, who could see Scott's bitter pain in his face and body language, felt an intense urge to hold him in her arms and tell him that Sara was going to be okay. However, feeling this overwhelming urge toward a man frightened her to the bone and caused her to become claustrophobic. Unaware of her own transference, she stood up, sighed, looked at her watch, and said, "It's time I went home. I have a lot of work to do and my report to Peckford must leave by midnight."

Scott did not want her to leave but knew that the time was not right to force the moment to its crisis. Although he had a lot more to say, he stood up, and careful not to seem disgruntled, extended his hand and said, "Thank you again for saving the Thornton's sanity at the expense of your valuable personal time."

"Glad to do it, Mr. Thornton."

"I thought you were going to call me Scott."

Debbie blushed, lowered her eyes, pulled her hand out of Scott's, and stuttered, "Ah, it seems so difficult to call you by your first name and I don't really understand why anymore."

"Could it be transference?"

"Oh, no. There is no transference here."

"But you just said that when a small thing causes a big emotion, there's transference."

At the mention of transference, Debbie became flustered, turned away, and without saying another word, walked towards the door. Scott followed behind and watched her open the door and step out alone into the stormy darkness. Without ever looking back, she mumbled a barely audible 'goodnight' and hurried to her car. He waited at the door while she fumbled for her keys, which because of the darkness and rain she had trouble finding. Then he rushed to her aid with an umbrella, helped her get into her Camry, and waited in the rain until she drove away. It was most peculiar, given the circumstances, that she did not say thank you or even wave goodbye before she took off.

Her hurried exit left a deep impression on Scott's mind. He sat on the living room sofa and began to excogitate. *"Why can't she call me by my first name? What's the big deal? There had to be transference, a big emotion for a small reason, but what is it? I wish I knew more about transference to decipher this situation. What's in a first name anyway? What? We use Mr. in formal address in order to keep a polite distance. First names are informal,* familiar, and much closer. *Closer? Distant? Oh, no, it must be distance then. Debbie must be more comfortable when she keeps her distance and must feel uncomfortable when she gets too close, too close to any man perhaps, but especially to an eligible man. That has to be it. There's no other explanation.*

That's what Jane told me in confidence. Debbie was date raped at fourteen and has never let a man touch her ever since. That's why she was in such a hurry to leave. She wanted to go home so that she could kneel in front of the statue of the Virgin on her dresser and pray until I will have passed out of her mind. She went home to pray to forget me. Oh, thank you Jane, but if she should ever find out that you had betrayed her to me, then all of us Thorntons would stand to lose her forever. I must be extremely careful. Yes, Scott Thornton, if you really want Debbie Hunt to keep her Thornton connections, you'll have to be extremely careful."

With Debbie gone and Sara asleep, Scott checked his e-mail, did the laundry, took a warm shower, sat in bed, and attempted to read some of his professional magazines. But no matter how hard he tried to concentrate, his mind wandered off towards Debbie, his new and most desperate obsession. He felt a strange urge to call her under some pretext and the only reason he didn't was because all the pretexts he could think of seemed too transparent. Thus far, he had never called her except when he needed her help with Sara. But with Sara asleep, if he were to call her at such a late hour, she would interpret his call as an advance and that could rekindle her transference and distance her further.   Sitting alone with insomnia, he rehearsed Jane's conversation over and over but no new ideas came to him. Exasperated, he thought of calling Jane but it was already past ten and definitely past her and Flora's bedtime. Crazed by his inability to suppress this newfound obsession with Debbie Hunt, he even thought of calling Breena Birdsong mainly because he knew that she would be delighted to hear from him regardless of the hour. But, this time, his automatic fingers refused to dial Breena's number and kept on dialing Debbie's instead. Of course, even though he dialed Debbie's number many a time, he never placed the call. At last, wilted with mental fatigue, his thoughts retracted for the night and surrendered him to sleep.

On that night of Saturday, November 18, 2006 sleep was extremely unkind to Scott Thornton. While all the women on his mind slept, Scott was suspended in quarter-sleep where his eyes were closed but his mind was awake with noise. No matter what he did, he could not silence a distant ringing in his ears except when he opened his eyes and sat up. But as soon as he lay flat and closed his eyes, the distant ringing returned. Unable to turn off this auditory hallucination, he decided to entertain himself by carefully studying the sounds. Only then, with his attention totally focused on the ringing, was he able to hear it clearly.

It came from bells, church bells, bells from far away in the distance, from the direction of Lake Hefner, from the direction of St. Michael's Church on the water. The bells were not only ringing, they were speaking in voices, first in the voice of Father Elias, the holy pastor, then in the voice of Father James, his young assistant who gave the homily, then in the voice of Scott Thornton protesting Father James's preaching on original sin. The words with which he had shocked the congregation rang loud in his mind: "I'm not a sinner, Father, nor is my innocent daughter Sara, or my wife Nancy. I am an honorable citizen who has recently finished two years of service in Iraq. We are a good family with a clear conscience and we live a peaceful, loving life."

Then the voices of the bells hopped over the boundary of quarter-sleep and chased Scott out of his bed. Open-eyed, he ran into the living room with his hands on his ears. He paced, sat on the sofa, paced again, but nothing stopped the voices of the bells. He went to the window where the curtains were still cracked and looked down the dark street; it was empty. He waited for Debbie's car but it did not appear. He returned to the sofa but instead of sitting in his usual place on the right, he sat on the left where Debbie had sat. As soon as he sat in Debbie's place, the voices of the bells disappeared. But when he moved back to his place on the right, the voices returned. He moved back to Debbie's place and the voices disappeared again. That's where Scott found himself when the sun, creeping in through the cracked curtains, woke him up. He was curled up into a ball on the living room sofa with his head on the side where Debbie Hunt had sat.

Stiff with bell voices, Scott stood up, stretched, and then he made his resolutions for the day. He was going to take Sara to church, to St. Michael's on the Water, and he was going to pray for her to have a good school week. He was also going to pray for his own peace and ask Jesus to make the voices of the bells disappear from his ears and never return. Then, after church, he was going to take Sara to visit her grandparents, a love visit that was long overdue.

With his new resolve, Scott's turmoil was replaced by a fresh sense of direction. He was going to raise Sara without anyone's help and take care of all her needs until she was grown. He was never going to call Debbie Hunt again nor depend on her to rescue his Sara from the pits of transference if it should recur. He was going to become the model of an independent, single father who would not need a woman's love to complete his life. These pacifying thoughts rejuvenated his self-confidence and washed away all his prior obsessions for Debbie Hunt and Breena Birdsong.

As for Peckford, his savior, he would always be his guiding light, his mentor, and the deepest love he had ever experienced except for his love for Sara. The final thought that hit Scott like an epiphany and helped him see his life with stark clarity were the profound realizations that without Sara's love, his life would have no meaning and without Peckford, it would have had no depth. But love, meaning, and depth could not complete a life. There was something missing, something of prime importance, something that Scott had never dared to face or embrace.

The only other thing missing from Scott's life was faith. His mentor's words rang truer now than ever before,

"Once fear conquers your heart, the only means to overthrow it is to hurl yourself back into it, over and over, until it runs away from you instead of you from it. Waste no time reasoning with fear, Scotty; its only antidotes are reckless courage and blind faith."

Scott knew within his heart that he needed to return to God in order to complete his life and rid it from fear and that Sunday, November 19, 2006 was going to mark the beginning of his return. Without a mother figure, the only one who could help him raise Sara and bring her fearless into the world was God. The church would have to become Sara's mother and within its bosom Sara would have to grow up and learn to conquer fear with faith.

Chapter Thirty-Five
(The Church Again)

Scott and Sara walked into St. Michael's Church holding hands. Many, who remembered Scott's last scene and also knew about his heroic rescue of Sara, took note of the two as they walked in. A whispering wave arose, and traveled from head to head all around the congregation until everyone had become aware of their presence. The only two that remained unaware of the commotion they had generated were Scott and Sara who, after crossing themselves, found seats in the inconspicuous pews of the middle section.

Somehow, word must have reached Father Elias and Father James because, all during the service, they kept glancing at Scott and seemed to conduct themselves with circumspect caution. But this time, by the grace of God, the homily that was given by Father Elias was not on the topic of original sin; rather, it was about fear in general and the fear of God in particular.

Holding Sara's hand, Scott listened politely and refrained from protesting when Father Elias proclaimed that the fear of God is key to the avoidance of sin while the awe of God was essential for the nourishment of faith. Scott, who had his own ideas about such matters, prayed for Sara's peace of mind and kept his disagreements to himself. When the service was over, several church members congratulated Scott, welcomed him back to the church, and hailed Sara with witty compliments.

As Scott and Sara were making their way out through the throngs, Sara suddenly squealed, let go of her father's hand, and ran towards the right exit door. By the time Scott caught up with her, Debbie Hunt was on her knees with Sara in her arms. The joy on Sara and Debbie's faces as they held each other glowed like a halo among the faithful crowd and caused Scott, who stood at a polite distance from the embracing couple, to smile with deep satisfaction. When Debbie was finally able to stand up and greet Scott, her first words to him were, "I had no idea you had become a man of faith."

"What on earth do you mean by that?"

"Well, I was at church that day when you stood up and protested to Father James that you were not a sinner. After that episode, you never returned."

"I had no idea you knew me then."

"Everybody knew you then."

"Oh, well, I kept my mouth shut today, didn't I?"

"What was it that you would have liked to protest against?"

"If you'll have lunch with Sara and me, I'll tell you."

When Sara heard the invitation, she tugged at Debbie's white dress and pleaded, "Please, Ms. Debbie, come to lunch with us, please."

Debbie glanced at Sara's adoring face, threw a sweeping look around to see if anyone was watching, blinked at Scott's smiling eyes, lowered her gaze, and with an animated voice said to Sara, "I'll be happy to join you for lunch, Princess. Other matters will just have to wait."

When the two walked out of the church holding Sara's hands, they appeared like a healthy young family and that's what Debbie was most concerned about. She did not want her church friends to think that she had changed her mind and begun dating. Nevertheless, for reasons that were too human to resist, she did sit next to Scott in the car and the three of them did take off while the entire congregation watched. Indeed, their unlikely liaison must have sparked a fiery wave of gossip judging by the number of long necks that tracked the car until it disappeared around the curve.

For lunch, the three went to the Mandarin Gazebo, a restaurant that Scott chose because of its cozy atmosphere and good service. The lunch conversation, constrained by Sara's presence, wandered upon safe paths and avoided prickly, personal matters. Debbie, who was most intrigued by Scott's show of faith, began by asking Scott the question that he had evaded earlier.

"So, what was it that you wished to protest against in

Father Elias's homily?"

"You really want to know?"

"You said that if I would have lunch with you and Sara, you would tell me."

"Well, what's this fear of God nonsense? The fear of God is key to the avoidance of sin? It sounds like an ultimatum and that's not how Jesus taught us."

"So you think that the fear of God should not be part of the creed?"

"Don't you see, Debbie, that doing what's right because of fear is doing it for the wrong reason. We should do what's right because we want to and not because we're afraid. Moreover, we should have faith and we should love God because we want to and not because we have to. Whatever is done under the threat of fear is done insincerely and therefore cannot be good."

Here Sara, who was also listening, interjected her own thoughts on the matter, "I think that fear is bad and because it's bad, it can't be good."

Debbie was taken by Sara's succinct syllogism. She smiled as she turned to Scott with a dozen questions in her eyes. Scott, who was also proud of Sara for coming to his support, returned Debbie's look with equal fascination. Sara had stated her point so well that there was hardly anything else anyone could say. Seizing the moment, Scott reversed the situation by asking Debbie if she feared God.

"Well, I don't think I fear him as much as I'm in awe of him. After all, look at all this beautiful creation and tell me that it doesn't give you a sense of awe."

"But awe is not fear; it is a form of love that is so sublime that it inspires great admiration. That's how Peckford explained it to me."

"And what else did Captain Peckford teach you?"

"He taught me that it was not possible for the one who instills fear to remain free from it."

"So you think that by instilling fear Father Elias could not be free from fear?"

"I don't think that Father Elias was instilling fear; he was doing something far worse than that."

"Oh, really? And what could that be?"

"By preaching fear he was committing the ultimate sin of blasphemy."

"Blasphemy, Mr. Thornton?"

"By condoning fear, he was in essence saying that God is the one who wishes to instill fear in us. And if that were true, then God could not be free from fear, and that is blasphemy indeed."

"Oh, Mr. Thornton. You wield dangerous reason upon my faithful mind. That's what the Sophists used to do. They could make a convincing argument for each side of any disagreement. That's where the word sophistry originated."

"I'm not a Sophist, Debbie, and even the Sophists couldn't have come up with a good argument for fear."

"Oh, yes they could have. They could say that fear is good as a survival asset and that without it we would not be able to recognize danger."

"But that's not the fear I'm talking about. I'm talking about the fear that ruins our lives and diminishes our souls. I'm talking about the fear that makes us live our lives like cowards."

"And I suppose that Peckford taught you that one too?"

"Here's what Peckford once said to me, 'Once fear conquers your heart, the only means to overthrow it is to hurl yourself back into it, over and over, until it runs away from you instead of you from it. Waste no time reasoning with fear, Scotty; its only antidotes are reckless courage and blind faith.'"

Debbie's face took on a distant, pensive look when she heard the quote and she became quiet for the longest while. Then, as if perturbed by her own silence, she took in a rueful sigh and exclaimed, "So true yet so hard to do. What other adages did Captain Peckford teach you?"

"He taught me to follow my heart."

"And where's your heart leading you, Mr. Thornton?"

"It's leading me to you, Miss. Hunt."

Debbie became visibly upset at Scott's remark and

turned away to hide her blush. Then she abruptly stood up, pulled her car key out of her purse, said goodbye to Sara, and got ready to walk out when she realized that she had left her car in the church parking lot. With no way to escape this awkward situation, she reluctantly sat down, turned to Sara, and began a new conversation.

"Did you like your food, Princess?"

"Uh-huh. But why are you so white, Ms. Debbie?"

Debbie covered her face with both hands as she answered, "Oh, I'm not white, am I?"

"You look pale."

"I, I don't know why I'm pale. But, perhaps if you sit in my lap, I would feel better."

Sara hopped out of her chair, climbed into Debbie's lap, and the two of them rocked back and forth in avoidant silence. Scott, who had by now regretted his amorous remark, asked for the bill, paid, and announced to the rocking couple that it was time to leave because Sara still had to visit her grandparents before going home.

Hand in hand, Debbie and Sara walked out of the Mandarin Gazebo with Scott behind them. On the way back to the church, Debbie sat in the back seat next to Sara and said nothing to Scott until they drove up to her Camry in St. Michael's parking lot. Scott jumped out of his seat, opened the door for Debbie, and whispered so that Sara would not be able hear him, "I'm sorry, Debbie, I didn't mean to rush you like that."

Debbie's voice was moist and tremulous when, with downcast eyes, she replied, "Give me time, Mr. Thornton. I'm not ready for all this yet and may never be. And, oh, don't forget, Sara has school tomorrow."

"I'll drop her at school on my way to work and I'll ask my mom to pick her up and keep her till I get off."

"You know that you can still call me if you need help with Sara."

"Thanks, but it's high time we manage on our own."

Saying that, Scott extended his hand to Debbie who pretended not to notice, turned away, got into her car, and drove off.

With her beret on, Sara was no longer averse to visiting her grandparents. Scott called his mom and dad who were overjoyed at the prospect of seeing their granddaughter. When Scott arrived, Jill and Howard rushed to the car with bundles of embraces in their arms. They whisked Sara into the house where play and chocolate-chip cookies were the hors d'oeuvres and multiple gifts of clothes and toys were the entrée. Sara, oblivious of her hair, reveled in the attention, laughed, giggled, and hopped from Jill to Howard's laps like a flighty songbird dizzy with spring.

Scott, on the other hand, did not get much attention till it was time to leave. At the door, he asked his mom and dad if they would mind picking up Sara from St. Helena School at three and keeping her till he came for her after work. The Thorntons seemed dismayed to find out that Nancy was no longer going to pick Sara up from school and with their silent faces asked a thousand questions. Nevertheless, although Scott did not explain the details of what had really transpired, it did seem that the Thorntons understood enough to leave the matter un-broached. Of course, they were delighted at the prospect of spending quality time with Sara and jumped at the chance of picking her up after school without hesitation.

As Scott and Sara were about to drive away and the Thorntons were about to close their door, Jill let out a cry and ran back to the car. Scott became alarmed when he saw his mother running towards them. He opened his window and cocked his head out.

"Don't forget Thursday at two."

"Thursday at two? What the heck are you talking about, Mom?"

"It's Thanksgiving, Scotty."

"Oh, this coming Thursday?"

"Yes, Honey. This coming Thursday is Thanksgiving. It'll be Jane and Flora, you and Sara, and your dad and me. The last two Thanksgivings you were in Iraq, remember?"

"You mean that I've not had your turkey and stuffing for three years?"

Jill playfully slapped Scott's face and turning to go repeated, "Thursday at two and don't forget to bring along our little Sara."

Later on, at the Bradfords, the reception was equally warm but with a hint of surprise on the faces of Peter and Francis caused by Nancy's un-explicable absence. While Francis was busy entertaining Sara, Peter took Scott to the side and asked him the sentinel question.

"Where's Nancy?"

"I really don't know, Sir. She doesn't seem to want to be with us anymore."

"We thought that you were back together; what on earth happened?"

"It all seemed to change when Sara came back."

"Change? In what way?"

"Well, it's too complicated to explain, Sir, but the result of it all is that Sara became afraid of Nancy and also Nancy became afraid of Sara."

"So, what does that mean for Sara's future?"

"Well, Sir, it seems that Nancy does not want Sara to live with her anymore. She indicated that she's ready to give me full custody."

"But why? It seems so unnatural for a mother to behave that way."

"I don't understand it either, Sir. She surprised the heck out of me when she told me that she no longer wanted to have anything to do with Sara or me."

When Sara and Scott left, the Bradfords' faces were tainted with the realization that Nancy, their only daughter, had indeed abandoned her only child. Scott spared Peter and Francis the painful details of the schism and left it to them to find out from Nancy what had really happened. However, he could not help but suspect that the Bradfords were half-aware of the situation because they appeared to be much more dismayed than surprised.

Back home, Scott paved the way for Monday by

mentioning school to Sara while she ate her bedtime snack and was thrilled to find out that she was looking forward to it. But, when he tried to lower the bedrail for the night, Sara became uncomfortable and asked him to raise it up again.

"I can't sleep with the fence down, Daddy."

"Why not, Baby? Are you afraid you'll fall?"

"No, I'm afraid that someone will crawl into bed with me."

"Well then, in that case, let's keep the fence up and also keep the lights on. We don't want any intruders, do we?"

That night Sara slept unexpectedly well, did not curl up into a fetal position, and did not suck her thumb. Scott, on the other hand, was the one who paced the house and had a difficult time finding sleep. Granted, there was so much on his mind but the thing that really kept him awake was the fact that he felt desperately lonely. And the more he examined his feelings of loneliness the more he realized that Sara's love was not enough to sustain him for the rest of his life. He needed a meaningful relationship, someone else to love, a real woman with whom to share his evenings, nights, weekends, and life. With Nancy out of the picture, Debbie on the run, and Breena rejected by Sara he felt abandoned, helpless, and defeated. Rescuing Sara, it seemed, had reduced his chances at having a normal life, a sacrifice that he did not at all regret in spite of the painful realities that came along with it.

The dual natures of loneliness and solitude vied for his attention and brought back to his mind the long discussion that he and Peckford had had about the matter. Peckford had taught him that solitude was desirable and voluntary because it reset the mind and promoted internal peace through self-analysis and self-knowledge. Loneliness, on the other hand, resulted from the lack of desperately needed love, which in Scott's case meant the love of a real woman. Pondering his deep love vacuum, Scott felt trapped between the banks of solitude and loneliness, swept by currents that he could not control, and hurled towards a stagnant pond where what flowed in did not flow out.

Realizing that he could not find an exit out of his mental maze, he began to feel cornered as if he were a helpless prey surrounded by a pack of wolves. It was from within this abject despair, when he felt trapped beyond rescue, that he took refuge in prayer.

He knelt in front of the living room sofa—the same sofa where the brown paper bag that held Sara's hair had sat and where Debbie Hunt had sat—closed his eyes, and with a supplicating Christian soul, opened his heart to Jesus.

Chapter Thirty-Six
(School)

With the first light, Scott was up and busy like a traveler embarking on a destiny trip. The wind of time filled up his sails and sped him across the morning with enormous energy. When all was done and he went to wake up Sara, he found her sitting in bed waiting for him.

"Good morning, Baby."

"Would you please help me out?"

"But, what's the matter now? I can understand why you need help climbing into bed but you've always been able to climb out."

Sara stroked her stubbles and with a reproachful look whispered, "It didn't grow back."

"But you have your beautiful beret."

"Uh-huh."

A melancholy mask colored Sara's face as she raised her arms and waited until her dad picked her up.

On the way to St. Helena, Sara repeatedly adjusted her beret and had little to say in response to her father's prodding. At the gate, Mrs. Mann, her teacher, helped her out of the car, gave her a great welcoming hug, and sent her on her way into the building. Scott watched Sara walk into the school without ever looking back or waving goodbye. The image of her slow, hesitant pace and bowed head as she walked in accompanied Scott all the way to the Hartland Bank. Unaware of all the eyes upon him, he too walked in with a slow, hesitant pace and bowed head as if his mind were still at the St. Helena gate. What startled him out of his reverie was the loud clamor of applause that exploded at his arrival. The lobby of the bank teemed with loud, welcoming hurrahs, clapping hands, and cheering faces that rushed at him from all sides. Not knowing how to respond to this dizzying hero welcome, he just stood there with a thousand hands patting his back and shoulders until Mr. McMaster, standing on a side table, rang the bell and delivered his oration.

When it was over and Scott was able to get to his office, he found a large bouquet of flowers on his desk with a yellow ribbon tied around it. The attached card, in Mr. McMaster's handwriting, read: "The Hartland Bank has never claimed a hero among its ranks until today. On behalf of our country, our city, and our dignity, we thank you for holding up the torch."

At noon, Breena Birdsong waltzed into Scott's office, sat down, and crossed her legs. When Scott ignored her, she whispered with a deliberately hoarse voice, "I waited all weekend for your call."

Without looking at her, Scott whispered back, "I'm sorry. Sara was needing every minute of my time."

"If you'll take me out to lunch, I'd forgive you."

Scott looked up and blinked as though his eyes were suddenly stung by Breena's fishnet hose and ultra-short skirt. He wanted to say that he had too much work, that he was so much behind, and that he was not going to take a lunch break for the rest of the year but, because of his profound loneliness, he didn't. Confronted by a wanton woman caused chills to run up his spine. As his mind was about to convince him that Sara didn't need to know about their lunch date and that he could make time for Breena while his mom and dad kept Sara after school, his cell phone rang. It was Sara's teacher, Mrs. Mann.

"Oh, what's wrong?"

"Well, nothing serious, but I thought you should know what happened before you pick Sara up this afternoon."

"My mom and dad will be the ones picking her up from now on."

"Oh, I'm glad you told me. We're kind of paranoid after what happened."

With Scott anxiously waiting, Mrs. Mann took in a deep sigh and began Sara's story.

"Well, you see, Mr. Thornton, children can be very cruel at times. There's a boy in Sara's class, Sid Jordan, who is kind of a bully. At lunch, he snatched Sara's beret and ran off with it. I'm proud of the rest of the kids because they didn't laugh or cheer; they simply watched as he ran through the dining room flaunting Sara's beret. Before any of us could stop him, Sara caught up with him and tripped him. He threw her beret into the air as he fell to the floor and the kid who caught it started to bring it to Sara but stopped when he saw little Sara jump on Sid's chest and hammer him with both her fists. By the time I got her off him, she had bloodied his nose and mouth."

"Is he all right?"

"Well, we called his mom and she took him home."

Scott, not knowing if he should smile or frown, scratched his head, looked at Breena's fishnet hose, and asked, "Should I call and apologize to his mom?"

"As a matter of fact, the mom, who like all of us here, had followed Sara's story on TV and in the papers, made it a point to apologize to Sara. She felt so ashamed of her son's behavior that she told me in private that she was glad he got what he deserved."

"And how's Sara doing?"

"She seems fine. Oh, and about her beret, she gave it to me and said that she didn't need it anymore."

Scott recognized the feeling. He remembered the moment when he lost his fear after the Baghdad meeting. He remembered asking Peckford if Jonathan Brighton's mother was Iraqi, remembered his ensuing catharsis after the find, and remembered telling Peckford, "Oh, Sir, all of a sudden, I'm no longer afraid." Scott, who understood perfectly well what Sara's gesture meant, became overjoyed and could not hide his smile. *My Sara just lost her fear of being seen with a bald head,* he thought. *"Blind faith and reckless courage, that's what it took. I wish I could tell Peckford."* With all of this at once in his mind and with his eyes still fixated upon Breena's thighs, Scott left Mrs. Mann utterly confused when he said, "Throw the beret into the fishnet then and let's forget that she ever wore it."

"I beg your pardon?"

"Oh, what I meant to say was—please put the fishnet

in a brown paper bag and I'll pick it up when I bring her to school tomorrow."

Mrs. Mann let out a polite laugh, paused to give Scott time to recover, and then added, "Mr. Thornton, I do appreciate the enormous stress you're under and I think I understand that you'd like me to put Sara's hat in a bag and give it to you tomorrow morning when you drop her at school."

Unaware of his multiple faux pas, Scott thanked Mrs. Mann and, looking at Breena with a triumphant face, declaimed, "Let's go to the Metropolis; I hear their lunches are out of this world."

At lunch, Scott and Breena tiptoed around delicately intertwined conversations gossamered with genteel apprehensions. Each time Breena titillated, Scott shied away and when she intimated he feigned misapprehension. It was clear to her that he was interested yet reluctant just like a hungry fish lured by bait yet still cautious enough not to bite. By the time lunch was over, Scott had acquiesced to stopping by her apartment for a drink. The time was left open, however, until Sara would have made the necessary adjustments to her new routine. When Breena and Scott walked out of the Metropolis it had become clear, though never stated, that the winter of their relationship had ended and its spring was on the gates.

Lonely men have been known to do desperate things and Scott Thornton was no exception. On his way back to the bank, he hardly said a word to Breena. While she small-talked, his mind was with Peckford. One of Peckford's quotes had come to his mind and he mumbled it to himself as they awaited the elevator, "Yet many a man is making friends with death for lack of love alone." Breena looked at him with curious eyes while he mumbled unaware.

"Are you talking to yourself, General?"

"Oh, something came to my mind, something from a long time ago."

"Is it a secret?"

"No, it's a quote from a poem."

"Who's the poet?"

"I have no idea."

"If you give me the name of the poem, I can Google it for you."

"I don't know that either."

"Well what's the quote? I might be able to find it just from that."

The elevator's ring interrupted the conversation. Scott and Breena rushed in and lost their privacy in the lift's congestion. At the ninth floor, they parted with a soft au revoir and went back to their work.

After work, Scott hurried to his parents' home to find Sara sitting between his mom and dad having a snack with no head cover except her two-week-old stubbles. There was renewed confidence in her eyes as she told her dad about her first day at school. Scott had learned enough from Debbie to know not to inquire about Sara's hat. The hat, the chase, and the wrestling match remained unmentioned by Sara who seemed blissfully oblivious of the eventful happenings on her first school day. On the way home, Scott was too thrilled with Sara's progress to dwell on his own loneliness. After all, Breena Birdsong and he could become a couple when Sara became less needy and that time, given Sara's striking progress, did not appear to be too far away.

A little excitement crept into Scott's soul as he pondered his life to come. For the first time since Sara's kidnapping, he felt that his love emotions might become rekindled by Breena and his lost freedoms might become reinstated. As their relationship evolved, he could learn to love Breena and, in time, so could Sara. Meanwhile, however, he was intimately tethered to Sara regardless of the limitations inherent in that responsibility. Tacitly, he resolved not to expose Sara to Breena again until he felt that she was ready to accept her as a new member of the family.

At bedtime, Scott was surprised to find that Sara had

regressed a bit. She insisted on having her bedrails all the way up and asked Scott to lift her into her bed again. She also wanted the bedroom lights on, the door open, and she again slept in a fetal position with her thumb in her mouth. Scott had hoped, of course, to find her fearless after winning her first wrestling match. But, for that to happen, she had to await another breakthrough, which was not foreseeable from that point in time.

That Monday night, with a relatively clear mind, Scott had time to think. Life had dealt him a few tragedies followed by a few victories and while his tragedies seemed to be retreating, his victories seemed to be blossoming. Recognizing that life could never be perfect, he was rather content that his life had become perfect enough for the time being. For a long while, Breena Birdsong had had a crush on him and for a long while he had resisted encouraging her. But, for whatever reason, Breena Birdsong had suddenly become attractive to his senses, perhaps because she had diluted his loneliness with her flippancies. Still, deep in his heart, he had to admit that he could never marry her because he knew that she could not be the mother that Sara needed.

After that thought, his mind went to church. There was a singles club at St. Michael's Church that he was welcome to join and through it find the right woman. He wouldn't mind having another child to cement his marriage if his new wife proved to be a good mother to Sara. Then his mind took him to family, friends, and coworkers who could also match him with a compatible lady. Then, there was the Internet and all the datelines within its cyberspaces. With all these possible avenues, he felt reassured that in time he would be able to find his new soul mate and rebuild his life. Meanwhile, he would concentrate on his work and on Sara and, like so many other single parents, would do all he could to normalize their life together.

The next two days passed without mishaps as things returned to normal and routines became reestablished.

Breena flirted with Scott at the office and he flirted back. When on Tuesday she came into his office with a bunch of files in her arms, Scott noticed that she was wearing regular pantyhose and told her that he'd rather see her legs through the fishnet spaces. Her surprised eyes giggled at his remark and her face reveled in the pleasure of knowing that, indeed, he had noticed. On Wednesday, when she brought him the new loan files, she walked in wearing a wry smile, sat down, fluffed her hair, crossed her fishnet legs, and droned, "And I thought that you never noticed."

"Well, I do have eyes, you know."

"Eyes, yes, but I wasn't sure about the man behind them."

It was just after that wry comment and before Scott could repartee that Mr. McMaster walked into Scott's office, handed Breena an envelope with ten $100 bills in it, and said, "Would you please give this money to the janitors when they come in to clean, this evening. There are five of them and each gets a $200 tip for Thanksgiving. They usually come in half an hour after we close. I've always given it to them myself but today I need to leave early."

"Sure, Mr. McMaster, I'll be more than happy to do it. Besides, I can use that half hour to get caught up on some of my delinquent work."

After that, Mr. McMaster exchanged a few courteous remarks with Scott, wished Breena and him a happy Thanksgiving, and walked out.

Sara was happy to go to school, happy to be picked up by her grandparents, and eager to be reunited with her dad after he returned from work. Not once did she mention her mother and, of course, not once did Nancy call to check on her. Tuesday, on the way home, Sara asked her father when they were going to see Ms. Debbie again. Scott explained in a kind but firm voice that, "When we need her, she'll make time for us. But, when we're doing fine, she needs to spend her time with the other children who need her more."

Coming back home on Wednesday, Sara started the

conversation with, "I miss Ms. Debbie. Why can't we invite her to dinner?"

"Well, Darling, she's busy with other children."

"But I think she loves me more than she loves the other children, doesn't she?"

"I'm sure she does, Honey. But, she has a life to live and we don't want to get in her way, do we?"

"Uh-huh."

"Besides, tomorrow is Thanksgiving and we're gonna be with Grandma Jill and Grandpa Howard all afternoon. Aunt Jane and Flora are also coming. We're gonna have such a good time together and you're gonna be the queen of the party."

"But why can't Ms. Debbie come along with us?"

"Because she's gonna be with her own mom and dad."

"Uh-huh."

Observing Sara's doleful face through the rearview mirror brought pangs to Scott's heart and forced an unpleasant reality upon him. It was clear to him that Sara and Debbie had bonded. It was also clear that Sara was going to resist bonding with any other woman that he might choose. What was not clear, however, was whether Debbie felt as strongly towards Sara as Sara felt towards Debbie. This dilemma accompanied Scott all the way home and stayed with him for the rest of the evening. How could he possibly reconcile these two dissonant, emotional forces? Sara had bonded with Debbie as if she were her mother and had rejected Breena as her father's potential friend. Debbie, on the other hand, was resistant to the notion of wifehood and had clearly rejected his advances. Entangled in this dilemma, Scott felt even more alone and his loneliness grew darker with the advancing night.

After lifting Sara into her fenced bed and watching her curl into a fetal position with thumb in mouth, he left the bedroom with lights on and door open and retired to his study. At his desk, he tried to distract himself with e-mails and world news but all he saw was Sara's doleful face. He yearned to talk to Peckford but Peckford was in Baghdad. He wished he could visit the bench in order to clear his mind but to do that he would have to leave Sara alone. He tried to pray to Jesus but found out that he couldn't even pray. Mesmerized by Sara's face, all he could do was stare at his computer screen and see nothing. That was Scott's mental state, when at 10 p.m. on Thanksgiving's eve his cell phone began to vibrate.

"Hello?"

"Scotty, please, I need you."

"Nancy?"

"Oh, I feel so sick I could throw up."

"Nancy? Is that you? Your words are slurred."

"They are, agh... wait a minute, agh... agh..."

"Where are you calling from?

"From jail."

"Jail? What jail? What did you do?"

"I'm drunk and I ran a stop sign. They towed my car away. I need you to come and get me."

"Don't you have to post bail?"

"Oh, yeh, I forgot, fourteen-hundred dollars."

"Who has that much cash? Anyway, everything's closed till Friday morning."

"Oh, Scotty, I'll die if I stay here. It's horrible. Please come and get me."

"What jail are you in?"

"The Oklahoma City Municipal."

"Would you like me to call your parents?"

"Oh, no, please, I don't want them to know any of this."

By the time the call was over, Scott was covered with cold sweat and his head was fuming with indecision. He could not let Nancy spend the night in jail, nor could he get the needed cash, nor could he leave Sara alone to go get Nancy, nor could he wake Sara up to take her with him. His mind began to cave in under the weight of so many traps and his head began to feel too heavy for his neck. In despair, he laid his head on his desk, closed his eyes, and tried to pray but no words came to his mind. As he languished in this wet, confused state, the cell phone began to vibrate again. It was 10:30 p.m.

"Hello, General. Just calling to say good night and to wish you a Happy Thanksgiving."

"Breena?"

"Who else but the fishnet girl would call you so late?"

"Oh, Breena, I'm so glad you called. I sure have a problem on my hands."

After Scott finished telling Breena Birdsong the story, she burst into loud laughter, which left Scott even more confused. Apparently, the janitors did not show up half an hour after the bank closed and so Breena waited another half hour. But when they had not shown up by 6 p.m. she went home with the thousand dollars in her purse. She also had two hundred dollars of her own money and so did Scott. Between them they could muster the entire sum and all they had left was to figure out how to get it to Nancy.

After much deliberation, Breena came over to Scott's home and while she watched Sara, Scott paid Nancy's bail and drove her back to her apartment. When he returned it was after midnight and, by the grace of God, Sara was still asleep. Scott was so relieved and felt so indebted to Breena that he walked her to her white Mercedes, kissed her on the lips, and then traced her with his eyes until she disappeared behind the night.

Chapter Thirty-Seven
(Thanksgiving)

When Scott went to bed, it was already Thursday morning and when he woke up, the sun was already high in the sky and Sara was sitting by his side staring at him. Before he could give her a good-morning hug and applaud her climbing out of bed without his help, she said, "I'm hungry."

"And what would my little angel like for breakfast?"

"Eggs and toast."

"And how would you like the eggs done?"

"Just like Ms. Debbie did them when you were gone."

"And how did Ms. Debbie do them when I was gone?"

"I don't know. Can we call and ask her?"

"Oh, just tell me what they looked like and I bet I can do them just like hers."

"They were fluffy."

Scott scrambled the eggs just like Debbie did, browned the toast to perfection, and putting them before Sara said, "Voila."

Sara stared at the eggs but did not touch them and when Scott tired to entice her to eat by quipping, "I thought you said that you were hungry." she sighed but did not answer. Then Scott made a tactical error. Instead of holding her in his arms and distracting her, he pressed the issue to the edge of tears by holding an egg-loaded fork to her lips. With lips pursed, Sara flicked the fork away, scattering the eggs all over the kitchen floor, got up, and ran back to her room.

Perplexed, Scott cleaned up the mess and, deciding to leave her alone for a while, went to take his shower. An hour later, he tiptoed to her room but she was not there. He checked the kitchen, the other rooms, the garage, the car, and even the closets. Then he ran out, looked all around the house, checked the backyard, and was about to call the police when he felt an urge to look underneath the living room sofa. There was Sara curled into a ball and asleep with thumb in mouth. Next to her head lay the brown paper bag with her hair in it, which Scott had shoved under the sofa and forgotten about.

It was close to noon when Sara emerged from underneath the sofa with the brown bag in her hand. Her first words to Scott—who was patiently sitting on a nearby chair waiting for her to wake up—were, "This is my hair."

"What would you like us to do with it?"

"I'd like to give it to Ms. Debbie."

"And what would she do with it?"

"She'll keep it with her until my own hair grows back."

"And then what?"

"I don't know but she'll know. Can we call and ask her?"

"You know, today is Thanksgiving and we need to get ready to go to Grandma Jill and Grandpa Howard's. Aunt Jane is coming and Aunt Flora and it's going to be a lot of fun and you're going to be the party queen."

"Is Ms. Debbie coming?"

"No, Baby, Ms. Debbie is going to her own folks. That's what families do; they get together for Thanksgiving."

"But I thought that we were her family."

Scott decided not to respond to that last statement. Instead, he took Sara onto his lap and tried to distract her. She was stiff and did not want to cuddle. When he tried to take the brown paper bag out of her arms, she clung to it as if it were her Barbie doll. When he tried to coax her into getting dressed and ready, she said that she did not want to go anywhere. And when he tried to entice her with all kinds of rewards, she said that she didn't want anything. Indeed, all of Scott's fatherly attempts to soften her stubborn rejection ended up in failure. She was still pouting in his lap when the doorbell rang and startled the two out of their seats. It was one o'clock.

Scott carried Sara and her brown paper bag to the door. There was a taxicab parked in the driveway and a man at the door with a gift bag in his hand.

"Are you Mr. Thornton?"

"Yes."

"And is this pretty girl Miss Sara?"

"Yes?"

"Well, this gift is for her from Ms. Debbie."

Sara's excitement at Debbie's gift was uncontainable. She overflowed with exuberance as she opened the package to find a beautiful pink dress with a burgundy velvet jacket. In the package, the card read, "Happy Thanksgiving, Princess. I love you. Debbie." After that, Sara needed no help getting dressed and ready. Her sudden transformation from withdrawn to exuberant knocked on Scott's head and begged an explanation. Question after question assailed his mind and before he could answer one, another would take its place and another and another until he felt like a beehive teeming with mystery. The only plausible explanation he could invoke to explain Sara's sudden mood switch was love. The gift, the note, the timing, and the choice of colors all said that Ms. Debbie loved her and missed her terribly.

As Sara reveled in her new attire, Scott wrestled with his feelings of rejection. With the coming of the gift, two facts had crystallized in his mind—Debbie loves Sara and Debbie does not love him. Although he needed a woman's love as much as Sara needed a mother's love, Debbie Hunt was ready to give hers to Sara but not to him. Peckford's quote rang loud in his mind again, "Yet many a man is making friends with death for lack of love alone." But, determined not to let Sara or his parents see through his grief, he put on a cheerful front, donned a light gray suit, selected a red necktie, and took off as planned.

On their way to his parents' home, Scott and Sara frolicked like teenagers with much talk of little substance. When they drove into Jill and Howard's driveway, it was 2:15 p.m. and Flora and Jane had already arrived.

Scott's mom met them at the door and, gloating over Sara's dress, flaunted her to the rest of the group. Throughout the entire affair—before, during, and after the meal—Sara was the pièce de résistance that everyone partook of. The joy imparted by little Sara was unsurpassable and made for a blithe Thanksgiving that overflowed with boisterous merriment. Sara was, as her dad had promised, the queen of the event and the one who had the best time of all. There was no doubt in anyone's mind that the Sara they knew had returned, seemingly unscathed, back to her family's bosom.

Small gossip arose here and there but always away from Sara's ears. Jane asked Scott where Nancy was; Flora asked Scott where Debbie was; the Thorntons asked Scott about the Bradfords. Scott, on the other hand, asked himself where Peckford was and wondered what kind of Thanksgiving they were having in Baghdad. Then his mind traveled to Breena and her face-saving kindness towards Nancy. And then his thoughts alighted on Debbie's rejection of him and her unilateral love for Sara.

After coffee with all bellies full, fatigue began to evince its long, pale face, gossip died down and was gradually replaced by yawns, and Sara's eyes began to close as she nestled into her father's lap. It was near evening when, with many a goodbye-kiss and a thank-you-hug, the group splintered and the couples went their separate ways. When Scott arrived home, Sara was asleep in her car seat. Afraid to wake her up, he carried her into her bed without taking her pretty dress off, made sure the bedrail was up, the light on, the bedroom door wide open, and then retired to his study. Sara and he had traveled far since the kidnapping and Thanksgiving this year was a thanks giving indeed.

Alone, at last, he obsessed again and again over the many meanings behind the gift that toppled Sara's mood. "*Really, why did she send it and how did she know to time it so perfectly? What caused Sara to become so suddenly enthralled? What was the transference that had brought about such an overwhelming change? Perhaps I should call Debbie and ask her? But what if she interprets my gesture as an advance, runs away, and refuses to give me another chance? No, I better not. But, isn't it time to accept reality and settle for what I can get? Breena is kind, playful, beautiful, sexy, and not as serious or mysterious as Debbie. But Debbie loves Sara and Sara loves Debbie. I don't know why it still hurts me to be outside their love duet. It's all about love, isn't it? All about love."*

As soon as Scott confronted the love link, he began to ask himself some severe questions. *"Was I ever in love? Have I ever loved anyone but Peckford and Sara? Is that why I'm so attached to the two of them? Is that why I'm hesitant about Breena? Could it be because I know that I couldn't really love her? Could that mean that my first need is to love a woman? Love a woman? I have never loved a woman. I've only loved another man and a child. I loved Sara before she was born, before I knew her, before I saw her. How can that be? Oh, how confusing.*

Perhaps I'm afraid to love a woman. Perhaps I'm just like Debbie, afraid to succumb to love. Oh, how confusing, indeed. Surely, Sara is not the only reason I want Debbie in my life. Surely, I feel drawn to her for other reasons. She's strong, smart, and reminds me of Peckford. She's beautiful and military like Peckford and has his deep-green eyes. She's a real woman just like Peckford is a real man. Could she be my transference? Could I be falling for her because she reminds me of Peckford now that Peckford is no longer in my life?

But why is it then that I think of her more than I think of Peckford? Why is it that whenever I try not to think of her she ends up on my mind like an obsession that is somewhere, everywhere, and nowhere all at the same time. Oh, no, I shouldn't fall in love with her. She's a dead end. No, I don't need more dead-end roads. I've had enough of those. But why do I feel so empty inside, so unfulfilled, so unsatisfied? I have a good job, a good life, and good parents. I have Breena waiting for me and I have my daughter back. So, what is it that I'm lacking? What is it that I'm afraid to face? I'm a hero on the outside and a coward on the inside. I resist my emotions and refuse to face them. I have no joy anymore. It can't all be transference. Oh, Peckford, Peckford, where are you now when I need you to set my mind free and to help me live for love and joy."

Unable to settle his own arguments, Scott left his study and began to pace the living room. He paced like a sleepwalker, open-eyed but dazzled. He paced unaware that he was pacing as if his head and body had become estranged from one another and no longer cared to communicate.

A far away light blinked through the curtain crack. It was an approaching car coming down the street. Scott sat by the window, leaned forward in his seat, and positioned his face right behind the curtains so that he could see without being seen. The car lights became brighter as they got closer, climbed up his driveway, and then turned off. It was too dark to see the car but when the door opened and the inside lights went on, he saw her. In disbelief, he rubbed his eyes and looked at her as she closed the car door and slowly walked towards the house. Then, midway, she stopped, went back to her car, got in, and sat there for the longest time. He vacillated between going to her or waiting for her but while trying to make up his mind, she started her car, backed out of his driveway, and drove away. He watched her reach the end of the street, stop, turn around, come back up his driveway, kill the engine, and sit alone in the darkness. He wanted to walk up to her and invite her in but found too late that he couldn't move.

Frozen in his seat, he watched her get out of the car again, walk towards his door, and tap it almost inaudibly. Not sure that he heard anything, he waited until she tapped again. At that point, there was no doubt in his mind that she was not a ghost. His limbs creaked; he got up, took a few paces, and opened the door. There she stood shivering, pale, blue-lipped, and wordless. He pulled her in, sat beside her on the sofa, and said nothing. Perhaps he feared starting a conversation without knowing where it would end. But when the silence became more painful than any words, he whispered, "Would you like some tea?"

"Yes please."

"I'll be back in a minute."

In the kitchen, Scott found himself becoming

frightened but did not understand why. His fear became so ominous that he was even afraid to let his mind do any thinking. Back into the living room with two cups of tea, he sat next to her and said nothing. The steaming cups on the side table remained untouched. Everything remained frozen in the silence of the moment. The only sounds that reached Scott's ears were his own heart beats. Then, with a hoarse, doleful voice and eyes glazed to the plumes rising from the teacups, she whispered, "Peckford is dead."

"What?"

"He was killed in an Al-Qaeda explosion this morning."

"Oh, my God..."

"Did you listen to the news?"

"News?"

"Al-Qaeda retaliated this morning. A series of car bombs and mortar attacks killed 215 people and injured 257 others. The Iraqi government placed Baghdad under 24-hour curfew and shut down the Baghdad International Airport."

"And where was Peckford?"

"They knew about the attacks and were trying to protect the inhabitants of Sadr City when a car bomb took him and four other members of his team."

"Debbie, are you sure?"

"It's official."

"I feel numb."

"Me too."

"Did you love him?"

"He was my uncle."

"Your uncle?"

"My father's brother."

"How come your name is not Peckford?"

"I changed it."

"Why?"

"To run away from my past."

"Oh? What kind of past?"

"There was a car accident. A boy was killed. His parents blamed me. I went away to college and changed my name before I returned to Oklahoma."

Scott and Debbie sat and watched the teacups get cold. The ominous silence, punctuated by sniffles and sighs, twisted the moments into contorted piles of rubble. Midnight crept cautiously among the wreckage of realities littered with shards of memories and splintered hopes. A light snore stole into Scott's ear and was followed by slow, rhythmic purrs. Cautiously, he turned towards the soft, sonorous sounds. Debbie had fallen asleep on the sofa, her head lay over her chest, and her hair hung over her face like a brown veil. Scott's heart sank under the profound weight of utter loneliness. Gently, he laid Debbie down on the sofa, placed a pillow under her head, covered her with a throw, turned the lights off, and retired to his room haunted by Debbie's eyes. *"She has Peckford's deep-green eyes. Must be the niece that Peckford talked to me about. No wonder I was drawn to her. She's all I have left of Peckford. Now I understand my déjà vu."*

Chapter Thirty-Eight
(The Chimes)

The remains of the night were unkind to Scott Thornton. He lay in bed among his bleak realities and inconsolable insomnia. Everyone was asleep, it seemed, but him. Debbie, Sara, Jane, Flora, his mom, his dad, and even Peckford lay still under the vast pergola of night except him. With the lights off and his eyes shut, he still saw everything that he did not wish to see. He saw the beheadings, heard Sara's tears from inside her box in the closet, saw Debbie being raped, and saw Peckford being blown up with his team. Then he saw Nancy in the Oklahoma City Municipal Jail looking disheveled like a tramp, slurring her speech, calling him names as he helped her into her apartment, and not once with her foul, alcohol breath did she thank him or ask about Sara. One o'clock chimed.

He thought of going to the bench; perhaps he could find peace in the stark cemetery night air. He thought of surfing the news; perhaps he could see some pictures of the Baghdad carnage. He thought of the vengeful cunning of Al-Qaeda and their strategic strike on Thanksgiving. He thought of raising Sara alone, watching her blossom, and releasing her into a vicious world where he could no longer protect her. The world seemed like a dungeon full of creeping creatures praying on the innocent flesh of its inmates. The whole bed shook with his drumming heartbeats as they pounded the silence at rhythmic intervals. Two o'clock chimed.

The bitter taste of death swirled in his Lazarus mouth as he pondered Peckford, his savior and mentor, the one who taught him how to think and how to question, how to love and how to believe, how to confront fear and how to rise to patriotism, and how to overcome heroism's praise by espousing humility. He thought of life without Peckford and found it intolerable. Peckford was his mind, his soul, his heart, and his worldview. He wanted to go to the bench, to hold it, to stretch on it, to confide his loneliness to it, to become one of its solid bars that embrace the seasons unmindful of the elements. Three o'clock chimed.

Suddenly he remembered Peckford's gift, the beautiful Baghdad painting that he planned to frame and hang in his office. He tried to recall all the meanings it carried among its river gardens, lonesome palm trees, cobblestone streets, serpentine allies, and mighty minarets that obelisked its horizon. Then he recalled Peckford saying to him, "We live dangerously here, Son. It needs to be in a safer place, where beauty is truth and truth, beauty." Then he rehearsed Peckford's last words to him, "Baghdad is a very sad place, my boy, sad for those who are staying and sad for those who are leaving. Where there's no art, there's no joy. Save yourself and the painting, Son, and leave us to our woes. Better say goodbye now, Soldier. In Baghdad, we never make promises." Four o'clock chimed.

Muffled footsteps and a shadow floated through the bedroom door, groped for the bed, lay down, and inched towards him. A hand with a trembling set of fingers spidered up his chest, slipped through a crack in his pajama top, wandered among his chest hairs, and settled on his heart. A head rolled up his shoulder and buried its hairs into his neck. A tear dripped through his undershirt and sprawled onto his skin among smothered sniffles and stifled sighs. A shuddered voice full of all the unfulfilled yearnings of humanity whispered in his ear, "Scotty, would you hold me please?"
Scott, who believed that he was hallucinating, wrapped his arm around the dream and, finding it corporeal, gasped.
"Debbie?"
"Uh-huh."
"You called me by my first name?"
"Uh-huh."

"Is that really you?"
"Uh-huh."
"You sound like Sara."
"Uh-huh."
"Debbie."
"Yes, Scotty."
"I like it when you say my name."

The silence wept, the moments slept, and not a hand or finger crept. Five o'clock chimed.

Debbie's warm, humid breaths ebbed and flowed against Scott's neck like sea waves. He wanted to hold them between his lips and gasp them into his chest as if he were a deep-sea diver who had just surfaced after almost drowning. His loins fumed underneath the covers while he lay mired in the anguish of indecision, struggling against sleep paralysis, and still unsure if he were dreaming or awake.

"Scotty, would you kiss me please?"
"Uh-huh..."
"Scotty, please, don't swallow me."
"I'm sorry..."
"Scotty, Scotty, oh, no, please be careful with my clothes. I have to look proper for Sara when she wakes up."
"I'm so sorry. I forgot my manners. I'll be gentle, gentle..."

The moments fled, the heartbeats sped, the darkness shook with famished dread.

"Oh, no, be careful, not so fast, Scotty, please, slower, I'm not used to... I haven't done..."
"I'm so sorry. I'll stop, I'll stop..."
"No, no, don't stop, yes, oh, yes, Scotty, Scotty, Scotty..."

The silence sighed, the moments cried, the rapid

breathing groaned and died. Six o'clock chimed.

"Scotty, are you awake?"

"I don't really know."

"What are you thinking about?"

"Peckford."

"Is he talking to you?"

"How did you know?"

"He talks to me too."

"I was afraid to tell you. Didn't want you to think that I was crazy."

"What's he saying?"

"The same line, over and over."

"What line?"

"Yet many a man is making friends with death for lack of love alone."

"You missed a small part. 'Yet many a man is making friends with death, *even as I speak* for lack of love alone' is how it really goes."

"You know it?"

"I know the sonnet."

"Oh, I thought it came from a poem."

"A sonnet is a poem."

"Who's the poet?"

"Edna St. Vincent Milay."

"A woman?"

"A real woman."

"Would you say the whole thing, please?"

"I'm not sure I can say it to the letter."

"Would you try? I need to know where that line came from because, for some reason, it haunts me."

"Let me see..."

Debbie sat up in bed, held Scott's open palm to her chest, and with a hesitant voice recited:

"Love is not all, it is not food nor drink
Nor slumber nor a roof against the rain
Nor yet a floating spar for men who sink
And rise and sink and rise and sink again."

Debbie choked on her tears and paused awhile before she continued.

"Love will not fill the thickened lung with breath
Nor clean the blood nor set the fractured bone
Yet many a man is making friends with death
Even as I speak..."

Here Scott interrupted Debbie and with unconcealed excitement finished the line for her, "for lack of love alone."

Debbie stopped, put his palm in her lap, and droned, "So, now you know where your haunting line came from."

"Is there more?"

"Yes, a sonnet is fourteen lines and you've only heard the first eight. Would you like to hear the rest?"

"Yes, please."

As if he wouldn't be able to hear it unless his hand was on her chest, Debbie put Scott's palm back between her breasts and with the same hesitant voice continued:

"It may well be that in a difficult hour
Pinned down by pain and moaning for release
Or nagged by want past resolution's power
I might be driven to sell your love for peace
Or trade the memory of this night for food
It may well be, I do not think I would."

Scott pulled Debbie back onto his chest and quipped, "You wouldn't sell my love for peace?"

"I think that I've already sold my peace for your love. How about you? Would you sell the memory of this night for food?"

"I'd rather starve to death."

There was naught more meaningful, more poignant, more apropos that either of them could have uttered. The sonnet had stated their feelings for them, released them from the bondage of the unsaid, and set their fretful hearts ablaze.

Love, frightening love, comatose love, frozen love that was long presumed dead was miraculously resurrected by death, by sacrifice, by Peckford, and by Thanksgiving. With this epiphany, sleep rescued Debbie and Scott who lay entangled into each other like a pair of spiders with not a cover but the merciful shroud of night. Seven o'clock chimed.

Chapter Thirty-Nine
(The Trinity)

Friday morning surprised the burnt-out, exhausted couple. The sunrays slipped their fingertips through the curtain crack, reached for the bedroom, and pinched the solemn darkness on the cheek. Scott and Debbie gazed into each other's eyes and glowed with embarrassment. The incoming light brought with it laced realities that were concealed by night. Their arms, their legs, and their athletic bodies lay intertwined like two trees that had grown into each other over the years and had become inseparable. Debbie blushed as she tore her body away from Scott's, pulled the covers over her chest, and whispered, "Is the door locked?"

"What door?"

"The bedroom door."

"Oh, you mean Sara…"

"Close your eyes."

"Why?"

"Scotty, close your eyes so I can get up and lock the door."

"Oh, sure, I'm sorry."

Debbie did not return to bed after she locked the bedroom door. She furtively collected her garments, strewn all over the floor, and ran into the bathroom. Then she stuck her neck from behind the bathroom door and said, "Scotty, you need to get dressed."

While Debbie got dressed in the bathroom, Scott put yesterday's clothes back on, went into the kitchen, and began making coffee. Debbie soon followed, sat at the breakfast table, and started to fidget. Scott, without saying a word, sat next to her and held her hand. By the light of day, they were more comfortable with silence than words and avoided each other's eyes until the coffee pot beeped. Scott returned to the table with two cups of coffee and while Debbie gazed at the rising plumes of steam, he began the inevitable conversation.

"How did you overcome your fear?"

"What fear?"

"Your fear of men."

"How did you know that I was afraid of men?"

"Jane told me."

"She shouldn't have. That was our secret."

"It's still our secret."

Scott and Debbie quietly sipped their coffee while the sun glared at them through the window. They had so much to discuss but, that early in the morning, they were still reticent to venture into life-altering discussions. Debbie, afraid of being found out, wanted to leave before Sara awakened. She pushed her coffee cup away, stood up, and yawned.

"No, please, don't leave just yet."

"Sara shouldn't find me here when she wakes up."

"It's only eight. She's not been waking up before nine."

"But, what if she does?"

"We'll just say that you dropped by to see if her dress was a perfect fit or if it needed to be altered."

"Oh, I'm so embarrassed."

"How did you get over your fear?"

"Well, I trusted you, perhaps too much."

"Please, Debbie, talk to me."

"It's so hard to be sure."

"I know that you know. Please tell me how did you lose your fear."

"And why should I tell you?"

"Because I have a need to know and you have a need to tell, because fear is the only thing that can separate us, and because fear was the force that pulled you, Sara, and me back together."

Debbie nervously walked up to the counter, refilled her coffee, and came back to her seat without saying a word. She gazed at the steam spiraling out of her cup and remained silent. Scott, seeing how anguished Debbie looked, cleared his throat, shifted in his seat, and patiently waited. Then, after a polite interval, he took her hand, pressed it against his lips, and lowered his head as if in fervent prayer. This kind, beckoning gesture must have touched Debbie in the core and helped her open up her heart. With downcast gaze, as if she were talking to the steaming coffee cup between her hands, she slowly related what had happened.

"We listened to the Baghdad news when I was at my parents. I became worried but couldn't let them know it. When I returned home, it was about six-thirty. I checked my e-mail link, read the official report, and collapsed on the floor. When I was able to return to the screen, I read the report over and over hoping to find that I had misread it. Still, it read that Peckford was dead, that he was killed in an explosion, that his death was a great military loss, and on and on... Then I noticed that there was another e-mail sent by Peckford at 5 a.m. Baghdad time. It was one line. 'Debbie, please take care of yourself and of Scotty; you need each other and I love you both.' He must have written it just before he left for Sadr City suspecting that he might not return."

"Is that why you came?"

"Yes. Until I read that last line, I thought that I didn't need a man in my life. But something happened to me after I read it. I started to obsess about you and me and Sara as a family and the more I tried to resist that thought, the more it haunted me. I felt a very strong compulsion to obey it, perhaps because it was Peckford's last wish, or perhaps because it was about time I grew up and behaved like a real woman. I didn't even try to understand why my mind suddenly changed. All I knew was that I had to come to you. In spite of that, I resisted and resisted until I exhausted all my energies. That's when I gave up and came."

"So it was Peckford who broke your fear."

"I guess. He must have loved you as much as he loved me and because of that I could allow myself to trust you and to want you."

Scott kissed Debbie's palm and murmured, "You're not going to run away anymore, are you?"

Debbie looked at her watch and did not answer. Scott kissed her palm again and whispered into it, "Can you learn to love me for me and not for Sara?"

"I think I already do. Maybe that's why I was so afraid of you."

"Afraid of me or afraid of love?"

"Maybe I was afraid of loving you because that meant that I would lose control."

"Control of what?"

"Of my emotions."

"And that's what you're really afraid of, losing control, isn't it?"

"Stop analyzing me Scotty; it makes me feel uncomfortable."

"Do you love Sara?"

"You know that I do."

"Is that why you sent her the dress?"

"Maybe."

"You didn't know about Peckford when you bought the dress. What did you want the dress to say?"

"Maybe that was my way of saying I'm sorry."

"Sorry for what?"

"Sorry for rejecting you."

"Did I frighten you that much?"

"No Scotty. You didn't frighten me at all. I frightened myself because I had a secret awe of you, a sort of hero worship, and I was afraid that I might not be able to resist you."

Debbie's eyes quivered with held-back tears. It was an agonizing confession, much like giving birth, and Scott was the one to extract it by forceps. It was time to decompress, to dilute the tension, to change the topic, and Scott mercifully did so. Pretending not to notice Debbie's tears, he cautiously inquired, "Do you know about the bench?"

"Peckford's bench?"

"Yes."

"I was the one who commissioned it."

"Do you know that Peckford and I used to meet

there?"

"I also know that at times you went there alone."

"And how do you know that?"

"It's part of my job."

"Is part of your job to spy on me?"

"It's part of my job to keep an eye on you."

"What else do you do that I don't know about?"

"That's all I can say, Scotty. Please don't pressure me to say any more; I'm not allowed to."

Feeling a bit intimidated, Scott let go of Debbie's hand as he pondered the matter. He knew that the Homeland Security had kept him under surveillance but, for some reason, it bothered him to find out that Debbie was part of the surveillance team. Not knowing how to deal with his sudden feelings of intimidation and violation, he gazed at Debbie with surprised eyes, as if he had never seen her before, as if he were discovering her anew, and as if he were no longer sure if she were virtual or real. Then, from behind his veil of confused emotions, he pleaded,

"Would you go there with me?"

"Go with you where?"

"We'll take Sara to lunch and then we'll go visit the bench together, like all the bereaved families that visit the cemetery on holidays."

Reading Scott's painful confusion, Debbie stroked his hand and prodded, "Why the bench, Darling? Is there anything in particular you wish to say to Peckford?"

"I want to thank him for bringing us together and for giving us another chance at life. Going to the bench is the only way I can communicate with him now that he's really gone. And how about you? Wouldn't you like to say something to him too?"

"I'd like to thank him for helping us conquer fear with love. I also want to ask him how come, two days earlier, he sent me the first four lines from a sonnet and insisted that I should learn them by heart. I got the feeling that, somehow, he knew that I would want to say them to you one day."

"And did you learn them by heart?"

"I did as he said."

"And are you going to say them to me?"

"They'll make us cry."

"Soldiers don't cry. How could four lines make anyone cry?"

"I cry each time I say them to myself. They haunt me just like that other love line haunted you."

"I wouldn't mind crying then as long as we do it together. Would you please say them? Maybe they'll help us feel better about things."

Debbie stared through Scott as if he were a distant fog and hesitantly breathed her four lines into the tearful room:

"How I have loved you all my life and yet
'Twas only yesterday that we had met
My only fear is losing you and all
The wasted years apart my one regret."

Holding hands like teenagers, Debbie and Scott silently pondered the four haunting lines from Peckford's sonnet. They had waited too long and wasted too much life apart. But instead of regrets they now had hopes, and instead of fears they now had love, and instead of death they now had living memories. Debbie, who desperately needed to love and be loved, now had both Scott and Sara inside her heart. Scott, who had never loved or been loved by a woman, now had Debbie inside his. They were still young and fecund and their future lay ahead, pregnant with hopes and dreams.

Preoccupied with pondering their new lives together, Debbie and Scott forgot all about Sara. She only came to mind when, a little after nine, she called for her dad to come help her out of her bed. Scott jumped as if startled, took two steps forward, stopped, turned back towards Debbie, and whispered, "Why don't you go and get   her. She'd love the surprise."

"Are you sure?"

"Very sure."

"I don't know why I feel so nervous all of a sudden."

"Could it be transference?"

"What transference are you referring to?"

"Why don't you go and find out for both of us."

The symbolism of Debbie coming to Sara's rescue proved overwhelming. Ever since her kidnapping, the first one Sara saw upon awakening was her father. The many layers of meanings that lurked within the role reversal that was about to take place were transparent to both Debbie and Scott. What Scott seemed sure about and Debbie was not was how Sara would react to such a surprise. Nevertheless, the morning beckoned and, although still apprehensive, Debbie seized the moment and took the chance.

With Scott tiptoeing behind her, Debbie walked to Sara's room with a thousand butterflies fluttering inside her chest. She stood at the door and with a meek, hesitant voice cooed, "Good morning, Princess."

Sara's eyes gaped with disbelief. She held her breath as if she were about to dive from a high cliff, scaled the bedrail with reckless disregard to gravity, fell flat on her face, got up, flew into Debbie's arms, and burst into tears.

Debbie carried her into the kitchen, waited for her to stop sobbing, and then playfully inquired, "What were you crying about, Princess?"

"My bed."

"Your brand-new bed?"

"Uh-huh."

"What about your bed?"

"I don't like it anymore."

"And why's that?"

"It made me fall."

"Would you like a different bed?"

"Uh-huh."

"What kind of bed would you like this time?"

"The kind without a fence."

The End

Epilogue

What ever happens to Frightened People? Do they really overcome their fears, do they outgrow them, or do they bury them into their unconscious and suffer them for life? And are we not all, at some level, Frightened People?

Would Sara ever date a dark-skinned gentleman, a smoker, or a suitor with a shaven head? Would she ever wear her hair short? Would she always prefer an SUV to a sedan? Would she panic if the elevator electricity should suddenly go out and leave her trapped in the dark between floors? Would she ever lie with a man behind closed doors? Would she ever want to reconnect with her biological mother?

Would Debbie insist on a female gynecologist? Would she ever drink beer or go to a lake cabin for a weekend? Would she overreact if her teenaged son came home smelling of alcohol?

Would Scott want to watch the July 4th fireworks explode in midair? Would he resist buying Sara an SUV? Would he visit a historic, underground cave? Would he ever wear a turtleneck?

Was the US frightened into invading Iraq, boycotting Cuba, and competing in the nuclear arms race? Did the US frighten Japan into surrender? Did conquistadors use surprise to frighten their embattled enemies? Do dictators use fear to exact submission? Is not the history of humanity—with all its revolving myths and beliefs—but the history of the ebb and flow of fears across the ocean of years?

Mark Twain once said that if a cat sat on a hot stove, it would never sit on a stove again, not even if the stove were cold. By the same token Sara would not let anyone push her around, Debbie would not tolerate the company of a drunken man, and Scott would not sleep until Sara would have returned home from her date.

Fear is the most powerful emotion that we can ever experience and it has the longest memory. So much of what we dislike in life is based on unconscious fears. Most of our emotional overreactions are transferences from old fears interred in our unconscious. Moreover, words that carry emotional heft also come from historical transferences that have seeded our unconscious. Think of the repulsion you feel when you hear certain negatively charged words such as communist, socialist, terrorist, jihad, and genocide. All such words evoke unconscious fears that surface into our consciousness as dark threats.

Naturally, all the branches of the fear tree grow out of one main trunk, the foreboding Fear-of-Loss trunk. Evidence supporting the veracity of this generalization abounds and, barring medical anxiety disorders, one can hardly find an exception to this rule. Whatever we are afraid of translates in our minds into a fear of some kind of loss. Thus, disease is the loss of health, pain—the loss of pleasure, death—the loss of life, captivity—the loss of freedom, violation—the loss of sovereignty, shame—the loss of dignity, poverty—the loss of property, age—the loss of youth, ugliness—the loss of beauty, weakness—the loss of power, infirmity—the loss of independence, loneliness—the loss of love, misery—the loss of joy, and despair (hell)—the loss of hope (heaven).

Traumatic experiences are especially frightening because they cause both emotional and physical pains that imprint indelibly upon our psyche, grow up to become our demons, and engage us in mind-to-mind combat for the rest of our lives. From within such haunting fears, the dragon of the Post-Traumatic-Stress-Disorder-Syndrome rears its multiple ugly heads and bites us with its thousand poisonous fangs.

Back From Iraq is an exposé of the pernicious and infinitely protean presentations of fear and its fiendish offspring, the Post-Traumatic-Stress-Disorder-Syndrome. Fear is a bomb—once it explodes, we are doomed to suffer its terrifying consequences. To defeat it is to defuse it before it explodes and that's where our preemptive energies need to be employed.

HAS
8.21.09

About The Author

I was born in Lebanon in 1946, studied medicine at the American University of Beirut, and came to Oklahoma in 1971 for post-graduate training in internal medicine and infectious diseases. Of my sixty-four years, I have spent the last thirty-nine in Oklahoma where I have been productive as physician and writer. Back From Iraq is my third novel and I am currently working on a book of short stories. More information is available on my web: hannasaadah.com

Other Books by Author

Poetry:
Loves and Lamentations of a Life Watcher (1987)
Vast Awakenings (1990)
Familiar Faces (1993)
Four & a half Billion Years (1997)
Novels:
The Mighty Weight of Love (2005)
Epistole (2007)
Back From Iraq (2010)

Other Writings by Author

Web: hannasaadah.com > Blog > Literary
Thought Of The Day
Poem Of The Week
Essays
Etc.